Praise for Leslie Meier and her

Silver Anniversary
"The frenzied pace of the city, effectively contrasted with the more tranquil atmosphere of a small town; the reappearance of familiar characters; and numerous plot twists all contribute to the appeal of this satisfying entry in a long-running series."
—*Booklist*

British Manor Murder
"Counts, countesses, and corpses highlight Lucy Stone's trip across the pond . . . A peek into British country life provides a nice break."
—*Kirkus Reviews*

Candy Corn Murder
"Meier continues to exploit the charm factor in her small-town setting, while keeping the murder plots as realistic as possible in such a cozy world."
—*Booklist*

French Pastry Murder
"A delight from start to finish."
—*Suspense Magazine*

Christmas Carol Murder
"Longtime Lucy Stone series readers will be happy to catch up on life in Tinker's Cove in this cozy Christmas mystery."
—*Library Journal*

Easter Bunny Murder
"A fun and engaging read. It is quick and light and has enough interesting twists and turns to keep you turning the pages. If you like this type of mystery and this is your first meeting with Lucy Stone, it will probably not be your last."
—*The Barnstable Patriot*

Books by Leslie Meier

MISTLETOE MURDER
TIPPY TOE MURDER
TRICK OR TREAT MURDER
BACK TO SCHOOL MURDER
VALENTINE MURDER
CHRISTMAS COOKIE MURDER
TURKEY DAY MURDER
WEDDING DAY MURDER
BIRTHDAY PARTY MURDER
FATHER'S DAY MURDER
STAR SPANGLED MURDER
NEW YEAR'S EVE MURDER
BAKE SALE MURDER
CANDY CANE MURDER
ST. PATRICK'S DAY MURDER
MOTHER'S DAY MURDER
WICKED WITCH MURDER
GINGERBREAD COOKIE MURDER
ENGLISH TEA MURDER
CHOCOLATE COVERED MURDER
EASTER BUNNY MURDER
CHRISTMAS CAROL MURDER
FRENCH PASTRY MURDER
CANDY CORN MURDER
BRITISH MANOR MURDER
EGGNOG MURDER
TURKEY TROT MURDER
SILVER ANNIVERSARY MURDER
YULE LOG MURDER
HAUNTED HOUSE MURDER
CHRISTMAS SWEETS
INVITATION ONLY MURDER
CHRISTMAS CARD MURDER
IRISH PARADE MURDER

Published by Kensington Publishing Corp.

GOBBLE, GOBBLE MURDER

LESLIE MEIER

KENSINGTON BOOKS
www.kensingtonbooks.com

KENSINGTON BOOKS are published by
Kensington Publishing Corp.
119 West 40th Street
New York, NY 10018

All Kensington titles, imprints, and distributed lines are available at special quantity discounts for bulk purchases for sales promotion, premiums, fundraising, educational, or institutional use.

Special book excerpts or customized printings can also be created to fit specific needs. For details, write or phone the office of the Kensington Sales Manager: Kensington Publishing Corp., 119 West 40th Street, New York, NY 10018. Attn. Sales Department. Phone: 1-800-221-2647.

Kensington and the K logo Reg. U.S. Pat. & TM Off.

ISBN-13: 978-1-4967-2626-1 (ebook)
ISBN-10: 1-4967-2626-X (ebook)

ISBN-13: 978-1-4967-2625-4
ISBN-10: 1-4967-2625-1
First Kensington Trade Paperback Printing: October 2020

10 9 8 7 6 5 4 3 2 1

Printed in the United States of America

Contents

TURKEY DAY MURDER

CHAPTER 1

"Look at that face. I ask you. Is that the face of a cold-blooded killer?"

In her usual seat in the second row, part-time reporter Lucy Stone perked up. Until now, she'd been having a difficult time paying attention at the Tuesday meeting of the Tinker's Cove Board of Selectmen, even dozing off for a few moments during the town assessor's presentation of the new valuation formulas.

Lucy studied the face in the photograph Curt Nolan had propped up on an easel in the front of the hearing room, allegedly the face of a multiple killer: big brown eyes; an intelligent expression; a friendly, if somewhat toothy, smile. He didn't look like a mass murderer to her—he looked like a plain old mutt.

"Kadjo's not just some mutt," continued Curt Nolan, his owner and advocate at the dog hearing. "He's a Carolina dog. I went all the way to North Carolina to get him from a breeder there. He's descended from the dogs that accompanied humans across the Bering land bridge from Asia to America thousands of years ago. He's a genuine Native American dog." He paused for emphasis and then concluded, "Why, he's got more right to be here than you do."

That comment was aimed at Howard White, chairman of the

board of selectmen, who was chairing the dog hearing. White—a tall, thin, distinguished-looking man in his early sixties—didn't much like it and glared at Nolan from behind the bench where he was sitting with the four other selectmen as judge and jury.

This was more like it, thought Lucy, studying Nolan with interest. Most people, when called before the board for violating the town's bylaws, exhibited a remorseful and humble attitude. Nolan, by contrast, seemed determined to antagonize the board members, especially Howard White.

Even his clothing declared he was different from the majority of people who resided in the little town of Tinker's Cove, Maine. Instead of the usual uniform of khaki slacks, a button-down shirt, and loafers, which was the costume of choice for board meetings, Nolan was wearing a fringed leather jacket, blue jeans, and cowboy boots. His glossy black hair was brushed straight back and tied into a ponytail with a leather thong. A second leather thong, this one decorated with a bear claw, hung from his neck. His face was tanned and deeply creased, as if he spent a lot of time outdoors in the sun.

"We're not interested in the animal's bloodlines," growled White. "We're here to decide if he's a threat to the community. I'd like to hear from the dog officer."

Cathy Anderson stepped to the front of the room and consulted a manila folder containing a few sheets of paper. Lucy had struck up an acquaintance with Cathy over the years and knew she hated speaking in public, even in front of the handful of citizens who regularly attended the selectmen's meetings. Cathy flipped back her long blond hair and nervously smoothed the blue pants of her regulation police uniform. That uniform didn't do a thing for her well-upholstered figure, thought Lucy.

"The way I see it," said Cathy, taking a deep breath, "the problem isn't the dog—it's the owner."

Hearing this, White exchanged a glance with Pete Crowley. Crowley was a heavyset man who tamed his thick white hair with Brylcreem so that the comb marks remained permanently visible. Also a board member, Crowley was Police Chief Oswald Crowley's brother and a strict law-and-order man.

"Mr. Nolan has refused to license the dog," continued Cathy, "in clear violation of state and town regulations. He also lets the dog run free, which is a violation of the town's leash law. If the dog was properly restrained we could avoid a lot of these problems."

Crowley beamed at her and nodded sympathetically.

"Can I say something?" Nolan was on his feet. Without waiting for permission from White, he began defending his pet. "Like I told you before, Kadjo is practically a wild dog. He's closely related to the Dingo dogs of Australia and other wild breeds. He needs to be free—it'd be cruel to tie him up. And licensing him? That's ridiculous! We don't license bear or moose or deer, do we?"

"You're out of order!" White banged his gavel, startling his fellow board member Bud Collier.

Collier, a retired gym teacher, slept through most board meetings, rousing himself only to vote. Lucy often debated with herself whether she should mention this in her stories for the paper, but so far she had refrained. He was such a nice man, and so popular with the townsfolk, that she didn't want to embarrass him. Nevertheless, she wasn't entirely comfortable about covering up the truth.

"Ms. Anderson has the floor," said White, raising a bristly white eyebrow. "Please continue."

"Thank you." Cathy glanced at Nolan and gave him an apologetic little smile. "I'd like to call a witness, if that's all right with the board."

White nodded.

"I'd like to call Ellie Martin, who lives at 2355 Main Street Extension. Ellie, would you please tell the board members what happened last Monday?"

Ellie Martin stood up, but remained by her chair in the rear of the room. She was a pleasant-looking woman in her forties, neatly dressed in a striped turtleneck topped with a loose-fitting denim jumper. She was barely five feet tall.

"We can't hear you from there," said White. "Step down to the front."

Clutching her hands together in front of her, Ellie came forward and stood next to Cathy.

"Just tell them what happened," prompted Cathy.

"I don't want to make trouble," began Ellie, glancing back at Nolan. "I only filed the report because I want to get the state chicken money."

"What state money is this?" demanded board member Joe Marzetti. Owner of the IGA and a stalwart of the town Republican committee, Marzetti was strongly opposed to government spending.

"It's to reimburse people whose livestock has been destroyed by dogs," explained Cathy. "It's actually town money mandated by state law—it comes out of the licensing fees."

"But you said Nolan hasn't licensed the dog."

Lucy resisted the urge to roll her eyes. Trust Marzetti to find an excuse—any excuse—that would save the town a few dollars.

"That doesn't matter," said Cathy. "It's a state law."

"Well, if it's a law, how come I never heard of it?" Marzetti had furrowed his forehead, creating a single fierce black line of eyebrow.

"Well, it hasn't come up in a long time. Not many people bother to keep chickens or sheep these days."

"What kind of money are we talking here—how much are the taxpayers going to have to cough up?"

"Thirty dollars."

"Thirty dollars for a chicken!" Marzetti's face was red with outrage. "Why, I sell chickens for a dollar nine a pound in my store! That's ridiculous."

"Thirty dollars total," said Cathy. "Mrs. Martin had a dozen hens and she'll get two dollars and fifty cents for each one."

"Oh, that's more like it," said Marzetti.

"The dog killed the chickens? Is that what this is about?" demanded Pete Crowley, who was growing impatient.

"You'd better tell them," said Cathy, giving Ellie a little nudge.

"Well, it was like this," began Ellie. "I was busy inside the kitchen, cleaning the oven, when I heard an awful commotion in the yard outside. I went to look and saw the dog, Kadjo, chasing the chickens. They're nice little pullets, Rhode Island Reds. I raised them myself from chicks I got last spring. They'd just started laying and I was getting five or six eggs a day. That is, I used to. The dog got every one." Ellie's face paled at the memory. "It was an awful sight."

"Every one?" Sandy Dunlap, the newest board member and the only woman, was clearly shocked at the extent of the carnage. She was also sympathetic. When she'd run for election last May, she'd promised to be sympathetic and she'd stuck to her word. Nobody with a problem got short shrift from Sandy. "That must have been awful. I think the least we can do is vote to reimburse you for the chickens. I'd like to make a motion."

"That's not the question," snapped White. "She'll get the money. What we're here to decide is if the dog should be destroyed or banished or what."

"Hold on a minute," said Nolan, jumping to his feet. "I haven't heard anything here about it being my dog. How can you be sure it was Kadjo?"

White banged down his gavel. "Mr. Nolan, I'm warning you."

Nolan sat down, perching on the edge of his seat.

Lucy gave Nolan points for trying, however. In her opinion, White tended to be something of a small-town dictator.

Ellie smiled apologetically at Nolan. "Curt, you know perfectly well I'd recognize Kadjo anywhere. After he'd finished chasing all the birds, he picked one up in his mouth and brought it over and put it at my feet, like a present. He was real proud of himself. It was Kadjo, all right."

"Well, Ellie, he was just doing what comes naturally," said Nolan in a soft voice that made Lucy wonder exactly what their relationship was. "It's his instinct, you know."

White reached for his gavel, but was interrupted by Crowley.

"Is the dog vicious?" Crowley asked. "That's what we've got to determine. I'd like to hear from the animal control officer."

"Ms. Anderson—come on now. It's about time we had your report," said White.

Cathy Anderson leafed through the thin folder. She gave a big sigh.

"The way I see it, the dog isn't vicious. He isn't a problem dog. This is the first complaint I've had about him. Kadjo needs a little training and he really ought to be neutered. Frankly, I think that would take care of the problem."

"Neutered!" Nolan was back on his feet, his face bright red

with anger. "That's outrageous. Besides, he's a pedigreed dog and I plan to breed him."

White banged the gavel and glared at Nolan, who promptly sat down.

Watching Nolan, Lucy saw that he was having a hard time restraining himself. He seemed tightly coiled, like a spring, ready to explode.

"A lot of people feel that way but it's really kinder in the long run. He'll have a longer, healthier life," said Cathy. She turned to White. "That's my recommendation."

"Thank you," said White. "Do I have a motion?"

"You'd like that, wouldn't you?" demanded Nolan, unable to contain himself any longer. "Face it. It's what you've been doing to my people for thousands of years. Trying to wipe us out. It's not enough that the U.S. government has waged a sustained policy of genocide against Native American people for hundreds of years. Now you're after our dogs, too. You can't let wild Native American dogs breed, can you? Nope. All you want are Welsh corgis and Scottish terriers and Irish setters—Old Country breeds."

"Order!" snapped White, banging down his gavel. "You're out of order, Mr. Nolan. That vote isn't until next week."

Suddenly, a little lightbulb went on in Lucy's head and she understood the tension between White and Nolan. Nolan was a Native American, one of the town's few remaining members of the Metinnicut Indian tribe, the original inhabitants of the area before European settlers arrived in the early eighteenth century. The tribe had recently applied to the federal government for recognition and had asked the board to endorse their application. That vote was scheduled for next week, and if Lucy had been asked to predict the outcome, she'd have to say the Metinnicuts' prospects weren't good with this board, especially White.

"Do I hear a motion?"

Bud Collier roused himself from his nap. "The dog's vicious. It's a killer. I move we destroy it."

Lucy snapped to attention, astonished. This was the last thing she had expected. In similar cases up until now the board had always voted to recommend a course of obedience training, perhaps followed with a probationary period. Collier's habit of napping had obviously prevented him from getting the correct information, which happened all too frequently. Usually, however, the board members amended his motion if it seemed inappropriate. In fact, Lucy noticed, Sandy Dunlap and Joe Marzetti were looking rather pointedly at Pete Crowley, as if urging him to amend the motion.

"Do I hear a second?" snapped White.

Crowley nodded his head. "I second the motion."

Lucy's eyes widened in surprise as she hurried to scribble it all down in her notebook. The board usually followed Cathy Anderson's recommendations, and she'd urged obedience training and neutering. She hadn't even mentioned destroying the dog.

"You can't do this!" shouted Nolan, jumping to his feet. In the front of the room, Ellie Martin was whispering frantically in Cathy's ear.

"Could I add something?" asked Cathy as Ellie placed her hand on Nolan's shoulder to restrain him. He got the message and sat back down, but his knee jumped as he nervously tapped his foot.

"Out of order," said White, shaking his head. "Do we have any discussion?"

"I'll start," said Crowley. "The way I see it, a dog starts with chickens and the next thing you know he's got a taste for blood and he's after everything that moves. Nip it in the bud, before he attacks a little child. We can't have this sort of thing going on in our town—predatory beasts going after our children."

"I think we're jumping the gun just a bit here," said Marzetti. "This is the first time the dog's come to the board's attention, and let's face it: We have plenty of dogs we see three or four times before we vote to have them destroyed. It's always been a last resort. I think we should give the dog another chance. We don't need to go around destroying people's pets. I mean, the dog is his property, after all, and he's got a right to it."

Bravo, thought Lucy, wondering how she'd found herself agreeing with Marzetti's conservative logic. On the margin of her notebook she jotted down *1:1.* So far it looked as if the ayes and nays were tied.

Sandy Dunlap was next.

"I, of course, want to make sure that children are safe in our town, and I did see a special on 60 *Minutes* about dog bites. Did you know it's the second major cause for emergency room visits in the United States for children?" Sandy Dunlap pursed her lips and nodded, making her blond curls bounce. "And of course, I have to agree with Mr. Crowley that an ounce of prevention is worth a pound of cure."

Lucy started to add a second stroke to the ayes.

"But we have no proof that Kadjo is really vicious. I mean, there's a big difference between chickens and people. My old dog, Harold—what a sweetie—why, he'll chase a rabbit or a squirrel but he wouldn't dream of biting a person."

Sandy gave a big sniff and blinked. "I know how awful I'd feel if something happened to Harold—I think we have to give Kadjo another chance."

Lucy added the stroke to the nays instead.

"What about you, Collier?" asked the chairman. "Are you voting to put the dog down?"

"Wh-a?" Bud Collier blinked.

"You moved to put the dog down. Is that how you're voting?"

"I moved to put the dog down?" Collier scratched his head. "I must have been mistaken. She says the dog's an old fellow who wouldn't dream of biting anybody. I don't want to put him down. I vote no."

Lucy let out a big sigh of relief and put another stroke with the nays.

White threw his hands up in the air. "That's three nos. The motion doesn't pass."

Nolan stepped forward to retrieve the photograph of Kadjo.

"Not so fast," said White, shaking a finger at him. "Be warned: The board won't be as lenient next time. You can be sure of that."

Nolan didn't respond, but Lucy noticed he had clenched his fists. Ellie Martin reached out to touch his sleeve and he suddenly grabbed the picture and marched out of the hearing room. Ellie hurried after him.

"Meeting adjourned!" declared White, banging down the gavel.

Adjourned for now, thought Lucy, as she closed her notebook and tucked it into her purse, but she'd be awfully surprised if this was the end of the matter. She had a feeling the board would be seeing a lot more of Curt Nolan.

And maybe, she thought, as she crossed the town hall parking lot to her car, just maybe, it was time *Pennysaver* readers learned exactly how their board of selectmen actually operated.

CHAPTER 2

Next morning, at the *Pennysaver* office, Lucy stared at the blank screen of the computer. Somehow, writing about the dog hearing wasn't as easy as she thought it would be.

Yesterday, as she had driven home in a fury of righteous indignation, the words and phrases had flown through her head and she'd practically had the whole story written when she pulled into the driveway of the restored farmhouse on Red Top Road she shared with her husband, Bill, and their three daughters. Toby, her oldest and the only boy, was a freshman at Coburn University in New Hampshire.

At dinner, Bill and the girls had laughed when she described the meeting.

"You should have seen the look on Howard White's face when Bud Collier changed his mind," she'd told them as she dished out the ravioli. "I've never seen anybody look so furious."

"What does Kadjo look like, Mom?" asked Zoe, who was in first grade and could almost read all by herself, even though it was only November. At the library, she always went for the dog stories.

"Kind of like Old Yeller in the movie," said Lucy.

"Old Yeller died." Zoe sighed and picked up her fork.

"I can't believe they were really going to kill Kadjo," said Sara, who was in fifth grade and was a member of Friends of Animals. Last summer she had volunteered at their shelter, caring for orphaned baby birds and other injured wildlife.

"If you ask me, maybe they should have," declared Elizabeth, who was a senior in high school and a contrarian on principle. She speared a chunk of lettuce with her fork and took a tiny bite. "He killed twelve chickens, after all. What about them?"

"Killing the dog wouldn't bring back the chickens, would it, Mom?" Sara's round face was flushed with the effort of reaching across the table for the breadbasket. "It would just be killing another helpless, innocent animal. And Kadjo is a special dog, an endangered breed."

"I don't know if *endangered* is the right word," said Bill, giving Sara a pointed glance as he passed her the bread. "If they've survived all these years, they're hardly in danger."

"Just because they've done okay up to now doesn't mean they're not endangered," insisted Sara, holding out her plate for seconds. "They're losing habitat. People are building houses where there weren't any—there's less and less room for wild animals."

"There's going to be less and less room for the rest of us if you don't stop eating like that," said Elizabeth, who had limited herself to four raviolis and a large helping of salad. "You're going to get fat, like that man on TV last night."

"He weighed 1100 pounds," said Sara, defending herself. "I only weigh one tenth of that."

"Right," said Elizabeth, rolling her eyes in disbelief.

"That's enough." Lucy then repeated what had become her mealtime mantra: "It doesn't matter how much you weigh—what's important is feeling healthy and having enough energy."

"Hey, Lucy, how's that story coming?" demanded Ted Stillings, editor and publisher of the *Pennysaver* and her boss, intruding on her thoughts and snapping her back to the present.

Lucy shook her head, to clear her mind, and looked at the computer screen. It was still blank. As much she wanted to write the truth about the meeting, she was finding it hard to overcome her old habit of reticence. "Discretion is the better part of valor" had been one of her mother's favorite expressions, and Lucy had grown up believing that, if you couldn't say something nice about someone, you didn't say anything at all.

But she was a reporter, she reminded herself. She had an obligation to tell the truth. She straightened her back and took a deep breath, as if she were preparing to dive off the high board into a deep pool. Then she began tapping at the keys, picking up speed as she went and quickly filling up the screen.

> Kadjo, a Native American dog, narrowly escaped the fate that overtook his human companions when Selectmen voted 3:2 to spare his life.

"Lucy, I think you need to tone this down a little bit," suggested Ted, after she had sent the story to him for editing.

"No way, Ted." Having taken the plunge, Lucy was in no mood to compromise. "I wrote it just the way it happened. Nolan didn't get a fair shake. Listen, I've covered a million dog hearings and they always give everybody a second or even a third chance. I think they were discriminating against Nolan because he's Indian—I really do."

Ted tapped the mouse and scrolled through the story again.

"Look here. You're sure you want to say that Bud Collier 'roused himself from his usual afternoon nap'? Let's cut out that phrase, okay?"

"Ted." Lucy had set her teeth. "He sleeps through every meeting. Every one. People have a right to know."

Ted shrugged. "He's been on the board for twenty years or more and keeps getting reelected. He must be doing something right."

"Ted! People vote for him because they don't know he sleeps through the meetings. How are they going to know if we don't tell them?"

Ted chewed his lip. "Okay. You have a point. I'm just going to cut 'usual afternoon nap' and put 'brief nap.' How's that?"

"It's waffling."

"It's using discretion, and that's the name of the game in community news."

"You sound just like my mother," said Lucy with a shrug. "It's your paper. I'm just the hired help."

"That reminds me. I have a feature for you with a nice Thanksgiving tie-in. And since you're so keen on Native Americans these days, you'll love it. It's about a woman who makes American Indian dolls and won a prize." Ted scrambled through a pile of papers on his cluttered desk. "Here it is. Ellie Martin. Lives on Main Street Extension."

"That's the woman at the hearing last night. You know, whose chickens got killed."

"I thought her name sounded familiar."

"Some coincidence." Lucy took the press release from the American Dollmakers' Association and studied it. "She seemed real nice. I'll give her a call. When do you want it?"

"To run on Thanksgiving. As soon as you can get it to me. Oh, and Pam asked me to remind you about the pie sale."

Pam was Ted's wife, and this year she was in charge of the pie sale that raised money for the Boot and Mitten Fund. Without the fund, a lot of children in Tinker's Cove wouldn't have warm winter clothing.

"Oh, gosh. I did forget," said Lucy, remembering that in a moment of foolish optimism she'd agreed to bake six pumpkin pies for the sale. "Now, if you don't have anything else, I've got to run. I promised I'd help Sue take the day care kids on a field trip, and I'm late!"

"I was getting nervous," said Sue when Lucy pulled open the door to the recreation center basement where the day care center was housed. "I was afraid you'd forgotten about the field trip."

Sue Finch, Lucy's best friend, had convinced penny-pinching town meeting voters to fund the center several years ago, and it had been such a success that now there was hardly a murmer when the budget item came up every year.

"I got here as soon as I could," said Lucy, smiling at the group of preschoolers who had gathered around her, eager for attention.

"Hi, guys. Who's here?" She went around the group, pointing a finger as she named each child. Harry. Justin. Hillary. "Where's Hunter? There he is, behind Emily. And who's this?"

Lucy had spotted an unfamiliar face: a slight little girl with pale skin and huge black eyes.

"This is Tiffani," said Sue. "Today's her second day with us and I was hoping you'd be her special friend. How does that sound, Tiffani? Will you let Mrs. Stone hold your hand?"

Tiffani didn't answer but studied her shoes. Lucy could see a fine little blue vein throbbing at her temple. She gave a questioning glance to Sue, then reached down and took the little girl's hand. She was surprised when Tiffani didn't snatch it away, but instead gave her a little squeeze.

"Okay, gang. Let's put on those jackets," urged Sue.

Lucy helped the kids zip and button their coats while Sue gave last-minute instructions to Frankie Flaherty, her assistant, who was staying at the center with the three infants. When it was Tiffani's turn, Lucy couldn't help noticing how thin and ragged her lavender hand-me-down jacket was; the quilted lining was worn through at the elbows and shoulders. It could hardly provide much warmth and was much too big, besides. Making a mental note to tell Pam that Tiffani was a prime candidate for the Boot and Mitten Fund's largesse, she once again took the girl's hand and they followed the others out to the minivan Sue had borrowed from the senior center for the trip.

"All aboard," cried Sue, cheerfully. "We're going to see the turkeys!"

"Is that where we're going?" Lucy asked, doubtfully. "Andy Brown's turkey farm?"

"Where else?" replied Sue, sitting down beside her. "It's Thanksgiving."

"I know," said Lucy. She glanced at the kids, who were so small that their legs stuck straight out on the adult-sized van seats. "Turkeys can be a little scary, especially when they're bigger than you are."

"Nonsense," said Sue with a wave of her beautifully manicured hand. "We've been learning all about turkeys. When we get back, we're going to make hand turkeys."

"Hand turkeys?"

"You know. The kids trace their hands on a piece of paper.

Then the thumb is the head and they color in the rest of the fingers for the turkey's tail."

"I remember when Toby made one in kindergarten," said Lucy, a tinge of sadness in her voice. "He was so proud of it."

"Do I detect a touch of empty-nest syndrome?" Sue peered at her. "Is Toby coming home for Thanksgiving?"

"He's coming Tuesday, right after classes, and he's bringing his roommate, Matthew. What about Sidra?"

Sue's daughter had graduated from college a few years ago and was living in New York City, where she was the assistant producer of Norah Hemmings's daytime talk show. Her engagement had just been announced.

"Not this year. She's going to *his* folks," Sue snorted, fidgeting with the silk scarf she'd tucked in the neck of her tailored tweed jacket. "They're not even married and it's starting already."

Lucy smiled. "Do I detect a touch of jealous mother-in-law?" she asked.

"Touché," said Sue, smoothing her neat pageboy and staring out the window at the passing fields and trees. "I'm just not used to the idea of her being engaged, much less married."

"It must be hard," acknowledged Lucy. "I can't believe how excited I am that Toby's coming home. I really miss him. It's like there's this big, gaping hole at the dinner table." She laughed. "Actually, I guess he took the bottomless pit with him. For the first time ever, I have leftovers."

Sue chuckled and turned to check on the kids. "You know," she said as she settled back in her seat, "you have to expect some changes in Toby. You never get back exactly the same kid you sent away."

"Oh, I know," said Lucy. "But that'll be nice: seeing how he's grown and changed."

"Sure," said Sue, giving her hand a little pat. "Okay, kids, we're almost there. Now, who can sing with me? 'Over the river and through the woods,'" she began.

"'To grandmother's house we go!'" screamed the kids.

They were still singing merrily when they arrived at the turkey farm. When Andy Brown had taken over his father's failing dairy farm, a lot of people in Tinker's Cove had thought he was crazy. He had proved them wrong, however, and had turned the farm into a local attraction. In spring the place was filled with lambs and bunnies and chicks and he held Easter egg hunts. In summer he sold fresh fruit and produce. In September it was apples and cider, and by October the fields were full of pumpkins and a dilapidated old barn had been transformed into a House of Horrors. Now, in November, some of those Easter chicks had matured into a flock of Thanksgiving turkeys.

"Hi, kids, I'm Farmer Brown," said Andy, greeting them at the bus. "Welcome to the farm." As usual, he was dressed in overalls and sported a bright red bandanna.

"Good morning, Farmer Brown," chorused the kids, prompted by Sue.

They all climbed out of the van and gathered in the barnyard, which separated the farmhouse from the barn. A parking lot was off to one side and beyond that stood a cluster of equipment sheds.

"Are you here to see the turkeys?" Andy asked.

"Yeah!" said Harry.

"And what's the noise a turkey makes?" Andy had shown lots of school groups around the farm. He knew the routine.

The kids all began making gobbling sounds, the boys vying to see who could be loudest. Tiffani was the only one who remained quiet, standing silently beside Lucy.

"I guess you all know that turkeys are called *gobblers,*" said Andy. "Come on. Follow me!"

Lucy took Tiffani's hand and they followed the rest of the group across the barnyard and around the barn. There, in a huge pen dotted with A-frame shelters, were several hundred white turkeys. It was an awesome sight.

"Wow!" said Sue. "Turkeys are bigger than I thought."

"And noisier," said Lucy, listening to the din. She was aware that Tiffani had slipped behind her, only taking occasional peeks at the turkeys.

"And smellier—phew!" said Harry, making them all laugh.

Studying the turkeys, Lucy decided they were remarkably ugly animals. The males were enormous and sported long, fleshy combs that dangled across their beaks, hanging down one side. Wattles, in lurid shades of blue and pink, dangled from their necks and a large tuft of course black hair sprouted from each male's chest. Their scaly, reptilian feet had sharp spurs in addition to their three-clawed toes. The females, although smaller than the males, were still substantial birds. They didn't have combs on the tops of their heads, but they didn't have feathers either. Their bald heads were covered with lumpy, knobby skin.

Oddest of all, thought Lucy, studying the birds with the fascination truly horrible sights seem to require, were their eyes. They had an odd reflective quality, and when they blinked it reminded her of a shutter on a camera lens.

"How do we know turkeys are birds?" asked Sue, who was holding up a large white feather.

Emily knew the answer. "They have feathers."

"That's right," said Sue. "What else makes them different from us? Do they have mouths with lips and teeth?"

The kids studied the birds, trying to decide.

"They have beaks," said Justin.

"Farmer Brown, what do they eat?" asked Sue.

"Mostly corn and grain. See over there?" He pointed to the opposite side of the pen, where a worker was emptying a sack of grain into a metal hopper. "He's feeding the turkeys."

"Isn't that Curt Nolan?" asked Lucy, recognizing him from yesterday's hearing.

"Yup. Curt helps out this time of year."

"Farmer Brown," asked Sue, intent on continuing her lesson, "how big are these turkeys?"

"These turkeys are Nicholas Mammoths. The females dress out to between fifteen and eighteen pounds, the males at twenty to twenty-five pounds."

"What do they wear when they get dressed?" asked Hillary, giggling.

"They don't wear clothes." Farmer Brown scratched his head. "Oh, I get it. Dressed means something different. It means after they're killed and ready to cook."

"Killed?" Emily's face was white. The kids had suddenly grown very quiet. Behind her, Lucy could feel Tiffani's little body stiffen.

Lucy and Sue exchanged glances. Suddenly the trip didn't seem like such a good idea.

"A lot of food comes from animals," said Sue, using her teacher tone of voice. "Cows give milk and chickens give eggs, but to get meat we have to kill the animals. That's the way it is."

"All of them?" Hillary was horrified.

"All except one," said Farmer Brown. "TomTom Turkey. Want to see him?"

"Sure," said Sue, stooping down and giving Hillary a hug. "Let's go see TomTom Turkey."

"Old TomTom won the blue ribbon at the county fair last summer. He's the biggest turkey you're likely to see."

Andy pulled open the door and they all followed him into the large, airy barn. Lucy inhaled the scent eagerly—a rich mixture that recalled the cows that had once lived there combined with the fresh, sweet smell of hay. She loved the smell of a barn; it reminded her of childhood visits to Uncle Chet and Aunt Elizabeth in Thompson's Ridge, where they had had a dairy farm.

Unlike their barn, which had been filled with cows, Andy's barn was largely empty. Bins and shelves for produce lined the whitewashed walls, and pens were set up for displaying baby animals in the spring, but these were all vacant now. The only inhabitant of the barn was TomTom, who lived in a wire pen in the southwest corner, where sun came through a high window.

"That's some bird," said Lucy, simultaneously appalled and amazed. Tiffani was tugging at her arms, so Lucy lifted her up. She could understand the little girl's desire to be safe in somebody's arms. TomTom didn't seem entirely pleased to have company. After cocking his head to study the group, he'd begun puffing out his chest and spreading his tail, strutting around his pen. The kids were definitely impressed and stood silently, watching warily.

"How big is he?" asked Sue.

"He weighed fifty pounds last summer and he's probably grown some since then. I'd guess close to sixty pounds."

"So he's older than the others?" asked Lucy.

"Yup. I've had him about a year and a half. He's full grown."

"What made you decide to keep him?" she wondered aloud.

"Well, that's a funny story." Farmer Brown was leaning against the wood and wire pen. "First year we raised turkeys we picked him out for our Thanksgiving dinner. But when we got all done and all the turkeys were sold, my wife said she didn't want to have turkey after all. Said it wouldn't hurt her feelings if she never saw another turkey in her entire life, in fact; so we went off to her sister's in New York for the holiday and we took along a ham. And that's what we're going to do this year, too. So it looks like Old TomTom here is safe for a while."

"What's he doing?" asked Justin.

Farmer Brown turned to see. TomTom had suddenly become agitated. His comb had become more erect and his wattles had inflated. He was rocking forward and backward, staring at Farmer Brown.

Brown laughed and removed his bandanna, waving it in front of the bird. TomTom seemed to puff up even more, if that were possible, and then charged at the bandanna.

The terrified kids ran for cover, cowering behind Lucy and Sue.

Brown laughed and waved the red bandanna again; TomTom went for it, hurling himself against the pen. The children shrieked, and Hillary began to cry. Tiffani buried her head beneath Lucy's chin and clamped her arms firmly around her neck. Lucy knew they should lead the children away, but she was fully occupied with Tiffani, whose body had gone rigid.

Just then, a side door opened and Nolan appeared. He made a sound like a turkey's gobble and waved his red cap; TomTom turned and stood facing him.

Lucy took advantage of the moment and loosened Tiffani's grip, shifting her to her hip. Sue took Emily and Hillary by the hand and started toward the door. The boys followed.

"Thank you for letting us visit," called Sue as they quickly exited the barn and headed for the van. Lucy was bringing up the rear and she turned to give Farmer Brown a good-bye wave.

He didn't notice. He was gesturing angrily at Nolan, who didn't look too happy. To Lucy, in fact, it seemed that the two were engaged in a heated argument. She gave Tiffani a little squeeze and hurried out the door.

CHAPTER 3

Ellie Martin looked at Lucy over the rim of her mug, filled with herbal tea, and chuckled.

"Boy, I've got to hand it to you. You sure like to live dangerously." She glanced at the copy of the *Pennysaver* that was lying on her kitchen table with the rest of the day's mail.

"Oh, I don't know," said Lucy, ready to defend her story. She looked around Ellie's neat kitchen, where the scent of baking filled the air and new loaves of bread sat cooling on the counter. Then she took a bite of warm, buttered anadama bread. "After I saw the way they treated Curt, I decided it was time to tell the awful truth about the board of selectmen. Inquiring minds want to know—at least I hope they do."

Ellie smiled, revealing perfect white teeth. "Don't get me wrong," she said. "I don't have any problem with what you wrote. Frankly, I think it's long overdue. I just hope you know what you're in for."

Lucy experienced a sinking feeling, unrelated to the fresh bread she had eaten. "You think people are going to be upset?"

"Oh, yes," said Ellie.

"Oh, well," said Lucy with a sigh. "There's nothing I can do about it now. It'll blow over. In the meantime, tell me about your dolls."

"Come on. I'll show you."

*   *   *

Lucy followed Ellie down the narrow hallway of her ranchstyle home into the third and smallest bedroom. "Now that the kids are grown, I finally have a room just for my dolls," said Ellie. "My husband died a little over two years ago. He made the shelves for me."

"I'm sorry," said Lucy, wondering if a romance was brewing between Ellie and Curt Nolan and trying to figure out how she could ask.

Ellie led the way into the room, pointing out her workbench, complete with sewing machine, set up in front of the single window. The rest of the walls were lined with storage units, cabinets below and shelves above. The shelves were filled with supplies: baskets containing bits of leather, jars containing colored beads, a rack holding every color of thread imaginable. Taking center stage, opposite the window, was a lighted cabinet with glass doors containing the finished dolls. Ellie opened the door and Lucy stepped closer to examine them.

"These are exquisite," Lucy said, genuinely impressed by Ellie's craftsmanship. Each doll was different and each seemed to tell a story. A mother, dressed in a buckskin dress with flowing fringe on the sleeves, sat with her legs tucked beneath her, holding a tiny baby. Two little girls were posed together; they were holding tiny baskets filled with minute blueberries. A little boy with a bow in his hand seemed to be bursting with pride; Lucy guessed it had something to do with the bulging game bag that hung from his shoulder.

Ellie opened it, revealing a tiny, beautifully crafted rabbit, perfect down to its little white cottontail.

"These are incredible," said Lucy. "How do you do it?"

"I start with wire frames," said Ellie, showing Lucy several forms she was experimenting with. "Then I model the bodies using a special resin—the hands and the faces are the hardest. It's important to get them just right.

"Then I paint the features and make the wigs and clothes and accessories. . . ."

"You make everything? Even the baskets?"

Ellie's cheeks flushed. "I make it all. I don't use any findings.

Of course, sometimes it takes a bit of thinking. Take the blueberries, for example. What do you think I used?"

"I can't imagine," said Lucy, bending closer to study the baskets.

"If you shake them, they roll around. They're not molded together or anything."

"I give up," said Lucy.

"Tapioca. I painted grains of tapioca with acrylic paint, and it was quite a trick, getting just the right color. In the end, I used several colors, even a few pinks and greens. Makes them look more realistic."

"That's amazing. It's no wonder you win prizes. Let's see," said Lucy, flipping open her notebook. "You won 'Best in Show' and 'Most Authentic Ethnic Doll' at last month's meeting of the American Dollmakers' Association."

"It's kind of like the Oscar of the doll world," said Ellie, a touch of pride in her voice.

"Was the competition stiff?"

"I'll say. Thousands of people enter every year."

"And which doll won?"

"You can't see it. I mean, I don't have the winners here. They're on display at the Smithsonian."

"Wow. That's a real honor," said Lucy, scribbling the information down in her notebook. "Do you ever sell them?"

"You bet. That's what got me started. I needed to make money and I didn't want to leave my girls. Angie's in law school now and Katie's at Dartmouth. So l started making dolls and selling them at craft shows. That's how I got started. I sold the first ones for five dollars each. Can you imagine?"

Something in her tone made Lucy suspect the price had gone up. She had to ask. Maybe she could get one for Zoe. "How much?"

"It depends on the doll. The mother there—she'd go for about twelve hundred."

Lucy gulped and decided Zoe would have to go without an Indian doll.

"That little boy—he's special. He'd probably go for eighteen. I know it sounds like a lot, but people buy them as investments.

I've heard of dolls I sold years ago for a few hundred dollars going for thousands at auctions."

"And you make only Indian dolls? How come?"

"Well, I'm part Metinnicut. I guess it's really been a way to affirm my heritage."

Lucy was surprised. She hadn't had the slightest inkling that Ellie was a Native American. Now that she knew that Ellie was Metinnicut, it helped explain her behavior at the dog hearing.

"Is that why you were so reluctant to testify against Curt?" she asked.

"In a way, I guess. I've known him all my life."

Lucy didn't want to blow the interview, but she had to ask. "And you're just friends?"

"Just friends," said Ellie firmly, changing the subject. "The dolls are all authentic, you know, in a generic way. I couldn't learn much about the Metinnicuts in particular, so I took patterns from other tribes in the Northeast. I call them 'Eastern Woodland Indian.' That way I can use designs from other tribes that appeal to me. Take the fringed dress, for example. I saw one in the museum in Cooperstown—that's in New York and modified it. Working on such a small scale I had to simplify it, anyway, but the spirit's there, if you know what I mean."

Lucy studied the expression on the doll's face, which seemed to capture not only maternal love but also the mix of anxiety of hopefulness that all mothers feel for their children. Then she nodded.

"Why couldn't you learn about the Metinnicuts? There's Metinnicut Pond and Metinnicut Road. There's even Metinnicut Island out in the bay. And isn't there a war club in the Winchester College museum?"

"There is, but it's actually the only remaining Metinnicut artifact. Except for the names, I haven't been able to find anything else. It's all disappeared: the language, the culture, everything. The tribe died out in the eighteenth century. A lot of people around here have some Indian blood, but it's mixed in with a lot of other stuff. Frankly"—Ellie gave a little laugh—"I've probably got more Italian genes than anything else."

"But if there's no Metinnicut culture left, why are folks like Curt Nolan making such a big deal about it? They even want recognition as a tribe from the federal government—the select-men are voting on their petition next week."

The question hung between them before Ellie finally spoke.

"Because of the casino."

"Casino?" Lucy wondered if those occasional lapses of attention during selectmen's meetings were getting out of control. This was the first she'd heard about a casino.

"That's why they need federal recognition," continued Ellie. "If they get it, they can build a casino. I've heard they even have the plans. They want to put it on Andy Brown's farm."

Lucy remembered the disagreement she had witnessed between Andy Brown and Curt Nolan the day before.

"And how does Andy Brown feel about this?"

"He's all for it. He'll make a lot of money. That's what it's all about: money." Ellie's voice was full of sadness. "It isn't really about Metinnicut heritage at all."

"How come I haven't heard about this before?"

"Because nobody's talking about it. They've kept it pretty quiet. I only know because Bear Sykes—he's the tribal leader—is my uncle. They're going to present the whole plan at the selectmen's meeting next week." Ellie smiled slyly. "I thought inquiring minds would want to know—off the record, of course."

Lucy said her goodbyes quickly, knowing she'd better get back to the *Pennysaver* office as fast as she could to check with Ted. She only hoped he'd be there. Thursday afternoon, after the paper came out, was typically a quiet time when he took care of personal errands like haircuts and dental appointments. When she arrived, however, she found he was still working and so was Phyllis. Both were talking on the telephone.

As Lucy hung up her jacket she wondered if Ellie had been right about her story. Maybe the voters were capable of outrage; maybe there was hope for the democratic system after all.

She sat down at her desk and booted up her computer. While she waited for it to complete whatever it was doing, the phone rang. Ted and Phyllis were still on the other lines, so she answered.

"I'm calling about the dog," said a woman with a quavery voice. "That Kadjo."

"If you have an opinion about that story, we'd welcome a letter to the editor," said Lucy. "That way, we could print it."

"I don't think that dog should be allowed to run around. It's a menace. My sister lived next to a man with a vicious dog, and that dog killed her cat."

"That's very interesting—"

"Not that the cat died right away. She got it to the vet and he did what he could but poor Misty never regained consciousness."

"This was in Tinker's Cove?"

"No, no, no. Maude lives in Chagrin Falls, Ohio."

Lucy was confused. "I thought the cat was named Misty."

"Misty is the cat." The quavery voice was definitely getting a little testy. "Maude's my sister."

"Right. And could I have your name?"

There was no answer.

"Hello? Hello?" said Lucy, finally concluding the line was dead.

"That was funny," she said to Ted and Phyllis. "A woman called about a dog that attacked her sister's cat in Ohio."

"It's been like that all day," said Phyllis, letting the phone ring. "The phones have been ringing off the hook. Everybody's got an opinion about that dog story."

"They're calling about the dog?" Lucy's eyebrows shot up. "What about the selectmen? Aren't people mad that Bud Collier sleeps through the meetings and Howard White is a megalomaniac and Joe Marzetti is practically a fascist?"

Phyllis smiled. "Sorry. They're calling about the dog."

"Yeah?" Lucy was disgusted to find she was relieved. "What do they say?"

"It's been about fifty-fifty," Phyllis continued, ignoring the ringing phone and taking a moment to examine her manicure. Then she sighed and picked up the receiver. *"Pennysaver."*

A sudden crash—Ted slamming down the receiver—made Lucy jump.

"No more dog stories, okay?" he snarled, glaring at her.

"No problem," said Lucy. "Actually, I think I'm on to something big. Very big. Maybe a scoop."

"Really?" Ted was skeptical.

"Maybe." Lucy was suddenly hesitant. "It's the first I've heard of it."

"Well, what is it?"

"Ellie Martin told me the Metinnicuts want to build a casino on Andy Brown's farm. They even have plans."

Ted stared at her, forgetting the ringing phones. "You're sure about this?"

"I'm not sure. It's just what Ellie said. But she is part Metinnicut."

"Yeah. She's Bear Sykes's niece."

"So she said."

"Well, I guess she'd know then." He paused. "I suspected something like this, but I didn't know it had gotten so far."

Lucy shook her head. "I don't know. A casino in Tinker's Cove— it's crazy."

Ted snorted. "Crazy is right. It's madness." He tilted his head toward the still-ringing phone. "This is nothing," he said. "When people in this town find out that the Metinnicuts want a gambling casino, all hell's gonna break loose."

CHAPTER 4

Thin November light filtered through the kitchen windows and fell on the big, round golden oak table in Lucy's kitchen. It wasn't bright enough to allow her to make out the tiny expiration dates on her coupons, so she had also lighted the milk-glass hurricane lamp that hung above the table. Spread out before her were a colorful array of magazines and coupon sections from the Sunday paper, the IGA flyer, and yesterday's food section from the newspaper.

The town might be on the brink of a tremendous furor about the casino, but Lucy had other things on her mind. She stared at the blank sheet of paper in front of her and bravely wrote *Thanksgiving Menu* at the top. This year, she thought, she'd like to try something different. She flipped through the magazines until she found the article she was looking for: "A New-Fashioned Thanksgiving."

Low in fat, rich in flavor, our easy-to-prepare Thanksgiving dinner is sure to please even the pickiest Pilgrims, promised the story, which was accompanied by artfully designed photographs.

She turned to the recipes with interest. Pumpkin soup served in hollowed-out pumpkin shells? She didn't think so. It looked like something unspeakable to her and the kids would never eat it. Never, ever.

Come to think of it, she decided, there was no point in serving a soup or appetizer course. It would just spoil appetites for the feast to come.

She paused, doing a quick head count. How many would there be? Herself and Bill, the four kids, Toby's roommate Matthew plus her elderly friend, Miss Tilley, who was practically one of the family. That made eight.

She smiled in satisfaction. Eight was a nice number. Her dining room, newly redecorated after a plumbing disaster last Christmas ruined the ceiling, could seat eight very comfortably; she had sterling for eight. There were even eight teacups remaining in the china service for twelve she'd inherited from her mother. Eight would be perfect.

But what to serve them? Turkey and stuffing, of course. Creamed onions—she liked creamed onions and only bothered with them once a year. She glanced at the magazine menu. There were no creamed onions; there were zucchini boats stuffed with corn kernels. What happened to "easy-to-prepare"? She checked out the other vegetable suggestion. Brussels sprouts?

She clucked her tongue and wrote *peas* on her menu. Her picky Pilgrims would never eat Brussels sprouts.

Oops, she forgot mashed potatoes. Bill loved mashed potatoes, especially with plenty of gravy, and there would be plenty of gravy. That reminded her. There had to be sweet potatoes, too, but not with marshmallows. She shuddered. Just a little brown sugar. And of course, cranberry sauce and pickles and celery with olives—really just an excuse to use her grandmother's celery boat shaped like a little canoe.

That should do nicely, she thought, adding nuts to her shopping list. Three kinds of pie: mince, apple, and pumpkin, followed by nuts. It was her favorite part of the meal: that second cup of coffee and the leisurely cracking and dissection of walnuts, pecans, almonds, and filberts. Not hazelnuts—good, old-fashioned filberts—and grapes from the centerpiece.

She put down her pencil and studied the menu. *So much for something new,* she chuckled to herself. It was the same Thanksgiving dinner she served every year—the dinner her mother had made, the same dinner she remembered eating as a little girl perched on a slippery telephone book at her grandmother's long linen-covered table.

At the IGA, Lucy pulled the Subaru into her favorite parking spot and grabbed her coupon wallet and list. She loved grocery shopping; she saw it as a weekly challenge. Getting the most she could for her 120 dollars. To her way of thinking, there was nothing more satisfying than finding a buy-one-get-one-free special and matching it up with a coupon that she could double—or even triple using one of her precious triple coupons—if the deal was sweet enough.

Reminding herself to buy some extra canned goods for the high school food drive, she reached for a cart and tugged it loose from the others. Whirling around, she almost bumped into Franny Small.

"Sorry, Franny. I didn't see you," she apologized.

"No harm done," said Franny, reaching for a cart.

Franny looked remarkably good these days, thought Lucy. The tightly permed gray curls were gone. She now had a sleek frosted do and had replaced her pink plastic glasses with contact lenses. Also gone was the faded pink raincoat she'd worn for years; today she was wearing a sporty golf jacket.

"How's business?" asked Lucy as they pushed their carts into the produce section. Franny had recently landed a contract with a major department store for the hardware jewelry she designed.

"I've got more orders than I can handle," said Franny. "I've got a catalog company that wants ten thousand pieces but I can't find enough pieceworkers. I'm supposed to meet with some community development people from up north next week. I'm hoping I can get them interested in setting up a home industry program with me." She reached for a bag of carrots. "It's kind of frustrating, you know. I've got so many ideas."

"It's marvelous—what you've done for the local economy," said Lucy. "The unemployment rate is under ten percent for the first time I can remember."

"It could go even lower if we get that new casino they're talking about," said Franny. "That'll provide a lot of jobs, not to mention a terrific marketing opportunity for my jewelry. I'm already working up some Indian designs."

So the word was already out, thought Lucy, speculating that the Metinnicuts were carefully leaking news of the casino, hoping to build grass roots support through a word-of-mouth campaign. "You're in favor of the casino? I thought you were a Methodist," teased Lucy.

"I am a Methodist," said Franny. "And I'd never dream of gambling myself. But other people don't see anything wrong with it. The Catholics have bingo, don't they? Who am I to tell other people what they can and can't do?"

"I don't know," said Lucy, adding a bag of apples to her cart. "Somehow it just doesn't seem right."

"You've got to change with the times," said Franny, checking her watch. "I've got to run. If I don't see you before then, have a happy holiday."

"Thanks. Same to you," said Lucy, watching as Franny flew down the aisle, headed for the dairy section. She wasn't through in the produce section, not by a long shot. She still needed potatoes, at least ten pounds, and fruit for lunches, not to mention a holiday centerpiece. And those nuts—where did they hide them?

Almost an hour later, Lucy pushed her heavily laden cart up to the checkout, where she got in line behind Rachel Goodman. The cashier, Dot Kirwan, was busy ringing up another customer, a sixtyish woman with her gray hair cut in a neat sporty style.

"I don't know what the world is coming to," said the woman. "Did you see the paper this week?"

Lucy pricked up her ears.

"You mean that dog? Kadjo?" asked Dot. "I think he deserved a second chance."

"Not the dog. What that reporter wrote about my Bud! Honestly, the man dozes off for a few minutes and she makes it sound like he sleeps through all the meetings or something. It's outrageous. I don't know how they can print lies like that."

"It's not a lie," Lucy found herself saying. The three other women all turned to face her. "I've been covering those meetings for years, and I have to tell you Bud sleeps through all of them."

Mrs. Collier wouldn't hear it. She was so angry that the little wattles under her chin were quivering. "You're Lucy Stone?"

"I am." Lucy braced herself for the attack.

"Well, you ought to be ashamed of yourself! Writing trash like that! And don't think for one minute that I won't be complaining to the publisher."

Taking her bundle from Dot, Mrs. Collier plopped it in her cart and sailed out through the automatic door.

Standing in her place in line, Lucy felt rather sick.

"Well, I guess she told you," observed Dot.

"Don't give it a second thought, Lucy," said Rachel. "It's about time the truth was known." She glanced at Lucy's overflowing cart. "Is Toby coming home for Thanksgiving?"

"Yup. With his roommate, Matthew. What about Richie?"

Richie, Rachel's son, had graduated from Tinker's Cove High School with Toby and was a freshman at Harvard.

"He's staying in Cambridge. He says it's a good opportunity to catch up on his work." Rachel furrowed her brow. "I think he feels a little overwhelmed."

"It's a big adjustment," said Lucy. "I can't wait to see Toby. He says everything's okay but I need to see for myself—if you know what I mean."

"I do." Rachel began unloading her groceries onto the conveyer belt. "In fact, Bob and I are driving down and taking him out for Thanksgiving dinner."

"That's a good idea—plus you don't have to cook," said Dot as she began ringing up Rachel's order. "I see you got a turkey anyway."

"For the freezer. At this price, why not?"

"I got two," confessed Lucy. "One for Thanksgiving and one for the freezer."

"So you didn't get the fresh ones from Andy Brown?" Dot was grinning wickedly.

"At $1.69 a pound, I don't think so," said Rachel. "Not with tuition bills to pay."

"When that casino comes, our troubles will be over," said Dot. "We'll all be rolling in money. I went to Atlantic City last fall and won twelve hundred dollars. On the slots. That's the way to pay those bills."

"You were lucky," said Lucy. "I don't think you can count on winning. Most people lose money."

"That's true," conceded Dot. "But think of all the jobs. That casino will be a shot in the arm for the local economy."

"I don't know," said Rachel doubtfully as she began bagging her groceries. "Casinos bring a lot of problems: organized crime, drugs, money laundering. I can't say that I'm for it. In fact, Bob's going to be speaking against it at the meeting next week."

Rachel's husband, Bob, was a lawyer.

"That's good. People ought to speak up," said Lucy. "This is a nice seaside town. What do they want to go and spoil it for?"

"For money," said Dot matter-of-factly. "That'll be $141.38."

"Ouch," said Rachel, pulling out her checkbook. "That hurts."

"I feel your pain," said Lucy, nervously eyeing her own cart.

"Can I sell you a scratch ticket?" asked Dot.

"No!" chorused Lucy and Rachel.

CHAPTER 5

Zoe was excited about being able to read.

"S-T-O-P," she read the letters off the red sign, pronouncing the letters carefully. "Stop! Stop the car, Mom."

Obediently, Lucy braked at the corner and turned onto Main Street, driving a block to the Broadbrooks Free Library, where she pulled into the parking lot.

Lucy had, until recently, been a member of the library's board of directors and was still struggling with the mixed emotions of guilt and relief over her resignation. She had been tempted to avoid the library, but that wouldn't be fair to the kids, especially Zoe. This Saturday morning Lucy had firmly set her emotions aside so Zoe could attend a special program. Dr. Fred Rumford, an archaeology professor at nearby Winchester College, was leading a workshop on flintknapping, teaching the kids how primitive people made weapon points out of rocks.

"P-A-T-R-O-N-S," pronounced Zoe, staring at the PARKING FOR LIBRARY PATRONS ONLY sign. "Pat-rons. Mom, what's a patron?"

"It's *patron*. It means a person who uses something," explained Lucy as they followed the concrete path that led around the library to the front door. When they rounded the corner of the building she noticed Curt Nolan, who was raking the last of the leaves, and she gave him a wave.

"We're going to the library, so that makes us patrons," she continued, as they climbed the front steps, "and we can park here. If we were going to the stores across the street, we couldn't park here."

"But you do park here sometimes when you go shopping. You parked here when I got my school shoes." Zoe pursed her lips primly. "You broke the rule."

"I'm sure we went to the library that day, too," said Lucy so firmly that she almost convinced herself.

"No, we didn't," insisted Zoe. "I'd remember."

"Maybe I meant to, but ran out of time," said Lucy, pulling open the door. "Now remember: It's the library, so you need to use your very best manners."

Zoe nodded solemnly and hopped over the sill. Passing in front of the glass display case containing a pewter tankard she started reading off the letters: "E-Z-E . . ."

"Ezekiel Hallett," said Lucy, taking Zoe firmly by the hand. "He owned that mug a long time ago."

She pushed open the inner door and glanced at the circulation desk, then felt annoyed with herself for feeling quite so relieved that it was unattended. This was ridiculous, she told herself. People quit jobs, especially volunteer ones, all the time. And she had a good excuse. Her paying job at the *Pennysaver* was taking up more of her time.

"Mrs. Stone, how nice to see you."

Startled, Lucy turned and smiled at the new librarian, Eunice Sparks.

"Well, you know how it is," said Lucy. "Work, kids—there's never enough time."

"Oh, I know," Eunice agreed solemnly. Her brown eyes seemed almost liquid, floating behind her glasses. "And I see your byline *all* the time. Do you know we're having a special children's program this morning. With Fred Rumford from the college. Such a *fascinating* man."

"That's why we're here," said Lucy. "Zoe and I want to learn all about the Indians."

"And Indian dogs," said Zoe.

"The workshop is just starting downstairs in the meeting room," said Eunice.

"Thanks—see you later," said Lucy, leading Zoe through the children's section. "We'll pick out some books afterward, okay?"

As soon as Lucy opened the door to the stairs they heard the voices of the children and parents gathered for the workshop. What Lucy didn't realize until they reached the meeting room was that all the other children, except for Zoe, were boys. They were accompanied mostly by their fathers, but there were a few mothers, too.

"Let's go, Mom," said Zoe, halting in the doorway. "I don't care about Indians."

"Nonsense," said Lucy, heading for the two remaining empty chairs. "Indians are interesting."

"That's right," said Fred Rumford, a tall man with thinning hair who had a pair of wire-rimmed glasses perched on his nose. "Indians are very interesting."

He was standing at the head of a long conference table with a plastic storage box in front of him.

"What I have here," he said, peering down at the group seated at the table, "is the only remaining genuine Metinnicut artifact— at least, it's the only one we know about.

"The Metinnicuts, as you all know, lived here for hundreds of years before the European settlers came. We don't know very much about them or how how they lived. We do know that they hunted for game—deer and rabbits and things like that—and they also ate a lot of shellfish." He paused and looked at the children. "How do we know this?"

"Fossils?" asked a little boy with a fresh haircut.

"Good answer. But the Indians only lived here in the past thousand years or so. Fossils, bones that have turned to rock, are much older than that. But we do have archaeological evidence we've dug up. What do you think it is?"

Lucy knew Zoe knew the answer. They'd read about an archaeological dig in a children's magazine last night. She nudged her, but Zoe remained silent.

"Arrowheads?" asked another boy, who was wearing a cub scout uniform.

"Yup." Rumford nodded. "We have found arrowheads and spear points. What else?"

"Treasure chests?" guessed a boy in a plaid shirt. Lucy heard Zoe give a disgusted snort under her breath.

"No treasure." Rumford shook his head. "What do you think we've found?" He was staring at Zoe.

She hesitated, and Lucy held her breath, willing her to find the confidence to answer. Finally, she did. "Shells and bones."

Predictably, the boys hooted. The answer must be wrong because a girl said it.

"That's right!" exclaimed Rumford, silencing them.

Inwardly, Lucy gave a silent little cheer for Zoe. She hoped her daughter would always be able to summon up the courage to give an answer, even a wrong one, but she knew the odds were stacked against Zoe. The older the little girl got, the harder it would become.

"We can tell a lot about what the Indians ate from their garbage piles. We find bones from animals they ate and big piles of shells. We also know from what's in this box that they didn't just kill animals. Sometimes, they killed people."

He had the boys' undivided attention as he opened the box and lifted out a decorated wooden object for them to see. It seemed to Lucy to be in two parts: a wooden shaft decorated with black designs that held a solid wooden ball.

"It's a Metinnicut war club, used to bash out the brains of their enemies."

"Yeah!" exclaimed the boy with the haircut.

"Yuck!" said Zoe, wrinkling up her nose.

"I'm going to put it back in the box and let you all take a look at it, and while you're doing that, I want each of you to take a pair of these protective goggles. Then we can start making some flints, okay?"

Once Zoe was settled with her safety glasses and chipping away at her piece of flint, Lucy got up and wandered around the room, examining the displays that Rumford had brought from the museum. These were mostly points of all sizes—many of which would seem to be nothing more than bits of rock to untrained eyes. The war club, however, was undoubtedly something remarkable. Examining the workmanship, Lucy knew that it would have been difficult to produce anything like it even with modern woodworking tools. How could a native craftsman, working only with crude stone tools, make such a finely crafted weapon?

As she studied the war club, Lucy wondered about Metinnicut culture and all that had been lost. What had their garments looked like? Their houses? How had they managed to survive in such a hostile climate for hundreds, perhaps thousands, of years? What did their language sound like? What were their songs and dances like? What games did their children play?

It seemed terribly sad to her that nothing remained of the Metinnicuts except for the war club. So much had been lost, impossible to recapture. She couldn't help wondering how different American history might have been if the European settlers hadn't considered themselves superior to the natives and had been willing to learn from them.

"Look, Mom! Look what I made!"

Zoe was standing next to her, holding a crude arrowhead in her small, plump hand.

"Wow! That's neat."

Lucy picked it up and turned it over. "Was it hard?"

"No, Mom. C'mon. I'll show you."

Lucy allowed herself to be led back to the table, where Zoe instructed her in the fine art of flintknapping. When they were through, she, too, had produced a passable arrowhead. When she finally looked up, she realized everyone else had gone.

"I'm sorry," she stammered, blushing. "Are we holding you up?"

"Not a bit," said Rumford. "It's great to see someone take such an interest."

"It's fascinating," said Lucy. "It's amazing when you think about it. We have refrigerators and freezers and cars and TVs and computers, and it's a national emergency when the electricity goes out. These people lived so simply. . . ."

"Exactly," said Rumford, starting to pack up. "And they were successful until disease, brought by the Europeans, wiped them out. They had no immunity to common illnesses like measles and smallpox."

"Can we help you with this stuff?"

"Thanks," he said. "We can go right out to the parking lot through the workroom next door. Saves going up and down the stairs."

In a few minutes they had packed everything into plastic totes and gone out to the parking lot, forming a little parade. Rumford led, carrying a pile of boxes, followed by Lucy, who also had a stack of containers. Zoe was last, proudly carrying the box with the war club.

"It's the gray van. It says *Winchester College* on the side."

"W-I-N . . ." began Zoe, then stopped abruptly as Curt Nolan threw down his rake and approached them. He stopped in front of Zoe, towering over her.

"What you got there?" he demanded.

Zoe didn't answer, but stepped closer to Lucy.

"Is it a war club?" Nolan bent down so his face was level with hers.

Zoe nodded.

"Aren't you awful little to be carrying something so important?"

Nolan was no longer addressing Zoe. He had stood up and was talking over her head to Rumford.

Lucy started to speak, defending her child, but Rumford beat her to it.

"She's a very trustworthy child," said Rumford. "She was doing just fine."

"Well, what's fine to you and what's fine to me are two different things." Nolan glared at him. "Of course, it's only an artifact to you, a curiosity. To me, it's my history and my heritage. It's sacred. And if you can't take proper care of it, you ought to return it to the people who can—the tribe."

"What tribe?" Rumford's voice was contemptuous. "There are no Metinnicuts left. There is no tribe. And that's what I'm going to tell the feds."

Nolan's face flushed purple and he made a move toward Rumford. His hands were clenched, he seemed ready to take a swing at the professor.

Rumford's face was also flushed and he seemed ready to chuck the boxes he was holding in order to defend himself.

Lucy stepped toward him, staggering and causing her boxes to slip. The professor reflexively braced himself, allowing her to steady herself.

"How clumsy of me," she said, chuckling nervously. "We'd better get these things safely in the van."

"Of course," said Rumford, turning and setting his boxes on the curb. Slowly, with shaking hands, he took the keys out of his pocket and unlocked the back door, pulling it open.

"How's your dog?" Lucy had turned to face Nolan and spotted Kadjo, sitting patiently in the cab of Nolan's pickup truck. "Is he staying out of trouble?"

Nolan didn't answer, but stood for a moment glaring at Rumford. He suddenly turned and stalked off, stopping to pick up the rake he had thrown on the grass and tossing it into the bed of his truck. He jumped in the cab beside his dog and drove off, leaving rubber.

"Thanks," said Rumford. "I really didn't want to tangle with him."

"He's not so bad," said Lucy, carefully taking the box with the war club from Zoe and handing it to Rumford. "Emotions are running high these days. The Metinnicuts have a lot at stake." She smiled. "He might have a point, you know. Didn't the Smithsonian recently return some Indian artifacts?"

Rumford's face hardened. "If they get recognition as a tribe, and that's a big if, then we'll have to reconsider." He snorted. "If you ask me, it's just a big bluff. They don't care about the war club or anything else. They only want to be a tribe so they can have a casino." He paused and looked at her. "I mean, if they care so much, how come they've never protested when the football team uses the club at their pep rally every year? I care about that club a hell of a lot more than any of these so-called Metinnicuts— that's for sure. I make the team captain sign a paper saying he understands how valuable it is and that he accepts liability if any-thing happens to it, but believe me, I'm not happy until the club is safely back in its case."

Lucy nodded. "I understand how you feel," she said. Then she smiled. "But if I were you, I'd smoke a peace pipe with Curt Nolan. I think you have more in common than you think, and he's not somebody you want to have for an enemy."

Rumford shrugged in response and got in his van, giving her a nod as he drove off. As Lucy watched him go, she doubted he'd follow her advice, and maybe he was right. Curt Nolan didn't seem eager to make peace with anyone.

CHAPTER 6

Sometimes controversy was a good thing, thought Lucy, as she pulled her cleaning supplies out from beneath the kitchen sink. Thanks to the fact that the Metinnicuts' petition was so controversial, the selectmen's meeting had been scheduled for Tuesday evening, instead of the usual afternoon time, so more people could attend. That meant Lucy had all day to get the house in shape for Toby's homecoming.

Cleaning was never her favorite activity, but today she really didn't mind. She wanted everything to be perfect for Toby and his roommate Matt—or at least as perfect as it could be considering the house was over a hundred years old and occupied by an active family.

Oh, she loved the old farmhouse that she and Bill had worked so hard to restore, but she had to admit the years had taken their toll. As she went from room to room with her dustrag and vacuum, she noticed the woodwork was smudged with fingerprints, the paint on the back stairway was scuffed, and the wallpaper in the downstairs powder room was peeling. In the family room, the sectional sofa was looking awfully worn and the rug was past cleaning—it needed to be replaced. She sighed. There wasn't any hope of getting new carpet anytime soon; Toby's college bills made that out of the question. She went into the dining room to cheer herself up. There, the ceiling was freshly plastered and new wall-paper had been hung last spring.

As she polished the sideboard with lemon oil, she wondered about Matt, Toby's roommate. What kind of home did he come from? Coburn University had a smattering of scholarship students like Toby, but most of the students came from families that had plenty of money and didn't even qualify for financial aid. Did Matt come from a home like that? Would he expect a guest room with a private bath when all she could offer him was the trundle bed in Toby's room? And that was if she could convince Elizabeth to move back to her old bed in the room she used to share with the other girls—a big if.

All of a sudden the room she had been so proud of didn't look that great after all. The furniture didn't match; she'd found the big mahogany table at an estate sale but the chairs came from an unfinished furniture warehouse and she'd stained and varnished them herself. The rug was a cheap copy of an Oriental and the sideboard's only value was sentimental because it had come from her grandmother's house.

She flicked the dustcloth over a framed photo montage that hung above the sideboard and paused, studying the kids' faces. The montage had been hanging there for quite a while. Zoe was still a baby, Sara still a chubby preschooler, and Elizabeth was actually smiling. Perhaps that was her last recorded smile, thought Lucy, her eyes wandering to the photograph of Toby.

It was one she particularly liked, snapped just after Toby had scored a goal playing soccer in his freshman year of high school. He looked so young and boyish, with his chipmunk cheeks and enormous adult teeth, and so thoroughly pleased with himself.

Her hand lingered over the photo. She would never admit it to anyone, not even Bill, but she had missed Toby terribly since he'd left for college. Maybe it was because he was her firstborn, maybe because their personalities were so similar, but she had felt as if a part of herself had suddenly gone missing. She smiled. But now he was coming home again and the family would be whole again. She would be whole again.

Hearing the school bus she glanced at her watch. Goodness,

where had the day gone? She'd been so busy she hadn't noticed the time, and no wonder. She'd cleaned both bathrooms and the kitchen and had tidied and dusted the entire house. Only one job remained: evicting Elizabeth. She went to greet the girls.

"Where's Toby?" demanded Zoe, breathless from running all the way up the driveway.

"He's not here yet," said Lucy.

"Why not?" demanded Sara, dropping her bookbag on the floor with a thud.

"It's at least a five-hour drive, and he probably had classes this morning. I bet he'll get here around dinnertime."

"Oh, goody," said Elizabeth, her voice dripping with sarcasm. "I can't wait."

Lucy bristled. "You still haven't moved your things out of Toby's room like I asked you to," she said.

"I'll take care of it," replied Elizabeth, draping herself languidly on one of the kitchen chairs.

"It's still his room, even if you have been using it. I don't want Toby to feel that this isn't his home anymore."

"Well, it isn't, is it?" demanded Elizabeth. "He's not here anymore. Why does he get a whole room that he's not even using when I have to share with these cretins."

"What's a—" began Zoe.

"Am not!" screeched Sara, spraying everyone, and the table, with milk and chocolate chip cookie crumbs.

"That's disgusting!" exclaimed Elizabeth, reaching for a napkin to wipe her face as Sara beat a hasty retreat.

"Sara! Get right back here and clean up the mess you made, including your backpack!" yelled Lucy, shouting up the stairs.

"And you . . ." Lucy had turned to glare at Elizabeth. "I want you to clear your stuff out of Toby's room right now."

Lucy narrowed her eyes and Elizabeth shrugged. "Okay."

"And as for you . . ." Lucy turned her baleful stare on little Zoe, who was struggling with a gallon jug of milk. "Let me pour that for you."

* * *

By 6 P.M. everything was ready for Toby's homecoming. Elizabeth had taken her things out of his room and Lucy had made the beds with fresh sheets.

The table was set for seven and Toby's favorite meal, lasagna, was cooking in the oven.

Lucy inhaled the aroma of herbs and cheese as she went from room to room, closing the blinds and turning on the lights. In the lamplight, she decided, the house looked attractive and welcoming.

"Hey," called Bill, as he pushed open the door and dropped his lunch box on the kitchen counter. "Where's Toby?"

"He's not here yet," said Lucy, taking Bill's jacket and hanging it on a hook.

"Not here? What's keeping him?"

"I don't know," said Lucy in a tight voice. "I haven't heard a word from him."

"Now, don't worry," said Bill. "I'm sure everything's fine. They probably left later than they planned. You know how kids are."

"I'm sure that's it," said Lucy, pushing thoughts of squealing brakes and ambulances to the back of her mind. "Besides, we'd have heard if . . ."

"Right," said Bill. "The roads are clear. It's not like there's a storm or anything. I'm sure they're fine."

"Fine," repeated Lucy, peeking in the oven. "I know. Let's have a glass of wine and I'll hold dinner for a while. Say fifteen minutes? After all, it's Toby's favorite."

Bill opened a bottle of chianti and they sat at the kitchen table, fingering their glasses.

"How was work?"

"Fine." Bill took a sip of wine. "How was your day?"

"Okay. I have a meeting tonight."

"What time?"

"Seven."

Bill looked at the clock.

"Don't you think we'd better eat?" he asked.

"I guess so," said Lucy with a big sigh.

CHAPTER 7

Zipping down Red Top Road on her way to the town hall, Lucy had only one thought on her mind: She didn't want to go. She wanted to stay home to wait for Toby. Instead, she would have to sit in an overcrowded meeting room, facing the members of the board she'd so self-rightously blasted in last week's paper. What would their reaction be? Would Howard White publicly admonish her from his lofty perch as chairman? Would Bud Collier give her hurt, reproachful glances?

Worst of all was the knowledge that Ted had offered to cover the meeting for her and she'd turned him down. She had been sure Toby would arrive earlier in the day and there would be plenty of time to catch up at dinner. What had she been thinking? she wondered. How could she have forgotten that college students operated on a different clock from the civilized world, staying up until all hours of the night and sleeping late in the morning?

She braked to turn into the town hall parking lot and groaned aloud. Every spot was filled. That meant she was going to have to park across the street at the library. Not a good sign. The meeting room was obviously packed with people eager to express their opinions; it was going to be a very a long meeting, indeed. She wouldn't be home until eleven, at the earliest, and that was assuming she survived the roasting the board was sure to give her.

Getting out of the car, she spotted Ellie Martin and gave her a big wave. This was better; she'd feel a lot more comfortable going into the meeting with a friend.

"Looks like a full house tonight," said Lucy, as they waited for a car to pass so they could cross the street.

"I hope there's room for everybody," said Ellie. "I don't want to be shut out."

"Oh, you won't be," Lucy reassured her as they stepped off the curb. "Open meeting law. If the room's too small they have to relocate the meeting."

"Really?"

"Really. Trust me on this. If they could get away with it, the board would meet in a coat closet!"

Ellie was quiet as they walked along the sidewalk; then she stopped abruptly as they were about to enter the building.

"How do you think it will go tonight?" she asked in a serious voice. "Do you have any idea how they'll vote?"

"Not a clue," said Lucy with a little laugh. "They're a pretty unpredictable bunch."

She pulled open the door and paused, wondering what was bothering Ellie. "Does it matter to you, how the vote goes?" she asked.

"I didn't think it did, but now I'm not so sure," said Ellie, who was twisting the handles of her purse. When she spoke, she sounded tired. "I guess it's six of one and half a dozen of the other. You've heard of a win-win situation? Well, I'm afraid this is a lose-lose situation. No matter how the vote goes, everybody's going to lose."

Lucy wondered what she meant as they entered the hearing room. She had feared they would have to stand, but discovered there were a few unoccupied seats in the last rows. They sat down together and Lucy rummaged in her bag for her notebook and pen. Flipping the notebook open, Lucy found the agenda she'd picked up last week and unfolded it, holding it so Ellie could also read it.

"Where's the Metinnicut proposal?" asked Ellie, scanning the long list of items that included new parking regulations for Main

Street, budgets for the cemetery, shellfish and waterways commissions, and an executive session to discuss upcoming contract negotiations with the police and fire unions.

"It's last," said Lucy, realizing with dismay that the meeting could run well past midnight. "We'll never get out of here."

"Maybe they're hoping everybody will run out of patience and go home," said Ellie, hitting the nail on the head.

"Not much of a chance of that," said Lucy, scanning the jam-packed room. 'These folks aren't leaving until they've had their say."

Even from her seat in the back of the room, Lucy could see that all the players were in place, almost as if in a courtroom.

In the front row, on one side, sat Jonathan Franke, executive director of the Association for the Preservation of Tinker's Cove and Bob Goodman, Rachel's husband and the lawyer representing the association.

Franke's once long hair and casual workclothes had gradually been giving way to a more professional look; tonight he was wearing a denim shirt and knitted tie, topped with a tweed sport coat.

Bob, Lucy noticed, looked as if he'd come to the meeting straight from a long day in court. His suit was rumpled and he definitely needed a haircut. He was bent over a thick sheaf of papers and occasionally consulted with Franke.

On the other side of the room, the Metinnicut faction seemed more relaxed. Bear Sykes, the tribe's leader, was sitting with his arms folded across his chest. His thick black hair was combed straight back, and when he turned to confer with Chuck Canaday, the tribe's lawyer, Lucy saw he was wearing a wampum bolo tie with his plaid flannel shirt.

Canaday, as always, was impeccably dressed in a neat gray suit. Tall and fair, he was a dramatic contrast to Sykes's stocky, barrel-chested figure. Next to him was Andy Brown, wearing his trademark farmer's overalls and a smug expression, as if he had counted his chickens and was certain they would hatch a casino. The three looked up when a fourth man approached them—a man Lucy didn't recognize.

From his city-tailored suit, with no vents in the jacket, Lucy guessed he probably represented a bank or a real estate development company. This guess was confirmed when he bent down and whispered to Sykes, who immediately left the room and re-turned a few minutes later carrying a cardboard box, which he carefully set on a table in the front of the room. Lucy figured they were going to be treated to an architect's model—plans for the casino had indeed progressed further than anyone suspected.

"Look at that," snorted Ellie, glancing at Bear. "They treat him like an errand boy."

"If the casino gets approved, he won't be an errand boy any-more," said Lucy. "As tribal leader he'll be a very influential man."

"That's what I'm afraid of," said Ellie. "When's this meeting going to start?"

Lucy glanced at the empty bench in the front of the room and checked her watch; it was already ten minutes past seven.

"It's a power thing," she said, leaning toward Ellie. "The board keeps everybody waiting so they know who's in charge."

"I'll let them know who's in charge come the next election," said Ellie. "I'm missing my favorite TV show."

"Hiya, Ellie! What's happening?"

It was Curt Nolan, sliding into the seat beside Ellie.

"Did I miss anything?"

"Nothing. They haven't started," said Ellie. Lucy couldn't help noticing her voice suddenly sounded a lot brighter than it had be-fore Curt Nolan arrived.

"Good." Curt settled himself in the chair, planting his feet firmly on the floor and letting his knees splay apart. His hands rested easily on his denim-covered legs.

Lucy checked her watch again—it was a quarter past. Time for the selectmen to appear. A side door opened and Lucy slid down in her chair, hoping none of the board members would notice her as they marched in and took their places behind the raised bench. Last to enter was Howard White, the chairman, who walked briskly across the room to his seat at the center of the bench and picked up his gavel.

"This meeting is called to order. First on the agenda: parking regulations."

Lucy sighed with relief and sat up a little straighter. If Howard were going to scold her, he would have done it first thing.

"Point of order." Joe Marzetti's voice boomed out, unnaturally loud. "I'd like to move that we table all other business and take up the Metinnicut proposal first."

Lucy raised an eyebrow and scribbled furiously in her notebook.

"I second the motion," announced Bud Collier before White even had a chance to ask for seconds.

"Any discussion?" From White's tone, it was a challenge rather than a question. Howard White was clearly unhappy at this evidence of rebellion in the ranks.

Lucy was surprised. In her experience with the board, she had never seen individual members take any initiative whatsoever. Someone must have put a bee in Marzetti's and Collier's bonnets, and she suspected it was Chuck Canaday, who had gotten his ducks in a row before the meeting.

"Considering the very great interest in the Metinnicut proposal, I think we should act as expeditiously as possible," said Sandy Dunlap.

Lucy doubted that Sandy had come up with such big words on her own; she was probably quoting Chuck. What a busy bee. Lucy wondered if he was working on a retainer or if he stood to get a share of the casino.

"Any objections?" White looked hopefully to Pete Crowley, who was usually a stickler for proper procedure.

Receiving no encouragement in that quarter, White called for a vote, and the motion passed with only one no vote.

"All right, then," said White with a disapproving humph. "We'll take up the matter of the Metinnicut proposal."

There was a buzz in the room as Bear Sykes stepped forward to address the board, reading nervously from a prepared statement.

"The Metinnicut Tribal Council has asked me to request your support, as the board of selectmen, for the tribe's petition for federal recognition.

"We all know that the history of the Metinnicut people is interwoven with the history of this town—Tinker's Cove. When I was a little boy growing up here, I shared many of the same experiences as most American boys. I was a Cub Scout. I played Little League baseball. I went to the public schools and served in the army.

"I was also aware, however, that because of my Indian ancestry I was descended from people whose culture and values were different from those of most Americans. I felt a desire to acknowledge this separate identity, but I was unable to do so. My tribe, the Metinnicuts, were not recognized.

"In recent years, I spoke about this with family members and others and learned I was not alone in my desire to reclaim my Metinnicut heritage. As time went on, we formed a tribal council and conducted genealogical research. Now we are now ready to request federal recognition as a tribe. As citizens of this town, we ask your support for this petition. Thank you."

There was scattered applause, which White quickly silenced.

"Do I have a motion?" he asked, casting an evil eye toward Marzetti.

Marzetti swallowed hard and raised his hand. "I move that the board support the Metinnicut tribe's petition."

"Second?"

Collier nodded.

"Discussion?" asked White, looking extremely annoyed as hands shot up throughout the room.

"Do I have a motion to limit discussion?" Lucy, for once, found herself agreeing with White. Unless discussion was limited, the meeting could go on all night.

This was met with silence by the board.

Defeated, White recognized Jonathan Franke.

"With all due respect to Mr. Sykes and his Indian heritage, I want to point out that the main reason the tribe is seeking federal recognition is so that they can negotiate a casino deal with the state government. It's important to recognize that fact and consider the possible impact such a project would have on our town."

There was a loud buzz from the audience and Chuck Canaday stood up.

"If I may . . ." he began, catching Howard White's eye but continuing without waiting for his permission. "Mr. Franke has brought up an important point, which we are prepared to fully address tonight. With us is Jack O'Hara of Mulligan Construction in Boston. Mr. O'Hara has plans and a model of the proposed casino project."

"Ah, Mr. O'Hara," said White, shooting his cuffs. "Didn't I see your name in the business pages of the *Boston Globe*? They say you're the top contender for my old golfing buddy Joe Mulligan's job when he retires next year."

As Lucy wrote the quote in her notebook she felt a rare surge of sympathy for Howard White. It must be quite a comedown for a man like him—the former CEO of a paper company—to find himself reduced to managing an unruly group of local yokels.

O'Hara shrugged off the comment. "You know, sir, you can't believe everything you read in the papers. But I'll be sure to give your regards to Mr. Mulligan."

White was charmed. "Heh, heh," he chuckled. "That's right. Well, let's see what you've got there."

O'Hara stepped forward and stood next to the table with the box, but didn't lift the cover.

"By way of preamble," he began, "I want to tell you that we at Mulligan Construction believe we were presented with a tall order: a request for a modern, innovative design that would also honor the unique tradition of our clients, the Metinnicut Indian tribe."

A hush of expectation fell over the room. Feeling a slight vibration, Lucy's attention was drawn to Curt Nolan, who was sitting a few seats from her. He was so tense that his knee was twitching; his hands were clenched anxiously. Ellie was watching him nervously.

"With all due modesty," O'Hara continued, "I think you will agree that we have risen to the challenge and exceeded it."

With a flourish he lifted the cardboard cover and revealed the architect's model.

Involuntarily, Lucy blinked. There was a stunned silence, then a collective gasp, as audience members absorbed the two gleaming hotel towers, each at least fifteen stories tall, and the accompanying casino, a monstrous version of a traditional Iroquois long house rendered in glass and steel.

Lucy wondered what Nolan's reaction was and looked curiously at him. His knee, she saw, was jumping and his knuckles were white.

"What may not be obvious," said O'Hara, flicking a laser point over the model, "is that the complex will provide parking for two thousand cars, accommodations for five hundred overnight guests, numerous gift shops, and a wide variety of restaurants catering to all tastes from fast food right on up to a five-star dining experience."

As soon as he'd finished speaking, hands shot up around the room and Curt Nolan was on his feet.

"This is a travesty, an outrage," exclaimed Nolan.

From his perch behind the selectmen's bench, Howard White was nodding in agreement. He made no attempt to silence Nolan but let him continue.

"This prop-proposal has nothing to do with Metinnicut heritage," said Nolan, so angry he was stumbling over his words. "Metinnicuts never lived in long houses—and they certainly didn't have skyscrapers. And what about that museum we were promised? If you ask me, the only thing this looks like is the Emerald City of Oz!"

He sat down with a thump, and Ellie gave him a little pat on the knee.

White, for perhaps the one and only time, was nodding in agreement with Nolan. Looking around the room, he next recognized Bob Goodman, certain that he, as the lawyer for the Association for the Preservation of Tinker's Cove, would also be against the proposal.

"Putting all aesthetic considerations aside," began Bob, pausing to remove his glasses and wipe them with a handkerchief, "I feel compelled to point out that, as presented here tonight, this design does not comply with the existing zoning and site plan regulations of this town."

Canaday was immediately on his feet. "Point of order," he said, managing to get everyone's attention without raising his voice. "We believe there is some precedent here. If built on land that is owned by the tribe, and that can be shown to have been traditionally occupied by the tribe, local zoning ordinances do not apply."

At this pronouncement, the room exploded in an uproar as citizens loudly debated with their neighbors whether this could possibly be true.

Howard White pounded his gavel, and gradually the roar subsided and order was restored.

"I want to remind everyone that the merits," he spat the word out, "of the proposed casino are not the issue tonight. The question is whether the board will support the Metinnicut petition for federal recognition. I'm going to close the public debate now and bring that issue back to the board."

Pete Crowley took his cue.

"I'm sympathetic, of course," he began, "to the desire of the citizens of our town who are of Native American heritage to reclaim that, uh, heritage. But let's face it: Most of these so-called Metinnicuts are just about as much Indian as I'm Swedish, and for your information, my maternal grandmother was half Swedish which, as far as I can tell, makes me one hundred percent American!"

This was met with murmers of approval.

"The tribe's real interest, as we've seen tonight, is getting this casino built and as far as I'm concerned a casino is just going to bring organized crime and a lot of other problems to our town."

Crowley paused and shook his head sadly. "I'm sorry. I've lived with these people my whole life and I don't see how they're an Indian tribe. They're just like the rest of us."

"Well, I'm Italian and proud of it," proclaimed Joe Marzetti. "It doesn't make me any less American, but in my family we enjoy Italian food. We keep in touch with relatives in the old country. And I understand what Mr. Sykes is talking about. He has a right to his heritage. And if recognizing that right brings certain advantages to our town, like legalized gambling, so much the better."

He turned to Bud Collier and, noticing he had dozed off, poked him in the side.

Lucy couldn't help rolling her eyes. Mrs. Collier might not have liked her story, but it apparently hadn't affected Bud Collier in the least.

He roused himself, blinked a few times, and spoke. "There aren't enough jobs in this town. The kids are all moving away. We're going to become a town of old people if we don't watch it. These Metinnicuts—they're fine people. I've lived with them my whole life. Give them what they want."

He paused and cast a baleful eye on the model. "There'll be plenty of time to talk about *that* later." His chin sank on his chest and he resumed his slumber.

"Oh, dear," fretted Sandy Dunlap as Howard White looked in her direction. "I just don't know what to say. I mean, I'm sympathetic to the Metinnicuts . . . but after what we've seen tonight . . . I can't say I'm in favor."

Concluding that he had three no votes, White seized the moment.

"Are we ready to vote?" he asked.

"I vote yes. We should endorse the Metinnicut petition," said Marzetti.

"Yes," said Collier, expending as little energy as possible.

"I vote no," said Crowley, narrowing his eyes at the others.

"I, of course, vote no," said White. "That makes it a tie. Mrs. Dunlap?"

"Oh, dear, I just don't know."

Lucy leaned forward, pen in hand, to get every word.

"Of course, I value the Metinnicut heritage, but this is such an important decision, it could change our town forever. Of course, we can't stand in the way of progress, but we do want to preserve our treasured way of life. . . ."

Suddenly, Sandy's eyes brightened and her curls bounced.

"I know! Frankly, this is much too important a decision for people like us to make. This is one time I think we should rely on the experts in the federal government."

Lucy glanced at White; she thought he would explode with rage.

"The folks at the Bureau of Indian Affairs have developed expert criteria for determining whether a tribe is really a tribe," continued Sandy. "We should let them do their job. I vote yes."

Again, the room exploded. There was celebration on the Metinnicut side, anguish and head shaking among the preservationists. Lucy only felt relief. She had the quotes; she had the votes—she could go home. She grabbed her bag and fled, never looking back.

CHAPTER 8

"You're cutting it kind of close, aren't you?" growled Ted when Lucy arrived for work on Wednesday.

It was ten o'clock, just two hours before deadline.

"Not to worry," said Lucy, glancing at Phyllis, the receptionist, with a questioning raised eyebrow.

Phyllis responded with a nervous grimace. Lucy knew she was in some sort of trouble.

"I worked at home this morning," she continued, "while my pies were baking. I've got the whole story on this disk."

"I can't wait to read it," said Ted. "I heard there was quite a little dustup."

"Just what you'd expect. Howard White almost had apoplexy a few times, but he managed to control himself."

"What about Curt Nolan and the Mulligan guy? What's his name?"

"O'Hara," said Lucy, wondering what Ted was getting at. "Nolan had a few words with him."

"From what I heard, it was more than words."

"I don't know what you're talking about," said Lucy, feeling her stomach drop a few inches. "I stayed for the whole meeting."

"This was after the meeting. Nolan took a swing at this O'Hara fellow and he's pressing charges. Nolan's going to be arraigned this morning—I was hoping to have you cover it."

"Oh, shit," said Lucy, sliding into her chair and pounding her fist on the desk. "This is big. I can't believe I missed it."

"Me, either," said Ted, looking rather put out. "I thought I could count on you. What happened?"

"I stayed until they took the vote," said Lucy, sounding defensive. "Toby was supposed to come home yesterday but he hadn't arrived when I left for the meeting. I was in a hurry to get home and see him."

Ted nodded.

"The stupid thing is, he wasn't there when I got home either. He didn't actually roll in until one-thirty, and then he showed up with three friends instead of the one we'd been expecting." Lucy rubbed her eyes. "It was absolutely crazy. I mean, I was so worried l had Bill calling hospitals and the state police. When Toby finally did show up I didn't know whether to hug him or smack him." Lucy paused for breath. "And I didn't have a clue where all those extra people were going to sleep."

"Where'd you put them?" asked Phyllis, who had been keeping a low profile.

" 'No problem, Mom,' " said Lucy, imitating her son's laidback attitude. " 'We'll just crash in the family room.' This, mind you, comes after weeks of delicate negotiations to convince Elizabeth to move out of his room and back in with her sisters. I mean, I could've used Madeleine Albright!"

Phyllis laughed, and even Ted gave a weak chuckle.

"How are you going to feed them all?" asked Phyllis.

"Don't ask me. That was my next stop. After dropping this story off, I was going to get some groceries—with my Visa card." She looked at Ted. "What am I going to do about the story?"

He shrugged. "Go the official route. We don't have time for anything else. Get the police to give you the arrest report. Court's still in session, so you can't get the DA—I'll call the clerk's office and see if Mabel remembers those chocolates I gave her for her birthday."

While Lucy waited for the computer to boot up, she tried to get control of her emotions. It was tempting to blame the whole mess on Toby. After all, if he'd come home when he was supposed to, she wouldn't have been worried about him and wouldn't have hurried out of the meeting and wouldn't have missed the fight. Now, thanks to his inconsiderate behavior, she'd missed the biggest story that had come her way in a long time.

No, she thought. Shifting blame was the sort of thing kids like Toby did. She had every reason to be angry and disappointed with Toby, but she'd chosen to leave the meeting and she would have to live with her decision. Maybe she could still save the story. She reached for the phone and dialed Ellie Martin's number.

"Ellie," she began, "this is Lucy Stone. I guess I missed all the excitement last night. Can you tell me what happened?"

Ellie was cautious. "Is this for the paper?"

Lucy sighed. "You can talk off the record. I won't quote you. I'm just trying to find out what happened after I left. I heard that Curt took a swing at O'Hara. Did you see it?"

"I wish I hadn't," said Ellie. "I mean, if he has to lose his temper, why does he have to do it in front of a roomful of witnesses? I think he really hurt O'Hara—they called the ambulance. Curt's in big trouble."

"Do you know why he was so mad?" asked Lucy, making a note to check with the hospital on O'Hara's condition.

"He felt O'Hara had tricked the tribe. They'd been promised a museum and the casino was supposed to have a traditional design." She paused. "I think Curt really thought the casino was a way to recapture the Metinnicut legacy."

"Does he have a lawyer?"

"I don't know." Ellie sighed. "This morning I was all set to go down to the courthouse to bail him out. Then I thought, if he's so good at getting himself in these messes, maybe it's time he figured how to get himself out."

Lucy understood completely.

An hour later, Lucy had finished the story. Thanks to Mabel, Ted had learned that Nolan had remained in police custody overnight and had been arraigned on assault-and-battery charges. He'd been assigned a court-appointed lawyer and released on his own recognizance. The hospital hadn't been willing to release any information about O'Hara but Phyllis checked with her sister, who was a nurse in the emergency room, and learned he had been treated and released.

Lucy didn't linger in the office after finishing the story. She told Ted to call her at home if he had any questions and headed straight for the Quick Stop. There she picked up extra gallons of milk and orange juice, a dozen eggs, and a pound of bacon so she could give Toby and his friends a decent breakfast. Well, brunch, since they were probably still asleep after their late night.

As she expected, the house was quiet when she got home. Lucy peeked in the family room and saw the kids were dead to the world in a tangle of couch cushions, sleeping bags, and blankets. She closed the door and stood staring at it, wondering what to do.

It was almost one. Surely they didn't want to sleep the entire day away.

In the kitchen, Lucy brewed a pot of coffee and whipped up some blueberry muffins. While they were baking, she got some bacon started in her big cast-iron skillet.

"'Morning, Mom."

She smiled at hearing Toby's voice and turned to greet him. Her jaw dropped. He was standing there in nothing but a pair of boxer shorts.

"Toby! Put some clothes on!"

"What's the big deal?" he asked, pouring himself a cup of coffee and sitting down at the table.

Lucy stared at him. Who was this person with the shaggy hair and wispy little beard and mustache?

"You can't sit there like that. I won't have it. Go and put some clothes on."

"Okay, okay," muttered Toby, heading upstairs.

Lucy poked the bacon with a spatula and wished she didn't feel quite so miserable. She'd looked forward to Toby's homecoming for such a long time and now nothing seemed to be going right.

Hearing the rattle of hot water pipes that announced the shower was being used, she opened the door to the stairs.

"Don't use all the hot water," she yelled. "The others might want showers, too."

She was turning back to the stove when Toby's roommate,

Matt, appeared. He, she was relieved to see, was wearing jeans and a shirt. The same ones he'd been wearing last night. Lucy suspected he'd slept in them.

"Toby's taking a shower," she told him. "There's coffee."

"Coffee," he repeated, making it sound like some sort of rare and exotic drink. "That's great."

She poured a mug for him and set it on the table with the cream and sugar.

Matt sat down and stared at his coffee.

"So how was your trip? Was there a lot of traffic?"

"No," said Matt, obviously a man of few words.

Lucy turned over a piece of bacon. "We expected you much earlier."

Matt noisily slurped his coffee.

"Was there a reason why you were so late?" persisted Lucy.

"Late?"

Lucy gave up. "Would you like some bacon and eggs?"

That got a more positive response.

"Sure."

Toby and Matt were just finishing their meal when the two girls appeared in the kitchen.

"Mom, this is Amy and Jessica," said Toby, tilting his head in their direction.

Lucy looked from one to the other.

"I'm Amy," said the plump, dark-haired one. "That's Jessica."

Jessica had light brown hair and was tall and extremely thin.

"Would you like some breakfast?'"

"Maybe just some juice," said Amy.

"How about a blueberry muffin?" offered Lucy.

"No, thanks. I'm a vegan. I don't eat animal products."

"You can't eat a muffin?" Lucy was incredulous.

"Made with eggs, right? Listen, I don't mean to be any trouble. A glass of juice is all I want, really."

"And what about you?" Lucy turned to Jessica, who was watching with a horrified expression as Toby mopped his plate with a piece of muffin, lifted it dripping with egg yolk, and popped it in his mouth.

"Just some water," she said.

"Okay," said Lucy brightly. "That's easy."

What wasn't going to be easy, she thought, was coming up with something for supper that the entire group would eat. She'd been planning to serve beef stew, but that obviously would not do.

"So what are your plans for the day?" asked Lucy, joining the group at the table to eat a bacon, lettuce, and tomato sandwich.

"I don't know," answered Matt. "Say, Toby. What's doing in this burg?"

"Not much."

"There's the pep rally," said Lucy. "Or you could help out at the pie sale."

"Pie sale?" Amy was intrigued.

"They have it every year. To raise money for the Boot and Mitten Fund."

"Don't ask," said Toby. "It's so poor kids can have winter clothing."

"You don't want to miss the pep rally, Toby," said Lucy. "All your friends from high school will be there. Besides, don't you want to support the team? The Thanksgiving game is the biggest game of the year."

Toby rolled his eyes. "Oh, yeah. The Tinker's Cove Warriors against the Gilead Giants. I wouldn't want to miss *that.*"

"Toby, I'm surprised," said Lucy. "You always used to enjoy it."

No sooner had she spoken than she realized she'd said the wrong thing. Toby didn't want to be reminded of his youthful enthusiasms in front of his college friends.

"Well, it's up to you," she said, picking up her plate and carrying it to the sink, "but this is the country. There isn't a heck of a lot to do."

"How about a movie?" asked Amy.

"Only on the weekends," admitted Toby.

"I bet there's an arcade," said Matt.

Toby shook his head.

"A mall?" asked Jessica in a hopeful voice.

"Nope."

"Well," said Amy, "we might as well go to the pep rally."

"Rah, rah," said Jessica in a slow drawl.

Lucy had been listening to them as she loaded the dishwasher. She had to hustle, she realized. It was past two and she was late for the pie sale. She was just turning the machine on when the phone rang.

"For you, Mom. It's Dad."

"Sweetheart," he began.

Lucy new he wanted something. "What is it? I'm running late."

"This'll only take a minute. You know my clients, the Barths?"

"Um-hmm," said Lucy. "The old Tupper place?"

"Right. Well, they're having a little trouble with their car. It's a Range Rover and the garage says they can't get the part before Friday at the soonest."

"Bill, we have a full house," she protested. "We can't put them up."

"No, I know that. Matter of fact, they're staying at the Queen Vic," he said, referring to a very posh bed-and-breakfast on Main Street. "I was wondering if we could invite them for Thanksgiving dinner. It seems a shame for them to have Thanksgiving in a restaurant, especially since any decent place has been booked for weeks."

"I guess two more won't matter," said Lucy, glancing anxiously at the clock.

"Great! Thanks, honey."

By the time Lucy got to the pie sale, which was held in the fellowship hall of the community church, it was in full swing. Several long tables at the front of the room were covered with an impressive array of homemade pies, which customers could buy whole or by the slice. More tables were set up in the rest of the room, where people could eat their pie along with a cup of coffee or tea. As always, business was brisk and the room was crowded and noisy. Lucy finally found Pam in the kitchen, filling a coffeepot from a huge urn.

"Looks like you got a crowd," said Lucy by way of greeting. "Sorry I'm late."

"No problem," said Pam, giving her a big smile. "Did you bring your pies?"

"Sure did," affirmed Lucy, pleased to have gotten something right. "Six pumpkin."

"Bless you. I've been worried about running short. Patty Wilson came down with the flu and you know she always makes a dozen."

"What can I do to help?" asked Lucy.

"Here, take this coffee around and see if people want refills," said Pam.

"Aye, aye, Captain. Will you save an apple for me and a mince one, too, if you have it?"

"Sure thing."

As she made her way among the tables, Lucy saw many people she recognized. Oswald Crowley, the chief of police, gave her a wave and she went over to his table. As she went, she heard snippets of conversation. Everybody seemed to be talking about the same thing: the casino.

"Here you go," she said as Oswald held out his cup to be filled. "Who else wants some more coffee?"

She looked at the faces gathered at the table and fought the impulse to flee. It seemed the entire board of selectmen, minus Sandy, was sitting there.

"If it isn't our own little newshound," said Joe Marzetti.

"I just write it the way I see it," said Lucy, keeping her voice light. "More coffee?"

"I'll have some," said Bud Collier, looking at her somewhat curiously. It suddenly dawned on Lucy that he didn't know who she was; he hadn't connected her face with her byline, which was the way she wanted to keep it.

"I've got no complaints about Lucy," said Howard, surprising her so much that she almost dropped his cup. "She's a good reporter. And I'm sure we can count on her to cover all sides of this casino issue fairly." He put great emphasis on the word *fairly.*

"Absolutely," said Lucy, passing his cup back to him. She gave Bud a big smile, just in case he was following the conversation. "And anything I hear today is off the record."

"So, Howard," she heard Fred Smithers ask as she filled his cup, "is it true that town zoning regulations don't apply to the Indians?"

"That's nonsense," said Howard, setting his fork down. "We have very strong zoning regulations in this town. I don't think the Metinnicuts are going to find they can just ignore our bylaws."

"That's right," said Jonathan Franke, who was sitting at the same table. "The zoning bylaws were revised just last year and passed with a large majority at a town meeting. It was a long, hard battle but I think we finally have an effective tool for controlling development."

"Any court is going to have to take that vote into account," agreed Bob Goodman, dropping a lump of sugar into his coffee and stirring it with a spoon. "I've noticed in quite a few recent decisions that the courts have given community character quite a bit of weight."

Someone snorted at the far end of the table. Lucy was surprised to see Curt Nolan digging into a big wedge of blueberry pie.

"It's amazing," he said, hoisting his fork and popping a piece in his mouth. "You see what you want to see."

"Out of jail so soon?" asked Jonathan Franke, glaring at him.

"On my own recognizance," said Nolan. "It's a nice place to visit but I wouldn't want to stay there."

"I wouldn't be so cocky," said Crowley, giving him a nod. "You might be going back . . . for a while."

"You'd like that, wouldn't you?" said Nolan, looking at Franke.

"I'd like nothing better," replied Franke, shoving away his empty plate.

"Now, now, don't get all excited," said Nolan, looking over the rim of his cup. "I'm just as against that Mulligan proposal as you guys are, but I don't see how you can stop it with the zoning bylaws. Not when you let Andy Brown put up electric signs and that mechanical talking pumpkin. And a train ride. How come the association didn't have any problems with Mrs. Lumpkin, the Talking Pumpkin?"

As Lucy watched, Howard White's face grew quite red. "I can assure you that Mr. Brown went through all the proper channels," said White. "He obtained variances for those improvements."

"If you say so."

"Just hold on," said Franke. "You saw that model, and there

was no sign of any museum. It looks to me like Canaday and Mulligan Construction are taking the tribe for a ride."

Lucy held her breath, waiting for Nolan's reaction.

"I wouldn't be so sure if I were you," he said, clenching his fist.

"If I were *you,* I'd listen to him," said White. "What he's saying makes sense."

"We don't need *him* to explain things to us," said Nolan, pointing at Franke and rising to his feet. "We're not a bunch of dumb Indians who can't look out for own interests, you know."

"Now, now, I didn't say that—" began White.

"Well, I'll say this," said Franke, standing and facing Nolan. "The tribe used to be strong advocates for the environment. In fact, quite a few were APTC members. But now that you all stand to make a lot of money from the casino, well, I guess the environment takes a backseat to the almighty dollar. It's pretty hypocritical if you ask me."

"You have a lot of nerve, talking like that," said Nolan. "You haven't exactly been working for the environment for free, have you? What do you make as director? Fifty, sixty thousand? You know what the average Metinnicut income is? It's under the poverty line. Being environmentalists hasn't been quite as profitable for us as it has for you."

Franke glared at him, facing off. Lucy fully expected them to come to blows. Then, suddenly, Franke turned and stalked off.

Nolan laughed, then sat down. He looked at Lucy, who was standing speechless, coffeepot in hand.

"How about some more of that coffee?" he asked, giving her a big grin.

"Sure thing," she said, wasting no time in filling his cup.

Lucy stayed until the last cup had been washed and put away, the tables wiped, and the chairs neatly stacked in a corner. Then she bought her pies, said good-bye to Pam, and headed over to the football field to meet the girls. Remembering the trouble she'd had finding a parking spot last year, she put her pies in the car and left it at the church parking lot, walking the few blocks to the high school.

As she walked down the tree-lined street, where bare limbs

reached up to the blank gray sky, she wondered what made Curt Nolan tick. He'd only gotten out of jail that morning and he had been arraigned on assault-and-battery charges, yet only a few hours later, he almost got in a fight with Jonathan Franke. He seemed nice enough, she thought, admitting to herself that she actually found him rather likable. But he always seemed to be involved in some kind of confrontation. In fact, he seemed to make a habit of provoking and angering people. Why did he do it? What satisfaction could he possibly get out of it? It seemed a terrible waste of energy to her, an exhausting way to go through life.

Stopping at the corner to let a car go by before she crossed the street, she realized how tired she was. No wonder. She'd gotten only a few hours of sleep; then she'd spent the morning baking pies and working on her story. Then there'd been the stress-filled hour or two at the *Pennysaver* office, the rush home to cook for Toby and his friends, topped off by the pie sale, where she'd spent a couple of hours on her feet running around with the coffeepot.

Maybe Nolan had it right, she thought, trudging up the hill to the field and keeping an eye out for the girls. Maybe it was her way, trying to please everybody, that was exhausting. Maybe she ought to tell Ted to cover meetings himself if he wasn't happy with the way she did it, and maybe Toby needed to understand he couldn't be quite so inconsiderate and maybe Bill could cook Thanksgiving dinner for the Barths himself if he was so keen on inviting them. And what gave those girls, Toby's friends, the right to be vegans? The way she was brought up, you took what you were offered and said thank you.

"Mom! Mom!"

Lucy looked up and saw Sara standing by the gate, holding on to Zoe's hand.

"Are you okay, Mom?" asked Sara.

"Sure. Why?"

"You looked kind of worried."

"You looked mad," volunteered Zoe.

Lucy laughed. "I guess I am kind of tired."

"Toby was late." Zoe's little face was serious.

Lucy thought for a minute. "You haven't seen him yet, have you?"

"Nope."

"Me either," added Sara.

"Well, maybe we'll see him here. He said he was coming."

There were so many people on the field, however, that Lucy soon gave up looking for him. Instead, she led the girls to the top of the grandstand, where they could get a bird's-eye view of everything.

They had just sat down when the high school band could be heard approaching. Rapt with excitement, Zoe stood up and clapped enthusiastically when the band members finally appeared in their red uniforms with brass buttons.

As usual, they were playing out of key and several members were straggling behind, finding it difficult to keep in step while playing an instrument. Finally, they formed a loose rectangle on the field and waited while the drum major climbed onto an elevated platform. He raised his baton and the band responded with a blast of sound; he lowered the baton and they began rearranging themselves, finally resting in a ragged zigzag.

"What is it, Mom? What is it?" demanded Zoe.

Lucy frowned and furrowed her brow. After a moment, enlightenment came. "It's a W for Warriors."

"That's not a W," insisted Zoe.

"I think it's supposed to be a W."

"If you say so, Mom."

The drum major raised both arms dramatically, the final chord rang out, and everybody clapped like mad as the cheerleaders ran onto the field.

"Look, Zoe. It's the cheerleaders. Aren't their outfits cute?"

Zoe was enraptured. Lucy guessed she was picturing herself in a red-and-white cheerleader's skirt.

"What are they holding?"

"Pom-poms."

"Can I get one?"

"I don't know where you get them."

"You have to be a cheerleader," said Sara.

Zoe's face fell.

"Maybe we can make some," Lucy said, "out of crepe paper or something."

"I'll help," promised Zoe.

"We'll see," said Lucy.

"Give me a W," yelled the cheerleaders.

"W!" yelled back the crowd.

The cheer finally ended with everybody screaming, "Warriors! Warriors! Warriors!"

The band played a drumroll and all eyes went to the end of the field, where two girls dressed in fringed deerskin dresses were holding a large paper hoop. The band began playing the Warriors' fight song and the crowd roared as quarterback Zeke Kirwan broke through the paper circle, followed by the other members of the team. They ran down the field and formed a circle around a big pile of wood that had been stacked at the opposite end of the field.

The music finally stopped playing and everyone was silent, waiting for the big moment. They were rewarded with the sight of the two girls in Indian dress holding torches, escorting team captain Chris White, who was carrying the Metinnicut war club.

Everyone began chanting together: "Go! Go! Go!"

Chris raised the war club above his head, gave the traditional Warrior yell, and sped down the field followed by the torchbearers.

Still holding the club above his head, Chris joined the circle of his teammates. The girls threw the torches onto the pile of wood and the crowd roared as the flames grew steadily higher.

All of a sudden, everybody seemed to be moving, gathering around the huge bonfire. Holding Zoe carefully by the hand, Lucy made her way down from the grandstand. They joined the throng and stood watching the fire, roaring in approval as a dummy dressed in a Gilead Giants uniform was thrown into the flames.

"Mom, we'll win the game, right?" asked Zoe.

"Maybe," said Lucy, who subscribed to the glass-half-full theory.

"Not a chance," said Sara. "Gilead's already in the finals for the state super bowl."

"Winning's not the important thing," said Lucy mechanically. She was wondering what to have for supper. Something everybody would eat. "It's how you eat the rice."

"You mean play the game."

"That's what I said."

Zoe and Sara looked at each other and laughed.

CHAPTER 9

Lucy was just putting the finishing touches on a brown rice and carrot casserole when the phone rang. She picked up the receiver and was surprised to hear Fred Rumford's voice.

"What can I do for you?" she asked as she slid the dish into the oven.

"I have to get something in tomorrow's paper," he said.

"I'm sorry, Fred, but it's too late. The deadline was noon."

"Damn," he said.

Something in his tone made Lucy suspect that, whatever it was, it was something a lot more important than an announcement for a bake sale or a flintknapping workshop.

"Is something the matter?" she asked.

"You bet something's the matter! The Metinnicut war club is missing."

Lucy's hand tightened on the receiver. This could be a big story. "Are you sure?"

"Of course I'm sure. When I handed it over to Chris White I made him promise to bring it right back to me as soon as the pep rally was over. We agreed on a meeting place—by the ticket booth—and I was there right on time. In fact, I was early and I stayed for an hour, but there was no Chris. I went back to the museum, thinking he might have misunderstood and gone there instead, but there was no sign of him. I called his house and his mother told me he wasn't home yet and she didn't expect him until late because it was the night before the big game."

"Did you call the police?"

"Of course I did. And they picked up Chris, drunk as a skunk."

"On the night before a big game?"

"Not just him. Most of the team!"

"No wonder we never win."

"More to the point, there was no sign of the war club. Chris said he was approached after the pep rally by someone who offered to return the club for him and he handed it over."

"I can't believe he did that," said Lucy. "Did he know the person?"

"Apparently not. But he did say he looked like an Indian, with long black hair and a bear claw necklace."

Lucy sighed. "That sounds like Curt Nolan."

"Exactly," said Rumford.

"Are the police looking for him?"

"They are, but so far they haven't had any luck. He wasn't home and nobody seems to know where he is. For all we know, he could have left the country."

"I wouldn't jump to conclusions," said Lucy, who had learned as a reporter that there were always at least two sides to any story. "We don't really know much for sure. It's not even certain that it was Nolan who took the club."

"Oh, I'm certain," said Rumford.

Lucy didn't like his tone. He sounded as if he were ready to act as judge, jury, and executioner.

"What now?" she asked.

"Well, I'd hoped to get the news out. Ask for anyone who has any information about the club or Nolan to contact the police." He paused. "But you say it's too late."

As much as she hated it, Lucy knew she had to tell him, even though it meant the *Pennysaver* would lose a scoop.

"You could call the Portland paper," she said. "And the TV station. Why not try the *Boston Globe*?"

"You think they'd be interested?" Rumford sounded doubtful.

"I'm certain they will," said a resigned Lucy.

As she hung up, she thought of Ted. He'd be furious that he'd missed such a big story, but that was the problem with publishing only once a week. It meant you lost out on news that happened the other six days of the week.

There was really no point calling him with the bad news, she thought, as she started cleaning up the mess she'd made preparing the casserole. He'd find out soon enough.

CHAPTER 10

On Thanksgiving day, Lucy woke up a half hour before the alarm was set to go off. It was a luxury she was unaccustomed to: time to herself. Careful not to disturb Bill, who was sound asleep beside her, she rolled on her back and stretched. Then she tried to work up some enthusiasm for the long day that stretched ahead of her.

Truth be told, Thanksgiving had never been her favorite holiday, consisting as it did of football and food. Food that she had to cook and dishes—lots of dishes—that she had to wash. This year she'd been able to summon up more excitement than usual, but that was because Toby was coming home.

She sighed. Somehow Toby's homecoming hadn't gone at all as she'd expected. He and his friends seemed interested in using the house only as a place to sleep and leave their stuff. Yesterday, much to her irritation, after she'd gone to the trouble of making that vegan brown rice and carrot casserole for supper, they'd gone on to Portland after stopping only briefly at the pep rally and hadn't returned until around eleven. She hadn't seen much of Toby, and the girls hadn't seen him at all. They'd either been asleep or at school when he made his brief appearances. There was plenty of evidence of his and his friends' presence, however, in the huge pile of sleeping bags and backpacks that practically filled the fam-

ily room, in the wet towels left on the bathroom floor, in the litter
of dirty snack dishes that filled the kitchen sink.

Lucy didn't know exactly what she wanted. Certainly not cozy
family games of Monopoly, such as he used to enjoy when he was
younger. But she had thought he would join the family at dinner.
She'd thought he'd be around for a while in the evenings, perhaps
watching a video with the rest of the family. And she had hoped to
have a little time with him by herself.

Now, she realized with a start, if she did get him to herself she'd
like nothing better than to shake some sense into him. She would
like to yell and scream and let him know he was behaving like a
pig. She'd like to make him understand how much he was hurting
her and how very angry it made her feel.

No, she thought. That wouldn't do. If he was the prodigal son,
it was her job to set aside her petty little negative feelings and welcome him. To kill the fatted calf in celebration—or in her case, to
cook the turkey and reheat the brown rice casserole.

Doing a quick count, Lucy realized there would be twelve for
dinner, instead of the eight she'd been figuring on, presuming
Toby and his friends deigned to eat Thanksgiving dinner with
them. She counted again. Herself and Bill and the three girls—
that was five. Toby and his friends made nine. Add the Barths and
Miss Tilley, the total came to twelve.

That meant she would need some extra chairs. She'd have to
round up all the strays from the bedrooms and Bill's attic office.
There were plenty of dishes, but her silver service only had eight
place settings, so she'd have to use the kitchen stainless, too. So
much for the elegant table she'd hoped to set. Oh, well, she told
herself as the alarm sounded, Thanksgiving was about being
grateful for what you had, not wishing you had four more sterling
place settings.

A few hours later, Lucy was savoring the sweet satisfaction of
revenge. The college kids weren't sleeping late this morning thanks
to Zoe, who wanted to watch the Macy's Thanksgiving Day Parade on TV. She had settled herself right in front of the TV, a bowl
of cereal on the floor, a spoon in one hand, and the remote in the
other. Any attempts to dislodge her—and there had been a few—

had been repulsed with fits of noisy squealing. She had now solid-
ified her position, calling on her sisters to act as reinforcements.
The college kids had finally given up and had begun the hours-
long ritual of morning showers.

Busy in the kitchen, peeling potatoes and mixing up stuffing
and arranging plates of condiments, Lucy thought smugly to herself that things had a way of working out. They hadn't eaten the
cassserole last night; they could jolly well eat it today. They didn't
want to behave like proper guests; the family didn't have to act
like gracious hosts.

Glancing at the clock, Lucy saw it was almost time to leave for
the football game. She turned on the oven and opened the door,
preparing to slide the turkey inside so it could cook while they
were gone, when Sara ran into the kitchen.

"You'll never believe it, Mom."

"What won't I believe?" asked Lucy, straightening up.

"I saw Katie Brown on TV!"

Lucy looked at her doubtfully. "How can you be sure it was her?"

" 'Cause she was with her dad and her mom and her brothers.
They were all there. At the parade, like she said they would be."

"Really? You saw them in New York?"

"Yeah, Mom. Isn't that cool? She told me in school yesterday,
to look for her, and I did and I saw her! I can't wait to tell her."

"That is pretty cool," said Lucy. "Is the parade almost over?"

"Yeah."

"Good, because it's almost time for the game. Would you tell
the others so they can get ready to go?"

"Sure thing, Mom."

A miracle. A small miracle. She'd asked one of her children to
do something and she'd done it willingly. *Treasure the moment,*
Lucy told herself as she checked the dining room table.

Everything was in place: the linen tablecloth and napkins, the
cornucopia of fresh fruit and nuts, the twelve place settings with
assorted flatware. Three pies—pumpkin, apple, and mince—were
sitting on the sideboard along with dessert plates and coffee cups
and saucers. It all looked very nice, she thought, pausing to ad-
mire the new wallpaper.

In the kitchen, the turkey was stuffed and roasting in the oven;

it would be almost done when they got home. The brown rice casserole only needed a few minutes in the microwave; the potatoes were peeled and in the pot, covered with water and ready to cook. Cranberry sauce, pickles, and celery with olives were arranged on crystal dishes and covered with plastic wrap, cooling in the refrigerator. So was the wine, and the coffeepot was set up and ready to go.

And so was she. Ready to go and cheer for the home team at the football game.

Taking her place beside Bill in the Subaru, Lucy firmly pushed all thoughts of Toby and his friends from her mind. They had transportation. They could come to the game if they wanted to. She wasn't going to worry about them. She and Bill and the two younger girls would have a lovely time on their own. Elizabeth, never a big football fan, had offered to stay home and keep an eye on the turkey. What a contrast to her thoughtless, irresponsible, selfish brother!

"It's a perfect day for football," said Bill, interrupting her thoughts.

Lucy considered. The sun was shining brightly in a cloudless blue sky, there was no wind to speak of, and there was just a slight nip in the air.

"It's perfect," Lucy agreed, hoping that Toby and his friends wouldn't miss the game. It would be a shame, on such a nice day, to stay cooped up in the house.

Instead of going straight into town, Bill took the long way round on the shore road. There, big, old-fashioned, gray-shingled "cottages" stood on the bluff overlooking the cove. The trees were bare, and brown leaves had drifted into the road, but tall, pointed fir trees provided a touch of green here and there. Beyond the houses they could see the sea, deep blue with a scattering of tiny whitecaps. Farther out, on the horizon, they could see the humped shape of Metinnicut Island.

"See the seals!" exclaimed Sara, pointing to a small cluster of rocks.

Bill pulled off the road and stopped the car. Lucy took a closer look and saw several seals lounging in the sun. As she watched, one slid into the water.

"It's not a bad place to live," said Bill as they turned back onto the road.

"Not bad at all," agreed Lucy, resolving to concentrate on her many blessings rather than dwelling on her problems with Toby. After all, he was in college. It wasn't as if he were in jail or unemployed or working at a dead-end job somewhere.

Traffic grew heavier as they approached the field, so Bill decided to park alongside the road rather than try to find a spot in the parking lot. They climbed out and joined the crowd of walkers on the sidewalk.

As they marched along, Lucy kicked the dry brown leaves that covered the sidewalk and sniffed their sharp, musky scent. She grinned at the girls and slipped her arm through Bill's. When they turned the corner, they could hear the band playing, and Lucy felt as if she were back in high school herself. She squeezed Bill's arm. A roar went up from the crowd already gathered in the stadium and Lucy guessed the teams were being introduced.

They took their places in the line at the ticket booth and soon were climbing up the stands to claim the few remaining seats near the top. Lucy held Zoe's hand, but Sara insisted on going ahead of them.

They sat down just in time for the kickoff. The Warriors had won the toss and elected to receive the ball; Bill approved of their decision.

"Brian Masiaszyk, the kid who was on the state all-star team last year—he's really fast. If he gets the ball they'll gain a lot of yardage."

Lucy thought she understood what he meant. Maybe. She held her breath as the ball soared throught the air and landed in Brian's arms.

"Yes!" said Bill, leaping to his feet.

Suddenly everyone was standing and cheering as the all-star player ran down the field, dodging and even slipping through the arms of the Giants to make a touchdown. The Tinker's Cove fans roared their approval. On the other side of the field, the fans of the Gilead Giants sat silently, looking glum.

"What happened?" asked Zoe, tugging on Lucy's sleeve.

"A touchdown, stupid," said Sara.

Lucy's eyes widened in surprise. "That was unnecessary," she said.

"I'm sorry," mumbled Sara.

Lucy knew that Sara often squabbled with her older sister, but she was usually sweet-natured toward Zoe. Lucy wondered if the fact that Toby had ignored her since her got home was upsetting her, causing her to vent her frustration on her little sister.

"Is something bothering you?"

"Nah."

"Are you sure?" Lucy reached out and touched Sara's arm.

"I'm sure," said Sara, shaking herself loose.

"Okay."

The Giants now had the ball and were making slow, steady progress down the field. Despite their brave showing at the beginning of the game the Warriors seemed unable to put up much defense. By the half the Giants were leading thirteen to seven.

"Want something to eat?" asked Bill, standing up and stretching as the teams straggled off the field.

"And spoil our appetites?"

Lucy was starving but didn't want to admit it.

"I'm starving," said Bill. "It's been hours since breakfast. How about some hot dogs and hot chocolate?"

"Make it popcorn and black coffee for me."

"You got it. Come on, girls—I'll need help carrying the food."

Left to her own devices, Lucy decided to head for the ladies' room. She was standing in line when Sue saw her and stopped to chat.

"How's it going?" she asked, flipping her tartan scarf over her shoulder and straightening her matching gloves.

To her surprise, Lucy felt tears pricking her eyes. She blinked furiously. "Great," she said.

Sue narrowed her eyes. "If things are so great, how come you look so miserable?"

"I'm just feeling sorry for myself, I guess. Toby looks great. He's doing fine at school. He has lots of friends."

"But he doesn't have any time for you?"

"No." Lucy shook her head and her bangs bounced.

Sue wrapped an arm around her shoulder.

"I told you. You never get back the same kid you sent away. When Sidra was in high school she was hard working and organized. She kept her room neat as a pin. She played field hockey every fall and stayed in shape the rest of the year by running. She'd bring me little things she found: a perfect acorn, a seashell, a pink pebble." Sue sighed. "She came back from her first semester a completely different person. She would only wear black. She spent the whole vacation lounging on the couch. When I suggested she get some exercise she actually growled at me. I didn't know what to do. I was frantic. Finally, I dragged her to the doctor."

"What did he say?"

"After he examined her, he took me into his office and wrote me a prescription for tranquilizers!"

"Did they help?"

"I didn't take them. I decided I just had to let her grow up. couldn't wreck my life worrying about her. It was time to let go."

"Easy to say," said Lucy, tempted to growl herself.

"Not easy to do," agreed Sue. "See you later."

Back in the stands, Lucy propped her popcorn in her lap and wrapped her hands around the paper coffee cup. The warmth felt good. She slid a little closer to Bill and rested her head on his shoulder. He turned his head, brushing her forehead with his beard.

"They've gotta turn it around," he said, as the teams lined up for the kickoff. "Go, Warriors, go!" he roared.

The Warriors' cheerleaders were doing their best, leading the crowd through the familiar litany of cheers. It seemed to work; the Warriors played a lot better in the second half and got two more touchdowns, thanks largely to the heroic efforts of Brian Masiaszyk.

By the fourth quarter, the Warriors were obviously tired and getting sloppy. The Giants started putting pressure on the Warriors quarterback, Zeke Kirwan. In a desperation move, he threw a long pass that missed and the Giants got possession of the ball. They didn't go for any flashy maneuvers. They just drove down the field like a machine to score a touchdown. When the Warriors got the ball back they couldn't make a first down and the Giants had the ball once again. The Warriors had lost their lead. The game was tied at nineteen to nineteen, and there were two minutes left to play when the hometeam finally got the ball back.

Nevertheless, hopes were high on the Tinker's Cove side of the field. Fans stood and cheered, hoping for a miracle as the teams lined up on the thirty-yard line. Maybe Masiaszyk could score again? Maybe it was time for Kirwan to try another Hail Mary pass?

The stands fell silent as the players crouched down, waiting for the referee to signal the snap. All eyes were on the field, practically everyone was holding their breath in the tension of the moment. Raising his arm, the referee seemed to move in slow motion. He had the whistle in his hand and was bringing it to his lips when, suddenly, a woman's high-pitched scream ripped through the stadium.

It was one of the cheerleaders, Megan Williams. She was standing on the sidelines, shaking and sobbing. An EMT approached her and she pointed behind the concession stand; then she collapsed in his arms as he wrapped a blanket around her. He stood holding her as a couple of police officers ran up to them. There was an exchange of words and one of the officers signaled that the game should resume.

Once again the players took their positions, but Lucy knew Ted would expect her to find out what was going on.

"I'll meet you at the car," she told Bill and made her way down from the bleachers. Once she was on firm ground she ran over to the refreshment stand, oblivious to the struggle that was taking place on the field.

Several more officers had arrived when she joined the small group of curious onlookers. Spotting her friend, Officer Barney Culpepper, she elbowed her way through and went up to him.

"What's going on?" she asked.

Barney considered for a minute, glancing left and right as he removed his cap. Then he brushed his hand through his crew cut and carefully replaced it.

"We've got a homicide."

Lucy gasped in shock. "Who?"

"Curt Nolan."

For an instant, Lucy didn't register the name. Then it hit her. Her hand flew to her mouth. "Oh, no."

"You know him?"

"A little."

Lucy tried to remember when she'd seen Curt last. Of course, it had been yesterday at the pie sale. She could practically see him raising a fork loaded with blueberry pie to his lips, a glint of mischief in his eyes.

"You're sure he's dead?" asked Lucy, unwilling to believe the bad news.

Barney nodded. "Brain's bashed in."

Lucy grimaced but Barney wasn't through. "Murder weapon was right there beside him. Some sort of Indian club."

The roar of the crowd rang in her ears and she was jostled aside as the police cleared the area. For a second, she got a glimpse of Nolan lying on his back, his face to the sky.

That's where he's gone, she thought. *Up above the clouds into the bright sunshine beyond.*

CHAPTER 11

"I can't believe it," moaned Bill as they were driving home. "Neither can I," agreed Lucy, whose face was white with shock.

"Absolutely no defense," continued Bill.

"I wouldn't say he was defenseless," said Lucy. "I would've thought he could take care of himself."

Bill gave her a sideways glance.

"Are we talking about the same thing? I'm talking about the game."

"Me, too," lied Lucy.

Bill stared at her. "No, you weren't. You were talking about Curt Nolan."

"Well, I am going to have to report on it for the paper."

"Reporting is one thing. Getting involved and trying to figure out who did it is another. You'd better leave that part to the police."

Mindful of the two girls in the backseat, Lucy didn't want to argue.

"Absolutely," she said, thinking it was time to change the subject. "So how did the game end? Did we win?"

In the back seat, Sara and Elizabth laughed. In the front, Bill snorted.

"The Giants intercepted the ball. Some guy ran seventy yards for a touchdown. I tell you, there's no excuse for that. Where was the defense?"

"No excuse," echoed Lucy. "No defense."

An hour later, alone in the Subaru as she went to fetch Miss Tilley, Lucy's thoughts returned to Curt Nolan. No two ways about it, she admitted to herself, he was confrontational. He loved an argument and was never one to go along just to get along. A man like that made enemies, no doubt about that. There were plenty of people in town who had their problems with him, but that didn't mean they would actually kill him. This was New England, after all. The more ornery and cantankerous a person was, the more likely his neighbors were to grant him a grudging respect.

Lucy felt tears sting her eyes and blinked. She was surprised at herself. She wouldn't have thought she cared that much about Curt Nolan.

She remembered the day at the turkey farm, when the kids had been so frightened and he'd come to their rescue by distracting TomTom Turkey. She thought of him at the dog hearing, where he'd defended his pet.

By now the tears were really flowing and she had to pull off the road. This was ridiculous, she told herself as she fumbled in her purse for a tissue. She hadn't even known the man, not really.

But, she realized with surprise as she blew her nose, she had liked him. And why not? There was something awfully attractive about a man who was so comfortable in his own beliefs that he wasn't afraid to stand up for them. Not to mention the fact that he was good with animals and children.

Then her heart felt heavy as she thought of Ellie. She was already a widow, and losing Curt would be another terrible loss for her. Even more difficult, in a way, because the death of a good friend didn't elicit the same sort of sympathy that the death of a husband did. It was an awkward situation and people wouldn't know what to say or even if they should say anything at all.

Making the situation worse, thought Lucy, was the fact that Curt Nolan had been murdered. Tinker's Cove was a small town where nearly everybody knew everybody else. There was no random crime here as you would expect to find in a big city. Whoever killed Curt Nolan had done it deliberately, for a reason.

Why? wondered Lucy. *Why kill him?* It hardly seemed that the murderer would have taken such a huge risk, assaulting him at a crowded football game, just because Curt was occasionally obnoxious. There had to be a reason, thought Lucy, flicking on her turn signal and pulling back into traffic. A reason worth committing murder.

Arriving at Miss Tilley's little antique Cape-style house, Lucy leaned hard on the doorbell. She knew Miss Tilley—whose age was a secret but who had been old for the twenty-odd years Lucy had known her—was hard of hearing. She also moved slowly these days, so Lucy waited patiently, giving her plenty of time to answer the door.

After it seemed at least five minutes had gone by, Lucy gave the doorbell a second try. When this ring also failed to bring Miss Tilley to the door, Lucy began to worry. Perhaps her old friend had fallen or had taken sick. It happened to frail elders all the time and sometimes they weren't found for days.

Lucy swallowed hard and tried the door. It opened and she went in, preparing herself for the worst.

"Hello," she called out loudly. Then she paused a moment in the little entry hall, listening for a reply.

"No need to yell," said Miss Tilley. "I'm right here."

She spoke slowly, without her usual snappish tone. Lucy thought she sounded tired.

"Is everything okay?" Lucy asked, entering the front parlor.

Miss Tilley was seated in her usual rocking chair by the fireplace but there was no fire in the hearth. The electric lights hadn't been turned on either, making the room dim.

"No. It's not all right. It's dreadful."

"Are you ill?"

"Oh, no. I'm fine. A horrid, decayed old wreck like me is perfectly fine and a big, strong young fellow like Curt Nolan is dead. Is that all right?"

"No, it's not all right." Lucy sat on the footstool and put her hand on Miss Tilley's knee. She sat quietly for a moment, then spoke. "How did you hear about it? It only happened a few hours ago."

"The radio. I was listening to the game."

This was a new side to Miss Tilley that Lucy hadn't suspected. "I didn't know you followed football."

"Just the high school team. I like to keep track of the youngsters." Miss Tilley had been the town librarian for many years and knew everyone. "Curt played, you know. He was a very good player."

"I'm not surprised," said Lucy, spying something in Miss Tilley's hand. "What have you got there?"

"A little change purse." Extending her wrinkled claw of a hand she held it out for Lucy to see. "Curt made it for me many years ago."

Lucy took the little deerskin purse and examined the fine beaded design and the fringe decoration.

"It's lovely."

"I've always treasured it." Even in the poor light Lucy could see her eyes brighten at the memory. "He was such a sweet child, so interested in Indians. He read everything in the library, then asked me to get him more books from the interlibrary loan. By the time he graduated from high school, he must have been quite an expert. I hoped he'd go on to college to study anthropology or archaeology, but he didn't." She sighed. "He gave this to me just before he left for the army. It was the Vietnam war and he was drafted. Imagine. He survived all that and came back to Tinker's Cove, only to die at the Thanksgiving football game."

It was later, when they were in the car, that Miss Tilley finally asked how Curt died.

"Didn't they say on the radio?" asked Lucy.

"No. Just that his body had been discovered."

Lucy didn't want to tell her. It would only upset her, but there didn't seem any way around it. She drove carefully, watching the road, trying to think of the best way to say it. Finally, she came to the conclusion there was no good way.

"He was assaulted with the Metinnicut war club."

Miss Tilley drew in her breath sharply. "You mean he was murdered?"

"I don't see how it could have been an accident," said Lucy.

"That's awful!"

"I know."

For a few minutes, they drove on in silence. It was when they were turning into Lucy's driveway that Miss Tilley challenged her.

"You have to find out who did this, you know."

"It's not that easy," said Lucy, braking. "Bill's already made it very clear he doesn't want me getting involved. And I'm sure the police won't want me poking my nose into their investigation. I can just imagine what Lieutenant Horowitz would say."

"You're a reporter, aren't you? Asking questions is your job and they can't stop you. Freedom of the press is a constitutional right."

Lucy was sympathetic, but she wasn't going to be bullied.

"You know perfectly well that means newspapers can print what they want within reason. It doesn't mean reporters have carte blanche to interfere in a police investigation."

"As a favor for me?"

Lucy found herself looking at Miss Tilley: her faded blue eyes, her wrinkled cheeks, her wispy white hair.

"Please."

The word hit Lucy like a bucketful of cold water. Over the years Miss Tilley had threatened and argued and cajoled her into doing many things she'd rather not have done, but she'd never before said that word, never said *please.*

Lucy blinked hard and smiled.

"Well, if you put it that way, how can I refuse?"

Besides, she told herself, she already had a suspect in mind.

Entering the hall, where she paused to hang up Miss Tilley's coat, Lucy heard voices in the living room, where Bill was entertaining the Barths.

"Lucy," said Bill, rising to greet them. "I'd like you to meet Clarice and St. John Barth."

"I'm so glad you could come," said Lucy.

The Barths were seated together on the couch, and they nodded amiably at her. Clarice was just as she had expected: tiny, trim, and toned, dressed entirely in black. Just looking at her made Lucy feel huge, out of shape, and hopelessly out of style. In contrast, St. John was shorter and pudgier than she expected. He seemed ready to burst out of his stiffly starched shirt and tightly knotted tie. Seeing Miss Tilley appear behind Lucy, he jumped to his feet.

"I'd like you to meet a dear family friend, Julia Tilley," said Lucy.

"Nice to meet you, Julia. St. John Barth, here, and this is my wife, Clarice."

Lucy's eyes widened in shock. No one, except a sadly diminished group of contemporaries, ever called Miss Tilley by her first name. Today, especially, Lucy didn't think she'd tolerate such disrespect.

"I'm afraid I'm hopelessly out of date," Miss Tilley purred. "I prefer to be called Miss Tilley."

That seemed pretty mild, thought Lucy, relaxing.

"No problem, Miss Tilley," said St. John with a smile.

"Thank you."

A gleam appeared in Miss Tilley's eye and she screwed up her mouth.

Oh, no, thought Lucy. *Here it comes.*

"Since we're speaking of names, why do you pronounce yours *Saint John?* Don't you know it's properly pronounced *Sinjin?*"

Clarice bristled and came to the defense of her husband. "It's a family name and that's the way the Barths have been saying it for generations."

Miss Tilley's back stiffened and Lucy jumped in, hoping to avoid bloodshed.

"The Barths are clients of Bill's," she said. "They've bought the old Tupper place and are restoring it. It's going to make a lovely home."

From her place on the couch, Clarice gave a small, smug smile.

"Would anyone like a glass of wine?" asked Lucy.

Receiving nods all around, Bill disappeared into the kitchen.
Lucy helped Miss Tilley get settled in an armchair, then perched
on a hassock. She tried desperately to think of something to say.
"Tinker's Cove must be quite a contrast to New York," she fi-
nally ventured to say.
"Oh, it is," agreed St. John.
Clarice was examining her fingernails, which were polished
bright red.
This was going to be tough, thought Lucy.
"I suppose you'll be using the house for vacations and week-
ends?"
"Actually, we're thinking of moving here year-round."
"Really?" Lucy was surprised. "Don't you have jobs in the
city?"
"Clarice works in fashion—she designs displays for outfits like
Guess and Banana Republic," said St. John, a note of pride in his
voice. When he continued, his voice had dropped and he was
practically mumbling. "I used to work for a big construction out-
fit, Mulligan, but I'm between jobs at the moment."
Lucy recognized the name immediately; she knew Mulligan
Construction had designed the plans for the casino. Before she
could ask about it, Clarice jumped in.
"St. John wants to write a book."
"A writer!" exclaimed Miss Tilley. "What's it going to be about?"
"He's not sure yet," said Clarice. "But it's sure to be a best-
seller, whatever he writes."
Just then Bill appeared with a tray of wineglasses and passed
them around. Lucy waited until he had pronounced a toast and
then she fled.
"I have a few things to do in the kitchen," she said.

When she got there, she discovered that Bill had started cooking the potatoes, and they were ready to mash. That was good, she
thought, guessing he wouldn't be able to keep the combatants in
the living room apart for long. But when she started ro whip the
potatoes, she discovered the centers weren't quite cooked. No
matter how high she turned the electric beater, stubborn lumps
remained. She finally gave up and spooned the mess into a dish,

plopping a big lump of butter on top. She tucked the potatoes in the oven, then went to peek in the family room, where the younger set, college kids included, were watching a video.

"Dinner in fifteen minutes," she said, noting with surprise that the news was well received.

"I'm starving," confessed Matt.

"Mom makes great stuffing," said Toby. "And wait till you taste her gravy."

Lucy beamed at him and smiled at the girls. She was pleased to notice that Amy and Jessica had changed out of their usual jeans and had dressed up for the occasion in attractive dresses complete with panty hose and heels.

Back at the stove she pulled the turkey pan out of the oven and set it on the counter, perched on a trivet so as not to burn the countertop. With one oven-mitted hand, she held the pan, and with her other hand she began loosening the turkey with a spatula. Plenty of greasy juice had cooked out of the turkey, which was great for the gravy but made the tricky task of getting the twenty-five-pound turkey onto the platter awfully difficult. Making matters worse was the fact that the bird had become firmly adhered to the pan. No sooner would she get one part loosened than she discover another stuck to the pan.

Finally, after poking away at the bird for what seemed an eternity, she thought she could risk lifting it onto the platter. She jabbed a fork into the breast and slid her biggest spatula under the bird and attempted to lift it. Halfway between pan and platter it slipped and crashed back into the roaster, showering her with greasy juice before the whole thing, pan and bird, slid off the tipsy trivet onto the floor.

Lucy slapped her hand over her mouth to keep from screaming. Lord knows she wanted to scream and wave her arms and stamp her feet, but that would only attract attention, which was the last thing she wanted to do. She was alone in the kitchen. She was the only one who knew what had happened. She was going to keep it that way.

"Mom?"

It was Sara, staring openmouthed at the turkey on the floor.

"Don't say a word to anyone, or I'll kill you."

Lucy wrapped a dishtowel around the bird and wrestled it onto the platter.

"You can't serve that. It was on the floor." Sara was shaking her head.

"Oh, yes, I can," growled Lucy. "Now go back to the TV room and act as if nothing is the matter."

"But, Mom," protested Sara.

"Go! Now! And remember: One word and you die!"

After Sara disappeared into the family room, Lucy began mopping up the grease that had spilled from the pan and covered the floor. As she wrung out the mop she wanted to cry, watching her beautiful golden turkey juice swirling into the soapy water. Finally, the floor was clean and she turned her attention back to the dinner.

So far she had mashed potatoes (lumpy) and turkey (dusty). No matter, there would be plenty of other food. She slipped the brown rice casserole into the microwave. Then she popped a pan of sweet potatoes into the oven to warm beside the mashed potatoes. She dumped a couple of packages of frozen baby peas into the steamer and set it on a back burner behind the double boiler filled with creamed onions.

There was no question of making gravy; the juice was gone. She found a couple of cans of pork gravy in the cupboard and emptied them into a saucepan, adding a little soy sauce to darken the pale glop. She gave the spoon a lick, grimaced, and splashed in some cooking sherry. Maybe it would help.

"How much longer?" It was Bill. There was a note of desperation in his voice.

"It was your idea to invite them," she said, glaring at him. "You can't imagine what I've been going through in here."

Bill wasn't moved. "You think it's been a picnic out there?"

Lucy laughed. "Just a few more minutes."

Finally, everyone was seated at the table. Zoe recited a simple grace and Bill began carving the turkey.

As she surveyed the table, Lucy crossed her fingers and took a deep breath. The turkey didn't seem any the worse for its fall to the floor. She didn't think anyone would notice (and she had wiped it off with paper towels). As for the rest of the meal, well, she couldn't guarantee it would taste good but it sure looked good.

Bill stood and raised a glass. "To the cook!"

"Hear, hear!" chorused St. John.

Lucy tossed back her glass of wine and held it out for a refill.

"What did I tell you?" Toby asked Matt. "Doesn't my mom make great gravy?"

"I've never had anything like it," said Matt. His mother would have been proud of his tact.

"It's certainly unusual," said Clarice, furrowing her perfectly plucked brows.

"More stuffing, anyone?" asked Lucy.

"Yes," said Miss Tilley, taking the bowl of potatoes. "How about you?" She had turned her beady eyes on Jessica. "No wonder you're so thin. You're only eating celery. Here, have some mashed potatoes. Put some meat on your bones!"

Jessica's eyes widened in horror as Miss Tilley waved the bowl of potatoes in front of her. Looking somewhat green, she rose and fled from the table.

"I'll see if there's anything I can do," said Matt, following her.

"And you?" Miss Tilley had turned her basilisk gaze on Amy. "At least you're not all skin and hones, but what is that muddy stuff you're eating?"

"It's delicious. It's brown rice and carrots."

"You can't live on that! You need protein." Miss Tilley plunked a drumstick on Amy's plate. "Try this."

Amy studied the burnt offering for a moment, then shook her head. "Excuse me," she said, leaving the table.

"What's the matter with her?"

"She's a vegan, for Pete's sake." Toby pushed his chair away from the table and left the room.

"They don't eat turkey in Las Vegas?" Miss Tilley didn't understand.

"No. It's vee-gan. They don't eat animal products," explained Clarice.

Miss Tilley stared at the drumstick. "Oh, dear."

"You certainly have a knack for clearing a room," said Lucy. "At the rate you were going, I was beginning to wonder if anybody would be left for dessert."

"Wouldn't miss it for the world," said St. John. "Pumpkin pie is my favorite."

"Mine, too," said Miss Tilley, eyeing him with new appreciation. "I had my doubts about you, Sinjin, but you're all right!"

CHAPTER 12

All in all, Lucy thought Thanksgiving dinner had gone pretty well.

"There were a few tense moments, but it never actually came to blows," she told Bill the next morning as they sat at the kitchen table, taking advantage of the fact that the kids were all sleeping in to enjoy a second cup of coffee by themselves.

"Not even one fatality," said Bill, grinning.

His joke reminded her of Curt Nolan's death and she guiltily remembered her promise to Miss Tilley.

"I have to go in to work," she said, staring out the window at the fog-filled yard.

"What about the kids?"

"Zoe's going to spend the day with Sadie, and Elizabeth and Sara are going to the food pantry to sort out the stuff from the canned goods drive." She paused. "As for the others, I don't know and I don't care."

Bill put his hand over hers. It felt warm and good. "I know you're upset about Toby."

"Don't I have the right to be upset?" demanded Lucy. "King Lear was right—an ungrateful child is sharper than a serpent's tooth. I can't believe he's acting like this."

"I can," said Bill. "Don't you remember what it was like when you first went away to school and didn't have to ask your parents for permission anymore? You could come and go, and there was nobody to ask you what the hell you thought you were doing. Nobody to tell you what you could and couldn't do. You just started getting used to all that freedom when, all of a sudden, it was Thanksgiving and you had to go back home."

"I remember," said Lucy, thinking of how she used to dread the holidays when she was in college. For the first time, she wondered how her parents had felt. Had she hurt them as much as Toby was hurting her?

"Just a few more days," said Bill, standing up and putting on his jacket. "They'll be gone Sunday."

"You're right," said Lucy, stroking his beard when he bent down to kiss her good-bye.

"Lucy, thank goodness you're here," said Ted, when Lucy finally arrived at the *Pennysaver* a half hour late. "I was afraid you weren't coming, what with the holiday and all your company."

"I had to drop the girls off," she said, giving her damp jacket a shake and hanging it up. "Any progress on Nolan's murder?"

"Nope. The state police are holding a press conference later this morning. Maybe they'll have something to announce then."

"I'll go," offered Lucy eagerly. She could think of a million questions she'd like to ask the police.

"That's okay," said Ted. "I can handle it. I want you to start working on Nolan's obit."

"Not the obit," groaned Lucy. She hated writing obituaries. It was the worst part of working for a newspaper.

"I've already got some information from the funeral home," said Phyllis, trying to be helpful.

Lucy gave Ted an evil look. "I don't suppose you'll be happy with that, will you? You'll want quotes."

"Just a few," said Ted in an apologetic tone. He knew how hard it was to call up grieving survivors and ask them to talk about a lost loved one.

"A lot of people didn't like him," began Lucy.

"You can say that again," cracked Phyllis.

Lucy clucked her tongue and continued. "Do you want me to get negative quotes, too?"

"Sure," said Ted, turning back to his computer. "But I think you'll find people don't like to speak ill of the dead. Curt's probably a lot more popular dead than he was alive."

"Maybe I'll use that for a lead," said Lucy in a sarcastic tone. She turned on her computer and waited for it to boot up. "You know Fred Rumford called me Wednesday night? He was all upset that Chris White hadn't returned the war club. I was worried we were missing a big story." She sighed. "It's funny how things turn out, isn't it?"

"I can't believe that Chris was so irresponsible," said Phyllis. "That war club is priceless."

Lucy and Ted, both parents, laughed together.

"Doesn't surprise me," said Lucy, remembering Nolan's reaction that day at the library when he'd seen Zoe carrying the club. "Maybe Nolan saw Chris fooling around with it or something. He always said the club belonged with the tribe instead of in the museum. Didn't the cops follow up? Why didn't they question him on Wednesday and get the club back?"

"They tried to," said Ted, "but he wasn't home. There was even an APB out on him but there was no sign of him until he turned up dead."

"You mean they think Nolan absconded with the club?" Lucy was puzzled. "But that makes no sense because he brought it back with him to the game."

"Maybe he didn't take the club," said Phyllis. "Maybe the murderer took it."

A thought occurred to Lucy. "Maybe nobody took the club at all. Maybe Rumford had it all the time."

"But that would make him the murderer," said Ted.

"Maybe he is," said Lucy, remembering how angry he was that day outside the library.

"*Professor* Rumford?" Phyllis was incredulous.

"Why not?"

"I don't think you're on the right track, Lucy," said Ted, check-

ing the clock. "But you've given me some good questions for the
press conference." He got up and reached for his jacket. "You'll
have that obit done when I get back?"

"No problem."

After he'd gone, Lucy stared at the blank computer screen
wondering who to call. Ted was right: Nobody would want to be
quoted saying what they really thought of Curt Nolan. Certainly
not Howard White or any of the other members of the board of
selectmen. All she'd get from them would be a lot of hypocritical
double-speak and she didn't have the stomach for it. Andy
Brown? He was Nolan's boss, after all. But he was out of town.

Reluctantly, she decided there was nothing for it but to call
Ellie Martin. She dialed Ellie's number quickly before she could
change her mind.

"Hi, Ellie," she began, speaking in a soft voice. "This is Lucy
Stone. I just wanted to tell you how sorry I am about Curt."

"Thank you, Lucy." Ellie's voice sounded distant, as if she were
very far away instead of just a few miles down the road.

"I'm working on Curt's obituary for the *Pennysaver.* I wonder
if you could tell me a little about him."

"I don't know. . . ."

"You knew him better than most people," coaxed Lucy. "Don't
you want people to know what he was really like and to remember
him that way?"

"I do." Ellie paused. "People didn't understand him, even people in the tribe. You know, I think that, if he'd lived in the old
days, when the tribe was still strong, he would have been a shaman
or something. He would have been a great leader. There would be
legends about him. He saw things differently from other people.
He saw behind appearances to the way things really are."

As she wrote Ellie's words down Lucy wondered if Ellie had
given her the motive for Nolan's murder. Had he seen something
that made him dangerous to someone? Had he known something
that the murderer wanted to keep secret?

"Can you think of a particular example?"

"Well, he was very committed to his Indian heritage. It was
more important to him than anything else. And it had to be the
truth—what he understood to be the truth. He didn't like it when

people tried to pretty up the facts, like saying Native Americans lived in harmony before the white men came. He'd say that was nonsense, that the tribes used to make war on each other." Ellie paused. "I don't think you should put that in the paper."

"Well, we could say he was committed to the cause of restoring and preserving Metinnicut heritage and culture," suggested Lucy.

"That's good."

"I guess we could say he valued the traditional ways, but not everyone approved of his unconventional and sometimes controversial tactics."

"I'm going to miss him," said Ellie, her voice breaking.

"Are you taking care of his dog?"

"Kadjo? Yeah. He really misses Curt. He won't eat. He keeps looking down the driveway, waiting for him."

"Are you going to keep him?"

"Oh, Lucy, I wish I could but I don't see how. Not if I want to raise chickens again next spring. You can't change dogs once they've got the taste. Sooner or later I'm going to have to give him up, and I guess it might as well be sooner before I get too attached to him. I called the dog officer but she wasn't too hopeful about finding a home for him. She says he's got a bad reputation."

"What happens if she doesn't find a home for him?"

"They'll destroy him."

"That's horrible!"

"I know." Ellie was sniffling on the other end of the line. "Would you be interested in taking him? You've got a big place and you don't have any neighbors to speak of. How about it? He's an awfully nice dog."

Lucy remembered Kadjo. She'd often seen him sitting in the cab of Curt's truck, usually grinning, with his ears pricked up, waiting for his master's return.

"Okay," she said, then thought better of it. What would Bill say? "Well, maybe. I guess I'd better take another look at him."

"Come on over. Anytime."

"In an hour?"

"Sure."

Lucy pounded out the obit and headed over to Ellie's. By the time she got there, she had made up her mind. As much as she would like to save Kadjo, she didn't really think she could take him. So far the family's only experience with pets had been a few assorted cats through the years, and after Elizabeth was diagnosed with asthma, they hadn't had any pets at all. Lucy had suggested getting a dog a few times but Bill had always nixed the idea. "Too expensive," he'd say. "Too dirty." If she pressed the point, she thought she could probably convince him to accept a small dog, like a Jack Russell terrier or a poodle, but Kadjo was enormous. Eighty or ninety pounds at least. Furthermore, he did have a reputation as a problem dog. She knew perfectly well what Bill's reaction would be if she brought him home and she didn't want to have to deal with it. So when she knocked on Ellie's kitchen door, she had resolved to say she was very sorry, but she would not be able to take the dog after all.

"Hi, Lucy. Come on in." Ellie waved her arm at Bear Sykes, who was seated at her kitchen table. "You know my uncle Bear. He was at the meeting the other night."

Lucy hesitated for a minute. She didn't want to intrude on a family meeting.

"Sit down," said Bear. "Take a load off your feet. I see you running all over town, chasing the news. I bet you could use a break."

Lucy laughed. "I sure could."

Bear's black hair was combed back from his face, and he was wearing a beaded choker under his plaid flannel shirt. His skin was ruddy, and with his high cheekbones and curved beak of a nose, Lucy thought he looked very much like the stereotypical Native American.

"Coffee?" asked Ellie. "How about a cup of tea?"

"Tea would be great," said Lucy.

Ellie put the kettle on and joined them at the table. She smiled but didn't say anything. Neither did Bear. The silence stretched on and Lucy felt she had to speak.

"I'm awfully sorry about Curt," she said. "I didn't know him well, but I know you'll miss him."

Bear glanced at Ellie. "Ellie was a lot fonder of him than I was," said Bear, picking up a spoon and stirring his coffee. "He had a big mouth."

"He did a lot for the tribe." said Ellie, defending him. "He made people proud of their heritage."

"I'll give him that," said Bear. "But the trouble with Curt was he didn't know when to stop. Wouldn't compromise. I could've killed him at the meeting the other night when he started talking against the casino." Bear slapped his fist on the table. "I mean, here we've worked so long and come so far, and he has to start throwing a monkey wrench in things. When we all stand together, folks are a lot more likely to take us seriously. But if it seems like we aren't agreed on what we want, well, then they're not going to stick their necks out for us. That vote could have gone either way, you know. We got lucky with that Dunlap woman."

The kettle shrieked and Ellie got up to make the tea.

"What do you think your chances are for federal approval?" asked Lucy.

"A lot better now that Curt isn't spouting off—that's for sure."

Ellie passed Lucy a cup of tea, then sat down. She pulled a handkerchief out of her pocket and dabbed at her eyes.

"I'm sorry, Ellie," said Bear, patting her shoulder. "I know you're upset about what happened."

Ellie nodded, sniffling. "I'm going to miss him so much," she said.

"Well, I've got to get going," Bear said, rising to his feet. "I've got a meeting."

"You always have meetings," said Ellie, blinking back her tears.

"Ain't that the truth," he said.

For a moment he stood behind her chair. Then he bent down and enfolded her in a big hug. After a moment he straightened up and headed for the door, giving Lucy a little salute.

After he'd gone, Lucy sat staring at the door, a thoughtful expression on her face.

"He talks tough, but he's upset about Curt, too," said Ellie, reading her mind and answering Lucy's unspoken thoughts. "It's funny about the tribe. It's like a big family. We get mad at each other, but if one of us gets hurt in some way, it's like all of us got hurt. He's a lot more upset than he's letting on, believe me. Especially since Curt was killed. Maybe whoever did it had it in for

Curt, or maybe they hate all Indians. It wouldn't be the first time."

"Curt made a lot of enemies," said Lucy.

"Yeah," agreed Ellie. "So you want to see the dog? I put him outside."

Lucy followed Ellie outside through the fog and drizzle to the empty chicken coop Ellie was using as a temporary kennel. Inside the wire fence, Kadjo was lying down with his chin on his front paws. He didn't get up as they approached. He just cocked an eye at them and sighed. It was a huge sigh—a sigh that seemed to express immense sadness.

"If I didn't know better, I'd say he's mourning for his master," said Lucy.

"He is mourning for him." Ellie pulled the hood of her jacket over her head.

"How could he know?"

"Dogs know. Always. Bees, too."

"Bees?"

"When a beekeeper dies . . ."

"I don't believe it," said Lucy, sticking her hands in her pocket for warmth.

Ellie shrugged and opened the gate. When they entered the pen, Kadjo got to his feet, but he didn't make any gesture. He didn't wag his tail in welcome; he didn't growl in warning. Ellie reached down and scratched him behind the ears. He looked up at her with sad yellow-brown eyes.

Lucy stroked his neck, feeling the muscles beneath his thick, coarse coat, which was beaded with moisture. "Poor old boy," she said.

He expelled another huge sigh and leaned his shoulder against her leg.

"I'll take him," she said.

"Great," said Ellie. "You won't regret it."

Lucy was regretting it already.

"But not until Sunday when my company has left and the house is quiet."

"That's good." Ellie patted Kadjo's massive head. "That way you'll be able to get acquainted in peace."

"Not likely," said Lucy. "This will probably cause a divorce."

"Look on the bright side—at least you'll have a dog."

"Might not be such a bad deal after all," said Lucy with a small smile. She started to go, then remembered something she'd meant to ask Ellie about. "Fred Rumford called me Wednesday night. He accused Curt of taking the war club from Chris White. Do you know anything about that?"

"Kids! Curt saw Chris and some other members of the team loading a keg of beer into a car. They also had the war club. They'd left it lying on the roof of the car, in fact, so he told them to give it to him for safekeeping. He was going to take it back to the college."

"Even though he thought it should belong to the tribe?"

"Of course. The tribe doesn't have a safe place for it now. He wanted it for the museum—the one that's supposed to be part of the casino deal."

"You're sure about this?"

"Absolutely."

"But the police couldn't find him Wednesday night. Do you know where he was?"

A look of peace settled on Ellie's face and she smiled. "He was with the ancestors, showing them the war club and promising to keep it safe."

Lucy nodded, as if she understood; then she realized she didn't. "And where did he find the ancestors?" she asked, hoping she wasn't being rude.

"On the island, of course. Metinnicut Island in the bay."

"Did he go alone?"

Ellie nodded. Then her face crumpled and Lucy wrapped her arms around the sobbing woman. They stood there together—two women and a dog in the cold November drizzle—for a long time.

CHAPTER 13

What had Lucy done? Was she out of her mind? How on earth was she going to convince Bill to accept Kadjo when she didn't even know herself why she had agreed to take the dog?

This was insane, she thought as she drove down Ellie Martin's driveway and turned onto Main Street Extension. It must be some sort of empty-nest syndrome, she theorized. Maternal instincts gone awry. Toby had flown off to college. He preferred his friends over his family, and she was reeling from the snub. What other explanation could there be?

All that was perfectly understandable, she could hear Bill saying as the Subaru wagon whizzed past the brown fields and bare trees, but why should the whole family have to suffer because of her motherly neurosis? Why should they have to put up with a huge, unruly, smelly beast of a dog that nobody wanted but her? A dog like that must eat an awful lot. How much did dog food cost? Did she have any idea? Not to mention vet bills. What if he got sick or was hit by a car? How would they afford that?

She didn't have any answers, she admitted to herself as she passed a deep stand of dark pine woods. All she knew was that she wanted to adopt Kadjo and she was determined to do it. Besides, she rationalized, she didn't ask much for herself. She never bought anything—clothing or shoes—that wasn't on sale, and when the kids asked what she wanted for Christmas or her birthday, she always told them to make her a nice card because that would mean more to her than anything they could buy. And it was true.

Now, for the first time in a very long time, she wanted something. She wanted Kadjo, and she decided as she pulled up at a stop sign that she was going to have him no matter what.

That settled, she found herself feeling remarkably cheerful and lighthearted. She could hardly wait until Monday when she could bring the dog home.

She had just pulled out onto Route 1 and was speeding along, eager to tell the kids about her decision, when an avalanche of guilt overwhelmed her. Here she was rejoicing in the fact that she was going to have Kadjo and entirely forgetting the reason why he needed a good home. Her good fortune had come at Curt Nolan's expense. If he hadn't been killed, she certainly wouldn't be getting the dog. And what about her promise to Miss Tilley? She'd been so busy feeling sorry for herself that she hadn't given much thought at all to finding Curt's killer.

The blare of a horn and the zoom of an accelerating car as it passed startled her. She was halfway home and she had no recollection of the drive. Shaken, she pulled off the road and tried to collect herself.

She took a deep, cleansing breath and closed her eyes, only to see Rumford's image pop up. Okay, she admitted, so he hadn't faked the war club's disappearance as she had suspected. But what if he had encountered Nolan at the game with the club? It was extremely unlikely Rumford would have accepted Nolan's explanation. They would have argued and Rumford might well have lost his temper and bashed Nolan with the club. It was a scenario that seemed all too probable, considering the argument she'd witnessed outside the library.

In fact, she thought, considering the number of times she'd seen Nolan embroiled in some conflict or other, there was no shortage of people who could have argued with Nolan at the game. After all, even Bear Sykes had admitted he wanted to kill Nolan at times.

Not that she thought for a minute that Bear had killed Nolan. It was just an expression. People said it all the time but they didn't really mean it. For instance, at this very moment she would like to kill Toby. She'd like to wrap her hands around his neck and shake some sense into him. Of course, she would never do it. But the urge was there. He certainly knew how to push her buttons. Was that what had happened to Nolan? Had he made someone, probably Rumford, so angry that Nolan had gotten himself killed?

Or had somebody seen some benefit in killing Nolan and cold-bloodedly taken advantage of the moment? That theory expanded the list of suspects even more. Nolan had managed to make enemies on both sides of the casino issue. By insisting on the rights of the tribe, he'd alienated the anticasino forces, and by criticizing the proposed plan, he'd made enemies of the procasino faction. There was no love lost between Howard White and Nolan, and she suspected Pete Crowley didn't think much of him either. Come to think of it, she'd even seen him arguing with his own boss, Andy Brown.

Andy Brown! He had more to gain from the casino than anybody, considering it was going to be built on his land. He'd be sitting pretty—no more pumpkins and turkeys for him!

Of course, Brown had an unshakable alibi. He'd been in New York at the Macy's Thanksgiving Day Parade on the day Nolan was killed. Sara had seen Katie and the rest of the Brown family on TV.

Suddenly, she had an unsettling thought. The Browns were in New York and Nolan was dead. That meant nobody had been taking care of poor TomTom Turkey. He must certainly need some food and water, and as it happened, she wasn't far from the farm. She couldn't just let the poor old thing starve, she decided, flipping on the directional signal and pulling back onto the road. Besides, it wouldn't hurt to check Andy Brown's alibi.

When she pulled into the driveway at the farm, Lucy was struck by the silence. When she'd been there before, it had always been crowded with people. In summer, Brown did a big business with his fruit and vegetable stand. September brought apples, and hordes of weekenders visiting the old-fashioned cider press. October was pumpkins and the haunted house, and in November, of course, it was the fresh turkeys.

That explained the silence, she realized. The turkeys were

gone. All the noisy gobblers had either been sold or frozen for Christmas. All except TomTom.

Lucy pulled up beside the barn and got out of the car. She felt a little bit like a trespasser, but she did have a good excuse for being there. She was on a mission of mercy. Entering the cavernous barn she went straight to the corner where the giant turkey was penned.

"Hi, there, TomTom," she said, studying the situation. "Are you hungry?"

The huge bird cocked his head and blinked at her. As she watched he began to fan his tail.

"Now, calm down," she told him. "I'm not going to hurt you. I just came to see if you've got any food."

Moving with stately slowness, the bird approached her, lifting first one enormous clawed foot and then the other.

Good Lord, thought Lucy, watching in fascination. Suddenly the relationship between birds and dinosaurs, which she'd read about in numerous books when Toby was in his dinosaur phase, didn't seem so preposterous.

Her instinct was to make a hasty exit, but TomTom's feed tray was indeed empty. Also, it was close to the side of the pen and she could probably fill it with feed without entering the cage. The water, however, posed a problem. The galvanized metal can hung from a chain attached to one of the rafters and was in the exact middle of the pen.

"This is a pretty kettle of fish," said Lucy, keeping a wary eye on the big bird as she explored the barn looking for the feed bin.

She found it under a window and next to it stood a sillcock with a hose.

Lucy first filled the feeder tray, hoping the bird would be too busy eating to bother her while she filled the water can. But as soon as she opened the gate he turned to look at her, once again spreading out his tail.

"Okay. Be thirsty. See if I care."

Realizing the hose was quite long Lucy decided to try to toss it into the container, which fortunately had no lid. After a few tries she succeeded, then turned on the faucet. From the sound of the water pouring in, Lucy guessed it had been empty. TomTom immediately marched over and took a long drink, lifting his beak to let the water slide down his long neck.

"You are indeed a strange creature," said Lucy, watching the performance. As she turned the water off, she wondered if it really was true that turkeys could drown in the rain because they wouldn't shut their beaks.

"Not even turkeys are that stupid," she told TomTom.

He blinked in agreement.

Returning to her car, Lucy congratulated herself. Between Kadjo and TomTom, she had really become quite a friend to animals. Furthermore, she'd made some progress on her investigation. She could now eliminate Andy Brown from her list of suspects. All indications were that he and the rest of the family were away from the farm. His alibi appeared to be ironclad.

CHAPTER 14

"Sara, will you get that?" Lucy was stripping the meat off the turkey carcass so she could make soup and her hands were too greasy to answer the phone.

"It's for you," said Sara, covering the mouthpiece with her hand. "It's Miss Tilley."

Lucy felt exactly as if the teacher had called on her in class and she hadn't done her homework. She washed her hands and took the phone.

"You caught me up to my elbows in soup fixings," said Lucy to explain the delay.

"Is that what you've been doing, making soup instead of finding out who killed Curt?"

"I've made some progress," said Lucy. "I've eliminated Andy Brown from my list of suspects."

"I wouldn't call that progress," said Miss Tilley, adding a little snort. "Everybody knows the Browns are in New York—they were even on TV."

"Well, I went out to the farm to make sure," said Lucy, wishing she didn't feel quite so incompetent. "That's one thing I've learned, you know. When it comes to an investigation like this, you can't take things for granted. You have to check and double-check everything."

"Maybe you'd like to double-check this," snapped Miss Tilley. "Rachel's here, you know, and she told me the police have some solid evidence. It's supposed to be very hush-hush but the police chief told Bob, Rachel's husband. Those two are thick as thieves, you know, Bob being a lawyer and all."

"What kind of evidence?"

"Rachel didn't know but she said it's something important."

"I wonder what it is," said Lucy.

"I thought you'd be interested," said Miss Tilley, sounding smug. "Rachel also said that Bob had a meeting with Howard White and Jonathan Franke and some other people who are opposed to the casino. Bob told her they were shedding no tears over Curt."

"I can see why," said Lucy, remembering the pie sale. "Curt could have been quite an embarrassment to them. He was claiming the town couldn't use the zoning regulations to keep the casino out because they'd ignored them and given Andy Brown preferential treatment."

"Of course they did," said Miss Tilley. "Electric signs, a talking pumpkin—it's scandalous. I never could abide Howard White, you know. He's the sort who puts overdue library books in the book return slot so he won't have to pay the fine. Sneaky—that's what I'd call him."

Lucy couldn't help smiling at this proof of Miss Tilley's willingness to think the worst of everyone.

"Oh, Howard seems okay to me," said Lucy. "And he's right. It was all by the book. Brown applied for variances, just the way he was supposed to."

"Well, maybe you'd better do some of your double-checking," said Miss Tilley, adding a humph. "If you ask me, I don't doubt for one minute that Howard White is capable of murder. He routinely returned books with broken backs."

"I'll look into it," said Lucy.

As she turned to put the heavy stock pot on the stove, Lucy's eye was caught by Elizabeth, who was making herself a cup of coffee. This was not the usual mussed-up version of herself that Elizabeth typically presented in the morning; today she had dressed and combed her hair before coming downstairs. She had even, Lucy noticed on closer inspection, applied mascara and eyeliner.

Lucy was dying to know what the occasion was, but she knew better than to ask. All would be revealed, she told herself, if she was patient. Biting her tongue, she wrapped the extra turkey meat into a neat package and tucked it in the refrigerator.

She was wiping off the counter when Toby and Matt staggered in, barefoot and unshaven, in the same rumpled T-shirts and jeans they'd apparently slept in.

"Do we have any eggs?" asked Toby. "Matt and I want to fry some up."

"Sure. Help yourselves."

Lucy poured herself a second cup of coffee and joined the girls at the table. Elizabeth, she noticed, was watching Matt as he and Toby jostled to open the refrigerator door.

"Would you make one for me?" asked Elizabeth.

Lucy's eyes met Sara's across the table.

"You never eat eggs!" exclaimed Sara.

"Is that true?" asked Matt, lifting up his shirt and scratching his stomach.

"Of course not," said Elizabeth, furiously batting her eyelashes. "I love a well-cooked egg and I bet you know how to make them just right."

"I am pretty good with eggs," admitted Matt.

"Yeah, right," said Toby, handing him the box. "Just try not to break all the yolks this time."

"Sure thing. Elizabeth, how do you want yours?"

"Oh, over easy," said Elizabeth, seductively drawling the words.

Lucy almost choked on her coffee. "So what are you guys going to do today?" she asked. "Are you going to the parade?"

"There's a parade?" Matt paused, holding an egg in his hand.

"Every year. Santa Claus comes."

"The elves, too," added Sara.

"Well, that is tempting," said Matt, cracking the egg on the side of the pan. "But I think I'll pass."

"Well, if you're looking for something to do, Pam Stillings told me they could use some help at the food pantry. It's open today and they're expecting quite a crowd."

Toby and Matt nodded. "Sure. We can help."

"I'll come, too," said Elizabeth. "After all, I was the chairman of the canned goods collection at the high school."

"You were?" Matt carefully lifted an egg with the spatula and flipped it over. "I bet it was very successful."

"This year was the biggest ever," said Elizabeth, coyly running her finger around her coffee mug. "Of course, it wasn't just me. I had a lot of help."

Lucy couldn't take it anymore. She finished her coffee and went upstairs to make the bed.

"I think Elizabeth likes Matt," said Lucy as she and Bill and the younger girls were driving into town to see the parade.

"No way," Sara said. "She told me he was a dork. Almost as much of a dork as Toby, but not quite because Toby is the king of the dorks."

Sara had a way with words, thought Lucy.

"That's right," chimed in Zoe. "She said Matt is Dork Number Two and Amy is Dork Number Three and Jessica is a bitch."

"Zoe!" Lucy and Bill spoke in one voice.

"Well, that's what Elizabeth said."

"She shouldn't have said it and you shouldn't have repeated it," said Lucy. "Besides, I think she may have revised her opinion—at least concerning Dork Number Two."

Bill parked the car on a side street, hoping to avoid the inevitable traffic jam that took place after the parade every year, and they walked along the sidewalk past neat white clapboard houses to Main Street. At the corner, they encountered Officer Barney Culpepper, who was standing behind a sawhorse and making sure no cars tried to sneak onto the parade route. The assignment wasn't very taxing and he had time to talk.

"Hi, Barney. It's a fine day for a parade, isn't it?" Lucy asked.

"Unseasonably mild," he agreed. "They say it's that El Niño."

"We'll get plenty of cold before winter's over," said Bill.

"Mom, can we go ahead?" Sara was clearly bored with this adult conversation. "We'll wait for you right in front of the news store."

"Okay. Catch you later."

Barney gave his whistle a short blast and waved a Ford Explorer onto the detour.

"Never fails." He shook his head. "There's always some that think they can drive right onto Main Street."

Lucy shook her head at this example of human folly. She wanted to ask Barney about the new evidence Miss Tilley had told her about but didn't want him, or Bill, to suspect she was more than casually interested.

"Wasn't that awful about Curt Nolan?" she asked. "Killed in broad daylight, right here in town."

Barney looked down at her from his considerable height. "I hope you're not planning on playing detective, Lucy. You'll just get yourself in a mess of trouble. Remember the last time at the lobster pound?"

Lucy shuddered at the memory and reached for Bill's arm, giving him a little squeeze. "No. I've given up investigating," she said, telling herself it really wasn't a lie if she judged by the progress she'd made in the case so far. "I was just wondering if there was any new information I could pass along to Ted at the paper."

"There was a press conference this morning at the station and Ted was there. Lieutenant Horowitz gave his usual spiel. 'The case is under investigation by the state police and we'll keep you informed.' Never gave us any credit at all, and it was our department that turned up the only piece of evidence that looks like it's worth anything."

Lucy knew the local cops resented the way the state police took over investigations of serious crimes and rarely acknowledged the ability and expertise of local officers who often had firsthand knowledge of both the victims and perpetrators.

"Sounds like the same old story," said Lucy, adding a sympathetic cluck. "You guys do all the work, but the state guys get the glory. It's really not fair. If you found something important, you should get the credit." She paused, letting him think it over. "Whatever it was, it probably wasn't that important, huh?"

"It might be, might not. It all depends. It could link the killer to the crime—that's why Horowitz didn't want it to get in the papers. They're holding it back."

Lucy knew this was standard procedure, but she couldn't help being curious.

"I won't put it in the paper, Barney. Promise. Scout's honor."

He laughed. "We had some fun times when the kids were Cub Scouts together, didn't we? Hey, Bill, remember that chuck wagon you and I built for the Chuck Wagon Derby? It's still going strong."

"That's great," said Bill. "Of course, we built it to last."

Lucy didn't like the turn the conversation was taking, "You really ought to tell me about the evidence, off the record, of course. That way I can make sure the department gets credit when the case is solved."

Barney considered.

"You know you can trust me," said Lucy.

He sighed. "Like I said, it might not be anything, but they did find a button in Nolan's hand."

"A button? What kind of button?"

"Leather, I think. Kinda woven. You know the type. 'Course it might've been dropped there by anybody and he just happened to pick it up. It didn't have to come from the murderer."

"That's probably what happened," said Lucy, determined not to show her excitement at getting the information. "But you never know."

"We'd better get a move on," said Bill. "We don't want to miss the parade."

"Have a nice time now," said Barney, raising his hand to halt a pickup truck.

When Lucy and Bill found the girls, standing just where they had said they'd be, Sara was holding a big pink cone of cotton candy.

"You're going to ruin your teeth," scolded Lucy. "It's nothing but sugar, you know. Empty calories."

"Want some, Lucy?" asked Bill.

"Sure."

Soon she was happily enjoying the way the cotton candy melted on her tongue and watching the other people in the crowd waiting for the parade to start. That was one thing about living in a small town like Tinker's Cove: Even if you didn't know everybody by name, almost everyone looked familiar.

"When's it gonna start, Mom?" Zoe asked.

"Pretty soon. I think I hear the drums."

Just then a siren blared, causing the girls to cover their ears and scream with delight. The parade was approaching, led as always by the fire department's gleaming white pumper truck. The town's pride and joy—a brand-new hook-and-ladder truck—would be at the end of the parade, carrying Santa in a crow's nest atop the ladder.

The high school band was marching past, and everybody was smiling and clapping in time to the music. The band was followed by a band of clowns driving funny little cars, actually Shriners in costume. Everybody laughed at their antics and the children scrambled to catch the candy they tossed.

Lucy was enjoying the spectacle when, suddenly, someone fell against her almost knocking her off her feet. As she staggered to keep from falling, Bill took in the situation and leaped to her aid.

"Here you go, fella," he said, grabbing the man by the upper arms. "Steady now."

"I'm so sorry," the man said.

Lucy was surprised to recognize Howard White.

Pale and drawn, he hardly seemed the imperious chairman of the board of selectmen.

"Are you all right?" asked Lucy. "Should we call the rescue squad?"

"Oh, no." White spoke with some effort, he was out of breath and his chest was heaving.

"The fire station's just down the street—I'll get an EMT," said Lucy.

"I'm all right." The words came out in a rush. White continued to breathe heavily. "I just need to catch my . . . my breath. It's the cold you see."

Lucy hesitated. Her instincts told her he needed help, but she knew White would hate the embarrassment of causing a fuss at the parade. Indeed, he did seem to be getting back some of his color and to be breathing more easily.

"How foolish of me," he said. "I was fooled by this mild weather and was rushing to meet my wife. I should have taken my time. It's this darned asthma."

"Shall I go and get her?"

"No, no. I'll be fine. I'll just go on slowly, as I should have in the first place. I apologize for being so much trouble."

"Not at all," said Lucy, watching as he made his way cautiously down the street.

"Poor old fellow," said Bill.

"Yup," agreed Lucy, mentally scratching another suspect off her list. Miss Tilley was undoubtedly correct that Howard White wasn't mourning Curt Nolan's death, but Lucy doubted very much that he would have been physically capable of committing the evil deed. That war club was heavy; Lucy herself had held it when Rumford had brought it to the flintknapping workshop at the library. There was simply no way Howard White could have lifted the club and delivered a fatal blow, especially since it had been at least twenty degrees colder on the day of the football game. If temperature triggered his asthma and he was having trouble on a mild day, he would have been in serious trouble on a really cold day.

The parade continued but Lucy wasn't watching; she was lost in her thoughts. She was thinking of the button Barney had described. It sounded like the sort of button that was often used on tweed sportcoats—the sort of sportcoat that Fred Rumford almost always wore. Once again she remembered that day at the library.

"Mom! Mom!" Zoe was screeching, waving madly at Santa atop his fire truck. "I want to tell Santa what I want for Christmas!"

"Okay. What do you want to do, Sara? Do you want to visit Santa Claus?"

Sara rolled her eyes in disgust. Her mother should surely know better than to ask a question like that of such a mature individual as herself.

"You take Zoe to see Santa," said Bill. "Sara and I will go on over to the football field and see who wins the prize for the best float. You can meet us there."

Taking Zoe's hand, Lucy headed for the fire station, where

Santa traditionally held court. By the time they arrived, however, the line of children eager to tell him their Christmas wishes was halfway down the street.

"I hate standing in line," said Lucy.

Disappointment clouded Zoe's little face and she stuck out her bottom lip in a pout.

Lucy pulled a schedule from her pocket and checked the time.

"Look. Santa's going to be here for another hour. Why don't we do something else for a while and come back in forty-five minutes or so? The line will be much shorter then."

"What could we do?"

"How about this," said Lucy excitedly, spying an opportunity to continue her investigation. "There's an open house at the college museum. You know you love the mummy."

Zoe nodded. She was fascinated by the exhibit of a drab and dusty mummy case that contained the well-wrapped remains of an ancient Egyptian workman.

"Okay," she said.

As they walked the three blocks to the museum, Lucy told herself she wasn't really involving her child in a murder investigation. Of course not. She was taking Zoe to see the mummy, which was just one of the many strange artifacts William Winchester had collected on his grand tour and later donated to the college he had created back in 1898. No, her main interest was amusing Zoe, but if the opportunity rose to question Fred Rumford, she would certainly take advantage of it.

As she had expected, few people were attending the open house at the college museum. Lucy and Zoe helped themselves to lemonade and cookies from the table set up in the lobby. Then they wandered through the largely empty rooms studying the old-fashioned glass exhibit cases.

One case contained artifacts collected in Polynesia, including spears, drums, and a plaster model of a woman wearing a grass skirt. Lucy looked at the faded photograph of William Winchester surrounded by several half-naked native women and noticed he seemed remarkably dour for a man in that situation.

"Come on, Mom. The mummy's in the next room."

Lucy followed as Zoe ran up to the glass case, then stopped short.

"Is it really a dead person?" Zoe asked.

"Yes, it is. But the person has been dead for a very long time. Thousands of years."

"Why did they wrap it up like that?"

"It was their religion."

"I wouldn't like to be tied up like that."

"Neither would I. Not if I was alive. But once you're dead, it doesn't matter. You don't know what's happening to you."

Zoe had crouched down, trying to get a better view of poor old Asherati the stonecarver, and Lucy wondered what the poor fellow would think of his new situation if he were able to. He had died secure in the knowledge that his remains would be properly prepared for the afterlife; he would probably be horrified to find himself a subject of curiousity in a New England museum.

Leaving, they passed the empty display case that usually contained the war club. Lucy paused for a minute, thinking sadly of Curt Nolan. When she was leaving, she spotted Fred Rumford coming out of his office. To her disappointment he was wearing a blue blazer with brass buttons.

"I see the police still have the war club," she said, approaching him. "Do you know when you'll get it back?"

He shook his head. "They say it's evidence. We may not get it back until after the trial—if there is a trial, that is." Rumford grimaced. "Considering they have to figure out who killed Nolan and catch him before they can even have a trial, it could be years before we get the club back."

"What if they don't make an arrest? What if the case is never solved? Do you get the club back?"

"That," he said with a grim nod, "is the sixty-four-thousand-dollar question. The answer I got was, 'maybe.'"

"I guess you could sue them," said Lucy, ignoring Zoe's tugs on her arm. She'd gotten the chance to question Rumford and she wasn't going to let it pass.

"I guess I'd have to if it came to that," said Fred. "The problem

is, of course, that the war club is centuries old. It's extremely fragile and needs special care. Controlled humidity and temperature.
Which I'm pretty sure it's not getting in some evidence locker at
state police headquarters."

Rumford's voice had gotten louder as he spoke; he was clearly
very upset. "It's bad enough that they take it out of the museum
and wave it around at the pep rally every year, but there's nothing
I can do about that. Believe me, I've tried. It's outrageous, but
people didn't understand how to properly care for primitive artifacts when William Winchester wrote his will specifying the annual display at the football game." He seemed to run out of steam.
"I've learned to live with it. I mean, it's been going on for nearly a
hundred years. And it was never a problem until now."

Lucy nodded, hugging Zoe to her side. The little girl was getting restless and Lucy didn't want her to wander off.

"I know how upset you were when Chris White didn't return it
after the rally."

"You bet. I called the cops and they were great. They tracked
the kid down, but no club. Chris couldn't be bothered getting it
back here—he gave it to Nolan. Of all people!"

"You know," said Lucy, looking at Rumford closely and watching his reaction, "I think Nolan might have been just as concerned
as you about the club. I heard he took it for safekeeping and intended to return it to the museum."

"That's ridiculous!" exclaimed Rumford. "You know as well as
I do that Nolan's always said the war club belongs with the tribe."

"Ellie told me he wanted it for the tribal museum—the one
that's part of the casino deal." Lucy held tight to Zoe's hand; the
little girl was squirming, trying to run away. "She's certain he was
going to return it to you. What I wonder is whether he tried to do
that at the game? Maybe you were the last person to see him
alive."

Rumford looked at her suspiciously. "You know, the police
asked me that same question."

"The police questioned you?"

"Oh, sure." His face reddened with the admission. "I guess I'm
a suspect." He looked around the museum, as if to reassure himself it was still there and he was still its director. Then he gave a

short, abrupt laugh. "Oh, well. I'm probably in good company. Half the town would have liked to kill him!"

That was exactly the problem, thought Lucy as she and Zoe left the museum: too many suspects and none at all. Reluctantly, she crossed Rumford from her list of suspects. Not because he couldn't have killed Nolan; Lucy thought that Rumford would have liked nothing better. It wasn't that he couldn't have committed murder, but he wouldn't have, not using the war club. He would never have risked damaging such a precious artifact.

"I'm going to ask Santa for a Barbie Bakes Cakes oven," said Zoe, her mouth full of cookie. "You're too big to sit on Santa's lap, aren't you?"

"Yes, I am."

"Then how does he know what you want for Christmas?"

"He just knows."

"He does? How?"

"Magic, I guess. Santa magic."

That was what it would take, she thought, to get what she really wanted for Christmas. Even Santa would be hard-pressed to come up with a lead in this case.

CHAPTER 15

L ooking out the laundry room window, Lucy saw it had started to snow. Not heavily, but scattered tiny flakes were drifting down and a light frosting had collected on the cars in the driveway.

It was almost noon on Sunday and Lucy had spent most of the morning doing laundry. The girls had been up for hours. Elizabeth had gone ice-skating with some friends, Sara was working on a school project at a classmate's house, and Zoe was at the Orensteins', playing with her best friend, Sadie.

Lucy pulled one of Toby's shirts out of the laundry basket and began to fold it. Snow had been forecast, and if the kids had been smart, she thought, they would have gotten up early for the drive back to Coburn. If they had, they would almost be there by now. But as it was, it was nearly noon and they were still asleep in the family room, and it would probably be snowing heavily by the time they got going.

Lucy didn't like to think of them driving on the interstate in heavy snow; she doubted Matt was an experienced winter driver. He probably would try to go 65 miles an hour in spite of bad visibility and slippery roads.

Pulling another shirt out of the basket—an expensive designer shirt Toby had received as a graduation present—Lucy groaned.

The pocked was ripped, a cuff was dangling loosely, and several buttons were missing. Whatever could have happened to it?

It was hard to understand how his clothes could become quite so stained and torn in the library, where he ought to be spending most of his time. Summer camp, basic training, survival courses— she could see how such programs would be tough on clothing. But French 101, freshman composition, calculus, and theories of government? It hardly seemed they could account for the sorry condition of Toby's wardrobe.

The pipes began to hum; the college kids were starting the series of showers with which they began every day. Lucy sent up a quick prayer to the plumbing gods, begging that the hot water heater would hold out.

It was at times like these that she missed her father. He had served in North Africa in World War II and had been a master of the one-minute shower. She smiled, remembering him acting out the process for her, fully clothed, of course, in the living room. He could teach these kids a thing or two about conserving water, she thought, as she headed for kitchen.

"I've got some clean clothes for you—don't forget to pack them," she told Toby, who was pulling a carton of eggs out of the refrigerator.

Matt was standing at the stove, cooking bacon, and Jessica was sitting on the floor, reorganizing her duffel bag. That was the only explanation Lucy could come up with for the mess of clothing and personal articles that was strewn all around her.

"Toby, a lot of your clothes are ripped. What have you been doing?"

Matt laughed. "I told you your mother would be ticked," he said.

"I was on the rugby team," said Toby.

"Don't they have uniforms?"

"It's a club sport."

"Oh. Well, from now on, if you're going to play, wear sweats, okay?"

"Okay," said Toby. Then, surprising her, he wrapped his arms around her and enveloped her in a bear hug. Lucy responded with a squeeze and ruffled his hair.

"Tough guy, huh?" Matt said, smacking him with the spatula. Toby grinned and put up his fists.

Watching them scuffle, Lucy hoped Toby's T-shirt, already ripped at the shoulder, would last a little longer. She tiptoed through Jessica's assorted piles and went into the family room, intending to put Toby's clean clothes by his backpack. The sight that greeted her, however, made her gasp.

The normally neat, pleasant room looked like a disaster area. The couch had been stripped of its cushions. Clothing, shoes, blankets, sleeping bags, and pillows covered the floor. And for some inexplicable reason, the shade had been removed from one of the lamps. The window blinds, of course, were tightly closed. What did she expect? she thought, snapping the cord. You couldn't sleep until noon if the light came in, could you?

She was sitting on the uncushioned sofa, staring glumly at the mess, when Bill came in.

"I wish they'd gotten an early start," he said, looking out the window. "The snow's starting to come down pretty heavily."

"It'll take them hours to pack all this stuff," she said with a weak little wave of her arm. "Maybe the storm will be over by the time they leave."

"Buck up, Bucky," said Bill, pulling a couch cushion out from under a tangle of bedding. "We can have them packed and on the road in no time."

"Aye, aye, Captain," said Lucy, jumping to her feet and rolling up a sleeping bag.

An hour later the snow had petered out, leaving a scant inch on the roads. Lucy and Bill stood on the porch, waving as Matt floored the gas pedal and sent his battered Saab lurching down the driveway.

"So how does your empty nest look now?" he asked, slipping his arms around her waist.

She stroked his beard and looked up at him. "There's something I have to tell you," she said.

Bill's back stiffened. "You're not pregnant, are you?"

"Oh, no," she said quickly. "It's not that. But we are getting a dog."

"That's okay, then," he said, nibbling on her ear.

Lucy wasn't sure he'd heard right, but she wasn't going to press the issue. "You know what?" she said, slipping her arms around his neck. "We've got the whole house all to ourselves."

"Darn," he said, pulling her closer. "Another boring Sunday afternoon. Nobody home. Nothing to do."

"Oh, I can think of something to do."

"You can?"

He was kissing her.

"Oh, yes," she said, taking his hand and leading him back into the house.

Lucy had promised to pick up Zoe at the Orensteins' at three o'clock. Since she was already out, she decided to swing by Ellie's house to get Kadjo, too. Zoe wasn't sure this was a good idea.

"Mom, what if he bites?"

"He won't bite. He's a nice dog."

"Are you sure?"

"Of course I'm sure. I wouldn't adopt a mean dog."

"We've never had a dog before. Why do we have to get one now?"

"Kadjo needs a home."

"But why does he have to come to our house? Why can't he go somewhere else?"

"You'll like him."

"I don't think so."

Lucy pulled into Ellie's driveway and braked, then turned to face Zoe. "We're taking Kadjo on a trial basis. If it doesn't work out, we won't keep him."

"Promise?"

"Promise."

Together they walked up to the house and knocked on the door. Ellie greeted them warmly and invited them in to the kitchen, where Bear was seated at the table.

"Tea for you, Lucy? How about some hot cocoa for Zoe?"

"Sure," said Lucy, sitting down. "You know, I bet Zoe would like to see your dolls."

"Would you like that?" Ellie asked Zoe.

"Yes," answered Zoe.

Ellie led her down the hall to her workroom, leaving Lucy and Bear alone.

"You're a reporter, right?" he demanded, scowling at her over his coffee cup. "You heard anything about Curt's murder? Have they got any suspects?"

"I heard they've been questioning a lot of people," said Lucy, unwilling to admit she didn't really know how the police investigation was going. "And they've got some physical evidence."

"What's that mean?"

"Something they think belonged to the killer." She paused. "They're not saying exactly what it is."

He narrowed his eyes. "You've been talking to people, asking questions?"

Lucy wondered what he was getting at. "It's my job."

He shrugged. "Nothing wrong with that. If you ask me, it's the cops that aren't doing their job."

The kettle whistled and Lucy got up and turned the stove off. Ellie had left the cups ready to add water. Lucy poured and brought the hot drinks back to the table.

"You surprise me," said Lucy, lifting the tea bag out and squeezing it with a spoon. "Last time I talked to you, you said you would have liked to kill Curt yourself."

His black eyes seemed to bore into her for a long time. Then he grinned at her, reminding her of a fox. "People say funny things when they're upset. Shock takes people differently."

Studying Bear's broad, impassive face, Lucy didn't think he would shock easily. She listened as he continued.

"No two ways about it: I had my differences with Curt. That doesn't change the fact that one of my people was killed in cold blood and nobody seems to be doing anything about it."

"These things take time," said Lucy, turning around to smile at Zoe and Ellie, who were returning to the table. "Your cocoa's ready." She patted the chair. "What did you think of the dolls?"

"Nice," said Zoe, taking a big slurp of cocoa.

Lucy laughed. "Is that all you have to say?"

Zoe pursed her lips and thought for a moment. "Thank you for the cocoa," she finally said.

Lucy's eyes met Ellie's and she gave an apologetic smile. "How are you doing?"

"Okay." Ellie glanced at Bear. "It's hard."

Lucy patted her hand. "I know."

"I really appreciate your taking the dog. It's a load off my mind knowing he's going to a good home."

"I'm happy to take him."

When they finished their drinks, Ellie led Zoe and Lucy out to Kadjo's pen.

The dog was on his feet, not barking, but watching them approach. As they drew closer, his tail began to wave.

"Hi, boy," said Ellie. "Are you ready to meet your new family?"

She opened the gate and snapped on a leash and Kadjo bounded forward. When Ellie handed the leash to Lucy, however, he suddenly halted.

"Good boy," said Lucy, holding her hand out for him to sniff. "We're going to call him Kudo."

"That's a good idea," said Ellie. "Give him a fresh start."

When Kadjo, now Kudo, was satisfied with her scent, Lucy gave him a little scratch behind his ears. When she led him toward the car, he didn't resist but trotted along beside her. She opened the rear hatch for him and he jumped in willingly. She slammed the door down and looked at him through the window; he gazed back at her.

Zoe didn't want to sit in the backseat, where she would be close to the dog, so Lucy let her sit in the front passenger seat. She made sure Zoe's seat belt was tightly fastened, then started the car.

Ellie came up and stood by the car door; Lucy opened the window.

"Remember to be firm with him and you won't have any trouble," said Ellie.

"I'll remember," said Lucy. "Thanks."

"I'm the one who should be thanking you," said Ellie. "By the way, I don't know if you want to come, but the funeral is tomorrow. Ten o'clock at the meeting house in Hopkinton."

"Thanks for telling me. I'll be there."

"Better come early if you want to get a seat." Ellie bit her lip. "I just wanted a private graveside service but Bear said that wouldn't do. He said Curt was a tribal leader and deserved a traditional ceremony. Personally, I think it's a big waste. It isn't as if Curt is going to know."

Lucy recited the usual platitude. "It's not for him. It's for the people left behind."

Ellie shrugged, holding her hands out in a helpless gesture.

Lucy gave a little wave and shifted into drive, checking that the driveway was clear before accelerating. Seeing Bear climbing into his truck, she waited, watching with disapproval as he carelessly careened down the icy drive holding a cell phone to his ear.

As she followed, driving slowly, Lucy checked the rearview mirror to make sure Kudo was behaving himself in the cargo area. He seemed to be doing fine, not minding the motion of the car. She braked carefully when she got to the road so he wouldn't be knocked off his feet; then she proceeded to turn. She had no sooner got onto the highway, however, than he jumped into the backseat, causing Zoe to shriek. Signaling, Lucy immediately pulled off onto the shoulder and stopped the car.

She climbed out of her seat and opened the rear door. Kudo sat on the backseat, grinning at her, his tongue lolling. He seemed to be saying he much preferred riding in the backseat, sitting like a person, to sliding around in the cargo area.

"We're not getting off to a good start," Lucy warned him, looking him straight in the eye.

She took hold of his leash and pulled, but Kudo resisted. Lucy snapped the leash and yanked him out of the car. To her surprise, once he was on the ground he followed her easily around to the rear of the car. She opened the hatch and he leaped in. She got back in the driver's seat and started the engine, checking the rearview mirror before pulling onto the road. In the mirror her eyes met Kudo's.

"You'd better behave," she said.

Kudo grinned.

Still not trusting the dog to behave in the car, Lucy chose to drive home over back roads rather than to risk being distracted on busy Route 1. She liked taking the less traveled route through the woods anyway, especially since today the trees and bushes were still frosted with snow from the morning storm.

"Aren't the woods pretty today?" she asked Zoe.

"Like a fairyland," agreed Zoe.

"Fairyland," repeated Lucy. "But only for a little while. It's already starting to melt."

Suddenly spotting a fast-approaching dirt bike that was apparently headed straight for her car, Lucy slammed on the brakes. Zoe lurched forward, but was restrained by her seat belt, and Kudo slammed into the seat back.

"Are you all right?" Lucy's arm had instinctively shot out across Zoe's chest.

"I'm fine, Mom."

Looking over her shoulder, Lucy saw that Kudo had recovered without any damage. He was standing with his chin resting on the top of the seat back, staring at her reproachfully.

"It wasn't my fault," she told him before proceeding down the road.

She had no sooner got started again, however, than the dirt bike reappeared in her rearview mirror. This time Lucy continued driving slowly, trying to get a good look at the biker. Although she could see he was dressed in black motocross leathers, she couldn't make out his face. It was hidden behind a black visor.

Once again, she heard the motorcycle engine roar and once again he zoomed past her with an ear-deafening vroom. She tensed, ready to brake if he stopped again, but this time he continued on his way, disappearing down a side trail.

When Lucy finally reached Red Top Road, coming out just a few hundred feet from her driveway, she was much relieved. She hadn't thought the dirt biker intended her any harm, but his antics had been dangerous. What if she had hit him? He seemed to be playing a very dangerous game. If he was going to seek thrills, she wished he wouldn't do it at her expense.

She flipped the lever, signaling the turn into her driveway and tapped her brakes. When she checked the mirror, she flinched at the unexpected reappearance of the dirt biker. He had pulled up on the side of the road, opposite the driveway, and he remained there, watching, as she hurried Zoe and Kudo out of the car and into the house. Once they were safely inside, she looked to see if he was still there, but he was gone. Standing on the porch, Lucy could only hear the faint sound of the motorcycle engine as it grew more and more distant and finally ceased altogether.

Satisfied that he was gone, she went into the house herself. She wondered if she should call the police and report the incident. Looking at the phone, trying to decide, she rememberd Bear Sykes and his cell phone. Had he called the biker? she wondered briefly before dismissing the thought.

She was reminded of more pressing duties by Kudo, who was rubbing his wet nose against her hand.

"Come on and meet the family," she said, pushing open the door to the family room.

CHAPTER 16

That evening, having reclaimed the family room, Bill switched off the TV at ten and he and Lucy headed for bed. Kudo had been sleeping at Lucy's feet, but as soon as she stood up, he also got up and stretched. Then he looked at her expectantly. She went through the kitchen and he followed, nails clicking on the bare floor. She opened the back door for him and he trotted out, obviously with a mission in mind.

Lucy decided she might as well use the bathroom herself; then she opened the door and called the dog. He appeared out of the darkness almost immediately and she let him in, pointing to the bed she had put down for him in a comer of the kitchen. Kudo approached it cautiously, suspiciously sniffing the expensive, flea-repellent bedding.

"Go on," said Lucy in a reassuring voice. "It won't bite."

Then she turned out the light and opened the door to the back stairs. As she started up, Kudo was right at her heels.

"Oh, no," she said, turning around and pointing him to the dog bed. "You sleep in the kitchen."

Kudo dropped his head and made a little whining sound.

"That's enough," said Lucy sternly. "Down you go."

The dog turned and went down a few steps, then paused, shivering pathetically.

"It's not cold in the kitchen. It's a lot warmer than my room—that's for sure," she told him.

He raised his head and looked at her, somehow turning his yellow dog eyes into pools of melting chocolate.

"Okay. You win," said Lucy, resuming her climb up the stairs. "Just for tonight. I know it's hard getting used to a new home."

"What's he doing up here?" asked Bill, who was in bed reading a homebuilder's magazine.

"He followed me up the stairs."

"You know, Lucy, I'm not at all sure why we have this dog, but he's sure as hell not sleeping with us."

Lucy looked wounded. "You said it would be okay."

"I don't remember that," said Bill. He got out of bed and snapped his fingers. "C'mon, boy."

Kudo stepped closer to Lucy and made a noise that began as a whine but ended with a throaty rumble.

Bill looked at the dog, narrowing his eyes.

"I think he wants to stay with me," said Lucy.

"That's obvious," said Bill as he climbed back in bed. "But do we want him to stay with us?"

"I don't mind," said Lucy. "Do you?"

Bill sighed. He'd lost this battle before, when the kids were little and wanted to sleep in their parents' bed. He'd believed the books that said children must learn to sleep by themselves, but Lucy could never stand to send them back to their cold, solitary beds, where frightening monsters lurked in the dark.

"I guess not," he finally said. "But not on the bed."

Lucy settled herself on the pillows, propping a book on her chest. Kudo stood beside the bed, resting his chin on the mattress.

Lucy gave her head a little shake and the dog expelled a huge breath and curled up on the carpet next to the bed. Lucy let her arm drop and gave his head a scratch.

The next morning, after Bill and the kids had left the house, Lucy pulled on a warm jacket and took the dog out for some exercise along the old logging roads that ran behind their house. Lucy walked at a good pace, enjoying the fresh air and sunshine.

Kudo ran ahead of her, sniffing the ground and chasing rabbits, but returning frequently as if to check that she was still there.

Lucy picked up a stick and threw it. Kudo ran after it and brought it back to her, grinning proudly. She threw the stick a few more times, then realized it must be getting late. She checked her watch and discovered it was time to go home if she planned to go to Curt Nolan's funeral service.

Back at the house she gave Kudo a fresh bowl of water and a dog biscuit, then hurried upstairs to change her clothes.

As she tugged on her black pantyhose, Lucy considered the best route to the Indian Meeting House in Hopkinton. The most direct way was along the back roads she had taken the day before, but remembering the dirt biker she decided to take the long way round on the highway. Chances were that the biker, whoever he was, was just some kid who'd been having fun at her expense. Sure, the leathers and helmet had looked menacing, but that was just the style. They all wore them. No doubt the biker was back in school today or maybe even back on the job.

Lucy slipped on one black leather pump and sat holding the other. Maybe the biker wasn't a kid at all. Come to think of it, dirt biking was an expensive sport when you added up the cost of all the equipment, and there weren't too many kids in Tinker's Cove who had that sort of money.

But if he were a grown man, she wondered, what was he doing harrassing her like that? It was the kind of stunt a kid would find funny, but it wasn't the sort of thing an adult would even think of doing.

She put the shoe down and slipped it on. Rocking back on her heels, she lifted her toes, then slowly lowered them and put her hands on her knees. Why had that biker been so interested in her and why had he followed her home? Had it been an intentional move to find out where she lived?

Even more disquieting was the thought that Bear Sykes might have summoned the biker, using his cell phone. What possible reason would he have for doing that? she wondered as she stood up and fastened her faux pearls around her neck.

Come to think of it, Sykes had seemed awfully interested in what she knew about the murder. That didn't mean he was involved in any way, she told herself. As the tribe's leader he would naturally want to know how the investigation was proceeding.

After one last check in the mirror to make sure her slip wasn't showing, she decided she was ready. She was probably being paranoid, but she wasn't about to risk another encounter. Today, she'd stick to the highway.

It was funny, she thought as she carefully closed the door behind so Kudo couldn't get out. She hadn't felt a bit nervous this morning when she was walking with Kudo; she had felt sure that the dog would protect her. But even in a car she didn't want to risk the same deserted roads by herself.

As she started the car, she thought it might be a good idea to pay attention at the funeral and see who was there and who wasn't and to keep an eye out for strange behavior.

Arriving at the plain little country church with only minutes to spare before the service was scheduled to start, Lucy felt a surge of sympathy for Ellie. Judging from the number of cars and the crowd of people, not to mention the large white trucks topped with satellite dishes bearing the logos of the Portland TV station and Northeast Cable News parked along the road opposite the church, it was going to be a three-ring circus. It was bad enough to lose someone you loved, but to have your private grief turned into a public spectacle made it all that much worse.

Lucy had to park at least a quarter of a mile farther down the road and had to hike back to the church in her uncomfortable high heels. She arrived, out of breath, just as the bell was tolling. As she drew closer she realized she hadn't needed to worry about getting a seat—this crowd wasn't interested in attending the service. The people gathered on the church lawn were demonstrators, content to stand outside in view of the TV cameras. A few were holding placards with a photograph of Nolan demanding *Justice for Our Brother.*

Lucy looked for a familiar face, but the only person she recognized was Bear Sykes. Dressed in a denim shirt with a beaded chestpiece worn over it, he was being interviewed by a TV reporter. As she mounted the steps, she heard him deliver a ringing declaration and stopped to listen.

"If Curt Nolan were white, you can be sure the police would not be dragging their feet in investigating his murder. We demand equal treatment—justice in life and in death!"

He raised a fist and the crowd of protesters erupted in cheers and applause. Placards were held aloft and someone began beating a drum.

The crowd began chanting, "Justice! We want justice!"

Watching the spectacle unfold before her, Lucy found herself reaching for her reporter's notebook and camera. She didn't have them, of course. She'd left her big everyday bag at home and had brought her small, dressy purse. Maybe Ted was here, she thought, hopefully scanning the crowd of reporters gathered outside the churchyard for his face.

There was no sign of him. Lucy wondered what to do. She had come to attend the funeral service, but maybe she should stay outside and cover the demonstration. A few police cars had arrived without sirens, but the barking of their radios could be heard and their roof lights were flashing. A certain tension seemed to be building among the demonstrators and their chanting was getting louder. Lucy remained on the steps, hesitating.

A few organ chords made up her mind and she pulled open the heavy door. Inside, the church was quiet and dim and smelled like old wood and chrysanthemums. She waved away the usher, declining to sit and instead remained standing in the rear of the church. From that vantage point she could see the whole church and the fifty or so people who had come to the service.

In the front row she spotted Ellie and two attractive young women she took to be Ellie's daughters sitting on her left. On Ellie's right, Lucy was surprised to see a man. She couldn't tell who he was from his back, but he was very solicitious of Ellie, who was leaning against his shoulder.

When the hymn began and everyone stood, the man turned around as if to check and see how many people had come. Lucy was astonished to recognize Jonathan Franke.

As the hymn droned on, Lucy struggled to make sense of this new development. Perhaps he was simply an old friend who had put aside his dislike of the deceased to offer support to Ellie. Or perhaps, thought Lucy, he was taking advantage of the death of a hated rival to advance his own case as a suitor. The final amen sounded and Lucy wrestled with a vague sense of guilt. Here she was in church and all she could think of was sex and murder.

"Let us pray," began the minister, a stocky, white-haired man with a ruddy complexion, and Lucy took the opportunity to check out her fellow mourners.

Just a few rows behind Ellie she saw Chuck Canaday and Andy Brown, along with Joe Marzetti. *Ah,* she thought rather cynically, *the business community.* Never ones to alienate customers, they showed up at almost every funeral.

On the other side of the narrow aisle she spotted a few more members of the board of selectmen: Sandy Dunlap and Bud Collier. There was no sign of Pete Crowley or Howard White; even this prime opportunity to win some votes had not been attractive enough to overcome their dislike of Nolan. She didn't see Fred Rumford either, even though he could have used the funeral as an occasion to bridge the widening gap between the museum and the tribe. Perhaps knowing he was a suspect, he hadn't wanted to draw attention to himself.

Listening with half an ear to the minister, Lucy followed her own thoughts. Maybe the absentees had been afraid of appearing hypocritical, since they had all had their differences with Nolan. Personally, Lucy thought they were mistaken. By attending the funeral they could have shown respect for Nolan and for the Metinnicut people.

A sudden increase in the noise level from the crowd outside drew Lucy's attention and she decided she'd better see what was going on. She tiptoed to the door and, opening it as little as possible, slipped through. Once outside on the stoop she paused, horrified.

Dozens of police officers in full riot gear were advancing on the demonstrators with raised shields and batons. At first the demonstrators stood fast, huddling together in passive resistance behind their leader, Bear Sykes. Then a sound like a shot was heard.

Lucy was never convinced it actually was a gunshot; she thought it was probably a backfire from a passing car. Whatever it was, it had the effect of terrifying the crowd of demonstrators, who suddenly broke ranks and began running for safety, pursued by police officers through the churchyard and adjacent cemetery. Sykes remained in place, vainly calling for order, until he was collared himself and led to a cruiser.

Lucy watched in dismay as the officers wrestled people to the ground and handcuffed them. She winced at the thwack the batons made when they connected with human flesh. She heard the screams of fear and pain. Nevertheless, she was able to remain a detached observer until she saw a young child in a familiar threadbare lavender jacket. Tiffani had apparently become lost and separated from her family and was wandering about, dazed, with tears streaming down her face.

Jumping down the stairs Lucy ran to the little girl and scooped her up in her arms.

"Hold it right there," said a gruff voice.

Lucy froze, hugging Tiffani to her chest and patting her back. Next thing she knew she was seized roughly by the shoulders, the screaming Tiffani was torn from her arms and her wrists were restrained.

"I'm not—" she began in protest, attempting to make eye contact with her captor.

All she saw was her own face, very small, reflected in his aviator sunglasses.

"Tell it to the judge," he said as he thrust her inside the crowded paddy wagon.

CHAPTER 17

Judge Joyce Ryerson wasn't interested in what Lucy had to say. She tapped her long polished nails on the bench impatiently.

"How do you plead?"

"There's been a misunderstanding."

Receiving a warning glance from the judge, Lucy decided this was not the time to argue. "Not guilty."

"Thank you," said the judge, with exaggerated politeness. "You're due back in court on December fifteenth."

"That's so close to Christmas," protested Lucy.

The judge ignored her and studied a sheet of paper.

"I see no reason not to release you on your own recognizance. See the bailiff."

She banged down her gavel and Lucy got in line behind the other accused lawbreakers at the bailiff's desk. When it was her turn she waited while he scribbled on an official-looking form.

"That'll be fifty dollars," he finally said without even raising his head.

"Fifty dollars?" Lucy knew she didn't have that much money in her wallet. She guessed she had something in the neighborhood of five dollars. "Can I write a check?"

He raised his head and lifted an eyebrow.

"Do you take Visa?"

He shook his head.

"I understand I get a phone call?"

He nodded and she was led back to the holding cell.

When she finally got her turn at the phone, Lucy didn't know whom to call. Bill was on the job and nobody was home. She could leave a message on the answering machine, but the odds of one of the kids actually listening to the message and taking action weren't good. She could call the paper, but suspected Ted was most likely out on assignment. Phyllis usually only worked mornings, which meant she'd have to leave a message and trust he'd check the machine before quitting for the day. Besides, it was getting late and the banks would be closing soon. She knew he refused to carry an ATM card and the chances he would have fifty dollars in cash were slim.

Her best bet, she finally decided, was to call Bob Goodman, Rachel's husband. He was a lawyer, after all. He would know what to do.

"The law office of Robert Goodman. May I help you?"

Martha Bennett's voice was music to Lucy's ears. "Martha, this is Lucy Stone. Could I speak to Bob?"

"Lucy, I'm afraid he's not in right now. Can I take a message?"

Lucy didn't want to tell this very proper, silver-haired lady that she needed bail, but she didn't really have a choice.

"I'm in a bit of a jam and need Bob to bail me out."

Martha Bennett didn't seem at all surprised. Lucy supposed she'd gotten calls like this before.

"Don't worry, Lucy. I'll page Bob immediately. How much do they want?"

"Fifty dollars."

"He's on his way."

This time, as Lucy was led back to the holding cell once again, she felt encouraged. Bob was on the way; Bob would rescue her.

She sat down on the steel bench, squeezing in between a rather heavy woman in flowing handwoven garments, who was obviously one of the protesters, and a tiny, shrunken woman, who was shaking uncontrollably.

"DTs," said the heavy woman with a knowing nod. "Better give her plenty of room."

She had no sooner spoken than the tiny woman doubled over and vomited on the floor. Some of the other women in the crowded cell made sounds of disgust; the gray-haired woman called for the guard.

Nobody came to clean up the mess. There was no place to go; no other seat was available in the crowded cell. Lucy concentrated on a brown water stain on the opposite wall. She tried to ignore the smell; she tried not to notice the woman's trembling. Instead, she tried to frame the story she would write for the *Pennysaver* about the morning's events.

The thing that most struck her, she decided, was the contrast between the quiet mourners inside the church and the pandemonium outside. To her, it seemed the protesters and the police were equally guilty of disturbing the funeral service.

Her thoughts turned to Ellie and the figure beside her: Jonathan Franke. There had been something in the way he'd angled his body toward Ellie, something in the way his hand lingered on her back, that made Lucy doubtful he was acting simply as a friend. She would have bet her bail money that Jonathan Franke was hoping to take Curt Nolan's place as Ellie's boyfriend.

If that was true, she thought, it gave Franke a real motive for killing Nolan. She remembered the pie sale, where the two had argued. Now that she thought about it, the two men had exhibited more animosity than could be accounted for by their differing views about zoning regulations. In fact, she remembered, Franke had been so angry he had stalked off without finishing his pie—a definite first for the pie sale.

The more she thought about it, the more convinced she became that Franke was a prime suspect for Nolan's murder. It was obvious the murder hadn't been premeditated; the murderer had acted on impulse. And everybody knew Franke had trouble controlling his temper. Years ago, when the Association for the Preservation of Tinker's Cove had been in its early stages, he'd been involved in a few scuffles and had even been charged with assaulting a contractor in an effort to halt a construction project in a watershed area.

Lately, however, he'd made a real effort to be more reasonable and professional in his role as the association's executive director.

He'd given up the wild, curly hair that had been his trademark and had taken to wearing casual business clothes instead of the jeans and plaid flannel shirts he'd once favored. Now he was usually seen in khaki pants and tweed jackets-the sort of jackets that had leather patches on the elbows and woven leather buttons.

The thought brought Lucy up sharply: woven leather buttons, just like the one that was found in Curt Nolan's hand.

Feeling pressure on her upper arm, Lucy glanced at the alcoholic woman next to her. She wasn't a pretty sight and Lucy struggled not to gag. The woman had passed out and was leaning against Lucy. A stream of saliva was dribbling down her chin and she reeked of booze and vomit.

"Lucy Stone," called the officer.

"Here," yelled Lucy, gently easing herself away from the unconscious woman and lowering her to the bench before presenting herself to the guard.

She watched impatiently as he fumbled with the keys. Enough, already. She'd been here for an eternity and couldn't wait to get out.

"What took you so long?" she demanded as Bob led her to his car. "Do you know what it's like in there? People were throwing up! It was disgusting! I don't know how they get away with treating people like that, keeping them in such appalling conditions! It's outrageous!"

"I knew you'd be glad to see me," said Bob, unlocking the car door for her.

"I must've been in there for hours," said Lucy, fuming as she fastened her seat belt.

"Well, you're out now—until December fifteenth. Want to tell me how you got in this mess so I can convince Judge Joyce not to lock you up and throw away the key?"

"She could do that?" Lucy was horrified.

"I'm exaggerating," admitted Bob. "But you've got to face the fact that this isn't over. You've been charged with assaulting a police officer, disorderly conduct, unlawful assembly, and kidnapping."

"That's absurd! I was there for the funeral. I wasn't involved in the protest at all. Then I saw one of the kids from the day care center wandering around and tried to get her to safety. I wasn't kidnapping her." Lucy stared out the window at the bare gray trees they were passing. "They grabbed her out of my arms. What's going to happen to her?"

"Probably social services is taking care of her until her parents can claim her. Were they arrested, too?"

"I don't know. All I know is her name is Tiffani. I don't even know her last name." She bit her lip. "I hope she's okay."

"She's in good hands."

"I wish I could be sure of that."

"All right," said Bob. "I'll check on her and let you know."

"Thanks," said Lucy.

"About time," said Bob. "Most of my clients are a lot more appreciative. This will definitely be reflected in your bill."

"I'll tell Rachel," said Lucy with a little smile.

"Touché," said Bob. "This will be pro bono."

"Thank you. That's really nice of you."

"Don't mention it," said Bob, turning into her driveway. "I'm just being realistic. If you couldn't come up with bail, what are the chances you could pay me?"

"My funds were temporarily unavailable," protested Lucy.

"Never mind," said Bob. "Just do me a favor and stay out of trouble between now and December fifteenth. Promise?"

"I promise," said Lucy.

CHAPTER 18

"**M**om, you're on TV."

Lucy tossed the sponge she'd been using to wipe off the kitchen table into the sink and hurried into the family room. There she watched herself being unceremoniously tossed into the paddy wagon.

"Is my butt really that big?" she asked Bill.

He didn't answer but walked right past her to answer the phone that was ringing in the kitchen.

She stood there in the doorway, watching the rest of the report. Bear Sykes got a lot of play; he was shown in action leading the protest and was also interviewed afterward, when he had been released from jail.

"Why do you want to get mixed up with a guy like that?" said Bill, returning to his recliner and picking up the remote.

"I'm not mixed up with anything," protested Lucy. "I explained to you. All I did was go to the funeral. I didn't even know there was going to be a protest. I got arrested because I saw one of the day care kids had gotten lost and tried to get her out of the scuffle."

"Don't give me that," said Bill. "The cops obviously don't believe that story and I don't either. You told me you weren't going to get involved in this murder, and here you are, charged with ten counts of sticking your nose where it doesn't belong."

Lucy shifted uneasily and looked over at the couch, where Zoe and Sara had gotten very still and quiet. Bill, however, was too angry to notice and continued his tirade.

"You had no business going to that funeral. It isn't as if there isn't plenty for you to do around here. The house could do with a good cleaning and Zoe got stranded at her scout meeting without a ride home. Anybody with two working brain cells could have figured out there'd be some kind of demonstration at that funeral but you never gave it a second thought and went off to get yourself arrested and forgot all about your responsibilities."

"That's not fair," Lucy began, ready to argue in her own defense but Bill was having none of it.

"And if all this wasn't bad enough," he said, cutting her off, "you know who just called? The Barths. They don't want to move here anymore. They just want me to finish up the house as quick and cheaply as I can so they can sell it—and I don't blame them either. Who would want to live in a place with murders and a gambling casino and demonstrations? Nobody in their right mind—that's for sure!" He glared at Lucy as if it were somehow all her fault.

"Bill," she began, then realized she might as well talk to a wall. He had retreated behind the newspaper and she knew from past experience there was no point trying to talk to him when he was in this kind of mood.

Besides, she thought guiltily, returning to the kitchen, he did have a point. She had had no business promising Miss Tilley she would try to find out who murdered Curt Nolan and she should never have attempted to conduct her own investigation. She could have saved herself a lot of trouble if she'd stayed home vacuuming or dusting instead of going to the funeral.

Angry and depressed, she yanked open the freezer and pulled out the emergency chocolate bar she kept behind the ice cube trays. She smacked it on the table, smiling with grim satisfaction as she felt it shatter into small pieces. Then she sat down and unwrapped it, popping a piece of chocolate into her mouth.

Sitting there with the sweet, delicious chocolate melting on her tongue, safe in the house she didn't seem to appreciate and surrounded by the family she had neglected, Lucy felt tears stinging her eyes.

She pictured once again Tiffani's frightened, tearstained face as she wandered in the midst of the disordered crowd, looking for a familiar face among the struggling police and protesters outside the church. She remembered the fear and outrage she'd felt when the police had grabbed her and how frustrated she'd been to find herself completely powerless, being carted off ro jail. Worst of all was the way everybody had refused to listen to her explanation. To the cops and the judge, she was just another docket number, another case for the system.

And what a system. She hadn't had any idea how people were treated when they were arrested. All jumbled together in that appalling paddy wagon and then confined in that filthy cell. As soon as she'd gotten home she'd taken a shower and changed her clothes, but the stench of the jail seemed to linger stubbornly about her. She could still smell the disgusting reek of vomit, booze, and body odor.

She reached for a tissue and gave her nose a good blow, then took another and wiped her eyes. If she was this upset, she thought, popping another piece of chocolate in her mouth, what must poor little Tiffani be going through? Was she spending the night with strangers in some foster home? Had some unfamiliar woman bathed her and dressed her in borrowed pajamas, then tucked her into a bed that wasn't her own? Was she terrified that she'd never see her family again?

Lucy sniffled again and Kudo raised his head from the dog bed, where he had been snoozing. He looked at her curiously. He got up slowly and stretched, then clicked across the floor to her and rested his head on her lap.

At least someone understands, thought Lucy, stroking the thick fur on the dog's neck. She hoped Tiffani had found some similar comfort, maybe a teddy bear, to get her through the night.

Bob had promised to check on the little girl for her, but Lucy wasn't entirely confident he'd remember. Tomorrow she'd check with Sue at the day care center and make sure Tiffani was back where she belonged. Then, she promised herself, she would drop the whole thing.

But what about Jonathan Franke? she asked herself as she sucked the chocolate off a piece of almond. She couldn't just forget about him, especially since he seemed to have such a strong motive for killing Nolan. No, she thought, picking up another piece of chocolate, she had to alert the police to her suspicions. Once she'd done that, then she could retire from the investigation and turn her attention where it belonged: to her home and family.

CHAPTER 19

When Lucy stopped at the day care center the next morning her heart almost stopped when she didn't see Tiffani playing with the other children.

"You look like you've seen a ghost," said Sue.

"It's what I'm not seeing," said Lucy, frantic with worry. "Where's Tiffani?"

"Her mom called. She's keeping her home today." Sue paused, giving her an odd look. "What's it to you?"

"She's home and everything's okay?"

"Yeah. Why?"

"It's a long story," said Lucy.

"I'm not going anywhere," said Sue, casting an eye at the roomful of children. "I've got plenty of time."

"Well," began Lucy, taking a child-size seat next to Sue's desk, "I saw her at the funeral yesterday. She'd gotten separated from her mother or whomever she was with and was wandering around lost in the crowd. I tried to help her, but ended up getting arrested myself."

"No!"

"Yes. It was horrible. Jail isn't all it's cracked up to be."

"I can imagine," said Sue, expertly surveying the play area, where the little girls were chattering in the dress-up corner and the boys were divided between the blocks and the sand table. "How come you went to the funeral? I didn't know you knew Curt Nolan."

"I didn't. I went to support Ellie Martin. I got to know her when I interviewed her for the story I wrote about the dolls. She and Curt were in a relationship, so this has all been pretty tough on her. I've been trying to help—I even took the dog."

Sue stared at her. "You've got a dog?"

"Curt Nolan's dog."

"Kadjo?" exclaimed Sue in disbelief. "The one that killed the chickens?"

"We call him Kudo now. He's not a bad dog at all really. I've gotten kind of attached to him."

Sue gave her a knowing look. "Ah, an empty-nest puppy."

Lucy shook her head. "Don't be silly. He just needed a home."

"Right," said Sue, furrowing her brow. "Harry, please don't throw the sand."

"I never heard anything so silly," continued Lucy. "It would be crazy to try to replace Toby with a dog."

"If you say so," said Sue. "Harry, this is a warning. If you do that again you'll have to go to time-out."

Harry threw down his shovel and went over to the shelves, where he took down a big dump truck and started pushing it around on the floor.

"You know," said Lucy, "I never did get Tiffani's last name. What is it?"

"Sykes." Sue was on her feet, keeping an eye on Harry while she poured glasses of juice.

"Sykes! Is she related to Bear Sykes?"

"You bet," said Sue, carrying the tray of juice cups over to a low table and setting it down. "She's his granddaughter."

Lucy brought over the graham crackers and unwrapped them. "I guess that explains what she was doing at the demonstration."

Sue nodded, passing out the crackers to the children. "You won't believe this," she said, whispering. "He wanted me to bring all the day care kids, but I told him it wasn't appropriate."

"He wanted you to bring the kids to the demonstration?" Lucy was appalled. "Where'd he get such an idea?"

Sue took a bite of cracker. "About half the kids here are Metinnicut, you know. He's been after me for quite a while to add Metinnicut songs and stories to the curriculum."

Sue lowered her head, studying her carefully manicured nails. Her face was hidden by a fall of glossy black hair, which Lucy happened to know was testament to her colorist's skill. "I know I should. I mean, I really try to be multicultural. We sing songs from all over the world, so why not Indian songs? I'm really not opposed to it," she said, lifting her head, "but I don't quite see what business he has coming into my day care center with a couple of young toughs and telling me what to do. I told him to get lost."

Sue's attention shifted to the snack table. "Don't grab, Justin. There's plenty for everyone."

She turned back to Lucy. "And then he told me I'd better start looking for a new job because when the tribe makes money from the casino they're going to open their own day care center and I'll be out of work."

Lucy could hardly believe her ears. "That's ridiculous," she said, sputtering.

"No it's not. Like I said before, about half the kids are Metinnicut. If they go somewhere else, there won't be enough children left to justify funding the center. In fact, I wouldn't feel right asking the voters for the money for so few children."

"You could fight back," said Lucy. "I'll put it in the paper, how he's using strong-arm tactics."

"It's not such a big deal really," said Sue. "I don't have to do this. I'm not sure I want to anymore. It filled a need when Sidra went away to college. I admit it. It was a way to fill my empty nest." She smiled down at the children, who were seated around the snack table. "But I've worked that out. I'm ready for something new."

"I had no idea," said Lucy, giving her friend a hug. "I didn't realize you were that upset when Sidra went away."

"It was terrible—I almost got a dog," said Sue, struggling to keep a straight face.

"Ouch!" exclaimed Lucy. "I'm not taking any more of this abuse. If I want abuse, I can go to work. At least Ted pays for the privilege."

But when Lucy got to the *Pennysaver* office, there was no sign of Ted.

"He's interviewing Bear Sykes," said Phyllis, "for a story about the demonstration yesterday."

"Oh," said Lucy, digesting this information while she hung up her coat. All of a sudden it seemed as if Bear was popping up everywhere. He was the man of the hour, and as yesterday's protest seemed to indicate, the tribe was falling in step behind him.

"Lucy," said Phyllis, breaking into her thoughts, "since you're here, would you mind keeping an eye on things? I've got to go to the post office."

"No problem."

Lucy sat down at Phyllis's desk, where she could answer the phone and keep an eye on the door. Since she was alone, it seemed a good time to call Lieutenant Horowitz and tie up that last loose thread. Then she could retire from the investigation in good conscience.

Lucy reached for the receiver, then hesitated. This wasn't going to be pleasant, she told herself, recalling previous encounters with the lieutenant, but it had to be done. Bracing herself, she dialed the number of the state police barracks in Livermore.

"Ah, Mrs. Stone," he said when her call finally got through to him. "I was wondering why I hadn't heard from you."

"I didn't know you cared," said Lucy, picturing his long rabbit face and his tired gray eyes.

"I care very much," said the lieutenant, adding a long sigh. "It's the new buzzword in the department: community policing. We're supposed to get the public involved, maintain good relations with the media. So what can I do for you?"

"Well, since you asked, I was wondering if Jonathan Franke is a suspect in the Curt Nolan investigation?"

There was a long pause. "Well, in an investigation like this, the umbrella of suspicion covers a lot of people. Why are you asking about Franke in particular?"

"I happened to see him at the funeral yesterday and he was being very attentive to Ellie Martin, who used to be Nolan's girlfriend."

"Hmm. Jealousy. Could be a motive."

Encouraged, Lucy continued. "Plus, he happens to wear a lot of tweed jackets with the kind of button that was found in Nolan's hand."

"Who told you about the button?"

From the lieutenant's icy tone, Lucy guessed he was no longer interested in cultivating good media relations. "I can't tell you that," said Lucy. "My sources are confidential."

"I could take you into court for witholding evidence," said Horowitz. "I don't think Judge Ryerson would look very kindly on you, especially considering the list of charges pending against you."

"You know perfectly well that's all a big misunderstanding. Now, to get back to Jonathan Franke, I think you have to consider him a suspect. First there's the motive: jealousy. Then there's the question of whether he'd be capable of committing murder. I can tell you he has a very hot temper and I've seen him almost come to blows with Nolan."

"Mrs. Stone, just hold on a minute. Curt Nolan almost came to blows, hell, he did come to blows—with lots of people."

"What about the button?"

"Every man in America has an article of clothing with that kind of button: a jacket, a sweater, a raincoat. Trust me on this."

"It isn't who's got buttons like that—it's who's missing a button," said Lucy, feeling rather pleased with her cleverness. "Have you checked his clothes?"

"Mrs. Stone, as a professional journalist—and I use the term loosely—you know perfectly well that I can't reveal the details of an investigation. But off the record, I will tell you that Jonathan Franke has been eliminated as a suspect in the murder of Curt Nolan."

"Eliminated? Why?"

"Again, off the record, he was having dinner with his mother at the time. Thanksgiving dinner."

"You believe that?" Lucy was incredulous. "You're taking the word of his mother?"

"Actually, no. He had proof. Turkey leftovers, wrapped in foil."

"You're teasing me. You know you are."

Horowitz chuckled. Lucy could hardly believe her ears. "You know, I understand your interest in the case. It's a big story. And I appreciate the coverage we've gotten from the *Pennysaver* in the past. The *Pennysaver's* always been supportive and cooperative. But I've got to tell you that an investigation like this is best left to the professionals. We're not talking about someone who steals Girl Scout cookies here—this is a real bad guy and he won't hesitate to kill again. Do you understand me?"

"Yes," said Lucy in a small voice.

"Good. Now I want to tell you about the department's unclaimed property auction next month. Got a pencil?"

"Sure," said Lucy.

She'd just finished jotting down the details when the bell on the door jangled and Ted came in. His jaw was set and he stomped across the office to his desk, tossing his notebook down. Then he pulled off his jacket and threw it across the room, missing the coat rack.

"What's the matter?" asked Lucy, ready to duck for cover.

"Bear Sykes—that's what's the matter."

"The interview didn't go well?"

Ted snorted.

"It wasn't an interview, it was a lecture. Sykes told me the kind of coverage he wants in the future, and he pretty much let me know that the *Pennysaver's* continuing survival depends on it. And he had a bunch of young fellows from the tribe to back him up, too. Guys with nothing better to do than look tough."

"Wow. I guess power's really gone to his head. Sue said he's been throwing his weight around at the day care center, too." She paused, remembering the selectmen's meeting when Sykes had presented the Metinnicuts' petition. Ellie had called him an errand boy when he'd run out to fetch the architect's model of the casino. "It looks like he's really consolidated his position as tribal leader," she said. "You should've seen him at that demonstration yesterday. And the cops just played into his hands—those arrests will unify the tribe even more."

"I dunno," said Ted, perching restlessly on the edge of his chair. "Somehow I have a feeling that Curt Nolan must be turning over in his grave. He took pride in his Indian heritage. I don't think he'd like what's going on. Sykes and his boys looked more like the Mafia than anything else."

Lucy's and Ted's eyes met; they were both thinking the same thought. Before either could express it, however, the door opened with a jangle. They both looked up. Lucy recognized Jack O'Hara.

"Hi," she said, stepping behind the counter. "Can I help you?"

"Yes," he said. "I'd like to speak to the editor. You can say Jack O'Hara from Mulligan Construction is here."

"I know who you are," said Lucy with a big smile. "I covered the meeting."

"I'm sorry. I should have recognized you." He grinned apologetically. "I'm afraid I have a terrible memory for faces."

Yeah, right, thought Lucy. She was pretty sure he'd gone into that meeting knowing exactly who would be covering it; Chuck Canaday would have primed him.

"We're pretty informal here," she said, tilting her head at Ted. "That's Ted Stillings. He's the editor and publisher."

O'Hara pushed open the gate next to the counter and walked over to Ted's desk.

"Nice to meet you, Ted. Like I said, I'm Jack O'Hara from Mulligan Construction." He stuck out his hand and Ted shook it. "Mind if I sit down?"

"Not at all. What can I do for you?"

O'Hara spread his feet apart and leaned forward, resting his arms on his thighs and shifting his gloves from hand to hand. Lucy had the feeling she'd become invisible; O'Hara was talking to Ted man to man.

"As you probably know, Mulligan Construction has been selected by the Metinnicut Nation to build their casino. It's a big project, and we know it's bound to he controversial. This is a small town, and people in small towns don't usually like change very much. They like things to stay the way they are and I guess that's understandable."

Ted glanced at his watch, signaling it was time to skip the preamble and get down to business.

O'Hara cleared his throat and continued. "I understand just how influential a local newspaper like the *Pennysaver* can be in a situation like this, and I want to be sure we're all on the same page here. If you have any questions, anything at all you'd like to ask me about the project, I'd be more than happy to answer."

"Well, that's real nice of you," said Ted, reciting his stock answer. "I'll keep it in mind and give you a call if I have any questions."

O'Hara didn't take the hint. "A project like the casino can mean a lot to a town like this. It will give the local economy a big boost, believe me. And more business means more advertising, right?"

"Hadn't really thought about it," said Ted. Lucy could tell he was getting a bit hot under his collar.

"We happen to be fairly big advertisers ourselves at Mulligan," continued O'Hara. "I'm not sure of the total budget, but I can assure you it's substantial. And we're very selective. We place ads where they'll get the most results. And of course, we tend to favor publications that support our general goals. We play ball with people who are on the team, if you know what I mean."

Lucy watched, waiting for Ted's reaction. This was the second time someone had tried to pressure him in one day and she knew he must be pretty fed up.

"We'll be happy to run your ads," Ted said, spitting the words out. "As for supporting your goals or playing ball, I don't work that way. The paper's a public forum and we try to give equal coverage to all sides."

O'Hara looked down at his shoes, then turned his gaze on Ted. "I understand your reluctance," he said, practically winking at Ted. "I can assure you we would definitely make it worth your while to write a positive editorial. I understand that your opinion is valuable—more valuable than you might think."

Ted sat there, his eyes bulging and his mouth gaping like a goldfish. "Are you saying you would pay me to write an editorial in favor of the casino?"

"Oh, no. You misunderstand me," O'Hara said smoothly. "We would work something out. I hear you have a son in college—perhaps he could win a Mulligan scholarship? How would that be?"

"Get out!" roared Ted, rising to his feet and pointing to the door. "This discussion is over! Get out of my office!"

O'Hara maintained his casual manner as he stood up and crossed the floor to the gate. He pushed it open, then paused.

"You're making a mistake," he said, slapping his gloves against his hand. "We can make things pleasant, or we can make them very unpleasant. It's up to you."

"Are you threatening me?" Ted took a few steps toward O'Hara.

"I think I've made myself clear," O'Hara replied, opening the door.

A moment later he was gone, with nothing to remind them of his visit except the jangling bell.

CHAPTER 20

"That was weird," said Lucy after O'Hara had gone. Ted didn't answer. He grunted and started flipping through the stack of papers on his desk. Then he shoved them aside, pushed his chair back and stood up.

"I'm going out for some fresh air," he said, dropping the stack of papers in front of her. "Would you mind typing in these listings for me?"

Lucy figured Ted had had enough for one day and needed to get away from the office for awhile.

"No problem," she said.

Once he'd gone, however, she realized it would take hours to go through the stack of press releases announcing club meetings and used-book sales and holiday bazaars. She was struggling to decipher a particularly confusing notice about an amateur production of *Amahl and the Night Visitors* when the phone rang. It was Miss Tilley.

"I wondered if you'd like to join Rachel and me for lunch," the old woman purred.

Rachel worked as a part-time caregiver for the old woman, driving and cooking for her.

"I'd love to, but I can't. I've got too much work to do."

"That's too bad. Rachel and I were hoping you could give us an update on your investigation."

Lucy squirmed in her seat, remembering her conversation with Lieutenant Horowitz.

"I don't have much to tell you," she said. "In fact, I've been so busy—"

"You can't fool me, Lucy Stone," snapped the old woman. "I know you must have some idea by now of who killed Curt."

"Oh, I have some ideas," said Lucy. "But I think I'd better keep them to myself for the time being."

"I wouldn't tell a soul," coaxed Miss Tilley.

Lucy glanced around the empty office. She was dying to discuss her thoughts with someone, and Miss Tilley was a gold mine of local knowledge.

"My lips will remain sealed," continued Miss Tilley.

"I know you'll tell Rachel," said Lucy.

"Well, Rachel won't tell anyone either. She's married to a lawyer and she's used to keeping secrets. She's nodding in agreement as we speak, and making a sign of zipping her lips."

Lucy chuckled. "This is just an idea, now. I don't have any real evidence. But it does seem that one person has benefitted from Nolan's death more than anyone else. It's the *cui bona* thing."

"Bear Sykes!" exclaimed Miss Tilley, confirming Lucy's suspicions. "I just knew it!" Then she added, "Rachel thinks so, too."

"This is just a hunch."

"I'm sure you're right. It's obvious when you think about it. He's always had a power complex, and Curt Nolan was the one person who stood in his way as tribal leader."

"He's definitely in charge now," said Lucy. "He's really been throwing his weight around, you know."

"I'm not at all surprised. Why, I remember when he was a little boy. He wasn't much of a reader, you know, but he was looking for a topic for a research paper. It had to be about a famous person who changed history. I suggested Eisenhower, the supreme allied commander and such a dear man, too—but Bear wasn't interested. He said he'd rather write about John Wayne and wanted books about him."

"John Wayne? Isn't that an odd choice, considering Bear is a Native American?"

"Now that you mention it, I guess it is. Of course, I had to tell him that John Wayne was only an actor, that he hadn't really changed history." She paused. "I finally suggested Napoleon and Bear really got interested. For a while there he was constantly asking for books about Napoleon. Such a horrid little man, I've always thought, but Bear absolutely adored him."

"I wonder why," said Lucy.

Miss Tilley spoke slowly. "I suspect it was the fact that Napoleon was ultimately defeated but was still considered a great general."

"Like Geronimo and Sitting Bull?" Lucy said.

"I think so."

"Well, he's certainly acting like Napoleon now. He's turning the tribe into something like the Mafia."

"I can't say I'm surprised," said Miss Tilley. "Do you think the police suspect him?"

"I don't know," admitted Lucy.

"Maybe you could help them. Isn't there some way you could get evidence?"

"I can't think how."

"Search his house or something."

"You want me to break and enter?" Lucy was astonished. "That's illegal. What if I got caught?"

Miss Tilley clucked her tongue. "What's happened to you, Lucy Stone? You used to much bolder, you know."

"Let's say I'm older and wiser, unlike some people I know."

Miss Tilley wasn't about to give up. "If you applied yourself, I'm sure you could trick him into confessing."

"And how would I do that without risking my neck? You know, I have a family and they depend on me."

Miss Tilley didn't answer immediately, but Lucy could have sworn she heard her wheels turning through the telephone line.

"Use the telephone! Like that Linda Tripp person. Record him and take the tape to the police."

"That's illegal—they've filed charges against her, you know."

Miss Tilley sighed. "It was just an idea. You're probably not clever enough to trick him into confessing anyway."

"Thanks for the vote of confidence," said Lucy.

"I have to go. Rachel says lunch is ready—it's shrimp wiggle today," said Miss Tilley, naming a favorite dish of Lucy's.

"You have absolutely no mercy," said Lucy.

She hung up and picked up the next press release. It was for a square dance, and although it gave more information than she needed about callers and cuers, it didn't state the time of the dance. Fortunately, there was a phone number so Lucy called it.

While she listened to the rings, Lucy noticed there was a record button on her phone. She pushed it just as the other party answered.

She got the information she needed, hung up, and dialed the code for the message system. Sure enough, she'd recorded the entire conversation. That was interesting, she thought, wondering if she dared call Bear Sykes, when the phone rang. She recognized Jack O'Hara's voice.

"I'm sorry," she said, "but Ted's not here. You can leave a message if you want."

"Actually, it's you I want to talk to," he said.

Lucy rolled her eyes; didn't this guy ever give up?

"You couldn't convince Ted, so now you're going to try me? You're wasting your time. I'm just the hired help. I have no influence whatever."

O'Hara laughed and Lucy found herself warming to the man despite herself.

"You can't blame me, can you? After all, this is a project I believe in. Not just because it will make a profit for Mulligan, but because it will improve the town's economy. You've got to admit there's an awful lot of poverty in your unspoiled rural paradise. I mean, people can't afford to buy mittens for their kids?"

Lucy thought of Tiffani and her ragged jacket. "I can't argue with you there."

"Andy Brown and I would like to go over the plans with you. I think you'll see that gambling is really just a small part. There will be shops, theaters, even a museum. In fact, it's been suggested we name it after Curt Nolan as a memorial. It's a lot more than just a casino. It's going to employ a lot of people and they'll be able to make a lot more money than they're getting from jewelry piecework—that's for sure. This could mean opportunity for a lot of people."

Lucy's first impulse was to refuse, but she hesitated. The man had a point. She hadn't really considered the benefits the casino could bring; she'd made up her mind against it based on her own prejudices. Thanks to her Protestant upbringing, she had an unshakable conviction that gambling was sinful and the only proper place for money was in a savings bank.

"Okay," she finally said. "When and where?"

"There's no time like the present."

"No can do," said Lucy. "I have some work I have to finish up before deadline."

"Say in a couple of hours? At Andy Brown's place?"

Lucy checked the clock. It was almost one and she had to be at the selectmen's weekly meeting at four.

"How about three o'clock? But I won't be able to stay long."

"Great. See you then. I'll have Andy warm up some of his famous cider."

"Sounds good," said Lucy, suddenly hungry as she hung up the phone. She hadn't eaten lunch and she was ravenous. She knew she ought to eat something, but she still had pages and pages of listings.

Her stomach growled and she came to a decision. She'd go home and eat something and finish working on the listings there. That way she could check on the dog and she'd be closer to Andy Brown's farm. She could easily swing by there on her way to the meeting.

Satisfied with her decision, she stood up and stuffed the papers into her bag. She turned the sign in the window to read *closed* and pulled the door shut behind. As she hurried to the car she debated what to eat: leftover stew or a peanut butter and jelly sandwich?

CHAPTER 21

L ucy was sitting at the computer in the family room, working on the press releases, when the girls got home from school at a quarter of three.

"Home already? Gee, I didn't realize it was so late," said Lucy, ejecting the disk from the machine. "How was school?"

"School sucks," said Elizabeth. "I can't wait to go to college."

Lucy gave her a sharp look. "Don't swear."

"My group only got a B on our South America project because Lizzie Snider left Argentina off the map—it's not fair!" wailed Sara, who wasn't much of a team player.

"Mrs. Wilson put my picture up on the wall," said Zoe, beaming proudly.

"Great," said Lucy, bending down and giving her a peck on her forehead. "Listen, guys, I've got to go to a meeting, so I want you to hold the fort. I won't be home in time for supper so, Elizabeth, you'll have to cook the franks and beans. Sara, you can make a salad and, Zoe, you set the table. Got it?"

"Got it." Elizabeth was reaching for the phone, which had begun ringing right on schedule minutes after the girls got home.

Lucy shrugged off the guilt that invariably accompanied her when she left the kids in charge of dinner and headed for the door. Kudo was right at her heels.

"Sorry," she told him. "I don't have time for a walk today and believe me, you wouldn't like the selectmen's meeting."

Kudo didn't seem convinced. He wagged his tail eagerly. Lucy reconsidered. She supposed she could take him along for the ride to the farm and drop him off at the house on her way to the meeting.

"You win, just this once," she said, opening the door.

A blast of cold air hit her, and she quickly shut the door, almost bumping Kudo's nose.

"Oops. Just a minute—I've got to get my coat zipped."

She slapped her hat on her head and pulled on her gloves.

"Now we can go," she told the dog, holding the door for him.

Kudo ran ahead of her to the car and waited by the rear hatch. As soon as she lifted it, he jumped in and stood in the cargo area wagging his tail and smiling.

"We're just going for a little ride," she warned him as she started the engine. In the rearview mirror she could see him grinning at her, his big pink tongue lolling out of the side of his mouth.

What a doofus, she thought. Though not quite so much of a fool as Jack O'Hara, who actually thought he could bribe Ted to support the casino. Maybe that sort of thing happened in the world of big business, but it certainly didn't happen at the *Pennysaver.*

As she drove along, she wondered if bribes were business as usual at Mulligan Construction. From what Howard White had said at the meeting, it seemed O'Hara was pretty important in the company. Hadn't he said O'Hara would be the next CEO? She had wanted to ask St. John Barth about him on Thanksgiving, when he'd mentioned he used to work for Mulligan Construction, but the opportunity had slipped by when the conversation took a different turn.

She glanced at the dashboard clock as she pulled into the yard at the farm and saw she was late; it was already ten past three. Brown and O'Hara would have to make their case for the casino quickly because she could only stay for a half hour at most if she was going to get to the meeting in time.

She debated what to do with Kudo. She would have liked to let him out of the car but she wasn't confident she could control him, even on the leash. It was cold and windy outside, but the sun was shining and the car would stay warm, so she decided to leave him.

"Be a good boy," she told him.

Kudo stared at her for a minute, almost as if he couldn't believe he was going to be left behind. Then he curled up in a ball for an afternoon nap.

As usual, there was an assortment of vehicles in the Browns' farmyard, but none of them looked like the kind of car O'Hara would drive. The shiny black pickup truck was Andy's, his wife drove the Caravan, and the battered Corolla with radio station stickers probably belonged to one of their kids. The motorcycle, she figured, could belong either to Andy or one of his boys, maybe even a farmhand.

Lucy wasn't sure if she should go to the house or the barn. There'd been mention of mulled cider, which seemed to indicate the house, but since the barn door was propped open, she thought she might as well check there before climbing the hill to the house.

After the bright, albeit waning, sunshine outside, it took a few minutes for her eyes to adjust to the dim light inside the barn. It was surprisingly warm, and she pulled off her beret and jammed it in her pocket.

"Over here!" yelled O'Hara, and she finally made him out standing by TomTom Turkey's pen.

As she got closer and her vision cleared, she was shocked to see he was wearing a leather motorcross suit.

"I took you for the kind of guy who drives a Lexus or a BMW," she said in a teasing tone.

"You'd be right," he said, smiling. "I've got a Lexus but I ride my bike whenever I can. It's great exercise and a lot more fun than sweating on a treadmill in some stinking gym."

"A lot more dangerous, too," said Lucy, thinking of the cyclist who had harrassed her on the back road and wondering if it could possibly have been O'Hara. She thought of Bear Sykes and his cell phone but dismissed the thought. It seemed unlikely that O'Hara would be at Sykes's beck and call; it must have been one of the young toughs Ted had told her about. She relaxed.

"Where's Andy?" she asked, glancing uneasily at the turkey, who was pacing back and forth in his pen. "I don't think old Tom-Tom here cares much one way or the other about the casino."

"That's where you're wrong," said O'Hara with mock seriousness. "Before you got here, he was telling me he loves to play blackjack."

"I think craps is more his style," said Lucy, wrinkling her nose.

"You may be right," agreed O'Hara, unrolling the plans and laying them out on a stack of hay bales. The sun was sinking lower in the sky and it streamed through the high windows, lighting the entire area in a golden glow. "Andy had to make some phone calls but he said he'd be right over."

Lucy stepped closer, studying the blue-and-white diagram.

"This is what they call an elevation," O'Hara said. "It shows what the casino will look like from the southeast, actually the main entrance."

Lucy looked at the rounded awning, which was reminiscent of a long house. She noticed the carvings of a bear and turtle that stood on either side of the doorway. Her eyes followed the soaring lines of the hotel tower and she counted the rows of windows.

"Fourteen stories. It seems so big. Bigger than anything we've ever seen in Tinker's Cove."

"I know. But what would you rather have? A tall building like this or a sprawling complex covering acres of land?"

"I guess I never thought of it that way," said Lucy.

"This is so much more economical. It's energy efficient." O'Hara paused, looking at her. "You know, I'll never understand you country folk. You've got all this empty land—acres and acres of it—and you all act like one building is going to spoil it. What gives?"

Lucy shrugged. "People around here like it the way it is."

"I noticed." He tapped the plans with his finger. "You can't hold back progress, you know. Whether you like it or not, things are going to change in Tinker's Cove, with or without the casino. If the tribe gets federal recognition, the whole balance of power is going to change. It won't be Howard White and his buddies calling the shots anymore. And your boss, Ted? He's awfully cocky for a guy whose entire livelihood is tied up in that rickety newspaper. I mean, think what one carelessly thrown match could do to that place."

Lucy's head jerked up and she stared at O'Hara. "Is that why you had me come here? To send a message to Ted that you're going to torch the *Pennysaver* if he doesn't support the casino?"

O'Hara had been getting the full force of the slanting sunlight; it was so bright it illuminated the dancing dust particles in the air. Beads of perspiration had formed on his upper lip and he wiped them away with his hand.

"You've got me wrong," said O'Hara, unzipping his jacket. "I just think people should think things through before they make big decisions."

"That's good advice for—" began Lucy, stammering to a halt as her eyes fell on the short black thread that dangled from the neck of his sweater. It should have held a button, a woven leather button just like the ones that remained.

"Well, for anyone," she continued brightly, hoping he hadn't noticed her staring. "It's just common sense," she babbled on, wondering if O'Hara's missing button was *the* missing button. "What my mother used to tell me: 'Think before you speak.'"

O'Hara nodded and leaned forward to pull out another plan, and she instinctively stepped back. He looked at her curiously.

"I think that, if you keep an open mind when you look at these plans, you'll have to agree the casino could be a real asset to the town. Look here. We've used a woodland theme. A brook with waterfalls actually runs through the gaming area and there will be recordings of birdsong. The furniture will be Adirondack style, like a lodge, right down to a gigantic fieldstone fireplace."

He tapped the plan with his finger, inviting Lucy to step forward and take a closer look. She knew she should do it, but she couldn't make her feet move. All she could think about was that missing button.

"I know casinos aren't everybody's cup of tea," he said, sensing her discomfort. "Let me show you the shopping concourse. It's truly magnificent. It has a four-story waterfall."

As he spoke, Lucy came to a decision. She had to get out of there. She'd make up an excuse, a little white lie, and leave.

"You know," she said, making a show of checking her watch. "I just realized that I have to pick up my daughter from Brownies."

Damn it. If only she could take her eyes off that darn sweater.

But no matter how hard she tried, her gaze kept returning to the sight of that dangling thread.

"I thought you said you had until four when the selectmen have their meeting." His eyes had become flat and his tone was insistent.

"I'm sorry. I just forgot about the scout meeting. I really do have to go," insisted Lucy, wishing she had never agreed to meet O'Hara.

"I only have a few more points to go over with you," he said firmly. "It won't take long."

Looking through the long barn, Lucy could see the door, still ajar. More than anything she wanted to go through it.

"I can't stay," she said. "I really have to pick up my daughter."

"Can't she wait for a few minutes?" His tone was unexpectedly vehement and it struck Lucy that O'Hara was a man used to getting his own way, a man who didn't like to be crossed.

"Ten minutes," she said, hoping he'd accept a compromise. Besides, she was probably just being silly. There was no sense jumping to conclusions. Lots of people wore those sweaters. What had Horowitz said? Every man in American had something with that kind of button in his closet. Furthermore, she knew they tended to fall off. How many times had she replaced the buttons on Bill's sport coat? Having a missing button wasn't a crime and it didn't mean O'Hara was a murderer. The sooner she went along with him, she told herself, the sooner she'd get out of there. Her best bet was to behave as normally as possible without giving him a hint of her suspicions. She could keep a poker face as well as anyone.

"How many stores in the shopping concourse?" she asked, trying to sound interested.

"Forty or so, ranging from high-end jewelry and fur boutiques to souvenirs and T-shirts."

"This is a much bigger project than I imagined," she said.

"Mulligan is one of the biggest construction companies in the Northeast," he boasted. "We only do big projects."

"Really?" Lucy decided to lay on the flattery. "And you're in line to be the next CEO?"

"I don't know where Howard White gets off saying stuff like

that." He glanced at TomTom, who was still regarding them suspiciously from his pen. "One thing I've learned in business is never to count your chickens, or your turkeys, before they're hatched. There are plenty of foxes sniffing around, believe me."

"From what Howard said, it sounded like a sure thing."

"No way. I've got a lot of competition for the job." He looked at the plans. "Of course, if I can make a go of this thing it would give me a real advantage." He paused and smiled smugly. "You see, this casino project is my baby."

"What do you mean? Didn't the Metinnicuts hire you?"

"No way. It was my idea," he said. "You see, I've known Andy for a long time. We went to college together. When he told me the local tribe was trying to get federal recognition, I approached Bear Sykes. He hadn't even thought of a casino until I mentioned it. I mean, of course they'd thought of it, but they hadn't come to any decision."

Lucy nodded. "From what Ellie told me they were mostly interested in maintaining their heritage and establishing a cultural identity."

"Whoa," said O'Hara, holding up his hands in protest. "If I hear those words one more time—I mean, what do they want? We've got bears and turtles and babbling brooks and fucking birdsongs, pardon my French. But that wasn't enough, not for Mr. Nolan. It wasn't enough that this casino can generate enough money for the entire tribe to go live in Tahiti if they want, for God's sake, but he's nitpicking every little thing. Talk about bad timing. Just when we need to grease the wheels he comes in throwing sand around. That guy made a big mistake when he tangled with me."

O'Hara suddenly realized he'd said too much. "Not that I had anything to do with his death."

"Of course not," said Lucy, backing away from him. "That never crossed my mind."

O'Hara's eyes were fixed on something in the corner. Lucy followed his gaze and recognized a maul—an oversize mallet with a steel head used to force a wedge through a log to split it into firewood.

"Of course, I'm not shedding any tears for him," said O'Hara, picking up the maul and checking its heft. "I guess you could call it a lucky break."

Lucy had split plenty of wood in the days when they'd heated their house with a woodstove, and she knew to the ounce exactly how heavy a maul was. She had once dropped one on her foot, which had turned black-and-blue for weeks. She didn't even want to think about the damage one could cause if it were used as a weapon. She looked toward the door, estimating the distance. If she made a run for it, would she make it? Not unless O'Hara was distracted, she decided.

"I've always believed you make your own luck," said Lucy, nervously backing up against the turkey pen and reaching in her coat pocket. Behind her, she could hear TomTom making throaty noises. "Things seem to be going pretty well for you. You wouldn't want to do anything foolish."

"One thing I know," he said, stepping toward her. "You don't get ahead by being indecisive—you can't be afraid to take risks."

He started to lift the maul and Lucy knew he planned to kill her, just as he'd killed Curt Nolan. She edged away from him and reached deeper in her pocket, finally finding what she was looking for: the red beret she had stuffed there earlier. She pulled it out, waving it and tossing it straight at O'Hara.

He instinctively ducked and grabbed for it, giving Lucy an opportunity to unlatch the gate of TomTom's pen.

Enraged by the sight of the red beret in O'Hara's hand, the huge bird went straight for his supposed rival. Caught off balance by the unexpected attack, O'Hara went flying and landed on his seat in a pile of straw.

TomTom cocked his head, blinked his eyes and decided he'd been so successful at cutting this guy down to size that he might as well finish him off. He puffed out his chest, spread his tail, and renewed his attack.

Lucy didn't wait to watch. She started to run for the door but stopped in her tracks when it flew open and Kudo ran in, followed by Barney Culpepper.

"Hold it right there!" bellowed Barney, reaching for his gun.

O'Hara froze, holding the maul at shoulder height and keeping a wary eye on the turkey. TomTom, however, was no longer interested in attacking him. He was checking out a new opponent: Kudo, who had faced off opposite him, growling.

"You're under arrest," Barney told O'Hara. "Put the maul down and put your hands behind your back."

"What's the charge?" demanded O'Hara, cocky as ever.

"Mistreating an animal will do for starters,'" said Barney, snapping on the cuffs.

Her knees shaking, Lucy stroked Kudo's thick ruff. He wagged his tail, then jumped at TomTom, sending the turkey scurrying for the safety of his pen. Lucy fastened the catch with trembling hands. Then she collapsed on her knees, burying her nose in the dog's fur and hugging him.

He tolerated this embarrassing display for a few seconds, then pulled away, cocking his head and pricking up his ears.

"You're right," said Lucy. "It's time to get out of here."

CHAPTER 22

Lucy had just put Kudo in the car when she heard sirens. So did the Browns, who began pouring out of the house and streaming down the hill to the barnyard. *About time,* thought Lucy, slamming down the hatch. *Where were you when I needed you?*

Andy led the group, marching up to Barney and demanding, "What's going on?"

Marian Brown stood a few steps behind him, wiping her hands on her apron and keeping an eye on the kids.

"I'm making an arrest," said Barney, lifting off his cap and running his hand through his brush cut before replacing it.

Andy peered in the back of the cruiser, then raised his eyebrows in shock when he recognized Jack O'Hara.

"There must be some mistake!" he declared. "That's Jack!"

"Excuse me," said Marian, stepping beside her husband, "but what possible reason could you have for arresting Mr. O'Hara?"

"Well, somehow I think it's for more than attempting to assault a turkey," said Barney as a couple of state police cars spun into the driveway with their lights flashing.

Barney went to confer with the new arrivals, leaving Lucy with the Browns.

"Do you know what's going on?" asked Andy.

"I'm not sure," said Lucy, "but I think your friend killed Curt Nolan."

Marian and Andy exchanged glances. Then Marian bustled off, shooing the kids back into the house. Andy hitched up his overalls and studied Lucy.

"Are you the one who came up with this bright idea?" he asked, hooking his thumbs in the straps of his overalls and looking down at her.

"It wasn't me," said Lucy, watching as Barney returned to the cruiser and drove off with O'Hara, followed by one of the state police cars.

"O'Hara asked me out here to show me the plans—at least that's what he said, but things got a little out of hand." She shuddered and looked at Andy. "What were you all doing? I must have been in the barn with him for half an hour. Didn't you notice you had company?"

Andy's face got a little red and he gave his overalls another hitch. "The boys and me were watching TV, one of them talk shows. It was about moms who steal their daughters' boyfriends." He grinned. "It got pretty wild there—pulling hair, fighting. They had to pull a couple of 'em apart." He shook his head. "They shouldn't allow stuff like that on TV."

Maybe you shouldn't watch it, thought Lucy as Lieutenant Horowitz approached them.

"I think we've got everything under control here," he told Andy. "Thanks for your cooperation."

"No problem," said Andy. "Do you mind telling—"

"I'm afraid I can't say anything right now," Horowitz told him. "Now if you don't mind, I have a few questions for Mrs. Stone."

Andy stood his ground for a moment, then realized he was being dismissed. He shrugged and went back to the house, leaving them alone.

Lucy took a deep breath and looked up at the sky, which was orangey from the setting sun.

"I thought we had an understanding," said Horowitz, scolding her. "I thought you were going to stay out of this."

"I was. I did," answered Lucy quickly. "Honest."

Horowitz spoke slowly. "O'Hara's a dangerous man."

"You don't have to tell me," said Lucy indignantly. "He was going to bash my brains out with a maul."

"I don't doubt it for a minute," said Horowitz, fixing his pale gray eyes on hers. "Once we started talking to people at Mulligan Construction, he became our top suspect. Nolan wasn't the first, you know. O'Hara was involved in the disappearance of a secretary, but there wasn't enough evidence to charge him. We got a lot of information from a former employee who was planning to move here."

"St. John Barth?" asked Lucy.

Horowitz looked at her curiously. "You know him?"

"My husband is restoring a house for the Barths, but they changed their minds. They want to sell it."

"Barth didn't want to be anywhere near O'Hara," said Horowitz by way of explanation. "Barth knew too much about O'Hara."

Lucy screwed up her mouth. She couldn't believe she'd had Barth at her dinner table the day of the murder and he'd had the answer. If only she'd asked him.

"Is something the matter?" Horowitz sounded concerned.

Lucy shook her head. "I never suspected him, not for a minute." She shivered, thinking what a close call she'd had. "Is that why Barney came? He knew O'Hara was here?"

"Not exactly. Your boss called. I guess your conversation with O'Hara was recorded somehow on the message system. When he found out you were meeting O'Hara he was worried about your safety. It seems O'Hara had threatened him earlier today."

Lucy shook her head. "I can't believe I was so stupid. O'Hara wanted me to take another look at the casino plans. He said I should keep an open mind."

"You never suspected he had killed Nolan?"

"No. I had my suspicions." She paused. "About somebody else."

"Ah." Horowitz put his long fingers together. "So I guess I was right and you were wrong."

Lucy grimaced. "I guess."

"I hope you'll keep that in mind in the future," he said. "Some things are best left to the professionals. Now, go back home to your family and count your blessings, Mrs. Stone. You were very lucky today, you know."

"I know," said Lucy.

She managed a little smile and he gave her a nod. Then he started across the yard to his car.

Lucy watched him go for a moment, then called out, "Lieutenant! Just thought I'd let you know there's a button missing from O'Hara's sweater—not that it means anything, of course, but it's worth checking out."

"Thank you," he said, giving her a salute.

Lucy took a last look at the sky, now a deep purplish blue, and opened the car door. Kudo was waiting for her.

"Extra rations for you tonight," she told him. "A whole can of turkey and giblets."

She had no sooner spoken than she could have sworn she heard a distant protesting gobble from TomTom in the barn.

"Did you hear anything?" she asked Kudo as she started the car.

There was no answer from the cargo area, but she did hear him lick his chops.

CHAPTER 23

It was a beautiful spring morning. Lucy had to admit that; who could argue with a cloudless blue sky, flowering apple trees, and gorgeous, lush lilac bushes covered with blossoms that bobbed in the warm breeze? It was the sort of day that lifted your spirits, put a smile on your face and a bounce in your step.

Nevertheless, her heart was heavy as she drove the familiar route to Andy Brown's farm. Today the ground-breaking ceremony for the new casino was to take place and she was covering it for the newspaper. Even though she knew the casino would bring jobs and money to Tinker's Cove, she hated to see the quiet countryside she loved become the site of a gleaming monument to greed and avarice. They called it entertainment but she knew better; gambling was simply another way to separate a fool from his money. Money that would be better spent on shoes for the children and groceries and mortgage payments.

Looking back over the last few months, Lucy could hardly believe how smoothly the casino project had progressed. One by one the expected obstacles had toppled. The Bureau of Indian Affairs had recently revised its policy on tribal recognition and had granted the Metinnicut people tribal status in record time. The state legislature, where both Democrats and Republicans were eager for increased tax revenue, had voted to approve the casino with little discussion. Faced with what appeared to be an unstoppable juggernaut, the members of the Tinker's Cove Planning Board had been unwilling to risk embroiling the town in expensive court appeals and promptly issued the necessary approval. In a matter of months the casino project had gone from a set of paper plans to reality.

She supposed the project's success would have assured Jack O'Hara the job he wanted so much that he was willing to kill for it. Perhaps he was taking some satisfaction from the fact that the casino would be built, from whatever section of the hereafter he was presently occupying. O'Hara hadn't been willing to face a trial and the likelihood of spending the rest of his life in jail. Instead, he had managed a spectacular escape and had been shot by pursuing police officers. "Suicide by cop," they called it, but Lucy suspected O'Hara was betting he could get away.

As Horowitz had told her, it was St. John Barth who fingered O'Hara in the first place. He had been the last person to see the missing secretary alive, getting in O'Hara's car, but although he'd told the police, they had never been able to make a case against O'Hara. Barth had left the company, figuring it would be prudent to get as far away from O'Hara as he could. As he had explained to Bill, when O'Hara had turned up in Tinker's Cove, he didn't think he could risk an encounter. So he and Clarice had decided to sell the house. Now, with O'Hara out of the picture, the Barths had moved in and St. John was working on a true-crime book about his former nemesis.

The thought made Lucy smile as she parked the car and climbed out, checking to be sure she had her camera and notebook. As she made her way through the crowded parking lot to the pumpkin field where the casino was to be built, she saw the crowd was divided into several groups.

Holding center stage was Sandy Dunlap, dressed in a red power suit and sporting a chic new hairdo, backed by Mulligan Construction executives and town officials sympathetic to the project. Rumor was she was considering a run for the state legislature, and Lucy had no doubt she'd win. As Ted had pointed out so often, Sandy was a terrific campaigner, but she didn't have a clue what to do once she got in office.

The Brown family was also there in force, all dressed in their Sunday best. Lucy wondered if they would stay on in the farm house, next to the casino, or if they'd take the money and settle somewhere else, someplace where there wasn't a tacky casino spoiling the landscape.

Also standing with Sandy and beaming approval were a group from the Business and Professional Women's Association of Tinker's Cove led by Franny Small. This newly formed group was having a definite impact on town politics, well out of proportion to its small size.

Last, but not least among the group gathered around the town officials, were Bear Sykes and the Metinnicut people, dressed in traditional Native American clothing decorated with fringe, beads, and feathers.

Another group was also waiting for the ceremony to begin, but these people had grim expressions on their faces and had arranged themselves in front of a Mulligan Construction bulldozer. Jonathan Franke was there, holding a placard that read, *Bet on the environment,* and so was Fred Rumford, holding a traditional deerskin drum. Ellie was absent, Lucy noticed, speculating that she would have found herself in an awkward position, having to choose between her loyalty to the tribe and her relationship with Jonathan.

There was a squeal from the microphone as Sandy began speaking and thanked everyone for coming.

"This project has not been without controversy," she continued, getting a few chuckles from the crowd, "but change is always controversial. Today we are embarking on a new adventure, which we hope will bring unprecedented prosperity to our community—to our whole community."

Everyone, except the protesters, applauded. They remained stubbornly in place, in front of the bulldozer.

Sandy raised her hand and the machine roared into life, she lowered her hand and it began rumbling forward, making the first cut in the field. The protesters stood their ground until the last minute. Then they scattered for safety to the sidelines, where they stood in a ragged row. Fred Rumford began beating his drum slowly, as if for a dirge.

Lucy had snapped some pictures and was moving among the crowd, collecting quotes, when it suddenly became much quieter. The slow drumbeats continued but the bulldozer had stopped and was idling in the middle of the field. The operator had jumped down and could be seen on his knees, pawing at the dirt.

Rumford passed his drum over to Franke, who continued the slow beat, and ran out to join the bulldozer operator. He, too, knelt and began gently brushing away at the soil. When he stood up his solemn expression had been replaced with a huge smile.

"We have archaeological remains," he exclaimed, and the protesters erupted into joyful cheers.

"What does that mean?" asked Sandy, looking puzzled.

"That means everything stops. Right now. We have to call the state archaeologist, who will determine if the site is historically valuable and should be preserved."

A little worried furrow appeared between Sandy's brows.

"You can't do that!" exclaimed Andy Brown. "This is my land and I say we're going ahead." He tapped the bulldozer operator on his shoulder. "You, get back up on the machine. Let's go."

The fellow shook his head. "Sorry. No can do." He tilted his head toward Rumford. "He's right. It's a state law. We have to wait for the archaeologist."

"How long will that take?" demanded Andy impatiently.

The fellow shrugged. "A couple of weeks maybe."

"And then we can go ahead with the casino, right?"

"Wrong." It was Rumford, looking as if he'd stumbled on the Holy Grail. "These are human remains, very old remains. And Metinnicut pot shards. If I'm right, and I'm sure I am, this is a gravesite dating from 1400 or earlier."

"So what? There's stuff like that all over the farm. Arrowheads, bits of this and that—I don't know what all."

"There are?" Rumford could hardly contain his delight. "All over, you say?"

"Yeah. What of it?"

"This is a priceless archaeological resource!" Rumford was bouncing on his toes. "It can't be touched! It's one of a kind! It will have to be excavated and researched! Do you know how rare this is? It's fantastic! It's what I've been waiting for my entire life."

"What about the casino?" insisted Brown.

"There's no question about that. You'll have to find another site for the casino."

Brown glared at him angrily, then stomped off to confer with the Mulligan executives.

Bear Sykes approached Rumford. "You say these are the remains of my ancestors?"

"I'd bet my life on it," said Rumford. "Heck, I'm going to stake my career on it. This land holds a wealth of information about the Metinnicut people."

Sykes nodded. "It is good," he said and began clapping his hands and singing a traditional chant. He was soon joined by other members of the tribe, and Franke picked up the beat on his drum. Someone produced a tightly knotted bundle of sage leaves and lighted it; fragrant smoke rose heavenward.

Lucy took a deep breath and savored the sharp scent of the burning herbs. She surveyed the field filled with friends and neighbors and looked beyond to the budding trees that rimmed the field. She looked up at the blue sky, where a single dark cloud had formed directly overhead blocking the sun. Then she thought of Curt Nolan.

She remembered the day he died, how his sightless eyes had looked up at the sky. Today, if he was up there, perched on that cloud and looking down on the human comedy in Andy Brown's pumpkin field, he must surely be smiling. As she watched, a gleam of bright light broke through the cloud. It split apart and the sun shone brightly once again.

A Lucy Stone Thanksgiving

Lucy Stone has cooked the same Thanksgiving dinner for years. In fact, it's the same dinner she remembers her mother and grandmother cooking when she was a little girl. Lucy has inherited her mother's china, and her grandmother's crystal and linen, and uses them to set the table. She takes great pleasure in taking them out for the holidays—she even enjoys ironing the linen tablecloth and napkins!

The menu is simple: New England home cooking based on recipes from *The Fannie Farmer Cookbook*. Lucy has the eleventh edition, which was published in 1965, and doesn't think much of the newer versions.

For a centerpiece, Lucy arranges colorful fall leaves on her best white damask tablecloth and piles fresh fruit and vegetables on top. The arrangement varies from year to year, depending upon what's available, but she likes to use apples, pears, and Concord or Fox grapes, punctuated with tiny pumpkins and squash. She doesn't use tropical fruits such as oranges and bananas, believing that only native-grown New England produce is appropriate for Thanksgiving. A scattering of mixed nuts in their shells completes the arrangement, which the family nibbles on after the meal. When the children were younger, Bill used to make little boats out of the walnut shells, continuing a tradition from his own childhood.

Five kernels of dried corn are placed at each place setting. That was the daily ration allowed to each of the Pilgrims during their first difficult winter in Plymouth Colony, and it is a reminder of the hardship they endured so they could enjoy the freedom we take for granted today.

Appetizer

Lucy tends to agree with her mother, who always maintained appetizers were too much trouble and only spoiled people's appetites, anyway. Sometimes, though, she does serve shrimp or oysters before dinner.

Shrimp are served chilled, on ice, with cocktail sauce and lemon slices.

Oysters are served raw, on the half shell, also with cocktail sauce.

Soup

What? And make more dishes to wash?

Main Course

Roast turkey with bread stuffing (Sensitive about her weight, Lucy now mixes chicken broth, instead of water and butter, with either Pepperidge Farm or Arnold stuffing.)

Giblet gravy

Mashed potatoes

Sweet potatoes or yams (the canned kind, heated in the oven while she makes the gravy)

Creamed onions (white onions from a jar in white sauce)

Petite peas (frozen, not canned)

Condiments (These are served in crystal dishes Lucy inherited from her grandmother.)

Cranberry sauce (whole berry)

Celery with pimento-stuffed olives

Sweet pickle mix (the kind with cauliflower and tiny onions)

Dessert

Mince pie (Lucy always uses a jar of Grandmother's brand mincemeat.)

Apple pie (Macintosh or Cortland apples)

Pumpkin pie (A good way to use up pumpkins left over from Halloween)

Coffee, fruit, and nuts

TURKEY TROT MURDER

For all the Turkey Trotters,
Especially
Greg, Ben and Abby, Matt and Sam,
Andy and Mandy,
Em and Ari, Leon and Debi

PROLOGUE

It was all over the morning TV news—the season's first killing frost. It came later than usual, probably due to global warming. That was the theory, anyway. But come it did, finally, coating each blade of grass with sparkly white rime, sealing automobile windows with a thick layer of frost, reducing late green tomatoes to black mush, and changing chrysanthemum plants, whose color had faded weeks before, into shriveled black stumps.

Alison Franklin didn't notice these changes, but she did sense the sharp nip in the air as she stepped out onto the flagstone patio of her father's house in Maine. She zipped up her fleece jacket and jogged down the long drive to begin her morning run. She usually went one of two ways. One route took her along scenic Shore Road with its ocean views and the other wound through the woods on old logging roads and circled around Blueberry Pond. A cold northeast breeze was blowing off the water so Alison chose the more sheltered woodland path.

She was rounding the loop that led to Blueberry Pond when she heard the cries. It was nothing more than a yelp at first, a cry that could be the call of a crow or perhaps the yip of a fox. The calls came louder and grew clearer as she drew nearer to the pond.

Realizing someone was calling for help she quickened her pace and soon spotted a familiar figure standing on the shore of the frozen pond. She'd been spotted so it was too late to turn around. Nothing for it except to make the best of the situation.

"Alison! Thank God you're here!"

"What's the matter?" she asked somewhat reluctantly.

"It's Scruffy! He ran out onto the pond and I think he's fallen through."

Alison studied the pond, which had a coat of new ice. "Are you sure? There are no tracks in the ice and I don't hear him crying."

"Of course I'm sure! Why would you doubt me? Listen, listen! Can't you hear him? Oh, the poor thing. He's growing weaker . . ."

Once again Alison turned to the pond, casting her eyes along the irregular shore which was littered with large boulders, glacial erratics, most now covered with a thin layer of soil that supported bushy balsam pines and gnarled blueberry bushes, all hanging on for dear life. This growth made it impossible for her to get a clear view of the entire shore or to see exactly where Scruffy had gone through. She concentrated on listening for the poodle, hoping his cries might direct her, but all she heard was the sighing of the wind in the trees and the groaning protest of bare branches thrown against each other.

"Stop dithering! Poor Scruffy. He can't hang on much longer!"

There was no way out, decided Alison with a sigh of resignation. The undergrowth along the shore was too dense for her to make her way around the pond without a machete, which she didn't happen to bring along on her morning run. The only way she could find Scruffy was by going out onto the freshly frozen surface of the pond.

The ice cracked ominously as she ventured forth, staying as close to the shore as possible, but it held and she gained confidence as she proceeded. A small spit of land covered with brushy growth extended into the pond and she made her way along it, grabbing onto overhanging branches for safety. Once she got to the end of the spit she figured she would have a better vantage point from which to spot Scruffy.

She was almost there when a patch of reeds forced her farther from the shoreline. There was a sudden loud crack and the ice beneath her gave way, plunging her into the frigid black water. Her cries for help were loud and strong, shattering the early morning calm, but no one answered.

CHAPTER 1

So the deep frost had finally come, thought Lucy Stone, stepping onto the back porch of her antique farm house on Red Top Road and surveying the withered mums that had been so bright and colorful only a few days ago. This recent long, extended spell of warm weather had been strange, even unsettling, she thought as she stretched her hamstrings. But today was more like it, she decided, grasping one ankle and pulling her foot to her bottom. This crisp weather was great for a run, a sentiment also shared by Libby, the family Lab. Libby was ready to go, and even though her black muzzle was now fading to white, she didn't need any warm-up exercises. She was circling eagerly, throwing expectant glances to Lucy as if to say "Enough of this nonsense. Let's go!"

"Okay," agreed Lucy, skipping down the porch steps and crossing the frosty lawn in an easy jog. She picked up speed once she reached the old logging road that wound through the woods behind the house, pushing herself to improve her speed. This year she was training for the Tinker's Cove annual Turkey Trot 5K race, and she thought she might actually have a chance of winning in her age division.

There were not many runners signed up in the women over-forty category, and those who were running were mostly casual runners interested in burning calories before they sat down to a big Thanksgiving dinner. That had been Lucy's attitude in the past, but this year was different. This year she wasn't going to be cooking a big turkey dinner for the whole family. This year, well, to be honest, she wasn't sure what she and Bill were going to do. Since it would be just the two of them perhaps they'd eat out in a restaurant, or maybe one of their friends would include them in their celebration.

Her feet pounded along the pine needle strewn path in a regular rhythm as she reviewed the various plans her children had made without consulting her. Of course, she hadn't expected Elizabeth to come home for Thanksgiving; her eldest daughter was busy with her job as an assistant concierge at the upscale Cavendish Hotel in Paris. It also wasn't practical for her only son, Toby, to sit down at the usual groaning board. Toby, his wife, Molly, and son, Patrick, had returned to Alaska where Toby had a government job working to increase and improve salmon stocks. It had been wonderful having the young family living in the old homestead while he took graduate courses at nearby Winchester College, and Lucy had really enjoyed spending time with her grandson, but that was a temporary arrangement. Now she stayed in touch with Patrick via Skype, setting aside a half-hour every Sunday afternoon.

But, she thought as she allowed a certain sense of resentment to carry her over a rather steep patch of trail, it had been rather inconsiderate of the two daughters who remained home to make separate plans for the holiday. Sara, who was studying earth science at Winchester College, had signed up for a field trip in Greenland led by one of her professors, arguing it was a once-in-a-lifetime opportunity and would strengthen her graduate school applications. Okay, muttered Lucy, huffing a bit from exertion, she understood. It wasn't her preference, but she could live with it. No, it was Zoe, her youngest, who had really driven in the knife with a nasty twist. Zoe had announced only days before that her friend and neighbor Renée La Chance had invited her to spend the Thanksgiving break with her at Concordia University in Montreal. Montreal, in Canada, where Renée was a freshman.

"Oh, well," said Lucy, speaking to the dog running beside her with her tongue hanging out of her mouth. "We can't always get what we want, can we?"

Libby didn't answer, but she was clearly enjoying herself, letting her drooping, silky ears flap behind and holding her tail aloft in an exclamation of doggy joy.

Realizing they were drawing close to Blueberry Pond where Libby might expect a drink of water but would find ice instead, Lucy decided to use the leash she had wrapped around her waist. She'd heard of too many dogs that had gone out on thin ice and fallen through. It was a story replayed every year when lakes and ponds began to freeze. Sometimes the owners were able to call for help from the fire department. Sometimes they were foolish enough to venture out on the ice themselves, which was usually a tragic mistake.

"C'mere, girl," she said, and Libby obediently approached, allowing her to snap the leash onto her red leather collar. Then they were off again, running side by side at a rather more sedate pace. The newly frozen pond would be pretty in the morning light and Lucy wanted to take time to appreciate it. This was something new, suggested by her friend Pam, who was a yoga instructor.

"Live mindfully," Pam had advised. "Be in the moment."

This was the perfect opportunity, thought Lucy as the pond came into view. It had frozen overnight, and the ice was smooth and glistening. The pointed firs on the opposite shore were a dark green, piercing a clear blue sky. She paused on the shore, holding Libby firmly by the leash, and took in the scene. *This could be on a calendar,* she thought. *Maine in late fall, preparing for winter.* Soon the pond would be covered with snow, the familiar woods would be transformed into a dreamlike fairyland, the little waterfall at the pond's outlet would become still, frozen into a freeform sculpture.

Lucy took a few deep breaths and banished all negative thoughts from her mind. There was nothing but her breath, the pond, and the panting dog leaning against her leg. She felt the warmth of the dog's shoulder against her thigh, and savored it. She closed her eyes, just for a moment, feeling the delicious heat. Then she opened them and saw something in the patch of reeds that shouldn't be there. Something pink.

Maybe it was just a bit of clothing, something that had gotten caught in the reeds. She studied the ice, which looked thick enough to support a single person, but she knew these early freezes could be deceptive and she didn't dare trust it. She needed to get closer to investigate that blob of bright pink, and she knew there was a narrow, hidden path occasionally used by trout fishermen in the spring. Now, however, after a summer's worth of growth it was going to be tough going and she didn't want to struggle with the dog as she battled her way through the thick underbrush, so she tied Libby to a tree. "Stay!" she added for good measure, then began making her way along the peninsula, pushing branches out of her way and scrambling over rocks until she was blocked by a thick curtain of leafless hanging vines that she suspected was poison ivy. She couldn't go any farther but was close enough to get a good look.

A bit of hot pink fleece, she realized, and more. Pink fleece and long blond hair. She gasped, her hand flew to her mouth. *Oh, no.* She reached for her cell phone, fumbling with the zipper on the pocket, and dialed 9-1-1.

As soon as the dispatcher assured her that help was on the way, Lucy made a second call, to her boss at the *Pennysaver*, Ted Stillings. She was a part-time reporter, feature writer, and copy editor at the weekly paper, and knew she'd stumbled onto a big story. And it was deadline day, too, which made it breaking news.

"A woman in the pond?" asked Ted. "Who is she?"

"I don't know," replied Lucy.

"And you're sure she's dead?"

"Not sure, but I think it's pretty likely," said Lucy, her voice tight with dread. "I couldn't get close enough for a good look. She's too far out from the shore and I sure wasn't going out there. The ice is too thin and the same thing would happen to me—I'd fall right through. I can't imagine why anyone would do such a risky thing."

"Well, stick with it, Lucy. Deadline's not until noon and I may

be able to get more time from the printer. I'll get right on that."
He paused, then added, "Get as many pictures as you can, okay?"

"Okay," promised Lucy, ending the call and making her way
back through the brush to the logging road.

She'd no sooner got there when Libby announced the arrival of
the first responders. Her loud yips and enthusiastic jumps threatened to snap the leash that kept her fastened to the tree. Lucy un-
tied her but held tight to the leash, watching as the town's special
brush-breaking truck lumbered into view. The regular fire trucks
were much too big to negotiate the old, uneven dirt logging road
so the rescuers had taken the smaller truck that was equipped to
fight forest fires. The truck was towing a trailer carrying an inflatable boat used for water and ice rescues, and an ambulance followed close behind, lurching from side to side as the driver
attempted to avoid boulders and potholes.

"Where's the victim?" asked Jim Carstairs as he leaped out of
the truck.

"Out there," said Lucy, pointing to the reedy patch.

"We'll need to use the inflatable," he said, spotting the bit of
hot pink fleece in the distance.

Lucy watched as two firefighters, apparently the youngest and
fittest members of the crew, suited up in bright orange protective
suits while the others unloaded the inflatable from the trailer and
carried it to the shore. The guys in the orange suits fastened toggle
straps that connected their suits to the inflatable, then began
pushing the inflatable out onto the ice. They didn't get too far before the ice gave way and one man plunged into waist deep water.
Then they both got into the inflatable and began using oars to
propel the craft through the mix of ice and water.

"I've never seen one of these ice rescues," said Lucy, speaking
to Jim, who as captain was supervising the operation. "It looks
really difficult . . . and risky, too."

"We train for them every year," he replied. "The guys know
what they're doing."

"Any chance that the victim is alive?" she asked, watching as
the two firemen struggled to lift the woman's body into the inflatable.

"Doubtful," said Carstairs, striding toward the crew members who had remained on the shore and blowing a whistle—the signal for them to begin pulling on the rope connected to the inflatable, bringing the victim and crew safely to shore.

Lucy snapped photos of the operation with her smartphone, noting that the victim remained motionless, showing no signs of life, and the crew members were subdued. The rescue operation had become a recovery.

When the inflatable reached the shore, an EMT examined the victim, then stepped away, shaking her head. Lucy found herself drawing closer for a better look and was shocked to see the victim was a beautiful young woman, dressed for a run in a pink fleece and black tights. Her long blond hair, which blew gently in the breeze, was held by a jaunty pink knitted headband and an earbud dangled from its thin white wire. Her running shoes were top of the line, her sodden gray gloves were cashmere.

"Any idea who she is?" asked Lucy.

"It's Alison, Alison Franklin," said one of the crew members, a young guy with longish hair. "I've seen her around."

"Is she related to Ed Franklin?" asked Carstairs.

Lucy knew Ed Franklin was an extremely wealthy new arrival in town, a retired CEO who had quickly become a force to be reckoned with. She'd covered numerous meetings and hearings where he'd tussled with local officials to gain approval for the oversized mansion he built on Shore Road. Once settled into the mansion, he quickly offered himself as a candidate for the board of health, promising to cut red tape and bureaucratic obstruction. Much to the surprise of the entrenched office holders, who took his candidacy to be a joke, he won by a landslide.

"Yeah," said the long-haired guy. "She's his daughter."

Somehow the realization that this young woman was not only beautiful but also a child of privilege made her death seem even worse.

"Wow," said Carstairs with a big sigh. "What a shame."

"Senseless," said another. "So much to live for."

"I see it all the time," said the EMT, shaking her head. "I'll bet she was high as a kite on heroin or oxy."

"It looks to me like she was out for a run," said Lucy.

"That's probably what her folks thought, too. But there's a shack not far from here that's a popular spot for drug users." The EMT gave a wry smile. "I'd be willing to bet on it. This girl was using. Why else would she go out on thin ice? Nobody in their right mind would do such a stupid thing."

A tug on the leash from Libby reminded Lucy that she had other responsibilities and it was time to be on her way. Ted was waiting for her story, but that wasn't her first priority, not according to Libby. Libby wanted her breakfast.

CHAPTER 2

"A monstrosity."
"Absolutely appalling lack of taste."
"Ridiculously ostentatious."

As a freshly showered and dressed Lucy drove along Shore Road, passing the Franklin house on her way to work, she recalled the reactions of some planning board members when they were presented with the plans. Ed Franklin hadn't gone before the board himself. He'd sent his architect and lawyer to seek the necessary approvals. And they'd succeeded because the plans had been cleverly designed to take maximum advantage of the town's zoning laws.

The structure was enormous, much larger than the other mansions on Shore Road, but at 14,999 square feet, it was actually one square foot less than the town's maximum of 15,000 square feet. It's true that the roof was topped with an inordinately large widow's walk, but those were allowed, and the house itself was only three stories high and just shy (by an inch) of the maximum height restriction. And while the roomy flagstone terrace seemed to extend forever, it actually stopped ten feet and one inch from the property line, more than meeting the required ten-foot setback.

Lucy had covered the meeting and had quoted the architect,

who had announced in a rather challenging tone, "We have not exceeded any of the local restrictions and have been mindful of traditional New England architecture."

She also remembered quite well the various reactions of the board members, who had no choice but to grant approval to the plans. Maisie Wilkinson had looked as if she had bitten into a lemon when she cast her vote, Horace Atkins had huffed and puffed for all the world like an outraged walrus, and Linc Curtis had glared at the applicants as if he could make them disappear by staring angrily at them. Committee chairman Susan Brooks had abstained, claiming a conflict of interest that Lucy suspected was little more than an excuse to avoid going on record as supporting the project. Only realtor Wilt Chambers had spoken in favor of the plan, saying it would increase the tax base and raise property values.

As she drove by the house, Lucy thought it could have been worse. It could have been a modernistic glass box, for instance, or a faux Tuscan villa with a red tile roof, rather than the overblown Federalist-style mansion that now dominated the neighborhood. And even though it was huge, everything was in proportion, with oversized windows and chimneys, and a dramatic carved pediment calling attention to the massive front door which was made from some rare Brazilian hardwood. Lucy had heard that when seen from a distance—it could quite easily be observed from a boat bobbing on the sea it overlooked—the house seemed quite in scale with its surroundings.

But no house, no matter how grand, could protect its inhabitants from the vagaries of fortune or shelter them from tragedy and grief. In fact, it seemed to her that wealth and success could almost tempt fate. She thought of John Kennedy, Jr., becoming disoriented and crashing his plane into the Atlantic, and Gloria Vanderbilt, who saw her son hurl himself from a fourteenth floor terrace, and now Ed Franklin, who had certainly not awakened this morning expecting to learn that he'd lost his beautiful daughter forever.

Lucy was uncharacteristically somber when she got to the office, prompting Ted to comment on her glum expression.

"Pretty rough morning?" he asked in a sympathetic tone. Ted

was the owner, publisher, editor, and chief reporter for the weekly paper.

"Who was it?" asked Phyllis, chewing on the earpiece of the jazzy reading glasses that either hung from a chain to rest on her ample bosom or perched on her nose. Phyllis's official title was receptionist, but she also handled ads, classifieds, and event listings.

"Alison Franklin," said Lucy, hanging up her barn coat on the coat rack.

"Ed Franklin's daughter?" asked Ted.

"That's what they say. I don't know much about Ed Franklin apart from the permitting process for his big house."

"That was quite a show, wasn't it?" said Ted, who had relished the controversy that prompted so many heated letters to the editor.

"She hasn't been officially identified," said Lucy, "but one of the EMTs recognized her."

"Well, write up what you've got," ordered Ted. "We'll say 'tentatively identified as'."

"Okay," said Lucy with a sigh, sitting down at her desk and booting up her PC.

It was an old machine and slow to wake up in the morning, so while she waited she mulled over possible leads for the story. Her eyes roamed around the familiar office, where an old Regulator clock hung on the wall above Ted's rolltop desk, which he'd inherited from his grandfather, a legendary small-town journalist. Wooden blinds rattled at the window and a little bell on the door jingled whenever anyone came in. Entering the office was like taking a step back in time, she thought, wishing for a moment that such a thing was really possible. If only the clocks and calendars could roll backwards to yesterday, then Alison would still be alive.

Lucy's computer announced with a whirr that it was up and running and she got to work.

When the paper came out on Thursday the story was front page news, but of course everyone in Tinker's Cove had already heard about Alison Franklin's fatal mishap. News, especially bad news, traveled fast in town, and the tragedy was the main topic of conversation in Jake's Donut Shack when Lucy arrived for her weekly breakfast date with her friends.

"Such a shame, a young girl like that with her whole life before her," declared Norine, the waitress, greeting Lucy when she entered the busy little café. "Your friends are already here," she added with a nod toward the table in the back where the group regularly gathered.

The four women had begun the weekly breakfast meetings as a way of keeping in touch when their children had grown and they no longer ran into each other at Little League games, bake sales, and PTA meetings.

"So young and so very rich, too," offered Sue Finch. With a perfectly manicured hand, she tucked a glossy lock of hair behind one ear. "Her father is enormously wealthy. Fortune Five Hundred wealthy."

"Money doesn't guarantee happiness," said Lucy, slipping into the vacant seat and greeting her friends with a smile.

"That's so true," said Pam Stillings, speaking from experience. She was married to Lucy's boss, Ted, and had wholeheartedly supported her husband's struggle to continue publishing the *Pennysaver* despite competition from the Internet, dwindling advertising revenues, and ever-increasing production costs. "Good health, family, friends—those are the things that really matter."

"Pam's right," said Rachel Goodman, who was married to Bob Goodman, a lawyer with a busy practice in town. "Simply possessing money doesn't guarantee happiness. In fact, it can cause lots of problems—guilt, lack of responsibility, family disruption." She had majored in psychology and had never gotten over it.

"I certainly wouldn't want to swap places with Alison's parents, not even if they had all the money in the world," said Lucy, glancing up as Norine approached with her order pad in hand. "But there's a big difference between having enough money and not having it." Her tongue went to the new crown she'd recently had to get when a tooth broke, spending the money she'd been saving to buy a new family room sofa.

"Okay, ladies. The usual for everyone?" asked Norine with a raised eyebrow. "Sunshine muffin for Rachel, granola yogurt for Pam, hash and eggs for Lucy, and"—she paused for a disapproving little snort—"black coffee for Sue."

Receiving nods all round, she retreated to place the order and returned moments later with a fresh pot of coffee. "You know," she said, filling Lucy's mug, "I've heard people saying that girl committed suicide. She must've wanted to die to go out on that thin ice."

Lucy shook her head, unwilling to entertain such an idea. "I don't think so. I hope not," she said, wrapping her hands around the warm mug. "That would be too sad."

"Depression is an insidious disease," said Rachel, adding a dab of cream to her freshly filled mug. "And so often it goes unrecognized and untreated."

"It was most likely an accident," said Pam, stirring some sugar into her coffee. "The ice might've looked much stronger than it actually was. People get fooled. We have an accident like this every winter. Remember last year, when Lydia Volpe had a close call? Her dog fell through and she tried to save the beast. Luckily for her, Eddie Culpepper saw them struggling and managed to get them out."

"That was the first thing I thought of, but there was no sign of a dog or anything like that," said Lucy as Norine arrived again and began distributing their orders.

"That's why folks are saying it must've been suicide," insisted Norine, putting down Lucy's plate with a thump that made the toast jump. "Or maybe she was high on something and thought she could walk on water."

"It looked to me like she was out for a run. She was dressed for a run," said Lucy, who was staring at the pair of sunny-side-up eggs sitting on top of a mound of hash and thinking she really didn't want eggs this morning. Truth was, she hadn't really had much appetite at all since she'd discovered Alison's body.

"I guess we'll never know," said Norine, tenting the little bill and setting it on the table.

"It comes at a bad time for Ed Franklin," said Sue. "His new wife is expecting a baby. Due any day from the looks of her."

"His wife's pregnant?" asked Lucy, doing some quick math. "If Alison was twenty, isn't it rather late to be adding to the family?"

"How old is this latest wife?" asked Pam.

"About Alison's age, I'd say," said Sue. "I saw her at the salon when I was getting these highlights." She tossed her head. "Expensive highlights, I might add, not that any of you have noticed."

"I noticed," said Pam, dipping her spoon into her yogurt. "I thought your stylist missed a few bits."

"Monsieur Paul does not miss any bits," said Sue, not the least bit amused. "And he was making an enormous fuss over the newest Mrs. Franklin. Mireille's her name. She's very young, very beautiful, and very pregnant."

"Exactly how many Mrs. Franklins are there?" asked Lucy.

"At least two, according to Monsieur Paul. There's Alison's mother, who must be at least fifty or so, and Mireille, who I doubt is old enough to buy a bottle of wine. Not that she would have any business buying wine, not in her condition."

"That does muddy the waters, doesn't it?" mused Rachel. "Imagine what it would have been like for Alison to have a stepmother who is her own age."

"And pregnant," said Pam.

"A constant reminder of this young stepmother's allure," said Rachel. "Not to mention her father's sexual potency."

"Yuck," said Pam.

Yuck indeed, thought Lucy, pushing her plate away. She thought of the Franklin home, the mansion perched high above the roiling sea below, and wondered what emotions were in play behind those massive walls, and if some primal forces drove Alison to her watery grave.

When Lucy got to work later that morning she discovered Ted had a completely different take on Alison Franklin's death.

"You know, Lucy," he said as she shrugged out of her jacket and hung it on the coat rack, "I've been getting a lot of calls about this Alison. People are upset and most of them blame drugs. That's what they're saying—that we have to stop this heroin epidemic that's claiming our young people."

"It's true," said Phyllis. "We've had at least three calls this morning."

"I've had some e-mails, too," said Ted.

"I've heard that theory, too, but I don't think it was drugs,

Ted," said Lucy, remembering the hot pink fleece jacket and the running shoes. "I think she was out for a run."

"Lucy, people don't run on thin ice."

"Maybe she didn't know about the way ponds freeze. Not everybody grows up knowing these things. Maybe she's a city kid. Maybe she made a very bad mistake. It happens—like when that trucker tried to take his semi under the old railroad overpass last month and got stuck."

"That was quite a hoot," said Phyllis. " 'Course, nobody dies of embarrassment."

"Well, all I know is that a lot of people are blaming this opioid epidemic and want some answers. It's about time we put Jim Kirwan on the spot and ask what he's doing to stop these senseless deaths."

"You want me to call the police chief?" asked Lucy, sitting down at her desk.

"Good idea, Lucy," said Ted as if it hadn't been his idea all along.

"Okay," said Lucy, anticipating the chief's reaction, "but he's not going to be happy."

As she expected, Chief Kirwan was immediately defensive when she asked what his department was doing to combat the opioid epidemic. "As you well know, Lucy, we are not the only town coping with this influx of drugs. Heck, it's a national problem. It's complex. There's high unemployment among youth, limited prospects for kids who don't go to college, folks can't get ahead, and heroin is cheap and plentiful. Truth is, it's easier for kids to get illegal drugs than to buy a six-pack. It's not like we're ignoring the problem. We've got a new program with the courts—we don't prosecute if the addicts agree to go to rehab . . . but oftentimes there's no rehab places available." He sighed. "Facts are facts. We're a small department with very limited resources and we're doing all we can."

"I know," said Lucy in a sympathetic tone. "People are upset over this latest thing. You know . . . Alison Franklin's death."

"Well, people shouldn't jump to conclusions," he said in a sharp tone. "The investigation is still ongoing and the cause of death has not been determined. We don't know if drugs were involved and we won't know until the toxicology results come in from the ME's office."

"When will that be?" asked Lucy.

He snorted. "I wish I knew. The state lab is underbudgeted and understaffed."

"I won't hold my breath then. Thanks," said Lucy, ending the call.

"Just as I expected," said Ted, who had been listening to Lucy's end of the call. "The same old, same old." He paused. "Well, we're not going to settle for lame excuses. I want to know what Alison's family has to say. I bet Ed Franklin wants some answers and he's the kind of guy who gets 'em."

"Ted, you're not going to make me call him, are you? The man just lost his daughter. . . ."

"And I bet he wants people to know what a wonderful girl she was, and how much he loved her," said Ted.

"The poor man must be beside himself with grief," protested Lucy.

"That's funny," observed Phyllis. "You called him poor, but he's not poor. He's probably the richest man in the state."

"You know what I mean," said Lucy, glaring at Phyllis.

"There's no rush," said Ted. "You've got till next Wednesday. Give him a call next week . . . when he's had some time to get over it."

People don't get over an unexpected, violent, tragic death of a loved one in a few days, thought Lucy, biting her tongue. Sometimes Ted got so involved in a story that he lost all sense of perspective or even decency. But noticing how he was hunched over his computer keyboard pursuing truth and combating evil one keystroke at a time, she admitted it was that determination that kept him going.

"Okay, I'll do it Monday," she said, booting up her computer to check her e-mails.

As it happened, she didn't have to wait until Monday to call Ed Franklin. She was just about to leave the office later that afternoon when the door flew open, setting the little bell to jangling, and the man himself walked in.

Lucy had never seen him in the flesh, but everybody had seen photos of the billionaire who was frequently in the news. He was most often featured in the business pages, announcing the construction of a new condo tower, golf course, or gambling casino. These projects were always described as fabulous, luxurious, or magnificent. Ed Franklin was a man who went in for superlatives and did everything in a big way.

The man himself, however, was shorter than she expected, although that mane of silver hair and the ruddy complexion were unmistakable. So was the expensively tailored suit that couldn't quite conceal his paunch. "Who's in charge here?" he demanded in the raspy voice she'd heard on TV.

"That would be me," said Ted, jumping to his feet. "I'm Ted Stillings. How can I help you, Mr. Franklin?"

"Look here," said Franklin, plunging right in. "I've had it with all this political correctness, this so-called tolerance. It's time we put a stop to these Mexican drug traffickers bringing heroin and marijuana here and poisoning our kids. Where is the outrage? There's supposed to be a war on drugs, but if this is how we fight a war . . . well, it's no surprise we're not winning. I'm going to get straight to the point. This is what I want you to do—I want you to run an exposé of this filthy business. Let people know where these drugs are coming from and how we can stop it. I speak from personal experience here. I just lost my daughter. A beautiful girl. Gorgeous, and smart, too. I know what I'm talking about. It's these filthy Mexicans and we've got to get them out of the country."

"I'm very sorry for your loss," said Ted, stunned by Franklin's outburst. "We all are," he added with a wave in Lucy and Phyllis's direction.

"You have our sympathy," said Lucy.

"You're in our thoughts and prayers," added Phyllis.

"That's neither here nor there," said Franklin in a gruff tone, brushing aside their condolences. "The question is, what are you going to do about it?"

"It's not clear that your daughter died because of drugs," said Lucy. "The toxicology tests haven't been completed."

"Well, what else could it be?" demanded Franklin. "She had everything to live for. And I mean everything. Looks. Money. Connections. Everything."

"As it happens, we did call Chief Kirwan today, asking tough questions about the current opioid epidemic," said Ted.

"That's a start," said Franklin, "but you've got to take it further. We have to get to the source and cut off this vicious trade. It's these Mexicans. They're like a plague, swarming across the border, bringing death to our kids and destroying our American values. Our American way of life." He paused and looked around the office, taking in the worn and shabby atmosphere. "Look, see here. I'm a businessman and I know these are bad times for newspapers. I'm always looking for good investments and I see a lot of potential here. What you need is capital so you can expand. Maybe start a magazine, an online edition of the paper. Hell, the sky's the limit if you've got vision and the cash to make it a reality."

"We're doing just fine the way we are," said Ted, his dander rising. "Thanks for stopping by."

"Ted . . . you don't mind if I call you Ted, do you?" Franklin asked, continuing without pause. "You know, I've seen a lot of guys like you. Frankly, I think you're one of those guys who'll go down with the ship, blaming the tides and currents. But you could be the captain of your destiny, if you'd take my advice. This is an issue that could make a dinky small town paper like yours into a national player." He shrugged. "But have it your way. There's nothing wrong with being a big frog in a small pond, if that's all you want to be." With that parting shot, Ed Franklin pushed the door open, making the little bell jangle, and let it slam behind him, causing the wooden blinds on the plate glass window to slap against the glass.

"Wow, he's a noisy guy," said Phyllis, smoothing her angora sweater over her chest.

"I'm pretty sure we haven't heard the last of him," said Lucy.

"Did he actually call me a big frog?" asked Ted, looking puzzled.

CHAPTER 3

Several days later, Lucy found herself in the basement meeting room at the town hall, covering the weekly meeting of the board of selectmen. The town meeting voters were a thrifty lot and didn't go in for frills so the room where the town's business was conducted was a very plain affair. The concrete block walls had been painted yellow a long time ago, perhaps in a misguided effort to lighten the gloom, but instead made everyone look slightly jaundiced. Fluorescent lights, rows of beige metal chairs, and gray industrial-strength floor tile certainly didn't help.

The detail that always amused Lucy, however, was the little raised platform where the five selectmen sat behind a long table. The platform was a mere six inches high, allowing the citizens in attendance to get a clear view of these elected officials while ensuring that they didn't get above themselves. Behind the table an American flag stood in one corner and the Maine state flag in the other. There were nameplates on the table for each selectman, as well as a microphones, now that the meetings were televised on local cable TV.

Attendance at the meetings had fallen off since people could watch the antics of the board members from the comfort of their homes, but a few stalwarts still showed up each week. Town curmudgeon Stan Wysocki was in his usual seat and local fussbudget

Verity Hawthorne had brought her knitting. When things got slow at the meetings, Lucy sometimes entertained herself by wondering exactly what the shapeless mass of moss green that grew larger every week was meant to be. A sweater for a yeti? An afghan for a cow? A cozy for Verity's aged Dodge?

"Hi, Lucy," said Corney Clark, slipping into the seat beside her. "I'm glad you're covering this meeting."

"I cover them all," said Lucy, stifling a yawn.

"Well, tonight's going to be worth your while," said Corney, making her eyes quite large and giving a little nod that caused her expertly cut blond hair to rise slightly and then fall back exactly into place. "Big doings, that's all I'm going to say."

"Give me a hint," prompted Lucy, who knew Corney had a tendency to overstate. She was the executive director of the town's chamber of commerce and worked tirelessly to promote area businesses.

"Nope, you'll just have to wait," she said, turning to give an encouraging wave to a very tall, very thin, very distinguished looking man who had just entered the room.

"Who's that?" asked Lucy, who knew everyone in town and couldn't place him, even though he looked familiar.

"Rey Rodriguez," said Corney.

"Not the TV chef?" inquired Lucy, who had seen his show.

"The very same," said Corney with a smug smile.

Perhaps this meeting would provide some surprises, thought Lucy, watching the board members file in.

They were led by the chairman, Roger Wilcox, who was a retired army man and maintained his military bearing despite being well over seventy. Next in line was Joe Marzetti, another longtime member who owned the town's IGA supermarket, followed by bearded and plump retiree Sam Bellamy and Winchester College professor Fred Rumford. The newest member of the board, Franny Small, brought up the rear.

Poor Franny's bottom had barely met her chair when Roger called the meeting to order, opening with the usual period for public comment. The public, being largely absent, had nothing to say, although there was a bit of a stir as some latecomers arrived. These were Police Chief Jim Kirwan, Fire Chief Buzz Bresnahan, both in uniform, along with Audrey Sprinkle from the board of health. The three seated themselves together in the front row, causing Rey Rodriguez to cast a questioning look in Corney's direction. She responded with a smile and an encouraging thumbs up.

This was interesting, thought Lucy, aware that the two chiefs rarely made appearances at board meetings unless there was a compelling reason, usually something involving public safety. Glancing at the agenda, she saw only routine business, which the board dealt with promptly. They voted to allow the Boy Scouts to erect a bench on the town green, approved the repair of a DPW truck, and authorized overtime for a police officer to provide traffic control at the upcoming Turkey Trot race.

When Roger moved on to new business, Corney stood up. "I'm here tonight to introduce Mr. Rey Rodriguez, who I'm sure you all know from his TV show, *Let's Go Global*, on the Food Channel. Rey is also the author of many best-selling cookbooks and is the culinary genius behind two highly regarded and successful restaurants in California, El Conquistador and Mission."

Corney paused and Rey Rodriguez rose, giving the board a polite little bow. "I am very happy to be here in Tinker's Cove," he said. "I have recently purchased a property, the Olde Irish Pub, and am looking forward to an exciting new chapter in my life in this most charming and beautiful part of the country."

"Well, on behalf of the board, I welcome you," said Roger, looking a bit puzzled. "I assume you are planning to reopen the Olde Irish Pub? In that case, you will need to request a transfer of the current liquor license."

"Mr. Rodriguez is aware of the licensing requirements," said Corney. "I just wanted to get the ball rolling as he is hoping to be open for Thanksgiving."

"That will be tight, but I think it's doable," said Roger. "We'll need to consider the transfer at our next meeting. You should make sure to get it on the agenda so it can be posted. Mr. Rodriguez will have to supply some information, and we will need time to verify it, but if everything is in order I think we will be able to vote."

"That's great news," said Corney.

"I do have a question," said Franny. "Can you tell us what you have in mind for the pub?"

"Will it be a Mexican restaurant?" asked Joe Marzetti. "Tacos and enchiladas, that sort of thing?"

"And margaritas?" asked Sam Bellamy with a twinkle in his eye.

"Not classic Mexican," said Rey. "I am going to completely reimagine and renovate the present building, which will be known as Cali Kitchen. It will feature a sophisticated fusion menu using fresh, local ingredients cooked in imaginative ways while drawing on traditional cuisines including Asian, Southwestern, and even New England Yankee."

"That does sound impressive," said Joe.

"And delicious," said Sam.

"If I may," said Police Chief Kirwan, rising to his feet. "I'd like to say a few words in support of Mr. Rodriguez."

"Of course," said the chairman. "You have the floor."

"Well," began Jim Kirwan, "Mr. Rodriguez has had discussions with me. He's aware of the lack of employment opportunities for our young people and the fact that many turn to drugs and get themselves into trouble. He's interested in setting up a program in cooperation with the department to offer employment to at-risk kids, setting them on the path to gainful employment in the restaurant industry. I have to say that this is something my department would welcome, as so often we see these youngsters getting themselves in deeper and deeper until they end up in the county jail."

Buzz Bresnahan was nodding along. He was a big, thoughtful man who never rushed into anything, but he offered his measured approval to the plan.

"It's not a secret that we have a big problem with opiate abuse here in town," he said, rising slowly to his feet. "Every week my EMTs are called out to deal with overdoses, and sad to say, they're not always successful in saving the victims. I'm in favor of absolutely anything that will help our youngsters."

"I don't want to rain on this parade," said Audrey Sprinkle. She was an attractive woman in her forties who was most often seen around town chauffeuring her three daughters to after-school sports events. "But am I the only one who sees a problem here? Where do these opiates come from? Mexico, right? And here we've got a . . . well, pardon my bluntness, but we've just had a terrible tragedy involving Ed Franklin's daughter. Well, Ed, who's chairman of the board of heath, couldn't be here himself, obviously, but he asked me to come and express his concern about the influx of drugs from Mexico and here we have an applicant who is Mexican—"

"Actually, I'm American," interjected Rey with some amusement. "My ancestors have been here in the US since the fifteen hundreds. I am proud of my Hispanic heritage. I am actually descended from the Spanish explorer Juan Rodriguez de Castillo, but I am thoroughly American and proud of my service in the US Navy."

Audrey's face reddened, but she hadn't finished speaking. "I thank you for your service," she said, "but as a mother, and speaking for a father who is going through unimaginable grief, I urge the board to be cautious about putting our kids, especially at-risk kids, under the guidance of a—um—newcomer. We need to be very careful." She paused and turned to Rey. "This is nothing personal. It's not against you. I'm just for our kids," she added before sitting down.

"Well, thank you for that," said Roger. "As I said earlier, all liquor license applicants go through the same process and must provide proof of good character, financial information, and criminal records check. It's quite a thorough vetting, I can assure you."

"If I may," said Rey, "I'd like to reassure the board that I am a father and I share this lady's concern. As it happens, my two children will be working at the restaurant. My daughter, Luisa, handles the business end of things, and my son, Matt, will run the kitchen. I will be the executive chef, creating menus and developing recipes, which I envision as a part-time position. I'm not so young anymore and I'm ready to let the youngsters take over."

"Quite understandable," said Roger with an approving nod. "I do have one question, however. Why did you decide on Tinker's Cove?"

"Ah," said Rey. "I have been a Californian all my life, but now, alas, I have had several bouts with skin cancer and my doctors tell me I must avoid the sun. Maine, it happens, is very cloudy and the sun hardly ever shines."

"Lucy," hissed Corney, grabbing Lucy's pen and stopping her note-taking, "don't put that in your story!"

The old saw about the variable New England weather, that if you didn't like it you should wait a minute, didn't hold true on Saturday for Alison's memorial service. The usually fickle sun put in a rare appearance, shining brightly in a clear blue sky as mourners gathered beneath the tall, white steeple in the simple clapboard Community Church.

Zoe accompanied Lucy to the service. Although the two girls hadn't been close, they were in the same class at Winchester College, located on the outskirts of town. Winchester was a small, liberal arts college that prided itself on fostering close relationships between students and faculty, and Lucy knew that Alison's death would be deeply felt by the entire college community. Young people weren't supposed to die, and Alison's death had been completely unexpected, so grief was compacted by shock and disbelief.

"It doesn't seem real," whispered Zoe as they stepped inside the dimly lit church. "I saw her on Tuesday. We sat together in American Lit. She had me laughing at the professor, imitating the way he said Thoreau's name. 'Not Thaw-row', he said, 'but *thorough*, rhyming with *borough*.' The way she—" Zoe broke off with a sniff, and Lucy plucked a tissue from the little packet thoughtfully provided in the rack for hymnals and gave it to her. "It was just so funny," continued Zoe, after giving her nose a good blow and wiping her eyes. "She was like that, and she was really nice, too."

"Death's never easy," said Lucy, "but it's easier to accept if a person is very old and had a good life, or if they've been sick and suffering for a long time."

"It really makes you think," said Zoe, and Lucy realized that this was probably the first time Zoe had truly confronted her own mortality.

As Lucy expected, the church was crowded and they were lucky to squeeze into one of the rear pews. Unlike the usual Sunday crowd, who greeted each other and chatted until the choir appeared, singing the opening hymn, this congregation was quiet and somber. The organist, Ruth Lawson, was playing a variation on the old hymn, "Amazing Grace," and Lucy followed the tune, letting it fill her mind and soothe her jumbled emotions.

"For the Beauty of the Earth" was the opening hymn and Lucy had a tough time singing the familiar phrases, thinking of the intense emotion with which she'd greeted each of her children, and how bereft she'd feel if she lost any one of them. She hoped Alison had been loved like that, enfolded with love from her first breath.

Lucy found her eyes straying to the bereaved family in the front pews.

She recognized Ed Franklin, with that head of carefully styled white hair. His young wife, Mireille, was standing beside him, but Lucy could only catch a glimpse of her back. Her long blond hair was a dramatic contrast to her black coat.

The hymn ended, but before the congregation could sing the final amen, a primal cry of pain and anguish disturbed the usual pregnant pause. All eyes were drawn to a sobbing woman in the front pew opposite the one occupied by Ed Franklin and his wife. She was supported by two men, one young and one middle-aged, as she collapsed into her seat and the sobs gradually subsided.

"Her mother, Alison's mother . . ." was the whispered message that rippled through the rather staid gathering of reserved New Englanders.

Rev. Margery Harvey, the minister known to all as Rev. Marge, was quick to move things along, calling upon those present to join in prayer. When the Lord's Prayer was completed, she thanked everyone for coming and offering their support to Alison's family—her father, Ed Franklin, her mother, Eudora Clare, and her brother, Tag Franklin, as well as her stepmother, Mireille Franklin, and stepfather, Jon Clare.

After a responsive reading of Psalm 23 the minister called upon Tag Franklin to deliver the eulogy. Tag was the young man who had attended Alison's mother, and he bore little resemblance to his sister. He was taller, had a more muscular build, and the shock of hair that fell across his brow was light brown. With his wide-set eyes, a straight nose, and very white teeth he looked as if he could have come straight out of a Lands End catalog.

He began with the usual fond remembrances of a shared childhood, occasional pranks, and even a few funny stories that elicited amused chuckles. But then his tone grew sharper, even accusatory when he directed his gaze at his father and said, "I wish I could say that my sister's brief life was happy and untroubled, but instead of receiving the unconditional love and support she desperately needed she encountered only selfishness. When she needed a warm embrace she got a cold shoulder, when she needed encouragement she got criticism, and when she most needed fatherly approval to sustain her she discovered that attention had been withdrawn and directed to another. Her beauty, her shining spirit, her intelligence, all went unnoticed and unappreciated."

Shocked, Lucy glanced at her daughter and saw with some surprise that Zoe was nodding along in agreement, brushing away a tear.

Then they were on their feet, singing the final hymn, "We Will Gather at the River." Lucy finally got a clear view of Alison's mother, Eudora, who was a tiny, very thin woman. Due to a puffy bouffant hairstyle, her head seemed much too large for her emaciated body. She was leaning heavily on her son and the other man, presumably her husband, Jon Clare. Unlike the hale and hearty Tag, Jon Clare was a lanky, weedy sort, with a narrow head, thinning hair, and long arms and legs.

"Do you want to go to the reception?" Lucy asked her daughter, who was stuffing a wad of damp tissues into her purse. "We could skip it. With all these people I don't think we'll be missed."

"Oh, no. I want to tell her folks how kind she was to me. You know, when I had that flu last month and missed some classes she offered to go over her notes with me." Zoe sniffed. "She didn't have to do that, you know."

"Okay," said Lucy as the usher released them from their pew, allowing them to join the stream of mourners leaving the church. She had been relieved when the pastor announced the interment of the ashes would be private, unsure of how Zoe would react to the grim business of seeing an entire human being reduced to a mere pile of dust. But, like most everyone at the funeral, she was somewhat curious and eager to see the interior of the Franklin mansion.

Shore Road was already lined with parked cars when Lucy and Zoe arrived, but it was a mild day and it was pleasant walking along the rocky bluff overlooking the ocean. Far below, the surf crashed against the rocks, sending up sprays of sparkling water.

The family was not yet present, still occupied with the burial, which loosened the usual sense of restraint felt by the gathered friends and neighbors. People were greeting each other with warm hugs, chattering vivaciously and helping themselves to the generous catered buffet. Zoe went straight to the reception line, which was already forming, while Lucy accepted a small cocktail sherry from the tray offered by a waiter in a crisply starched white shirt. She was making her way through the throng to the corner where her friends Sue and Rachel were standing, when a hush fell on the crowd and Ed and Mireille Franklin entered.

Ed held up his hand in greeting and said, "Thank you all for coming. The support of so many friends and neighbors means the world to me and Mireille."

Mireille, who was standing by his side, was remarkably pretty, very young, and extremely pregnant. She didn't speak but bestowed a sad little smile on her assembled guests.

"There is something I feel I must say," continued Ed. "My son, Tag, is no doubt deeply grieving the loss of his sister and that is completely understandable. However, I want to make it clear that Alison was a much loved daughter and both Mireille and I are devastated by this tragic turn of events. It was just this time last year when Alison had her biking accident, and unfortunately became dependent upon prescription painkillers. Mireille was a rock in those dark days and got Alison into rehab, but as often happens, recovery wasn't a simple process and wasn't as successful or complete as we hoped and it seems that Alison began using illegal opioids. These drugs are insidious, terribly hard to beat, and the dealers are relentless." He paused and swallowed hard. "Sometimes all the love in the world just isn't enough. Thank you for your patience."

"Nice comeback," said Sue, who had appeared at Lucy's side, along with Rachel. They were both holding glasses of sherry.

"I can see why he felt he had to say something," said Lucy, noticing that Tag wasn't present, and neither was his mother or stepfather.

"Do you believe him—Ed?" asked Sue, sounding somewhat skeptical. "It doesn't sound realistic to me—the trophy wife doting on the stepdaughter."

"I guess we have to give him the benefit of the doubt," said Lucy.

"Family members often have very different memories of important family events," said Rachel. "A brother and a sister, for example, might have very different interpretations of a particular birthday party. The brother might remember eating cake while the sister was upset because there was no ice cream."

"Alison's brother wasn't talking about ice cream," said Sue. "He seemed really angry about the way his father treated Alison."

"Or maybe he's projecting his own feelings toward his father and the new, young wife who displaced his mother," said Rachel.

They watched as Mireille and Ed began greeting the people waiting in the reception line, and were about to get in line themselves when Mireille suddenly began to sway and was caught by her husband. He supported her as they left the crowded room, accompanied by a solicitous older woman who followed them.

"Mireille's mother?" asked Lucy.

"I'd bet on it," said Sue, snagging a second sherry from a passing waiter.

Lucy noticed with some relief that Zoe had joined a lively group of young people. Deciding it was time to leave and tackle her long list of weekend errands, she thought she'd see if Zoe also wanted to leave or whether she'd prefer to hang with her friends.

"I don't want to interrupt," she began, joining the group, "but I really have to be going."

"I'll see you later, then," said Zoe, who was sipping on a soft drink. "We're going to stop by the cemetery together and say good-bye to Alison."

"That's a nice idea," said Lucy, rather surprised.

"It's the right thing to do" said one, a serious looking fellow with thick, black-rimmed glasses and a head of curly red hair.

"Are you sure you'll be all right?" she asked Zoe.

"It's something I want to do, Mom."

"Alison's not the first, you know," said a chubby girl with long, black hair. "There's been two others already this year."

"Drownings?" asked Lucy, shocked.

"No. Overdoses," said Zoe.

"Two at the college?" asked Lucy.

"From our class," said the boy. "Alison's the third."

"And there's been lots of close calls," added Zoe.

"We see the town ambulance on campus almost every day," said the girl.

"I'm really shocked," said Lucy. "I guess I thought college kids would be too smart to be using."

"You'd think so," said the guy. "But if they use even once, thinking they'll try it, it's all they think about. It takes over their lives. Believe me, Alison's not the last. There'll be more."

CHAPTER 4

Ted didn't greet Lucy when she arrived for work on Monday morning. He didn't even look up from his computer. "Don't bother to take off your coat," he said. "I need you to go straight to District Court."

"Okay," said Lucy, casting a "what's up?" glance toward Phyllis and getting an eye roll and a shrug in reply. "Mind telling me what this is all about?"

"The Downeast Drug Task Force made a big arrest last night. Three dealers. The arraignment is today." He pulled a sheet of paper off the printer and handed it to her. "Here's the press release with the names. Try to get photos, okay?"

"Will do," said Lucy, scanning the brief announcement that Carlos Cabral, 19, Manuel Perez, 21, and Eufry Victorino, 22, all from Queens, had been arrested following a three-month investigation. The three were caught in a Route 1 motel room with 50 grams of heroin, 40 grams of powdered cocaine, $5,750 in cash and several firearms. The street value of the drugs was estimated to be $15,000.

"I'm going to follow up on the official side," said Ted. "I'm sure the DA will want to get some credit, as will the Task Force."

"I always wonder why these investigations take so long," said

Phyllis. "What were they doing for three months? It doesn't take the buyers three months to find a dealer, does it?"

"That's one of the questions I plan to ask Detective Lieutenant Cunningham, who heads the task force," said Ted. "Now, go, Lucy. You've got to get over to Gilead by nine. Time's a-wasting!"

"Trust me," said Lucy, looping her purse strap over her shoulder. "They never start on time."

Despite the fact that trials seemed quite dramatic when presented on the TV news, Lucy knew that was because they were skillfully highlighted and presented for maximum effect. In truth, trials were extremely tedious and took a very long time to establish the most basic facts. Even arraignments, which were brief, required reporters to sit through a long list of other more minor offenders. Nevertheless, she felt a certain sense of excitement as she followed the familiar route to Gilead, the county seat, to cover what was sure to be a big story.

As she expected, the parking lot in the courthouse complex was packed and there were several satellite trucks from various TV stations. The Boston stations were all there, as was the regional cable news. She had to park in an overflow lot, which meant a long hike back to the courthouse, and by the time she made her way through the metal detector and had her purse examined by a gloved officer she was running late. Court was already in session, all the seats were taken, and she had to elbow her way into a spot in the back.

Judge Irene Thaw was clearly not pleased at the sudden intense interest in the proceedings in her courtroom, and she wasn't about to expedite matters for the benefit of the assembled members of the media. As usual on Monday morning, following the weekend, there were a number of cases to be dealt with including the usual allegations of driving while intoxicated, spousal abuse, and disorderly conduct.

The air in the courtroom had become quite stale and Lucy's back was aching when the case of the three alleged drug dealers was finally announced, causing the media crowd to snap to attention. Digital cameras and smartphones were readied, video cameras and tape recorders were switched on, notebooks were opened and pens were gripped to record the moment when the alleged offenders were brought into the courtroom.

District Attorney Phil Aucoin presented the charges himself, accusing Carlos Cabral, Manuel Perez, and Eufry Victorino of Class A aggravated trafficking in Schedule W drugs, illegal possession of firearms, engaging in interstate commerce for illegal transactions, resisting arrest, and driving a vehicle that did not have a current inspection sticker. That last caused a bit of a chuckle among the gathered crowd.

Aucoin had done his homework and went on to present the judge with the trio's criminal records, which Lucy thought were remarkably long for such young offenders. All three had spent time in juvenile facilities, and Victorino, the oldest, had recently been released from the EMTC correctional facility on Riker's Island where he had served eighteen months for assault and battery.

When Aucoin finished his presentation, the judge asked the court appointed attorney, Linda Blackman, if she had anything to add. Her attempt to defend the three was not terribly effective since she pointed out they were unemployed, or as she put it, "unable to find employment," and that situation had resulted in this misguided effort to make money by the only means available to them. She had no doubt, she said, that after further investigation the matter would be resolved as a misunderstanding. In the meantime, she wasn't going to ask for bail because, since the three were from another state, it was unlikely to be granted.

"Don't you want to at least go on record asking for bail?" inquired the judge.

"No, your honor," said Blackman, getting evil looks from her clients. She placed the case file in her brief case, shut it with a snap, and was out of the courtroom before the three alleged drug dealers were led away by the court officers to their temporary accommodations in the county jail.

"Wow," said *Portland Press Herald* stringer Pete Withers as he and Lucy joined the throng leaving the courtroom. "Their lawyer didn't want anything to do with them. That's cold."

"Well, they do sound like trouble," said Lucy. "And it's not as if they were local kids with families in the area."

When she stepped outside she realized there was another dimension to the case. A group of demonstrators had gathered on a grassy area in front of the courthouse and were holding signs that read BUILD A WALL! DEPORT THE DRUG DEALERS! and AMERICA FOR AMERICANS! She paused on the steps and snapped a few photos of the protesters, which prompted one of them to confront her.

"Why did you do that?" demanded a middle-aged man wearing a Carhartt jacket and a red-and-black–plaid hunting cap.

"I'm a reporter for the Tinker's Cove *Pennysaver* newspaper," said Lucy. "You're part of the story I'm covering. And besides, if you're standing out here in broad daylight demonstrating, I assume it's because you want people to know how you feel."

"I sure do want people to know how I feel," said the man, changing his tune. "These scumbags come up here from Mexico and they get welfare and food stamps and free educations and Medicaid if they stub their toes, all on the backs of hardworking real Americans. That's how I see it and it's about time it ended."

"Right!" yelled another protester. "You said it, George."

"Do you mind giving me your name, George?" asked Lucy, who had written down every word.

"George Powers. I'm from Gilead and I'm fifty-three years old."

"Thanks, George. I really appreciate your openness," said Lucy. But as she made her way back to her car, she was troubled by the demonstrators' sentiments. The three young men who had been arrested were most probably guilty, she thought, but that didn't mean that everyone who had a Hispanic name was a criminal. And this was America, where everyone was presumed to be innocent until proven guilty. Wasn't it?

She had just got settled in the car when Bill called her cell phone. "Did you forget your lunch?" she asked.

"Not my lunch," he replied. "My flip book. You know, that loose-leaf with photos of my work. I think it's in your car."

Lucy twisted around in her seat and spotted the book lying on the back seat of her CR-V. "Yup, it's here. Where are you?"

"I'm at the Olde Irish Pub. I'm meeting Rey Rodriguez to discuss some renovations."

"I didn't know you were involved with that," said Lucy.

"Me, either," said Bill. "He called this morning, asking if I'd be interested. I've got my laptop with photos, but he wants something he can keep for a few days, maybe show to his investors." Bill paused, most likely answering a question from Rey. "So how soon can you get here?"

"Twenty minutes," said Lucy. "I'm on my way."

When she arrived at the harbor, she noticed several cars parked by the Olde Irish Pub. Bill's truck was there, of course, but there was also one of the gray sedans used by town officials and a huge black Land Rover. She parked next to Bill's pickup, grabbed the book he wanted, and went inside.

When the Olde Irish Pub opened more than a decade ago it had been a big improvement over its former incarnation as the Bilge, a dive frequented by local fishermen and known for cheap beer and frequent brawls. The Olde Irish Pub was welcomed by locals, who enjoyed the friendly atmosphere, good food, and harborside location. As time passed, however, the owners seemed to lose interest and the level of service declined, as did the quality of the food, and people stopped going there. It hadn't been much of a surprise when the restaurant was closed and a FOR SALE sign appeared in the window. The property languished on the market for over a year before Rey Rodriguez expressed an interest in buying it.

"You can't beat the location," he was saying to Bill when Lucy arrived.

"I'd open up the windows to take advantage of the view," replied Bill, giving Lucy a wave. "Here's my wife with the book. Lucy, have you met Rey Rodriguez?"

"We haven't met, but I saw him at the selectmen's meeting. Welcome to Tinker's Cove."

"Lucy's a reporter for the local paper," said Bill with a smile, "so you better watch what you say or you might find yourself in print."

"Never fear. We're off the record," joked Lucy. Hearing raised voices, she turned to see the town's health agent, Jennifer Santos, and Ed Franklin emerging from the kitchen.

The two were arguing and Lucy wondered if she'd spoken too soon; this might be a situation worth a paragraph or two in the paper.

"I'm telling you, you can't do this," said Jennifer. "It's not legal."

She was an attractive woman about thirty years old, who wore her long, black hair in a pony tail and dressed for work in the same flannel shirts and jeans that the contractors she dealt with also wore. The idea may have been to blend in with the boys, but it wasn't entirely successful as Jennifer's slender body was curvy in all the right places.

"This is an environmental issue," said Ed, "due to the location here on the cove. There's no way I can approve a commercial septic system that would pour grease and detergent, including nitrates, into the harbor water. And that's before we even consider effluent from the restrooms."

"It's a perfectly legal system that's up to code and it's grandfathered," said Jennifer. "It was upgraded less than two years ago."

"What are you saying?" asked Rey, crossing the room which was filled with tables and captain's chairs tumbled every which way. "That the septic system isn't good?"

"That's exactly what I'm saying," said Ed, glaring at Rey. "The only way my board will approve a license for this property is if you agree to use paper plates. All tableware will have to be disposable."

"Like a fast-food place?" asked Rey, puzzled. "That's not the sort of business I have in mind."

"Too bad, amigo," said Ed. "I'm not, I mean, the *board* is not going to let you run dishwashers that will fill our beautiful harbor with grease and suds. No way, José. Got it?"

"Is this true?" asked Rey, directing his question to Jennifer.

Jennifer looked at Ed, then sighed. "I will have to look into it," she said, biting her lip. "I'm employed by the board of health and I answer to them." She cast a meaningful glance toward Ed. "The board doesn't have the last word, however. They are obligated to enforce the state sanitary code as well as local regulations."

"How soon can I expect an answer?" asked Rey. "Time is money and I want to get this restaurant open as soon as possible."

"I've been in business for over twenty years in this town. I've done lots of renovations and I've never run into anything like this," said Bill.

"And I've covered lots of projects for the *Pennysaver*, lots of board meetings, and I've never seen such a prejudicial attitude," said Lucy.

Just then the door flew open and a young man entered, greeting everyone with a cheery wave. "Hi, Pop. I'm here to take a look at the new place."

"This is my son, Matt," said Rey, introducing the newcomer. "He'll be managing the restaurant."

Matt was tall and good-looking, with longish black hair and very white teeth, and was swinging a pair of Ray-Ban aviator sunglasses in one hand. He was dressed in a leather jacket, designer jeans, and fancy driving shoes.

"What a great location, right?" said Matt, nodding his approval. "It's going to be fabulous."

"Well, we're running into some problems," said Rey. "This is Bill Stone. He came to discuss possible renovations. And this is his wife, Lucy. Ed Franklin and Jennifer Santos are from the town board of health, and they say we've got some environmental issues."

"Really?" inquired Matt, raising a dark slash of eyebrow. "I went over all the specs with an environmental engineer. He even did an inspection before we made an offer. He said everything was correct."

"Well, I'm the chairman of the board of health and I'd like to take a look at that so-called review," said Ed Franklin. "You can't just come into this town and start polluting the water with your greasy Mexican gunk. I know the sort of stuff you people eat—loads of lard and oil—"

"He says we will have to use paper plates like a fast-food place," said Rey.

"That has not been decided," cautioned Jennifer.

"What exactly is the process?" asked Matt, directing his question to Jennifer. "Do we have to get approval from him? Who is this guy? The king of sanitation?"

"Like I said, I'm the chairman of the board and they'll darn well do what I tell them to do," declared Ed. "And I can tell you that we don't want people like you—"

"Now I understand," said Matt. "It's because we're Latino, right?"

"Not now," cautioned Rey, placing his hand on his son's arm.

"Yeah, and three of your compadres were in the district court this morning. Drug pushers with guns. Not the sort of folks we want in Tinker's Cove."

"Not my compadres," said Matt. "Do you know our family came here from Spain in the fifteen hundreds? We were here long before the United States was created."

"Well bully for you," said Ed, turning to Jennifer. "I think we're done here."

"Here's my card." She handed one to Rey. "You can contact me anytime with questions." She seemed ready to add something, then glanced over her shoulder at Ed who was clearly impatient for her to leave, and decided against it. "It's been nice meeting you," she said, scurrying out after him.

"What do you think?" asked Rey, turning to Bill.

"Like I said, we take out these fake cottage windows and put in plate glass. Open up the kitchen, put in some new light fixtures, banquette seating. It's going to be beautiful."

"How long will it take?" asked Rey.

"Not long," said Bill. "A couple weeks if you go with stock items, which I recommend. Custom could take forever."

Rey was smiling and nodding along, sharing Bill's vision.

But Matt wasn't buying it. "And what about Ed Franklin?"

"In the end, the board has to follow the law, and the law's on your side," said Bill.

"Ed Franklin just lost his daughter. He's grieving." Lucy gave an apologetic smile. "People here aren't like him," she said, by way of farewell.

As she made her way to the *Pennysaver* office, she thought of the demonstration outside the courthouse and wondered if Ed Franklin was saying things out loud that many people had been thinking to themselves for some time. Maybe his hate speech would open the flood gates, unleashing a torrent of pent-up prejudice.

"What took so long?" Ted asked when Lucy arrived at the office carrying a bag from the Quik-Stop containing a pot of yogurt and a banana.

"Court took forever, then I had to grab something for lunch . . ." she said, noticing that Phyllis was holding up her hands in a cautionary sign, casting warning eyes in Ted's direction. Taking the hint Lucy decided not to mention her stop at the Olde Irish Pub, which was a personal errand, even though it meant not reporting the encounter between Ed Franklin and the Rodriguezes.

"I heard there was quite a demonstration at the courthouse. Did you get photos?" demanded Ted.

"Photos and quotes," said Lucy.

"Okay, write it up. And before you leave, I want to go over the week's news budget."

"Right, Chief," said Lucy, giving a little salute before hanging up her coat.

"No need for sarcasm," snapped Ted, who was hunched over his computer.

Lucy settled herself at her desk, eating her yogurt while she booted up her computer and scrolled through her e-mails. She was licking the last off her spoon when the phone rang and she answered it.

"Hi, Lucy," said Pam. "Something's come up and I need help."

Interesting, thought Lucy. Maybe this was the reason for Ted's bad mood. "What's the trouble?"

"Debi Long has pneumonia. She's in the hospital."

"That's too bad."

"Bad? It's worse than bad. It's a disaster."

"Pneumonia? They give you antibiotics, then you get better . . ."

"It's the Harvest Festival at the church! Debi always makes dozens of apple cider donuts and people snap them up. Some people come just for the donuts."

Lucy knew the Harvest Festival was a big fundraiser for the church, which in turn donated to numerous local causes, including the Hat and Mitten Fund that she and her friends had started to provide warm clothes and school supplies for the town's less fortunate children. She also had an uneasy feeling where this was heading.

"I wish I could help."

"Well, you can. You can make donuts, can't you? All you need is a deep fryer. If you don't have one I bet you can borrow Debi's."

"I have done it. I *can* do it, but that doesn't mean I *want* to do it," said Lucy, who used to turn out a steady stream of baked goods when the kids were little. Back then, she was always mixing up nutritious lunchbox treats like oatmeal cookies with raisins, peanut butter bars, and molasses hermits. To be honest though, she rarely bothered with donuts, considering them too much trouble, and unhealthy to boot. "I've always been more of a customer at the Harvest Festival."

"Well, I bet you'd like making donuts if you tried. It would come back to you . . . like riding a bike."

"It's the question of time," said Lucy, glancing at the rolltop desk where Ted was buried in a pile of papers. "Your husband here keeps me pretty busy."

"Never mind him. I'll take care of Ted. You take whatever time you need to make donuts. It doesn't have to be twelve dozen. Six would be good. Angie Booth said she can make six, too."

"What about Sue? Can't she do it?" asked Lucy in a last ditch effort.

"Sue is making peanut brittle, which she tells me is absolutely wonderful, though I don't know how she knows since I doubt she's ever actually eaten any." Pam paused. "Donuts aren't very hard, you know, if you use an electric fryer. You just pop them in and wait for them to float to the top, then flip 'em over." She paused. "Just be sure to let them drain well. They're icky if they're too oily."

Lucy knew from the tone of her voice that Pam was truly desperate. "Okay," she agreed reluctantly. "I'll dig out the fryer. Six dozen apple cider donuts."

"Thanks, Lucy. I knew I could count on you. You're absolutely super."

It was after four when Lucy finished writing her story about the arraignment and the related demonstration, and uploaded her photos. She jotted down some ideas for the news budget and checked her e-mails for last-minute announcements and changes to the official town calendar. Noticing something from the board of selectmen she saw a new item was added to the agenda for the upcoming meeting—a citizen's complaint about racial bias by a member of the board of health.

"This is going to be interesting," she told Ted, finally deciding to tell him about the discussion she'd heard at the Olde Irish Pub. "Ed Franklin was using derogatory words like *amigo* and *no way José* to Rey Rodriguez. And he was making up stuff about the septic system not being up to code, saying they might not be able to run a dishwasher."

"I'm not surprised that Rey is filing a complaint," said Phyllis.

"I'm not sure it's Rey," said Lucy, thinking that Matt had seemed awfully self-assured. "It might be his son, Matt."

"The hunk I saw filling up his 'Vette at the Quik-Stop?" asked Phyllis with a mischievous smile.

"Could be," said Lucy, laughing.

CHAPTER 5

When she got home that evening, Lucy was surprised to see Zoe using the old electric fryer to cook up a batch of Southern Fried Chicken. Each piece had a lovely brown crust and as they sat on a wire rack, they filled the air with a delicious chickeny aroma.

That aroma was clearly getting to Libby. Mouth watering, she was sitting expectantly at Zoe's feet.

"Is that for supper?" asked Lucy as she dropped her bag on the bench and began unbuttoning her jacket.

"Yup. I just got a yen for fried chicken," declared Zoe, carefully adding the last few pieces of crusty chicken to the wire rack to cool and switching off the fryer.

"Very impressive. I'm sure it's going to taste every bit as good as it looks. But I've got to ask, whatever possessed you?" Lucy knew her youngest daughter's forays into the kitchen rarely went beyond tossing a pack of popcorn into the microwave.

"I have a big American Lit midterm exam next week," admitted Zoe. "I'm avoiding studying because every time I open my notebook I think of Alison. According to my psych book it's called displacement activity."

"Oh, dear," said Lucy, concerned. "Maybe you should check

those psych books for a more positive approach—one that would get you back on track with your studying."

"I should," said Zoe with a sigh. "And I will. But every time I open my notebooks I think of Alison."

"It's tough, I know," said Lucy, giving Zoe a hug. "I think you just have to make yourself get started. Once you do, I think it will get easier."

"I hope so," said Zoe, plopping into one of the chairs at the round, golden oak kitchen table. "I'm thinking of taking next semester off. This new restaurant Dad's working at, Cali Kitchen, has got lots of help wanted signs up at the college. I'm sure I could get a job there."

Lucy had a horrible sinking feeling. She'd seen how this worked. First the kids dropped out of school, then with too much free time on their hands they began hanging around with other dropouts, and before you knew it, they started experimenting with drugs. "I don't think that's a good idea," she said, washing her hands in the kitchen sink.

"Don't panic, Mom," said Zoe in an amused tone, watching her mother pull some salad fixings out of the fridge. "It's just an idea."

"Maybe you could drop a course or two, and work part-time," said Lucy, ripping open a bag of lettuce and dropping it into a bowl.

"Yeah, maybe," said Zoe with a distinct lack of enthusiasm.

"In the meantime," began Lucy as she chopped a cucumber, "since you can't concentrate on American Literature, how about making apple cider donuts for me? I said I'd make six dozen for the Harvest Festival at the church."

"I could do that," said Zoe in a thoughtful tone. "I saw Martha Stewart make donuts on TV this morning and it didn't look hard."

Lucy wondered exactly how much time Zoe was wasting in this displacement activity as she watched her pick up the neglected notebook lying on the table and flipped through a few pages.

"Of course," said Zoe, "*Moby Dick* is a really complex book and I'm way behind. I already told Mrs. Hollis that I'm not going to be able to babysit for her this weekend and I'll need some gas money . . ."

Lucy had an idea where this was heading. "I'll pay you," she said in a small voice as she began coring a tomato.

"I'm pretty sure we can work something out," said Zoe with a satisfied smile. "When do you need the donuts?"

These days it seemed to Lucy that time was accelerating and the days flew by much too quickly before she could accomplish half the things she meant to do. The town calendar followed its usual pattern of regularly scheduled meetings and she found she had a permanent case of déjà vu, finding herself once again in the basement meeting room at the town hall covering the planning board or the finance committee, and most frequently, the board of selectmen.

At least today's meeting promised to be a little bit different, as the Rodriguezes complaint against Ed Franklin was on the agenda. When she arrived, Rey and Matt were already in attendance sitting side by side in a middle row, quietly conversing. They were dressed more formally in ties and business suits rather than the customary jeans and sweaters that was usual in Tinker's Cove.

She settled herself in her usual seat, then abruptly decided to shake things up a bit and moved to the opposite side of the room and sat beside Verity Hawthorne.

"Going rogue?" she asked, looking up from her knitting and giving Lucy a smile.

"Just thought I'd see if things look different from this side of the room."

"I think we're in for a bit of drama tonight," said Verity as Ed Franklin strode down the center aisle, planting his feet heavily with each step.

Reaching the row where Rey and Matt were sitting, he paused and glared at them, then continued on his way, taking a seat in the front row where he spread his legs wide apart and stretched his arms across the backs of the chairs on either side of him. The body language spoke loud and clear—Ed Franklin was a big, important man, much too big for one little chair.

The big hand on the clock behind the selectmen's dais clicked into place on the twelve and the board members immediately filed in. Following their usual order, they sat down at the long table, each behind his or her nameplate. Roger Wilcox called the meeting to order, they promptly dispatched the usual business, then moved on to the matter of the citizen's complaint.

Rey rose and politely addressed the board members, speaking in a somewhat regretful tone as he claimed that Ed Franklin overstepped his role as a board member when he inserted himself in the meeting with health inspector Jennifer Santos. "He had no place at that meeting, the purpose of which was simply to provide an overview of the project and discuss the relevant regulations. Mr. Franklin displayed a hostile attitude. He threatened enforcement of nonexistent regulations and interfered with Ms. Santos' professional responsibilities.

"I know a bit about the restaurant business," Rey continued in a deliberate understatement. "I have been in the business for nearly forty years. I have worked hard to earn an enviable reputation as a respected restaurateur and chef, so I can only conclude that Mr. Franklin objects to me personally because I am of Latino heritage. This, as you know, is a clear violation of national, state, and local equal rights legislation.

"I also want to add that I have come to believe that Mr. Franklin has been pressuring local suppliers and garbage haulers to refuse to do business with me. As my credit rating is excellent, that is the only possible explanation for the resistance I have encountered as I have tried to contract with local suppliers for necessary products and services. I might add that in all my years as a businessman I have never before encountered a situation like this."

Matt remained quiet in his seat while his father spoke but kept his eyes fixed on the back of Ed Franklin's head. That head remained immobile. Ed Franklin did not react in any way to Rey's accusations.

When Rey finished speaking, Roger thanked him for expressing himself so clearly and bringing the matter to the attention of the board. Then he asked Ed Franklin if he wished to respond.

"You bet I do," said Ed, remaining sprawled in his seat. His tone was conversational, as if he was merely repeating widely accepted truths. "Everybody knows Mexico has only two exports—illegal drugs and people—and both are trouble. We've all read in the newspapers about the gang wars on the border and the terrible killings. These folks have no respect for life. They kill anybody who gets in their way, including police officers. I have friends in Arizona, people who've been successful in business and were looking to enjoy a peaceful retirement, and they say they have to have dogs and fences and guns to feel safe from the illegals.

"Now maybe Mr. Rodriguez here is a law-abiding fellow. I've got nothing against him personally, and my wife says his cookbooks are great, fabulous, but when one Mexican moves in you get a lot more. They're like mice. You catch one mouse and think you've solved the problem, but believe me, it's just the tip of the iceberg. I think we've got a responsibility to keep Tinker's Cove a safe, pleasant place to live and that means keeping out undesirable elements. Mexicans should stay in Mexico. America is for Americans."

While Ed was speaking Lucy watched the expressions on the board members faces, trying to discern their reactions. At first, they seemed eager to display openness and a fair-minded willingness to hear his response to Rey's allegations, but as Ed continued, their expressions hardened and they began to fidget in their seats, growing more and more uncomfortable. By the time he finished speaking, Franny Small was biting her lip, Sam Bellamy's face was red and he seemed about to explode. Joe Marzetti was clenching his teeth and Winchester College professor Fred Rumford was shaking his head in dismay. Roger Wilcox was momentarily speechless, his head lowered as he stared at the papers on the table before him.

"Mr. Franklin," he finally said, "you have not answered Mr. Rodriguez's complaint that you personally interfered in a meeting with the health agent, overstepping your position as chairman of the board of health. What do you have to say?"

"Oh, no question, I was at the meeting. And I pointed out that there would most likely be problems complying with current septic regulations considering the location of the Olde Irish Inn."

Hearing this, Matt jumped to his feet. "He said we wouldn't be able to have a dishwasher, that we'd have to use paper plates like a fast-food place! That was a clear threat! Cali Kitchen will be a fine restaurant! Paper plates would be—"

"You're out of order," said Roger with a placatory smile. "Please let me continue questioning Mr. Franklin. If you feel you need to add something, you may speak later." He turned to Ed, raising a small booklet with a blue cover. "I wonder, Mr. Franklin, if you are familiar with this document. It is a concise summary of responsibilities and legal obligations that is given to every town official. I assume you were given one of these booklets?"

"Probably. I can't say it looks familiar," said Ed with a shrug. "A lot of paper comes across my desk. I don't get to read it all."

"I suggest you take this copy home with you tonight and read it very carefully," said Roger. "I believe you will find it helpful if you are going to continue as a member of the board of health in future."

"You're going to let him stay on the board?" demanded Matt, who was on his feet, hands clenched.

"For the present," said Roger. "But I will say this to Mr. Franklin. As much as we appreciate your service to the town, we expect you to follow all the policies the town has adopted, including the very specific requirement that every petitioner be treated respectfully, fairly, and equally. If you find yourself unable to comply with the fundamental rights guaranteed to all citizens by the US Constitution we will ask you to remove yourself from the board. Do you understand?"

"I have no problem with that," said Ed with a shrug. "I was misunderstood. That's all it was."

"We did not misunderstand you," declared Matt.

"Well, that's the thing with misunderstandings, right?" said Ed with an ingratiating smile. "I think one thing, you think another. But I guess it's all straightened out, right?"

"It better be," growled Matt as Roger banged down his gavel. Then turning on his heel, Matt marched out of the meeting room.

There was a rather stunned silence, then the newest member of the board, Franny Small, who rarely spoke, raised her hand.

"Ms. Small," said Roger, recognizing her.

"I have something to say." She spoke in a firm voice and unfolded some papers she'd taken from her purse. "It's a quote. I just happen to have it here. It was in the bulletin from last Sunday's service at the Community Church. I'd like to enter it into the minutes, if I may. It goes like this. 'First they came for the Socialists and I did not speak out—Because I was not a Socialist. Then they came for the Trade Unionists and I did not speak out—Because I was not a Trade Unionist. Then they came for the Jews and I did not speak out—Because I was not a Jew. Then they came for me—and there was no one left to speak for me.'" She paused. "It's from a man named Martin Niemöller. He was protesting the Nazis."

"I'd like to move that the quote Ms. Small just read be entered into the minutes," said Fred Rumford.

Sam Bellamy was quick to second the motion, which passed unanimously.

"Thank you all," said Roger, nodding his head. "I think we all need to remember that America is one country with people from many parts of the world. They came here for freedom and the guarantee of equal treatment under the law. Now, if there's no other business, the meeting is adjourned." He banged down the gavel and everybody started to leave.

Lucy went up to the front of the room to congratulate Franny. "I guess that was your maiden speech," she said, smiling. "Well done."

Franny was a very small woman well into her sixties, who'd had a remarkably successful career creating a profitable jewelry business. She'd begun by making the pins and earrings out of nuts and bolts and other hardware and selling them at craft fairs. She turned out to be a canny businesswoman and the company had grown and evolved through the years as major department stores began carrying the line. Now she was retired, and although she was probably the second richest person in Tinker's Cove, after Ed Franklin, she still lived in the modest house she'd grown up in and drove an ancient Honda Civic.

"Thanks, Lucy. I had to speak up. We simply can't tolerate this sort of intolerance in our town."

"I couldn't agree more."

Franny bent closer, whispering, "Have you seen his wife? She's young enough to be his daughter!" Her eyes widened. "And she's pregnant!"

"They've suffered a terrible tragedy," Lucy reminded her.

"The wages of sin, no doubt," said Franny with a knowing nod. "Have a nice evening," she added, making her serene way out of the meeting room.

Intolerance was a funny thing, thought Lucy as she gathered up her things. People rarely seemed to recognize their own prejudices, even when they were quick to condemn another's failings.

When she climbed the cement steps to the parking area, she was yawning, looking forward to a hot bath and bed. Hearing raised voices, she paused at the top of the stairs where she saw Matt angrily confronting Ed Franklin. The two were clearly illuminated by a street light, and a few bystanders were watching.

"We're not Mexicans," he yelled, face-to-face with Ed. "We're Americans. My father, his father, and his father going back for hundreds of years. They were all born in California."

"Get out of my way," growled Ed, attempting to edge around him. "I don't care who you are."

"Well, you better care," snarled Matt, blocking his way, "and you better call off your racist buddies . . . Becker and ProServe and Curtis Cleaners."

"I don't know what you're talking about," insisted Ed, attempting once again to make his way to his huge Navigator SUV.

"You know, and it's gotta stop!" yelled Matt, raising his arm.

"That's enough," said Rey, stepping between them. "Go home, Matt."

Matt stayed in place for a long moment, glaring at Ed, then marched across the parking lot to his Corvette. The car roared into life and he sped across the parking lot, swerving widely at the exit and zooming off down the road.

"I must apologize for my son," said Rey. "He's young and hot-headed."

"Like all you Mexicans, I guess," said Ed. "What do they call it? Latin blood?"

Rey looked like a man who'd been slapped in the face. He stepped back, shook his head, and walked slowly to his car.

"I have a feeling this isn't over," said Joe Marzetti, who had climbed the stairs and paused beside Lucy. "And it's not going to be pretty."

"I think you're right." She had noted the names Matt had mentioned, presumably outfits that had refused to do business with the Rodriguezes, and was jotting them down in her notebook.

Next morning at the office, she put in calls to ProServe and Curtis Cleaners, but both went straight to voice mail. She dutifully left messages, but doubted very much they would bother to return her call. Walt Becker, a local trash hauler, answered the phone himself.

"Hi, Lucy." His voice came booming through the phone. "What can I do for you?"

She had recently interviewed him for a story on recycling and he'd been extremely helpful, even taking her to the regional single-stream recycling facility for a tour. She didn't want to offend him by accusing him of racism, so she proceeded carefully. "Funny thing, Walt. I was at the selectmen's meeting last night."

"I'm sorry," he joked. "Nobody should have to go through that."

"I know," laughed Lucy. "It was pretty awful. But the reason I'm calling is that, well, Matt Rodriguez accused Ed Franklin of pressuring local businesses to refuse to contract with them and your name came up."

"Look, I know full well that it's against the law to refuse service because of race, color, religion, sexual preference, age . . . you name it. You call Becker Hauling and we'll haul it, as long as it's not toxic or radioactive or something like that."

"But did Ed Franklin pressure you in any way?"

"Sure. That's what Ed Franklin does. Thinks he's king of the universe. Said he'd fire me if I contracted with Rodriguez and wouldn't use my trucks anymore."

"What are you going to do?" asked Lucy.

"Look, nobody tells me how to run my business. If Franklin's unhappy with me, well, that's too bad. I've got plenty of happy customers."

"I'm sure you do," said Lucy.

"That's not to say that I've got to like everybody. Personally, I don't get that transgender thing at all, but I don't really care what bathroom anybody uses as long as they don't leave a nasty mess. And I'm not crazy about these Latinos or whatever they are. Did you see the news? Those three guys? The drug dealers?"

"Actually, I covered the arraignment," said Lucy.

"Well, then I don't have to tell you that those guys are bad guys. They're trouble and we don't need any more trouble. We've got enough of our own. But that said, business is business and I'm in the business of hauling trash from anybody and everybody who asks, just as long as they pay their bills."

"Then why did Matt Rodriguez name you as one of Franklin's buddies?" asked Lucy, determined to keep Walt wriggling on the hook. "It sure sounded like you refused their business."

"Well," said Becker, speaking slowly, "that was my girl here, Abby. She overheard Franklin threatening me and when Rodriguez called she said she wasn't sure if we could take on more business. I'll, uh, I'll give them a call and straighten it out."

"So it was just a misunderstanding?" persisted Lucy, suspecting it was nothing of the kind. She figured Walt had done a quick calculation and concluded that the bad publicity from a mention in the *Pennysaver* would be worse for his business than Ed Franklin's threats.

"Yeah," he said, quick to agree. "That's all it was. It was a misunderstanding."

There sure seemed to be a lot of misunderstanding going on these days, thought Lucy.

CHAPTER 6

The next morning, Lucy was dismayed to see, was a beautiful sunshiny day. A classic New England autumn morning with clear skies, golden-leaved trees, and crisp air. A perfect day for running and resuming her training program for the Turkey Trot, which she'd been neglecting.

She knew full well that she'd been avoiding running, using every excuse she could come up with—too rainy, too windy, she got a late start and didn't want to be late for work or for meeting the girls for breakfast. The truth was that Zoe wasn't the only one who was haunted by Alison's death. Lucy hadn't wanted to go back on the old logging road. The last time she ran there she'd discovered Alison's body and didn't want to relive that experience.

But she knew that she needed to train if she was going to be a serious competitor in the Turkey Trot and today was the perfect opportunity. It was early so she had plenty of time, and the weather was absolutely perfect. She had run out of excuses. It was time to lace up and face her ghosts.

When Libby saw her come into the kitchen in her running clothes, she leaped out of her doggy bed and began prancing around, tail wagging, eager to get going. The dog's enthusiasm was contagious and Lucy was smiling as she grabbed the leash and opened the door. She paused on the back porch and took a few deep breaths, then began her stretches.

Libby didn't approve of stretches. She was halfway across the yard when she stopped, realizing she was alone. She turned and barked a few times, as if to say "What's the holdup?"

"I'm coming," yelled Lucy, smiling to herself when she realized she was making excuses to her dog.

Then they were off, Lucy moving at an easy jog and Libby running just ahead, her tail up and ears flapping, her mouth spread open in a doggy smile. Lucy felt nicely loose and warmed up by the time the trail entered the woods, and she began to run harder along a flat stretch of dirt road that extended for a mile or so. She was panting and had worked up a sweat by the time the road began its uneven descent to the pond.

Her thoughts inevitably turned to Alison. *What was she doing, going out on the ice? It was such a foolish thing to do and she must have known the danger. Was she on drugs, like everybody thought? Or had there been a reason, like a dog or other animal in trouble?*

Lucy hadn't seen any sign of a struggling animal but that didn't mean it hadn't been there and either managed to get free or succumbed and sank below the surface of the icy water.

The other possibility, which nobody said out loud but which she was sure a lot of people were thinking, was that Alison committed suicide. A lot of young people encountered emotional difficulties in their early twenties, which was also the age at which mental illnesses like depression and schizophrenia manifested themselves. Suicide, sadly, was not uncommon at that age.

Lucy ran carefully, watching her footing as the path became more challenging due to ruts and rocks, but part of her mind was back in the community church, replaying Alison's funeral. She remembered Alison's birth mother Eudora, who had been so emotional and dramatic. Lucy had never quite overcome her somewhat repressive Calvinist upbringing, and couldn't help wondering if Eudora wasn't a bit of a drama queen. Then she sternly reminded herself that you never knew what people really felt inside, and that everyone dealt with grief in their own unique way. But still, it did seem a bit odd that Alison had been living with her father and his new young wife instead of with her birth mother.

Why did Alison choose to live with her father? Ed Franklin was a difficult man, to say the least, and Lucy suspected that Alison must have found him somewhat embarrassing. A young person of her generation was unlikely to share his bigotry, and even though she benefitted from his wealth, she would probably have been uncomfortable with the way he flaunted it. And then there was the young wife, Mireille, who was only a few years older than Alison and was pregnant. As Rachel had said, that must have been a difficult situation for Alison to deal with.

The fragrant balsam fir trees that lined the path, giving it a sense of enclosure, thinned as she approached the pond, opening up to reveal an open expanse of sky. Libby, who had been running ahead, suddenly stopped and began to whine; Lucy remembered her doing the same thing after they'd encountered a black snake sunning itself on a rocky part of the path last spring.

She must be remembering the dead girl, thought Lucy, bending down to grab the dog's ears and smooth her raised hackles. "It's okay, it's okay," she murmured. "Nobody here but us chickens."

She snapped on the leash and was about to resume her run. She knew a few tugs on the leash were all it would take to get Libby moving again. The old logging road circled the pond on one side, but there was a parking lot and swimming area on the other side that was accessed from a paved road. A narrow footpath also led from the old logging road to the parking area and Lucy decided to follow it and run along the paved road for another half mile or so before turning back.

She expected the parking area to be empty now that the summer swimming season was over, but noticed a small black BMW idling near the exit. She ran through the lot on the pond side, keeping well away from the car, which was exactly what she had been instructed to do at the women's personal safety workshop that Officer Barney Culpepper, Tinker's Cove Police Department's community outreach officer, offered from time to time. She was about halfway through the lot when a second car pulled in and then the two cars drove off together.

Weird, she thought, heading for the exit at the far end of the parking lot. She felt uneasy after witnessing the incident and was relieved when she reached the paved road, which was fairly well-traveled. She got friendly waves and toots of the horn from several passing drivers.

Reaching the rural mailbox that she used as a marker, she turned around and began the return route that would take her home. She considered continuing along the paved road, which met up with her own Red Top Road, but that would mean missing the uphill climb from the pond on the logging road, and she knew the Turkey Trot route had a similar incline. She really couldn't avoid it. She needed the workout the hill provided, so she headed back to the parking lot. There was no danger, she told herself, because the cars had left.

But as she drew closer to the lot Libby began barking, and sure enough, that little black BMW was back in the same spot, idling. Lucy picked up her pace, sprinting along the opposite side of the lot from the BMW and was almost through when an aged Caravan with a dented fender pulled up and stopped next to the BMW, driver's side to driver's side. She didn't stay to watch. She yanked the dog's leash and pounded across the remaining few yards of parking lot and entered the safety of the woods.

What was that all about, she wondered as she slowed her pace to allow her ragged, uneven breathing to even out and her racing heart to settle down. What was going on? There was something odd about the whole thing that simply didn't feel right. Was she paranoid? Maybe they were just bird watchers or nature lovers or something. Or maybe, she thought with a shock as she began the tough uphill climb, she had witnessed a couple drug deals. The parking lot was perfect for that sort of transaction. It was secluded from view, it was reliably deserted this time of year, and it had easy access to the paved town road. It was a no-brainer, she decided, wondering why she hadn't realized what was going on sooner. Drug deals! At Blueberry Pond.

But if she—a middle-class, middle-aged woman whose only experience of illegal drugs was a few puffs of marijuana in college—could figure it out, she figured it was hardly a secret. Everybody must know. And if everybody knew, that meant the cops must also know. So why were they ignoring it? Didn't they know there was an opioid epidemic? What was keeping them from making an easy arrest? Maybe even a lot of arrests, she thought, remember-

ing one of the EMTs who'd responded to Alison's drowning
telling her there was a nearby shack frequented by drug users.

Back at the house, Lucy couldn't stop thinking about the drug
deals she'd witnessed. It was shocking to her that this was happening so close to home. Blueberry Pond wasn't that far from
their house, and the logging road was passable by car. Were they
in danger from these criminals? Would they have to start locking
the doors to the house, something they'd never done in all the
years they'd lived on Red Top Road? And what about the stuff in
their shed? It was chock full of Bill's expensive power tools,
which a desperate user could steal and sell, probably for pennies
on the dollar, but enough to buy some cheap heroin. Maybe more.
She had no idea how much heroin or oxy or whatever they were
buying cost.

Even worse than theft, what about the home invasions she'd
heard about, she thought, as she stepped out of the shower and
wrapped a towel around herself. Remembering she was alone in
the house and feeling vulnerable, she turned the lock on the bathroom door. True, there'd never been a home invasion in Tinker's
Cove, and her fear was probably irrational, but it was there. She
didn't feel safe in her own home, and she was terrified for her
girls. She couldn't erase the memory of that terrible episode in
New Hampshire that had dominated the news for so long, when
two crazy men broke into a home and raped a mother in front of
her two preteen daughters, who they'd tied to their beds. After
strangling the mother they'd torched the house, and the girls died
from smoke inhalation.

The story went on for months as new details were revealed, the
suspects caught, and the trial unfolded. A scratch and whine from
the other side of the door, undoubtedly Libby looking for her
breakfast, reminded Lucy that those particular criminals had even
killed the family dog. Only the father, who'd been at work, was
spared.

"Okay, okay," she said, opening the door cautiously and allowing Libby to stick her nose through the crack. Summoning her
courage she opened the door and proceeded down the hall to her
bedroom, accompanied by the dog, who jumped on the unmade

bed and rolled around, legs in the air. Then she jumped off, ran to the door, and gave a sharp yip, reminding Lucy that Libby hadn't had her breakfast yet.

Lucy dressed quickly, throwing on her usual jeans and sweater. She combed and scrunched her damp hair, grabbed her shoes and socks, and hurried downstairs barefoot. In the kitchen, she dumped some kibble into Libby's bowl, poured some cereal into her own favorite bowl, and poured out the last of the morning coffee into a mug.

The headline in the morning paper, the *Press Herald*, wasn't encouraging. REGION TOPS IN OPIOID DEATHS. A quick read revealed that Massachusetts had the most overdoses, but Maine and the other New England states weren't far behind. And no wonder, she thought, tossing the paper aside with a snort, since the cops were letting the dealers operate in broad daylight.

When she arrived at the *Pennysaver* office, she wasted no time telling Ted what she had seen earlier that morning. "I couldn't believe it, Ted," she declared as she shrugged out of her barn coat and hung it on the coat rack. "There was a little BMW in the parking lot, idling there, and other cars came and went, stopping only for a minute. Sometimes they drove off together. It was creepy and scary. They're dealing drugs practically in my backyard."

"Right out in the open, at the pond?" asked Phyllis, furrowing her brows over the harlequin reading glasses perched on her nose. Today she was wearing a brightly colored floral print jersey topped with a magenta cardigan that closely matched the color of her dyed hair.

"Are you sure it was drug deals?" asked Ted in a doubtful tone. "Maybe they were sales reps, getting samples or price lists or something like that."

"No," said Lucy, shaking her head. "It was all very fast and furtive. They hardly spoke a word to each other, not chatty like colleagues would be."

"I guess you better give Chief Kirwan a call. Ask him if he's aware of the situation."

"And if not, why not? And if he is, why isn't he doing anything to stop it?" said Phyllis with a sharp nod that made the wattles under her chin quiver. "Especially since that poor little Alison

Franklin died there. She probably got the drugs that killed her from that guy."

"I'm on it," said Lucy, seating herself at her desk and booting up her PC. While she waited for the ancient machine to rouse itself, she worked out what she would say to Jim Kirwan. This was a delicate situation and she didn't want to put him on the defensive. If she was going to get any information out of him, she needed to make it very clear that she wasn't criticizing the department or his management.

"Good morning, Chief," she began. "How are you?"

"Just fine, and you?" he replied.

"Fine. In fact, I went for a run this morning. I'm training for the Turkey Trot."

"Good for you, Lucy, but I don't think you called to ask my advice on training regimes, did you?"

"Well, actually, I sort of am," answered Lucy, quick to seize the opening. "My usual route takes me past Blueberry Pond and I saw some activity in the parking lot that made me wonder if it was a safe place to be."

"What did you see?"

"A car was kind of lurking there. A black BMW with a man inside."

"Oh, you don't have to worry about him. We know all about him."

Lucy was shocked and troubled by the chief's comment and continued questioning him, determined to get to the bottom of this strange turn of events. "I'm not sure, but I think he's a drug dealer. And maybe he sold the drugs that killed Alison Franklin."

She heard the chief sigh. "First off, Lucy, the autopsy report isn't complete and we don't know what killed Alison Franklin. And second, I'm going off the record now, understand?"

"Off the record," said Lucy, eager to hear more.

"Okay, this discovery of yours isn't news to me or anyone in the department. We patrol the Blueberry Pond area regularly and keep an eye on the situation, but we don't interfere for a number of reasons. One is that we have quite a few people here in town who are struggling with dependency and we know who this dealer is—"

Lucy was quick to interrupt. "Who is he?" she demanded.

"He's responsible and his drugs are clean," continued the chief, ignoring her question. "If we cut off this supply, they'll end up going to riskier dealers, getting tainted stuff and dying."

"But wouldn't it be better if they went into rehab and got clean?" asked Lucy, shocked at what she was hearing.

"Sure, but this is the real world we're living in. I'm not saying this is a perfect solution. Personally I don't like it, but I have limited options. And I've got meager resources. I don't have all the officers I need and I don't have the budget I need to handle other priorities like domestic violence, highway safety, alcohol abuse, even animal control. We're strapped. That's the honest truth. We have to leave narcotics enforcement to the state police drug task force. They've got the knowledge and expertise and they focus on the big dealers."

"But those drug task force investigations take months," protested Lucy.

"Exactly." He paused. "That's because it's very difficult to prosecute these cases. Every *i* has to be dotted and every *t* crossed. These task force members know what they're doing and they do it well."

"Have you passed on information about this dealer?" asked Lucy.

"Yes, we have," he replied. "And now, I have other matters on my desk."

"Right," said Lucy, taking the hint. "And thanks."

Ted was all over her as soon as she ended the call. "Off the record? Did you agree to go off the record?" he demanded.

"I had to or I wouldn't have gotten anything out of him. It's a bad business. They know about the dealer. They know who he is, but the chief said all they're doing is 'keeping an eye on the situation.'"

"Are you kidding me?" asked Ted, looking puzzled.

"No. That's what he said. They have passed on his identity to the drug task force. He said his department is stretched to the limit without attempting to go after drug dealers."

"But people are dying," said Phyllis. "I think of that poor girl, drowning like that because of drugs. I can't get her out of my mind."

"This isn't acceptable," said Ted. "If the police aren't going to do anything, I think we have to. The dealing is bad, but the police cover-up is worse."

"I agree," said Lucy. "We can investigate this ourselves. We don't have to break my promise to the chief about keeping what he said off the record, I saw the dealer myself. We can follow up on our own."

"The chief's not going to be happy, and he's got a lot of relatives in town jobs. You'll never get a word out of any Kirwans in the future," warned Phyllis.

Lucy knew Phyllis was right. Dot Kirwan, the matriarch of the clan, worked as a cashier at the IGA, where she picked up a lot of newsworthy information that she passed along. Her numerous offspring, children and even grandchildren, had jobs in the police and fire department, the highway department, and the schools. Lucy would hate to lose Dot as a source, and more important, as a friend.

Ted, however, had no such reservations. "We'll do an investigative report," he said, warming to the idea. "We'll stake out the parking lot, take photos, figure out who this guy is."

"And what if we see the police observing him and doing nothing?" asked Lucy.

"We report it," declared Ted with enthusiasm. "That's what we do. We tell the truth, the whole truth, and this will be a big, breakthrough story. It will not only show that opioid addiction is a problem that crosses ethnic and class lines, that it touches all of us, but it will also show that the police, the people we expect to fight the war on drugs, are AWOL."

"So tomorrow . . ." began Lucy.

"We stake out Blueberry Pond," said Ted. "Bright and early." He paused, thinking. "Better dress warm."

CHAPTER 7

That afternoon, when Lucy returned home, she was surprised to see a snazzy Corvette parked in her usual spot. The only person she knew who had such a car was Matt Rodriguez and when she went into the house she found him in the kitchen with Zoe. The two were shoulder to shoulder, rolling out donut dough on the counter. Libby the dog was sitting on her haunches beside Zoe, watching every move in case a scrap of dough fell her way.

"Hi, Mom," Zoe sang out by way of greeting. Her face was flushed and Lucy didn't think the fryer had heated up the kitchen all that much. Zoe had an adorable smear of flour on her nose. "You know Matt, don't you? He's helping me make these apple cider donuts for the Harvest Festival."

"Hi, Matt," said Lucy with a smile as she plunked her bag on the bench by the door and hung her jacket on one of the hooks. "Thanks for helping Zoe."

"It's a pleasure," he said with a broad smile that revealed very white teeth and two deep dimples, one in each cheek.

He was remarkably good-looking, thought Lucy, seeing him up close. He had longish black hair and arched eyebrows over dark brown eyes, a hawkish nose, and wide mouth. Even his ears were small and nicely shaped. He was wearing designer jeans, fashionable ankle boots, and a tight cashmere sweater that showed off his toned muscles—not the baggy jeans and flannel shirts most young men in Tinker's Cove wore.

"I have to compliment you on your kitchen," he said, looking very serious. "It's functional, but also attractive and honest. It's a room with what my father calls *duende*. The closest English word is *soul*."

Lucy didn't quite know how to respond. In her mind, the kitchen was a mishmash of things picked up at yard sales. With its battered cabinets and golden oak table that gathered all sorts of clutter, it looked nothing like the sleek designer kitchens she saw in the magazines. The compliment made her wonder about this guy who she suspected was more interested in Zoe than in Lucy's decorating.

"Matt's a trained chef, Mom," said Zoe, who knew very well that her mother would want an explanation for Matt's presence in the house, which was a clear violation of the family rule against entertaining young men when no parents were home unless they'd been introduced and gotten the parental seal of approval. "We got talking when I interviewed for a job at Cali Kitchen and when I told him I had to make these donuts, he offered to help. He's already taught me so much about pastry. There's a lot more to it than I thought."

Lucy had reached for the jar of dog biscuits, a move that didn't escape Libby's notice, prompting her to abandon Zoe and transfer her attention to Lucy. Lucy raised a finger in the "sit" signal and Libby promptly obeyed, earning a biscuit, which she promptly took to the dog bed in the corner and chomped down.

"Zoe is going to be a great addition at the restaurant . . . if we ever get it opened," he said. "She's not only beautiful but she's definitely got a flair for cooking. She really ought to consider culinary school."

Lucy didn't like the sound of that one bit. "She's already attending Winchester College," she snapped, "and she hopes to go on to veterinary school."

He turned to Zoe with an expression of surprise. "You didn't tell me that! That's great! I love animals. I had the best dog when I was growing up. A beagle named Bismarck. He went everywhere with me." He paused. "I missed him more than I missed my folks when I went to college."

"Was that culinary school?" asked Lucy, wondering how old Matt was.

"No. I went to Pomona for a year and flunked out," he answered, turning around and leaning his back casually against the counter. "My dad wasn't about to let me be a dropout and pushed me to join the navy. That's where I really got interested in cooking. When my hitch was up I used the GI Bill and went to the Culinary Institute of America in New York state."

"And how long have you been working in the restaurant business?" she asked, busy adding up the years.

"About five, I guess," he said with a shrug and a big smile. "Time flies when you're having fun."

At least thirty, thought Lucy, which made him much too old for Zoe.

"And are you married?"

"No," laughed Matt. "Like I said, I'm having too much fun."

Not with my daughter, you're not, thought Lucy.

Libby, having finished her biscuit, rose from her doggy bed, gave a shake, and went back to her previous spot next to Zoe. Lucy, realizing she had little to no control over a situation she didn't much like, decided to go out and mulch the vegetable garden with compost for the winter.

When she returned to the house an hour later, Matt was gone and six dozen donuts were neatly lined up on paper towels and cooling on the counter. Lovely donuts, perfectly browned around the edges, with a light dusting of cinnamon sugar. Really, she ought to be grateful to the fellow, but she wasn't. She even resented the fact that she really, really wanted to eat one but knew she shouldn't. She heard the TV in the family room and went in, finding Zoe on the couch with Libby, watching a cooking show.

"Thanks for making those donuts. They're beautiful," Lucy said, plopping down beside the dog and scratching her behind her ears. On the TV, Ina Garten was adding a lot of butter to a pan of mushrooms.

"You should thank Matt," said Zoe. "I could never have made

such nice ones by myself. And they taste fantastic. He put in some spices I never would have thought of . . . like cumin and red pepper."

"Red pepper?" asked Lucy, alarmed.

Ina was cracking eggs into a bowl and whisking them.

"Just a tiny bit. He said it would 'liven' the sweet apple flavor."

"That will have to be our secret." Lucy could imagine how the usual festival customers would react to the idea of red pepper in their apple cider donuts. "What is she making?" she asked as Ina added grated cheese to the eggs.

"A mushroom quiche," said Zoe. "I have to say, I didn't think much of her pastry technique. She used a food processor and Matt says that makes a tough crust. You can always tell, he says, if the pastry was made by loving hands."

Ina was now outside her shingled house in the Hamptons, serving quiche to her husband, Jeffrey, who was sitting at a patio table. He really seemed to enjoy the quiche, even if the crust was machine made.

Or maybe it was the big glass of white wine, thought Lucy. "Matt seems really nice," she said, carefully weighing her words as the commercials began to roll, "but he's quite a bit older than you."

"What's that supposed to mean?" asked Zoe. "He's not my boyfriend or anything."

"He clearly seemed attracted to you," said Lucy. "Guys don't make six dozen donuts for girls they don't like."

"That's the silliest thing I ever heard," said Zoe, laughing.

"Well," admitted Lucy, also laughing, "it was a unique situation. But you've got to admit guys are nice to girls they're attracted to, and offering help is one way to get acquainted. You're very pretty. He even said so."

"He was just being polite," said Zoe.

"Maybe a bit too polite, too charming. I think you should keep things on a professional level. He's really too old, too worldly for a girl your age." Lucy sighed. "There are lots of nice boys at Winchester. Boys like Hank," she said, naming a boy Sara had dated the previous winter. "He was so nice. I don't know why Sara dropped him."

"For your information, Hank DeVries is a big loser and a druggie," said Zoe, clicking off the TV and picking up the textbooks and notebooks lying on the coffee table. "I've got to study."

"You must be thinking of somebody else," protested Lucy. "Hank was really into diving. Sarah met him at the college dive club. He was very fit and athletic . . . and smart, too. I thought he was a really nice boy."

"Mom, you should hear yourself," said Zoe, tucking the books into the crook of her arm. "*Nice* is just a code word for white and Protestant. You say that you don't approve of Matt because he's too old for me but what you really mean is that he's Latino, he's got dark skin and black hair, and he's probably Catholic. You'd rather have me go out with Hank, who's blond and Episcopalian and wears L.L. Bean boat shoes without socks year round."

"He wears duck boots in winter, like everyone else," said Lucy, stung by Zoe's accusation. "And I don't object to Matt because of his skin or hair. It's because of his age and the way he's so slick, so polished. It's nothing but charm. He's not sincere, and I don't trust him."

"But you trust Hank? That's a laugh. He's a dropout. He hangs around the college to score drugs."

"I can't believe that," said Lucy.

"Well, it's true. His family is all screwed up. He had a brother who was killed in a skiing accident. His parents are divorced. His father is a beach bum somewhere in the Caribbean and his mother sells crystals in Sedona."

"I had no idea," admitted Lucy, picturing the SCUBA enthusiast she remembered. "He seemed so clean-cut and helpful and open. I thought I could read him like a book."

"Well, it turns out the Book of Hank has some plot twists," said Zoe, leaving the room.

"I guess so," said Lucy, following her into the kitchen.

Zoe continued up the back stairs to her room, and Lucy began the job of packing the donuts on trays and covering them with plastic wrap.

Next morning, the phone rang while Lucy was getting ready for the stakeout.

"I've got that stomach virus that's going around and I'm not leaving the house," said Ted. "Believe me, nobody would want to be anywhere in my vicinity."

"That's too bad," said Lucy sympathetically, cradling the earpiece on her shoulder and pulling on a second pair of socks. "I was kind of looking forward to going undercover."

"Go ahead without me," said Ted. "This is an important story and we need to get right on it."

"I don't think I should go by myself," said Lucy, shoving her foot into a duck boot. "It might be dangerous."

"There's plenty of cover at the pond," said Ted. "And these folks are probably pretty focused on contacting the dealer and scoring. They won't be noticing the scenery."

"From what I saw the other day it seems they do come and go pretty fast," said Lucy, remembering that Chief Kirwan had told her the dealer was known to the department and wasn't considered dangerous. "I'll give it a try, but if I don't feel comfortable I'm getting out of there."

"That's my favorite investigative reporter!" declared Ted. "Uh, gotta go," he added quickly, ending the call.

Lucy wiggled her other foot into a duck boot and checked her appearance in the full-length mirror. She looked pretty pudgy, she decided, and no wonder since she was wearing many layers of clothing. She'd started with her usual bra and panties, adding a thermal top and leggings. Then she'd slipped on a turtleneck shirt, a pair of jeans, a sweater and a fleece vest. She'd topped it all off with a pair of camo-print hunting pants she borrowed from Bill, as well as a pair of his thick socks, which were making her duck boots feel awfully tight.

Of course, she told herself, she wasn't dressing for a fashion show. She was dressing for a chilly morning in the Maine woods. Once downstairs she filled a thermos with hot coffee and put on her warmest parka, as well as a wool hat with a pompom and a pair of lined gloves. She was tempted to add Bill's big mittens over the gloves, but figured they would be too cumbersome for taking photos.

Libby had watched her every move as she prepared to leave,

growing more and more excited every minute, certain that she would also be going on this outdoor excursion.

"Sorry," said Lucy, patting her on the head. "Next time."

The nippy air stung her cheeks when she stepped out onto the back porch and she congratulated herself on dressing so warmly. She was going to need every layer if she was going to stay out in the cold for several hours. She felt like the Michelin tire man as she made her way to the car, which she decided was her best option for getting to the pond, and in case she needed to make a quick escape. As Ted had reminded her, there was plenty of cover from evergreens, and she planned to leave the car on the old logging road a short distance from the parking area.

As she drove down the unpaved road, she felt a sense of mounting excitement. This was a lot better than sitting in that awful basement meeting room at the town hall and listening to the local power players argue about authentic historical paint colors or raising the price of a dump sticker. She loved getting out of the office and away from the computer, chasing down stories that really mattered. That was the best part of her job and she didn't get to do it enough.

She was really getting pretty fired up. Her sunglasses were getting foggy and she was perspiring. No wonder, she realized, glancing at the indicator on the dashboard. Somebody, probably Bill, had set the heat at seventy degrees. She switched it off and opened the windows, letting the cold air blow in for the last quarter mile or so. Finally reaching the spot she had in mind, she pulled the SUV into a small clearing, parked, and got out.

Once standing, she discovered she really needed to pee. She should have thought of this before she left the house, and before she'd pulled on all those clothes, she decided as she struggled to undress enough to relieve herself. That task done and her clothing rearranged, she made her way down the path toward the parking area beside the pond, carrying a big tote bag with her camera, notebook, coffee thermos, and energy bars. As she drew nearer, she scouted for a good observation post and was pleased to discover a bushy young fir tree growing beside a large bulletin board where various notices were posted. It was especially good for her purposes because there was a small gap between the tree and the sign which gave her a good view of the parking lot.

She set her tote bag on the ground and pulled out her camera, checking the battery level and peering through the viewfinder at the empty parking area. Reassured that she could get a clear shot, she looped the cord around her neck, letting the camera rest on her chest, and pulled out her notebook. Flipping it open she wrote down the date, time, and place. Observing there was still no action in the parking area, she tucked the notebook into her pocket and grabbed the thermos. After filling the cup, which felt pleasantly warm in her hands, she wished she'd thought to bring something to sit on. Her back was starting to ache a bit and it would be nice to be able to get off her feet.

Nevertheless, she told herself, it was a lovely morning. Chickadees were flitting around in the trees, some even perching on nearby branches and giving her a once over.

"Dee-dee-dee yourself," she whispered, taking a sip of coffee. There was nothing like hot black coffee on a chilly morning, she decided, savoring each swallow and promptly draining the plastic cup.

She was beginning to wonder if perhaps she'd arrived too early in the morning to catch any drug-dealing activity. Now that she thought about it, it seemed that drug-dependent individuals might not be early risers. Maybe they had to sleep off their high, like drinkers with hangovers. She poured herself another cup of coffee and sipped it while she peered through her peephole.

The coffee cooled rapidly in the chilly air, and her cup was soon empty again. She was reaching for the thermos to refill it when she realized she was going to have to pee again, and soon. What to do? She suspected that the moment she finally freed herself from her clothing and squatted down to relieve herself would be the very moment the drug dealer decided to make his appearance. She was simply going to have to hold it, she told herself, noticing that a chickadee had now perched on the handle of her tote bag and was cocking his black-capped head one way and another, apparently believing she kept sunflower seeds in there.

"Shoo!" she hissed, afraid that the little birds gathering around her were probably used to begging from swimmers and picnickers and would give her away. The birds were unmoved, which was probably for the best. A cloud of birds rising all at once would certainly have tipped off the drug dealer. Not that there was a drug dealer or any customers in the parking area.

Lucy checked her watch and discovered she'd been watching and waiting for over an hour and nothing had happened. Maybe drugs were only sold on Tuesdays and Thursdays but never on Fridays. Maybe the delivery had been late. Maybe the dealer had been arrested. Maybe it was time to call it a day, head home, and have a nice, long pee in the comfort of her downstairs powder room.

It was a tempting idea, especially since she was beginning to shiver in the cold. She was stamping her feet and waving her arms, trying to warm up, when she heard the purr of an engine. A car! This was it! She grabbed the camera and raised it to her eyes, clicking away as the black BMW came into view. It was followed by an aged orange pickup truck, a truck that she recognized because it had been parked in her driveway many times last winter.

Lucy watched with dismay as she recognized the familiar figure of Hank DeVries leaning down from the window of his truck to give something to the person in the BMW. The deal completed, the BMW zoomed off, but Hank lingered, sitting in the truck.

Horrified, Lucy broke cover and marched right over to the truck. "Hank! What do you think you're doing?" He'd grown thinner, she saw, and needed a shave and a haircut. It looked as if he'd been wearing the same clothes for too long. His hooded sweatshirt was grubby and shapeless.

Startled in the act of rolling up his sleeve, Hank jumped and dropped the bit of rubber tubing he was holding. "What are you doing here?" he demanded.

"Bird watching," said Lucy. "What are you doing?"

Hank hesitated as if trying to think up a plausible excuse, then gave a big sigh. "You know what I was doing. I was going to shoot up."

"That's terrible. You have to stop. You'll end up killing yourself."

"I'd like to stop. Believe me," he said.

Lucy did. "I know it's hard . . ."

"It's more than hard. It's impossible." His eyes were dull. He'd lost the sparkle and energy that had made him so attractive last winter.

"You should go to rehab. There are places that can help you."

He snorted. "They'll help you if you've got ten thousand dollars. I don't."

"There must be a way," said Lucy. "What about your folks?"

Hank was fidgeting. Dirty fingers picked at the worn, frayed cuff of his sweatshirt. "They've got their own problems. They don't need me to add to them."

Lucy guessed that he didn't want his parents to know about his addiction and she understood why. He wanted them to be proud of him, to approve of him. "There must be programs—"

"Ten thousand dollars. That's what they want. Then they'll let you in." He was beginning to shake, and Lucy realized he needed his fix.

She wanted to help him but knew it would be cruel to prolong his agony. "Well, I gotta go. But do you really mean it? Do you really want to go to rehab? If I find something for you, will you go?"

He was wrapping the rubber tube around his fingers. "I'll do it," he said.

Her heart sinking, Lucy walked away, picturing Hank injecting himself with heroin like the actors she'd seen faking it in countless TV shows. This was real, though, and she knew that sooner or later he'd overdose.

But please, God, not today.

Fearful that he might overdose, she went back to her post behind the bush and waited until he drove off. Then she picked up her tote bag and walked slowly back to her car, determined to find a way to help him.

CHAPTER 8

"Lucy Stone, you never made those donuts yourself," accused Sue Finch when Lucy proudly presented them at the festival. Sue had dressed for the Harvest Festival and was wearing a professional chef's apron over her chic buffalo plaid flannel shirt and skinny black jeans.

Transporting six dozen donuts had presented quite a challenge, and Lucy was proud of her solution. She'd borrowed the Legos she kept for her grandson Patrick to play with and had constructed a six story tower which she'd placed inside a sturdy picnic cooler. She was carefully unpacking the trays of donuts, arranging them in a neat pyramid on the baked goods table, which was already loaded with a mouth-watering assortment of homemade cakes, cookies, and pies.

"What do you mean?" she protested. "I'm a good cook."

Once her donuts were safely arranged on the table, she took a look around. The entire fellowship hall at the Community Church had been turned over for the festival and was filled with row upon row of folding tables offering gently used books and household items, homemade knitted items, baskets, and other crafts, all watched over by volunteer salesladies. The festival was very popular and even though the doors hadn't yet opened a small crowd had gathered outside. Inside, the volunteers were chatting, catching up on gossip, and admiring each other's contributions to the sale.

"You must have bought them!" exclaimed Sue, still dubious about the provenance of Lucy's donuts. "And if you did, where did you get them? They look fabulous."

"I didn't buy them," said Lucy. "Zoe made them with help from Matt Rodriguez."

"The cute kid with the 'Vette?" asked Sue.

"He's no kid," replied Lucy, "but he is a trained chef. His dad is Rey Rodriguez. You've probably seen his TV show."

"Oh, right. I have one of his cookbooks. Really creative, delicious recipes."

"Well, Rey has bought the Olde Irish Pub and plans to turn it into a fusion restaurant called Cali Kitchen, and Matt is going to manage it. Zoe interviewed for a job there and Matt took a shine to her and that's how I have these beautiful apple cider donuts."

"They sure are beautiful," said Pam, stopping by for a quick chat before the sale opened. "You've put us all to shame."

"I can't take credit for them. Zoe made them with help from Matt Rodriguez," confessed Lucy again.

"It looks like the Stone family will be enjoying world-class cuisine if Matt continues to court Zoe," said Sue.

"Zoe has a new boyfriend?" asked Pam.

"I sincerely hope not," said Lucy. "Matt Rodriguez is much too old and sophisticated for her. The very idea makes me uncomfortable."

"You're sure you're not being prejudicial?" asked Pam.

"Oh, probably," admitted Lucy. "But it's not his Latino heritage that bothers me. It's his age. He must be at least thirty, and Zoe's only eighteen."

The sound of a teaspoon tapping on a glass silenced Lucy and the other volunteers. Festival chairman Bessie Bone thanked everyone for their efforts and announced the sale was now open. There was a smattering of applause as the doors were opened and the eager customers rushed in.

The Harvest Festival had become well-known through the years for the quality of the crafts that were offered, especially the knits and baskets, and there was a good deal of rushing about as patrons searched out their favorites. Lucy and Sue's table was at the rear of the hall and didn't attract much attention at first, but word soon spread about the donuts, which people said were better than ever this year. They were all gone when Rachel arrived with Miss Tilley; all that remained on the baked goods table was a single blueberry pie with a rather burnt crust.

Julia Ward Howe Tilley—nobody but her closest and oldest friends dared to call her by her first name—was the retired librarian of the Broadbrooks Free Library and the town's oldest resident by at least a decade. Rachel was her home health aide, a position that had evolved from her friendship with the old woman following an automobile accident.

"Well, where are the donuts?" demanded Miss Tilley. "I always buy a half-dozen."

"Sorry," said Sue, "we're all sold out. All we have is this blueberry pie."

"My mother always used to say a pie doesn't have to look good to taste good," said Lucy, attempting to close the deal. "I think we could offer a substantial discount."

"Blueberry pie is a Maine tradition," said Rachel.

"Are they Maine blueberries?" asked Miss Tilley, eyeing the pie suspiciously.

"I'm sure they are," said Sue. "Franny Small made that pie and nobody is more Maine than Franny. She wouldn't use berries from the supermarket."

"You could ask her," said Pam, waving to Franny, who was standing at a nearby table.

Franny spotted Pam's frantic waving and came over, a big smile on her face. "The sale is a big success. My table is sold out."

"Miss Tilley is thinking of buying this pie you brought, but she wants to know if it contains Maine berries," said Sue.

"Of course it does. I wouldn't use anything else. I picked them myself out by Blueberry Pond and froze them. Last summer was a good year for berries. I got tons." Franny paused, and a shadow fell over her face. "But I don't know if I've got the heart to pick next summer—not after that poor girl died at the pond. I know that's all I'll think about now, every time I see that pond."

They all fell silent, thinking about Alison's tragic death, and even though they all had something they wanted to say, nobody wanted to be the first to speak.

It fell to Miss Tilley to break the awkward silence. "So sad when a young person dies."

"And a lot are dying from this opioid epidemic," said Rachel. "They overdose or get tainted drugs."

"I'm working on a story about drugs here in town," said Lucy.

"Here in Tinker's Cove. My goodness," said Franny, her eyes wide.

"Drugs are everywhere," said Sue. "It really is an epidemic."

"I simply don't understand why they do it," said Pam. "I'm high on life. I wouldn't risk my life for some synthetic version."

"I doubt very much that Alison Franklin died of an overdose," said Miss Tilley.

They all turned to look at her.

"Why do you say that?" asked Lucy.

"Because she was so healthy and athletic. I used to see her running by my house every morning when I opened the door to get my morning paper. She was always on time and she used to give me a big smile and wave at me."

"That doesn't mean she wasn't using drugs," said Rachel. "Or maybe it was her first time."

"Nonsense," snapped Miss Tilley. "I've been around for a long time and, well, you just get a feeling for people. She gave every impression of being a happy, healthy person. She radiated optimism."

Lucy couldn't help thinking that Miss Tilley was drawing a lot of conclusions from very little evidence, but didn't want to contradict her.

Sue had no such compunctions. "That's ridiculous!" she exclaimed. "You couldn't tell all that from seeing her run past your house."

"Do you know her father is married to a woman the same age as Alison?" asked Franny. "And she's pregnant."

"Her father is Ed Franklin," said Pam. "Imagine being related to him."

"He is terrible, I admit that," said Miss Tilley. "That big gold *F* on his chimney! So tasteless. But I have observed that very often the more horrible and vulgar a man is, the nicer his relations are. It's as if they're aware of his shortcomings and attempting to make amends. Just think of that basketball coach we had a few years ago. His wife was the loveliest woman."

"Well, if you don't think she overdosed, how exactly do you think Alison died?" asked Lucy.

"Well, I've heard all sorts of theories about drugs and even suicide or a tragic accident," said Miss Tilley. "But I think she was murdered." She didn't even pause for breath after making that astonishing comment but went on to ask, "How much for the pie?"

Lucy was still thinking about Miss Tilley's provocative comment after the festival was over and she went on to work at the *Pennysaver* office. Phyllis had taken the afternoon off to help her husband, Wilf, who was having cataract surgery, and Ted was covering a regional conference on flood insurance, so she had the place to herself. After she'd uploaded the photos she took at the sale, she googled drug rehab programs and made a few phone calls. She was surprised to learn that Hank was right and the programs did require up-front payment.

"These folks are drug addicts," said the admission counselor at a place in New Hampshire called New Beginnings. "We want them to commit to getting clean. Recovery is not easy. Our program is four weeks long and even with the big financial cost we have dropouts."

"What about health insurance?" asked Lucy, who had opened a file in her computer and was entering the counselor's comments with an eye to including them in the series on drug addiction. "Drug addiction is a disease, after all."

"It varies depending on the policy," said the counselor. "But it's an unusual patient who has coverage. By the time they come to us, they've pretty much bottomed out. Health insurance is usually tied to employment and most of our folks don't have jobs."

"So how do they come up with the money?" asked Lucy.

"Family, friends, people who love them. Parents often patch together the money using several credit cards."

"Ten thousand dollars is a lot of love," said Lucy, "especially if you're paying twenty percent interest."

"It is indeed," said the counselor. "But it's not uncommon. We actually have a waiting list."

"Let's add my young friend to the list," said Lucy on impulse, figuring that it was worth taking a chance. Maybe, just maybe, something would come up and Hank could go to rehab. In any case, the difficulty of getting into a rehab program would definitely be part of the series on drug addiction.

She remained at her desk after completing the call, cleaning up the file which she'd typed while talking on the phone. The whole situation was depressing, she thought, thinking of the mess these young people got themselves into and the difficulty of getting out. What future did Hank have if he couldn't get clean? She hated to think of him becoming a homeless straggler, relying on the food pantry for something to eat, or even worse, dying of an overdose. What a waste of a promising young man!

The sound of a police siren penetrated her dark mood and she brightened up, realizing it was signaling the start of the high school football team's pregame parade and rally, which she was supposed to cover for the paper. The team was having a successful year and would play on Saturday in the semifinal for the state championship. She quickly put on her warm jacket and grabbed her bag, heading out to join the folks lining Main Street where a police cruiser with flashing lights and wailing siren was leading the procession.

The parade was a homegrown affair, featuring the high school marching band, civic groups, and of course, the town's four fire trucks. The highlight of the parade was a flatbed truck carrying the uniformed team members, most looking rather self-conscious at all the attention.

Lucy waved and clapped as the various marchers went past, joining the cheerful watchers standing on the sidewalk. She snapped photos of the high school kids in the marching band, the team members, and Jason Marzetti (Joe Marzetti's kid) dressed for some reason as Uncle Sam and walking on stilts. The ladies from Fran's Famous Fudge tossed wrapped candy to the kids, and she got a great photo of a little blond tyke catching a piece in mid-air.

The kid was adorable, a fair-haired and ruddy-cheeked angel, and Lucy found herself wondering if she would characterize a black child with a curly Afro as adorable and angelic, but hoped she would. She was suddenly looking at the crowd with new eyes, realizing that it was entirely white and mostly adult. Of course, Maine had a very small minority population, but somehow she had never realized that fact. How had she lived in this town for several decades without realizing this?

She had grown up in New York City, riding the subway to her high school, sharing the train with all sorts of people—Hasidic Jews in hats and long black coats, elderly Asian women with shopping bags, mixed-race couples holding hands. She visited Boston from time to time, and there she saw Muslim women in head scarves, African-American women wearing kente cloth dresses and turbans and big gold earrings, and lots of kids of all races.

Looking at the rather thin crowd with new eyes, she was shocked to realize most of the people were senior citizens. It wasn't only Tinker's Cove, she knew, that was largely old and white. It was most of rural New England, and no wonder. Property was expensive, housing was limited, and good jobs were even scarcer than affordable houses. There had even been warnings from demographers that the trend couldn't continue, as there wouldn't be enough young workers to care for the aging population. She hadn't really paid attention, but there it was—the proof—right in front of her. Not only was she getting older, all her friends and neighbors were, too. And their children hadn't stayed in Tinker's Cove but had left following high school to attend college elsewhere and make their lives in economically vibrant places like Portland, Boston, and New York.

Yet another siren was announcing the arrival of the cheerleaders, and Lucy made sure to catch some good photos of the girls atop the hook and ladder. They were dressed in the school colors and, unlike the boys on the team, were tossing candy to the crowd and enjoying all the attention.

Putting her camera down, she gave the girls a big wave and one tossed a miniature chocolate bar her way. She caught it and tore off the wrapper, eating it as she walked along the street to the

262 Leslie Meier

church where she'd parked her car that morning. As she walked, she thought about the circuitous path that had brought her to Tinker's Cove.

She hadn't been born and raised in the little Maine town. Her family had been New Yorkers way back, tracing their ancestry to the early Dutch settlers of what was then Nieuw Amsterdam. Through the centuries, there had been various additions from Sweden, England, and Germany, but it was a matter of pride to her father that his ancestors had fought in the American Revolution, the Civil War, and two World Wars. While in college, she'd met Bill, whose ancestors included more recent arrivals from Ireland. After working for a few years on Wall Street, he'd begun dreaming of a simpler life as a restoration carpenter and they'd moved to Maine, buying the ramshackle farmhouse on Red Top Road and fixing it up.

Their story was typical, she thought. Everybody in America, except for the Native Americans, came from someplace else. And Americans didn't tend to stay put, either. Members of both their families had gone west and south. Bill's parents now lived in Florida; she had cousins in Texas and Virginia. The country was a big jumble of people from all over, who continued to restlessly follow their dreams. That was the whole point about America, she thought, beginning with the earliest settlers.

The parade over, the crowd was breaking up and the sidewalk was filled with people heading home. The afternoon light was already fading and the sky was taking on a pinkish hue. She'd reached Sea Street when she got stuck behind a young mother pushing a stroller and dragging along a tired preschooler, and was trying to get past when she heard people shouting. Turning toward the noise she looked down Sea Street to the harbor where she saw a crowd gathered in the parking area.

She was tired and hungry, having skipped lunch, and wanted to go home, but she was a reporter and duty called. Reluctantly, she turned left and walked down Sea Street to see what the fuss was all about.

As she drew closer, she realized the group was somewhat organized, engaged in a protest in front of the former Olde Irish Pub which now had signs in the window announcing new ownership.

COMING SOON! CALI KITCHEN! She knew that Bill had planned to meet Rey there this afternoon to go over the final plans for the renovation and spotted his truck in the parking lot.

Some of the people in the crowd also had signs. AMERICA FOR AMERICANS was one. Another read MEXICANS GO HOME.

She was snapping photos when the camera was snatched from her hand and she turned to protest. "Give that back!" she demanded, facing a man she recognized.

It was Jason Sprinkle, who owned a plumbing business.

"No photos," he growled in a threatening tone, giving the camera back. "And if you know what's good for you, you'll get out of here."

"What do you mean?" she demanded as a thrown rock smashed one of the restaurant windows, shattering the glass and shredding the paper sign.

CHAPTER 9

Lucy instinctively ducked and moved away from the group of demonstrators. Seeking shelter, she found it in the harbormaster's shack where Harry Crawford was watching the scene from the open doorway. As soon as she stepped inside, he closed the door and locked it. The little waterfront office was about the same size as a highway tollbooth, and gave a 360-degree view of the harbor and parking lot. He quickly began closing the miniblinds, at the same time calling the police department to report the situation.

"They're throwing rocks," exclaimed Lucy, who was standing by a window and peeking through the slats of the miniblind. "My husband's in there with Rey Rodriguez." The sun was sinking fast and the sky was now a fiery red, casting a lurid glow that was reflected in the pub's remaining windows.

"I've got a situation down here at the harbor," Harry said, speaking into the phone. "There's a mob protest that's turning violent."

Lucy was hanging on every word, at the same time following the action outside, terribly fearful for Bill's safety.

When Harry put the phone down, his worried expression wasn't encouraging.

"I don't think we're going to get much help, at least not right away. All the officers are working the pep rally." He still bore traces of the tan he'd acquired during the summer when he was out on the water every day patrolling the harbor. Peeking through the blinds, he was also keeping an eye on the protesters, and he remained on the line, updating the dispatcher on the demonstration. Turning to Lucy he asked, "Who's out there anyway? The dispatcher wants to know."

"I recognized Jason Sprinkle and Link Peterson. He used to play Little League with my son, Toby," said Lucy. "I think it's mostly those guys who hang out at the roadhouse on Route 1, like Zeke Bumpus. Not exactly up-and-comers."

Harry nodded. "I call 'em Left Behinds, guys like me, except they weren't lucky enough to get full-time jobs with benefits. Those guys have a lot of resentment. I've felt it when I've had to deal with them for going too fast in the no-wake zone or fouling the water."

"This isn't a spontaneous thing. It didn't just happen. Somebody must have organized this," said Lucy, watching nervously as a handful of bearded and leather-suited newcomers arrived on motorcycles, roaring into the harbor parking area to join the demonstration. They were greeted with a loud roar from the crowd, some of whom were holding signs that they waved enthusiastically. The lights in the parking lot had now switched on and Lucy could clearly see the crowd's enthusiastic reaction. There was a great deal of hand shaking and backslapping, and a roar of approval when one of the motorcyclists produced a heavy chain from his saddlebag and displayed it in a menacing manner.

"I don't like this at all," said Lucy, thinking of Bill and Rey, who were trapped inside the restaurant. "Where are the cops? This is more important than the parade. What about the sheriff or the state troopers?"

She was nervously shifting her weight from one foot to the other and biting her lip as she peered out the window through the slats of a miniblind.

Harry came to a decision. "It would take them a half hour to get here, minimum. It's up to me. I'm gonna go tell them to disperse," he said. "I'm responsible for security here at the harbor. It's my job. I can't just hide in here."

"You can't go out there by yourself, all alone," protested Lucy. "There's at least thirty of them and only one of you. You need reinforcements with riot gear."

"The cavalry's not coming," said Harry, ducking through the door just as a woman's scream pierced the chilly air.

All heads turned, including Lucy's. She had stepped into the open doorway and immediately spotted Ruth Lawson, the Community Church organist, standing between two parked cars, shrieking and pointing into the larger one, a black SUV parked beneath a tall streetlight.

"He's bleeding!" she yelled.

Harry immediately changed direction, abandoning the demonstrators and running toward the frantic woman. He yelled over his shoulder to Lucy, telling her to call 9-1-1 and to bring the first aid kit that hung on the wall.

Lucy grabbed the kit and began running toward the SUV, using her cell phone to call for help. She and Harry were the first to reach Ruth, a tall woman whose steel gray hair was tightly permed, but the demonstrators soon came charging across the lot from the restaurant to the line of parked cars. Lucy realized the SUV was Ed Franklin's Range Rover, and a quick glance through the shattered driver's-side window revealed he was beyond help. A good part of his skull was gone and blood was spattered everywhere, as well as globs of matter she thought must be bits of his brain. The first aid box was useless. Recoiling at the gruesome sight, she turned to Ruth, wrapping her free arm around the shaking woman's shoulders. She didn't feel all that steady herself, she realized, as she led the sobbing woman away.

Harry had placed himself between the restless crowd of gawkers and the Range Rover and was warning everyone to stand back. "This is a crime scene. Police are on the way."

"I saw him in the car, like he was sitting there waiting for someone," babbled Ruth. "But the angle of his head wasn't right. I thought he might've been taken ill or something, so I went closer to check on him and then I saw the—"

"I know, I know," said Lucy, guiding her to the harbormaster's shack. "Don't think about it."

"We should help him!" protested Ruth. "Get an ambulance!"

"Help is coming," said Lucy. "Harry's there. He's got things under control."

But even as she spoke, she doubted that Harry could actually control the rowdy crowd for very long. They'd been shocked into silence at first, but who knew how long that would last. Sooner or later they'd be looking for someone to blame, and she was afraid that person would be Rey . . . or even Bill, guilty by association.

She tried not to worry, focusing on Ruth, who was badly shaken. Reaching the harbormaster's shack she set the first aid box down on the wooden step and awkwardly opened the door, still supporting Ruth who was leaning heavily on her arm. She guided Ruth inside and helped her into the office chair, then switched on the electric kettle Harry kept in the shack. He was a tea drinker and all the makings were handy, so Lucy dropped a tea bag into a cup with shaking hands, and yanked up the blind so she could watch out the window while waiting for the water to boil.

The kettle was finally starting to steam when she saw one of the town's two police cruisers coming down Sea Street with lights flashing and siren blaring, followed by the fire department's ambulance. The two vehicles drove smoothly down the steep hill and into the parking area, stopping just short of the crowd. She continued to watch, glancing away only briefly to fill the cup with steaming water and to add two packets of sugar, then saw her friend, Officer Barney Culpepper, getting out of the cruiser. The flashing lights on the ambulance and cruiser were like a visual drum beat, ramping up the tense atmosphere, as he faced the crowd.

Barney was a big man who had been a cop for most of his life and wore his uniform easily, expecting and getting respect, even if it was sometimes granted grudgingly. Only a very foolish person would attempt to tangle with him. He immediately began ordering the onlookers to step back, then after a quick look into the Range Rover got right onto his radio, reporting the death. He also cautioned the EMTs who were unloading a gurney from the ambulance, holding up his hands in a stop signal so they wouldn't touch the body. The two EMTs shoved the gurney back inside the ambulance, then climbed back inside the cab, awaiting further instructions.

Lucy held the tea bag by the string and nervously jiggled it a few times to hasten the steeping. As soon as the water turned the proper shade of amber she handed the cup to Ruth, ordering her to drink it and telling her she had to go out but promising to return as quickly as possible.

Lucy hurried, winding her way through the rows of parked cars to the Range Rover, which was now illuminated by a spotlight. The crowd was still in place, refusing to disperse. She quickly snapped some photos, then drew close enough to hear what people were saying.

"We know who did it," claimed Link, getting a loud buzz of approval from the demonstrators.

"No we don't," said Barney, planting himself firmly on his thick-soled regulation black oxfords and staring the crowd down. "You'll get your chance to talk. The state police are on the way. Nobody leave. They're going to want to question everyone."

That silenced the crowd momentarily until Jason Sprinkle spoke up. "We got nothing to fear. It wasn't any of us. It was that Mexican kid, Matteo, who shot him. I saw him standing right here in this spot," he claimed, pointing at the Range Rover. "I even heard a pop, but I didn't think nothing of it. It's noisy here at the cove. Guys are prepping their boats for the winter, you know."

"That's ridiculous. You don't know what you're talking about," declared Rey, who had left the restaurant along with Bill when the cruiser arrived. He'd heard Jason's accusation.

"You calling me a liar?" challenged Jason, practically nose to nose with Rey.

"I'm just saying that my son would never shoot anybody," said Rey, stepping back. "He doesn't even own a gun."

"Who was shot?" asked Bill, taking his place beside Lucy.

Relieved that he was in one piece, she slipped her hand into his.

"Ed Franklin." She saw Rey start as if he'd received an electric shock, then quickly recover, adopting a serious expression. "Ruth Lawson discovered the body. She's in the shack," Lucy continued, speaking to Barney. "Is it okay if I take her home? She's pretty shaken up."

"No problem," said Barney with a nod, taking down Ruth's name in the leather-covered notebook he preferred to the electronic tablets recently issued by the department. "I know where you both live" He turned back to the crowd. "As for the rest of you, let's keep it peaceful. The state police are on the way and they're going to want to interview everyone, so nobody else leaves." He surveyed the group, letting his eyes rest on each and every one there, letting them know they'd been seen and noted. "And I don't have to tell you that the DA won't hesitate to prosecute anyone interfering with the investigation or anyone taking the law into their own hands."

Lucy sensed a certain rumbling hostility among the demonstrators, but took heart from the fact that the state police were on the way. After receiving a reassuring squeeze from Bill, she reluctantly withdrew her hand from his then went back to the shack. She wasn't entirely comfortable about leaving the scene, feeling that it was her responsibility as a reporter to cover the shooting, but also aware that she had a rare opportunity to question the prime witness.

When she reached the shack she found Ruth sitting motionless in the desk chair, her mug of tea in her hands, untouched.

"We've got permission to leave," Lucy told her. "I'll take you home."

"Are you sure?"

"I'm absolutely sure," said Lucy. "I told Officer Culpepper that you discovered the body . . ."

"Body!" whispered Ruth, trembling so violently that Lucy feared she would spill the tea. "You mean he's dead?"

Lucy pried Ruth's hands from the mug and set it down on the desk before answering. "I'm afraid so."

"Oh, noooo," wailed Ruth. "That's awful!"

"I think we should get moving before the state police arrive and the parking lot is blocked off," Lucy said, taking Ruth's hands and pulling her to her feet. "Let's get you home."

"I still don't feel right about leaving," protested Ruth. "I was the one who found the . . . the body."

"I told Barney all about it and he said they'll interview you at home where you'll be a lot more comfortable." Lucy opened the door. "My car is right over there."

Ruth stopped short in the doorway. "But what about my car?"

"You can pick it up tomorrow. I'll drive you over if you want. But right now you're in no state to drive."

"Well, I don't know—" protested Ruth.

"I do," said Lucy, giving her a hug. "You've had a traumatic experience and you're in shock."

"So much blood," said Ruth, allowing herself to be led out of the shack and across the parking lot to Lucy's SUV. "I never saw so much blood."

"It was awful." Lucy opened the passenger side door and helped Ruth climb in.

She sat passively while Lucy fastened the seatbelt.

Then Lucy went around the car, got behind the wheel, fastened her own seatbelt, and started the car. "Did you see anyone near Ed's car? Anyone at all?" she asked as she backed out of the parking space.

"No. I saw that bunch at the pub, the old pub, and wondered what it was all about. It made me think twice about parking at the harbor. I almost went back to my car to park it somewhere else. I was on my way to the church—I like to practice the hymns before Sunday, you know—and I knew I wouldn't find a parking space there because the volunteers would be cleaning up after the Harvest Festival and folks would also be parking there for the pep rally parade." Ruth was gaining strength as she spoke, finding relief in the distraction of conversation.

"The festival always attracts a big crowd and this year was no different," said Lucy, turning onto Main Street just in time to see State Police Detective Lieutenant Horowitz's unmarked car coming the other way, blue lights flashing.

"The crafts are rather expensive, in my opinion," said Ruth, eager for the distraction of chatting, "but of course it all goes to a good cause. I asked Sue Finch to save me a nice mince pie. They're not very popular these days. I guess they're rather strong tasting for a lot of people, very spicy you know, but they're my aunt's favorite and I always try to have one for her."

"My mother loved mince pie," said Lucy, thinking that at this rate she'd never get any information from Ruth. "I made—well, actually it was my daughter who did the cooking. She made six dozen apple cider donuts."

"My goodness! That must have been quite a job."

"It was indeed, but she had help from a friend," said Lucy, who was struggling to reconcile Link Peterson's accusation against Matt with the agreeable guy who'd helped Zoe make the donuts. "I'm just curious. What made you look in Ed's car? Did you see something suspicious? Did you hear anything? See anyone?"

"I'm afraid I was just being nosey," admitted Ruth. In a hushed voice she defended herself. "I'm not usually like that, you know, but I'd seen that car around town and I wondered what it was. It's not like the other cars, you know, the ones like this one. You see a lot of these and I suppose they're very nice and all . . ."

"Do you mean SUVs?" asked Lucy, somewhat amused.

"If that's what they're called, I suppose so. Hondas and Toyotas and Nissans . . . they're all Japanese, aren't they?"

"Ford and Chevy make them. Jeep too. I think every car manufacturer makes SUVs. They're very popular."

"Well, my father always used to say to buy American, and I've found my Dodge to be very satisfactory."

"They have a very good reputation," said Lucy, turning into Ruth's empty driveway. "But you were curious about Ed Franklin's Range Rover?"

"I was," said Ruth, picking up her handbag and squeezing the handles. "It's taller than the other UVS cars and it's the only one that looks like that. I wondered what it was, so I walked over and saw it's called a Range Rover. I think those are English or something."

"They are."

"I suppose they're very expensive, since he is so rich," said Ruth, suddenly realizing the need to correct herself. "Since he *was* so rich and all."

"I imagine so," said Lucy.

"I noticed that the windows are all tinted, not that I would have looked into the car. That's sort of a private place. But the driver's side window was down . . ."

Actually, shattered by the bullet that killed Ed, thought Lucy.

"Well, anyway, I could see right in and I wish I hadn't," concluded Ruth, reaching for the door handle.

"Do you want me to come in? Just to make sure you're all right."

Ruth looked at her with her muddy brown eyes and grabbed her hand in a surprisingly strong grip. "I don't want to be any trouble, but it would be so kind of you."

"No problem," said Lucy, hoping to get more information out of her.

"You see, I never lock my door," said Ruth as they walked up the path together toward the door, eerily illuminated by a yellow bulb that was not supposed to attract moths. "It always seems such a bother, but I suppose it's rather foolish. Anyone could walk in and steal me blind." Reaching the stoop, she paused. "Or worse."

Lucy knew that locked doors were a rarity in the little town where everybody knew everybody. "Well, I always think that if somebody wants to break in, a lock isn't going to stop them."

"I suppose you're right," said Ruth, who had stopped in front of the closed front door. "I mean, even if Ed Franklin had locked the doors of his car, it wouldn't have made any difference."

"No, it wouldn't," agreed Lucy, wondering why Ruth wasn't opening the door to her house. "Shall we go in?" she prompted.

"I know there's really nothing to fear but . . ."

"I'll go first," said Lucy, turning the knob and switching on the light.

The door opened into a small hall with a stairway; the floor had been painted gray and spattered with beige, yellow, and white in the old-fashioned style, and a braided rug served as a doormat. A prim and proper living room dominated by an upright piano was on one side of the hall, a dining room with a polished mahogany table holding a milk glass bowl of obviously fake fruit was on the other, with the kitchen behind.

"Nobody here," reported Lucy, after taking a quick look. "I'll just run upstairs."

Upstairs she found two neat and tidy bedrooms, each with white ruffled curtains and a double bed covered with a white candle-wick bedspread. She considered peeking in the closets and looking under the beds but decided that would be overkill. The house was definitely empty.

Going downstairs she found Ruth in the old-fashioned kitchen where a small table with two chairs painted red sat on a linoleum floor beneath a plastic wall clock shaped like a rooster.

Ruth was filling the kettle at the porcelain sink; an ancient red plastic dish drainer sat on the large drain board.

"I think a cup of tea is called for," she said. "All things considered."

"Absolutely," said Lucy, suddenly drained of energy and sinking into one of the chairs. "And if you have any, I'd really love a cookie or two."

Ruth produced some homemade oatmeal-raisin cookies and Lucy nibbled on one while they waited for the kettle to boil. Ruth couldn't seem to sit still and kept popping up to check the kettle and adjust the burner.

"A watched pot never boils," said Lucy with a smile.

"I know. It's just, well, I can't help worrying." Ruth paused, twisting her hands nervously. "You know, I'm a real fan of mystery shows on TV, and I know from watching them that the person who finds a body is always a suspect."

Lucy's jaw dropped. "You think the police will suspect you of killing Ed Franklin?"

"I'm afraid so," admitted Ruth.

Lucy glanced around the prim and neat house, and considered Ruth's work as a church organist. "I don't think you have anything to worry about."

Just then the kettle shrieked and Ruth grabbed a pot holder and snatched it off the stove.

"That's certainly a relief, Lucy," she said, filling the teapot. "But just to be on the safe side, I think I'll take my Glock into the station. They'll be able to tell that it hasn't been fired."

"Your Glock?" asked Lucy, shocked to her core.

CHAPTER 10

Lucy had enjoyed a half-dozen of Ruth's homemade oatmeal cookies, but she hadn't gotten any more information about her gruesome discovery. She had learned, however, that Ruth's father had given her the Glock many years before, and Ruth went straight to the shooting range every Sunday after church to practice. She had blushingly admitted she was quite a good shot, a fact that Lucy was mulling over when she finally left to go home. She had made numerous calls to Ted to tell him about Ed Franklin, but the messages had all gone to voice mail.

She was pouring herself a glass of chardonnay and wondering if Bill would be content with soup and sandwiches for supper when Ted finally called.

"Are you sure about this? Ed Franklin is dead? Shot in his car in broad daylight?"

"I'm sure," said Lucy in a grim tone. "I saw him. Blood everywhere."

"Wow," said Ted. "Any chance it was suicide?"

She paused, forcing herself to recall the sight of Ed Franklin's bloody body before she'd recoiled in horror and looked away. Ed was leaning away from the driver's side window, and all that remained of the window were a few shards of glass.

"I don't think so," she said. "The driver's side window was

broken and Ed's body was leaning away from the window. If he'd shot himself and the bullet also broke the window, I think he'd be leaning the other way. Also, I didn't see a gun in the car with him, but I didn't look for one, either. It was pretty gruesome." She paused and gulped down some wine. "There was an anti-Mexican demonstration going on in front of the old pub. It was pretty noisy so I guess nobody heard the shot. Ruth Lawson discovered the body."

"The church lady?"

"The organist."

"My word," said Ted.

"One of the demonstrators—it was actually Jason Sprinkle—claimed he saw Matt Rodriguez standing next to Ed's car. Even claims he heard a popping sound, but Rey insists his son doesn't have a gun."

"But he would have a motive," said Ted. "Ed was giving the Rodriguezes a lot of trouble."

"I bet Ed Franklin gave a lot of people a lot of trouble," said Lucy. "He was just like that. And don't forget, this is the second death in the Franklin family in a couple weeks."

"What are you saying, Lucy? That there's some sort of vendetta against the Franklins?"

"I don't know," admitted Lucy. "But it's certainly worth looking into."

That was the question Lucy pondered all weekend, and the one she wanted to pose when she went to the District Attorney's press conference on Monday morning, but she had to wait a good long while. The conference was late getting started as the conference room in the county complex proved too small for the large number of reporters assigned to cover the sensational death. Ed Franklin was a household name, known by one and all as typifying the American Dream of achieving success and untold wealth, and his murder was attracting a lot of interest.

After everyone had relocated to a larger space, actually a vacant courtroom, Phil Aucoin began by introducing representatives from the various law enforcement agencies involved in the investigation and congratulating them at length on their spirit of cooperation. Then there was a bit of a flap until the press releases he planned to distribute were found, apparently mislaid in the switch. Once found, it took only moments for the reporters to read the few printed lines and begin loud demands for more information.

"All this says is that Franklin was killed execution style by a person or persons unknown," began Deb Hildreth, who worked for a local radio station. "Do you have a theory, a motive? Are there any suspects?"

"I am unable to provide more information at this time," said Aucoin, "as it might hinder the investigation."

"Do you think Franklin's outspoken opposition to immigration might be the reason he was killed?" demanded Pete Withers, a stringer for the *Portland Press Herald*.

"I can assure the public that we are following a number of leads," said Aucoin.

"Franklin was involved in a number of failed businesses and even filed for bankruptcy a couple times," alleged Stan Hurwitz, from the *Boston Globe*. "Could the shooter be a disappointed creditor?"

"Could be," said Aucoin. "As I said, we're following a number of leads."

"Any ties to organized crime?" asked another reporter, speaking with a thick New York accent. "There were rumors . . ."

"There are always rumors about high-profile people," said Aucoin.

"What about his family?" asked Angela Hawkins, from NECN. "He had a very bitter divorce."

"Once again, we're following a number of leads," said Aucoin. "We will certainly be taking a look at everyone who had dealings with him, including his family."

Finally Aucoin pointed his finger at Lucy and she got her chance. "It's quite a coincidence that his daughter, Alison, died in a suspicious manner just a few weeks ago. Do you think there may be a vendetta against the Franklin family?"

The question caused quite a hubbub. Many of the reporters were new to the story and hadn't known about Alison Franklin's drowning and they began shouting questions.

"What happened to the daughter?"

"When was this?"

"How did she die?"

"Quiet down. One at a time." Aucoin waited for the unruly crowd of reporters to settle down. When everyone was back in their seats and quiet restored, he spoke.

"We have no reason to suspect foul play in Alison Franklin's death." He paused. "And with that, I'd like to thank you all for coming," he said, ending the conference.

Aucoin and the other officials made quick exits, leaving Lucy to deal with the out-of-town reporters' demands for information about Alison's death. "You can read about it on the *Pennysaver* website," she said as mikes were thrust in her face.

"C'mon, Lucy, just give us the gist," urged the guy with the New York accent as she tossed her notebook into her bag and started to make her way through the crowd to the doorway.

"I've got it!" crowed Pete Withers, peering at his smartphone and reading from Lucy's story. "Right here. 'Alison Franklin, daughter of billionaire Ed Franklin, drowned in local pond' . . . blah blah blah . . . oh, get this. 'DA Phil Aucoin cautioned that the cause of death has not been determined. In light of the recent opioid epidemic, he said he is waiting for toxicology test results from the state lab, but added that these tests are now routinely mandated for all unaccompanied deaths.'"

"So they think little Alison overdosed?" asked the New Yorker, blocking Lucy's path.

"I have no idea," said Lucy, shaking her head and trying to slide by him.

"What do most people think? This is Hicksville. People talk. What are they saying?"

"You'll have to ask them," said Lucy, finding a gap and slipping through.

"Hey!" somebody yelled. "There's Deb Hildreth. Ask her! She works for the local radio station."

Poor Deb, thought Lucy, abandoning her to the media scrum as she stepped into the airy lobby and the door closed behind her.

It was a typical November day, gray and miserable, and Lucy's spirits plunged as she made the drive from Gilead to Tinker's Cove. It was horrible to think that things like this could happen in the little town that she loved. Alison's death was bad enough—it was always awful when a young person died—but Ed's brutal murder overshadowed everything. The man was shot in broad daylight, right in the heart of town. It seemed incredible that such a thing could happen. Who would do such a thing? And why? Whoever killed Ed must have really hated him, she thought, finding it difficult to imagine how anyone could simply pull a trigger and blow off another person's head.

Of course, it happened all the time. Gun shootings were common occurrences in the US, and there were the constant reports of suicide bombings and assassinations and attacks on innocent people in Europe and the Middle East. Come to think of it, she decided with a sigh, it seemed that there were actually an awful lot of people who were not the least bit reluctant to take other people's lives.

"Wow, you look like you lost your best friend," observed Phyllis when Lucy arrived in the office later that morning. Phyllis was dressed today in a harvest-themed sweater featuring a design of apples and pumpkins, and her hair was tinted a flaming orange.

"Not yet, but you never know, the way things are going," Lucy said glumly, dropping her bag on the floor with a thunk so she could unbutton her jacket.

"How was the press conference?" asked Ted, who was staring at his computer screen.

"Crowded." Lucy hung up her jacket, then bent down and picked up her bag. From the way she moved you would have thought it was filled with bricks. "There was even an obnoxious guy from New York and lots of people from TV stations."

"Well, Ed Franklin was famous," said Ted. "Any new developments?"

Lucy sank into her desk chair and leaned her elbow on her desk, propping up her chin as if her head was much too great a load for her neck to bear. "Killed execution style. I guess we could've come up with that on our own."

"Talk about stating the obvious," muttered Ted. "No suspects?"

"Aucoin's playing his hand close to his chest," said Lucy.

"Dot Kirwan says it's all hands on deck, overtime for everybody—vacations and off-time cancelled," reported Phyllis. "She's real upset since Patsy was scheduled for maternity leave next week. Now she's going to have to work until she pops."

Patsy Kirwan was the police department dispatcher, just one of Dot's many relations who worked in the town's police and fire departments.

"Of course, you can see why they're so anxious to get the killer," continued Phyllis. "Talk about cold-blooded. It gives me the willies every time I think about it."

In spite of herself, Lucy found herself smiling. "Somehow I don't think we need to worry about getting shot in our sleep by some sort of serial killer maniac."

"Lucy's right," said Ted. "Ed Franklin was targeted. He was killed because somebody wanted him dead."

"Well, the one I feel bad for is that little wife of his," said Phyllis. "She's pregnant, you know, and even if she is a gold digger like everyone says, it must be awfully hard on her losing her husband like that. Of course, she's probably going to make out fine financially and all."

"That reminds me," said Ted. "I bet AP's got a file obit up for Ed Franklin. Want to check that for me, Lucy? Give it a local twist, get some quotes from the town's movers and shakers."

"Roger Wilco," said Lucy, relieved to be given a simple, undemanding assignment. And besides, she was interested in learning more about Ed Franklin's past. The past, she knew, often held the key to understanding the present and the obit did yield some surprising information.

It began with the usual summary of Ed Franklin's achievements—graduated from Dartmouth where he played football, went on to Harvard where he earned an MBA, began climbing the corporate ladder, ending as CEO of Dynamo where his high-profile leadership style made him a household name. It was Franklin's family history that caught her interest. His grandfather was a German immigrant, Emil Franck, who ran a beer hall on the Lower East Side of New York City. The beer hall was successful and he soon ventured into real estate, buying up tenements and renting them to Jewish and Italian newcomers in the early 1900s. His son, Ed's father, was thus armed with a sizeable fortune and an ambitious wife who wanted to join the highest ranks of New York society, which necessitated obscuring his immigrant origins. He changed the family name from Franck to the more American-sounding Franklin, and his wife was soon invited to join the boards of the Metropolitan Museum of Art and the New York Historical Society.

Lucy chuckled as she read this, wondering if Rachel would say Ed Franklin's hatred of Mexican immigrants was an effort to compensate for his family's immigrant past, which he somehow found embarrassing or shameful. It struck her as ironic that the man whose family fortune was originally built by exploiting newcomers to the country would become a proponent of anti-immigration policies. But maybe, she decided with a sigh, he only wanted to prohibit immigrants from Mexico and Latin America. Perhaps he would find Europeans more acceptable.

When it came to getting quotes from locals she decided to start with the folks he worked most closely with, his fellow members of the board of health. She was only able to reach one, Audrey Sprinkle, and had to leave messages with all the others, which she doubted would ever be returned.

Audrey was hesitant to say anything about Ed, perhaps fearing he would reach out from the grave in retaliation. "I don't really know what to say except this is the most awful thing that's ever happened here in Tinker's Cove. My heart just goes out to his whole family, and that includes his first wife, Eudora. That poor woman has lost her daughter, too, you know."

"I understand," said Lucy in her most sympathetic voice, "but what was it like to work with him on the board of health?" She was dying to ask Audrey if she agreed with Ed's anti-Mexican sentiments as her son Jason certainly did, but resisted the temptation, opting to stay in safer territory. "What was his leadership style?"

"Ah, well, I guess you could say he was a strong leader," said Audrey. "But he always had the best interest of the town in mind."

"I see," said Lucy. "Any examples?"

"Sorry, Lucy, I've got to run," said Audrey, ducking for cover. "There's someone at the door."

Moving right along to the board of selectmen, Lucy called the chairman, Roger Wilcox.

"A fine example of public-spirited service," he said. "Ed Franklin donated untold hours to the town, giving us the benefit of his unparalleled business knowledge and abilities."

"But weren't some of his actions rather controversial?" asked Lucy.

"Dear me," said Roger, "my wife wants me to walk the dog. Says it can't wait."

Joe Marzetti was always a safe bet for a quotable quote, but he didn't have much to say about Ed Franklin, either, when she reached him at his supermarket. "Helluva businessman, I got a lot out of that book he wrote—*Never Let 'Em See You Sweat: How to Win in Business and Life.*"

"Did he apply here in Tinker's Cove any of the concepts he wrote about in the book?" asked Lucy.

"Aw, gee. I gotta problem with one of the checkouts. Gotta go."

Lucy plugged away, working down the entire list of town officials, but nobody seemed to have much to say about Ed Franklin. She knew Ted wouldn't be pleased with the story, but she filed it just before leaving for the day, hoping to put off the inevitable rewrite.

When Lucy arrived on Tuesday morning, as she'd expected, Ted wanted more. "I know the guy's dead, but this story needs some livening up. It doesn't give the reader any idea of who Ed Franklin really was." He leaned back in his chair, chewing his lip. "What about his family? You haven't tried them."

"Oh, Ted," she protested. "They've got enough to deal with. I don't want to bother them. Phyllis was right. His wife's pregnant and her husband was shot . . ."

"She'll probably welcome the opportunity to talk about her late husband. She'll probably want everyone to know how wonderful he was." He paused, smirking. "Lord knows, nobody else seems to have liked him."

"Okay," said Lucy, hoping the phone at the Franklin mansion was unlisted. Unfortunately for her, the automated 4-1-1 operator offered her the option of placing the call.

A woman answered the phone, and Lucy assumed she was a

maid or some other employee, and after identifying herself asked to speak to Mrs. Franklin.

"Oh, poor Mireille. She's taking a nap," said the woman. "I'm her mom. Everybody calls me Mimsy. Maybe I can help you?"

Whoa, calm down, Lucy told herself, feeling as if she'd hit the mother lode. "Well, first of all, let me say how very sorry I am about your son-in-law's tragic death. I'm working on an obituary for the local paper and I just wanted to give family members an opportunity to say how they'd like him to be remembered."

"Ed was a great guy," said Mimsy. "He was crazy about my Mireille, and you know, a big famous guy like him, not to mention rich. Well he didn't need to, but, you know, he actually came to our house and asked my husband, Mireille's father, you know, for her hand in marriage! Isn't that the sweetest thing you ever heard? And it was especially nice since poor Sam was on his death bed. He had cancer and didn't live to walk little Mireille down the aisle."

Personally, Lucy thought it was probably a bit of a con, even going so far as to take advantage of a dying man, but she wasn't about to say so. "That is amazing," she said, doing her best to sound sincere. "Like he was just a regular guy."

"Trust me, Ed Franklin was really a regular guy. You'd never know he was a big shot. And good to our little girl! You shoulda seen the diamond ring he gave her. It's too bad she can't wear it now. Her fingers are awfully swollen. She's got it put away in a safe-deposit box. It's too valuable to keep around the house. That's what I told her. Better safe than sorry. After all, I told her, it may be the only thing she gets to keep, after that first wife of his gets through with her. She's already contesting the will, you know."

"Is she really? What a nerve!" replied Lucy, finding it only too easy to join this gossip fest.

"The way he left things, everything was to go to his children—poor Alison and the one Mireille's expecting. In the case of only one child surviving, that child would scoop the loot. No children, then it's a crap shoot. The executors have to distribute the estate equably, whatever that means."

"But what about the older son, Taggart?"

"Taggart wasn't actually his child. Ed adopted him when he married Eudora. Tag was from Eudora's first marriage, and Ed said in the will that he had previously made generous settlements to him."

"So Eudora doesn't think it's fair that Ed's wealth all goes to Mireille's baby?" asked Lucy. "That she and Tag don't get anything?"

"You said it! She seems all fragile and sensitive and artistic but believe me, that woman is really a crazy bitch. The things she's said to my Mireille! Vicious, nasty stuff. I'm not kidding. A mind like that, she really oughta be committed. Scary stuff."

"You don't say."

"I do say! And here she's gone and decided to drag Mireille into court and poor Ed's hardly cold. He's only been dead for three days. The papers were delivered to her this morning."

"That's too bad," said Lucy, well aware she could never use this material in a news story without inviting a libel uit, and she already knew that Eudora wasn't averse to legal challenges. "What about the funeral? Do you know what's being planned?"

"Haven't got a clue. Poor Mireille, she got up her courage and called Eudora thinking it was only proper to include her in the planning. And you know, what? Eudora told her not to bother, that Ed's lawyer was taking care of the details. Can you imagine? That's what these folks are like. It's all about the money. They don't care if he gets a decent funeral or not." Mimsy paused. "I guess you could give Munn a call. That's Howard Munn. He's Ed's lawyer. He's got an office in Boston."

"Thanks," said Lucy, wishing every interviewee was as forthcoming as Mimsy. "Please let Mireille know how sorry I am for her loss, and if there's anything she wants to add, she can reach me here at the paper."

"Will do. It's been real nice talking to you, Lucy."

Lucy shook her head after hanging up, thinking that things just kept getting stranger and stranger as suspects kept popping out of the woodwork. Matt Rodriguez was the prime suspect, of course, named by a witness. Then there was Ruth, a self-declared and extremely unlikely suspect, but there was the troubling matter of the Glock. Who knew what other weapons she might be hiding under all those hand-crocheted afghans? And now it turned out that Mireille had a very strong motive for killing her much older husband, since her baby would inherit his entire fortune. As the mother of this tiny billionaire, she would certainly have access to the estate and might actually control it. Come to think of it, thought Lucy, Mireille might also have figured out a way to kill Alison, clearing the way for her baby to inherit every last penny. And then there was Mimsy herself. It wouldn't be the first time that a cold-hearted killer used charm and an apparent willingness to help to distract investigators. It was certainly something to think about, Lucy decided as she googled Howard Munn.

CHAPTER 11

The lawyer's number was easily obtained and Lucy got right on the phone to his Boston office where, much to her surprise, the man himself answered the phone. Caught off guard, she blurted out her thoughts.

"I didn't actually expect to get through to you," she confessed before identifying herself. "Sorry, I'm Lucy Stone from the Tinker's Cove *Pennysaver* newspaper."

Munn chuckled. "Well, I've got a small office, just me and a couple associates. We find that it's best to keep things simple and direct, and our clients seem to appreciate our approach. I detest those recorded messages and why should I have a girl to answer the phone when I can do it myself?"

"Absolutely. I couldn't agree more. Believe me, I spend a lot of time trying to negotiate phone systems that I suspect are designed to make callers give up in frustration. They say every call is important to them but they sure don't act like it."

Munn seemed to appreciate that and gave a little laugh.

"I won't take up much time," said Lucy, addressing the reason for her call. "I just need the details for Ed Franklin's funeral for his obituary."

"Of course. The service is at eleven o'clock Saturday at Trinity

Church in Boston, followed by a reception at the Copley Plaza Hotel. Unfortunately for your readers, it's by invitation only."

"Of course. He was a very important person and I suppose a lot of other very important people will be attending."

"Yes," said Munn. "We know there's a lot of interest, however, and I do have a limited number of press passes. Shall I reserve one for you?"

Lucy was floored. In her years as a part-time reporter for a small town weekly she knew only too well that she was at the bottom of the media food chain. "That would be great. Thank you."

"No problem. I know how much Ed loved Tinker's Cove and how active he was in local affairs. He'd want to include his neighbors, but given the situation it's not practical to invite the whole town."

Lucy found this reaction encouraging and decided to press for more information. "I've been told that Ed Franklin's first wife is challenging his will. Is that true?"

There was a pause before Munn answered. "No comment, I'm afraid."

Now it was Lucy's turn to chuckle. "Can't blame a girl for trying."

"Not at all," he said. "I respect people who work hard."

"Is there anything you want to say about Ed Franklin for the story? I expect you've known him for a good number of years."

"I have indeed," he said in a thoughtful tone, "and I'm shocked and saddened by his death, especially so because it was clearly an assassination. I knew him well, personally and as a client, and I can think of no reason why anyone would want to kill him. This is a real tragedy. Ed's death is a great loss to many, and most especially to his wife, Mireille, and his entire family."

"Considering the fact that his daughter also died recently in rather suspicious circumstances, do you think there's a vendetta against the Franklin family?"

"I fear poor Alison's death was simply a tragic accident and unrelated to her father's murder." He paused. "I will overnight that press pass to you. You should have it in the morning."

Lucy knew the call was over and there was no point trying to prolong it. "Thank you. I really appreciate this opportunity."

Ted, however, wasn't impressed when she told him she'd been invited to the funeral. "A funeral's a funeral, even if it's in Trinity Church," he said, swinging around in his swivel chair and facing her. "There'll be music and people will say a lot of nice things about Ed Franklin that may or may not be true and then they'll party afterwards, glad it's over."

In her corner by the door, Phyllis gave an amused snort.

Lucy couldn't believe what she was hearing. "This is a big deal, Ted. There are going to be a lot of VIPs there, and maybe even his killer."

"I'm sure the killer will wear a sign or something to identify him or herself. One of those smiley face stick-ons—Hello My Name Is Hit Man."

Phyllis thought this was hysterical and she was struggling, shoulders shaking, to keep from laughing out loud.

Lucy, however, wasn't amused. "The funeral's by invitation only and I bet they haven't invited any locals. I'd be representing the whole town." She paused, dredging for something that would convince him. "We really owe it to his wife and the people Ed knew here, all the folks who worked with him on committees."

"You mean all the folks he fought with," said Phyllis.

"Well, yeah," admitted Lucy. "He was involved with a lot of people. He affected a lot of lives here in town." She could see Ted's expression softening.

He was definitely considering letting her go.

"I'll do it on my own time, Ted," she offered, sweetening the deal. "I won't even put in for gas."

"Well, when you put it that way, I suppose we do owe it to our readers," he said, turning back to his computer. Then, giving a little start, he slapped his hand against his head. "Did I hear you say something about his first wife challenging his will?"

"Yeah, that's what Mireille's mom told me."

"I wonder, do you think she's been blabbing to everyone who calls, or do you have a scoop? A scoop you've been sitting on since yesterday?"

"Well, if she told me, she's probably told others," said Lucy, defending herself. "She sounded like quite a character. Very chatty."

"Yeah, but you know Samantha Eggers," said Ted, naming the court clerk. "You wrote a flattering story about her, didn't you, just a few months ago?"

"I don't know if I'd call it flattering," said Lucy, feeling the need to defend her journalistic integrity. "It was part of that series we did on the county court."

"You did kind of suck up to her," said Phyllis with a knowing nod.

"She was very helpful," said Lucy, still defensive. "She's nice. That's not a crime, you know."

"Well, get on over there and see if she's got anything on this so-called lawsuit, okay?"

"Okay, boss," said Lucy, only too eager to get out of the office . . . and out of town.

Ed Franklin was gone, but somehow the combative attitude he'd brought to Tinker's Cove was lingering on. Paranoia and discord seemed to be spreading like some sort of infectious disease.

Heading back to Gilead for the second time in two days, Lucy stopped at the Quik-Stop for gas and picked up a hotdog for a quick lunch she could eat while she drove. It seemed to her that she was plying the same route to Gilead, the county seat, quite a lot. Fortunately, the trip was quite scenic, taking her past lovely old homes and giving her peeks at numerous coves and inlets dotted with pine-covered islands. As she drove and ate her hot dog, she thought about how Maine was changing.

When she'd first moved to Tinker's Cove, lots of people sold homemade items like quilts and whirligigs, setting them out on their lawns for tourists to buy. Now, most of those displays were gone, replaced with neat signs advertising art galleries, acupuncture, and computer services. The region, indeed the whole country was experiencing a changing economy, and those who didn't have college educations were joining Harry Crawford's group of Left Behinds.

Approaching Gilead, which was nestled in a valley and dotted with tall white steeples, Lucy thought it was quite an attractive New England town, apart from the county complex that included the 1960s brick courthouse and the grim granite jail with its chain link fence topped with coiled razor wire.

In the past, she had been able to come and go freely in the courthouse, but after 9/11 everything changed and now she had to present her bag for a search and step through a metal detector. Once inside, she went straight to the clerk of court's office, where Samantha Eggers had brightened the atmosphere by stripping away the dog-eared and faded notices that used to be taped any which way on the walls and replacing the dusty old Venetian blinds with attractive striped valances and simple Roman shades. The budget hadn't stretched to cover new furniture, however, so the same old tired tables and chairs remained as well as the old-fashioned card files that stood against one wall. The computer revolution had not yet arrived in the county court, where lawsuits were still entered on index cards and filed away alphabetically in drawers.

Lucy noticed there was a line of people at the counter, which was staffed by two assistant clerks, so she went straight to the drawer marked CH-CO but found no card for Clare v. Franklin. That meant she also had to join the line filled with people filing lawsuits or inquiring about suing someone or checking on the progress of their case. Samantha Eggers was visible, busy at her desk behind the counter where she was available for consultations when necessary.

She glanced up from time to time to check on the progress at the counter and when she saw Lucy, she got right up and drew her aside to the far end of the counter. "What brings you here today, Lucy?"

Samantha wore her gray hair in a short, no-nonsense cut and wore suits and low-heeled shoes. Today she had left her jacket hanging on the back of her desk chair and was wearing a flattering light blue cashmere turtleneck and a gray skirt.

"A little birdy told me that Ed Franklin's first wife is contesting his will," said Lucy, speaking in a very low voice. "But I didn't find anything in the card file."

"It just came in and we're processing the paperwork," said Samantha.

"Any chance I could take a peek?"

Samantha looked away as if studying the effect of the new window treatments, then smiled. "I don't see why not. It's going to be public soon enough. Come on in."

She raised the counter and opened the gate beneath, allowing Lucy to step inside the office area, which caused a bit of a stir among the people waiting in line. Samantha ignored them, and took Lucy to a vacant desk in the rear where she presented her with the original petition then went back to her own desk.

Eudora Huntington Clare and Taggart Huntington Franklin v. Estate of Edward Franklin consisted of twelve typewritten pages prepared by Eudora's lawyer who happened to be her husband, Jon Clare. The words they contained were nothing more than various combinations of letters from the alphabet, but Lucy felt her face reddening as she read them. It felt as if they were alight and burning her skin.

The suit alleged that Mireille had alienated the affection of Eudora's husband, Edward Franklin, and had poisoned his mind against his lawful wife by knowingly making false accusations against her. The alleged accusations included claims that Eudora was mentally unbalanced and accused her of spousal abuse, infidelity, and incest, such charges being wholly unfounded and entirely false.

The suit also claimed that the aforesaid Mireille Wilkins had falsely claimed to be pregnant with Edward Franklin's child, which situation caused him to initiate divorce proceedings against Eudora Franklin. Furthermore, the suit continued, after her marriage Mireille Wilkins Franklin had continued to slander Eudora Franklin and had influenced Edward Franklin to disinherit her and her son Taggart Huntington Franklin, whom he had legally adopted upon his marriage to Eudora Huntington.

In addition to accusing Mireille of lying and slanderous behavior, the suit alleged that she had alienated Alison Franklin, the daughter of Edward and Eudora Franklin, against her birth mother. The most terrible accusation was last and claimed that Mireille had "knowingly and with malice intentionally provided illegal opioids to Alison, causing her to become addicted to said substances and contributing to her untimely death."

When she finished reading, Lucy sighed and looked up, meeting Samantha's sardonic expression.

"Do you want me to make a copy for you?" Samantha asked. "It'll cost you."

"How much?" asked Lucy.

"Twenty-five cents a page."

"Quite the bargain," said Lucy, handing the papers to Samantha, who promptly unstapled them and fed them into the huge copy machine. The machine was old and slow and produced the copies at a stately pace, but Lucy left the office with a complete set folded in her bag.

When she was crossing the parking lot she noticed several reporters she'd seen at the press conference, making their way to the courthouse. She assumed that Mimsy had been at work and the word was out; she could only hope that Samantha wouldn't be as helpful to these others as she had been to her.

Fearing she had no time to waste before the media horde turned its attention to Jon Clare, Lucy put in a call on her cell phone to the law firm named in the letterhead which was the prestigious old-school Boston firm of Bradstreet and Coffin. Unlike Howard Munn, Bradstreet and Coffin had an automated phone system that provided the names of associates and their extension numbers. When Jon Clare's name was not mentioned, Lucy took the option of pressing star for the operator.

"I will connect you," said the operator without providing an extension number.

That made Lucy wonder exactly what relationship Jon Clare had to the office.

He did pick up, however, and confirmed that he was representing his wife, who was contesting Ed Franklin's will. "It's a story old as time, an attractive young woman stealing the affection of an older man and destroying his family."

"I saw the suit. There are an awful lot of terrible allegations against Mireille," said Lucy. "I find it hard to believe that a hard-headed businessman like Ed Franklin could be so easily manipulated."

"Well, it will all come out in court, and more," said Jon. "I can promise you that this is just the beginning. It's going to be a sensational trial." He sounded quite gleeful at the prospect.

Lucy found it disturbing. Once again she wondered about his

professional status. "In future, if I need to reach you, what number should I use? I noticed the firm hasn't given you a telephone extension."

"Um, right. I'm just here temporarily. A friend is letting me use an office that happens to be empty. I'm actually, uh, retired," he said. Something in his tone made Lucy wonder if that was the truth. Perhaps no law firm wanted to hire him, or perhaps being married to Eudora was a full-time job. "Use my cell," he added, giving her the number.

By the time Lucy got back to Tinker's Cove she discovered the media frenzy had begun. There were several vans from TV stations parked in front of the police station, and she spotted several reporters she recognized filming segments for the evening news.

At the office, she presented Ted with the copy of the lawsuit, but admitted she didn't think she had a scoop. "I saw a bunch of reporters at the courthouse, just behind me, and they're already filming reports out there on Main Street. For all I know, Samantha is handing these out to everybody."

"Somehow I doubt that," said Ted, and as it turned out, he was right.

That evening, when Lucy tuned in to a Boston channel, she noted with satisfaction that Michelle O'Rourke could only report that police investigations into Ed Franklin's death were continuing, and that a court official had confirmed that Ed Franklin's will was being contested but could provide no details as the paperwork was still being processed.

The rumor mill continued to grind during the week, however, and Wednesday morning's *Boston Herald* had front page photos of Ed's mansion in Tinker's Cove and Eudora's mansion in nearby Elna, superimposed with head shots of Mireille and Eudora under the headline CURSED HOUSES. The little weekly *Pennysaver*, however, was the only paper that would have complete details of the suit when it arrived in subscribers' mailboxes the next day.

CHAPTER 12

Lucy wasn't aware of her big scoop on Thursday morning as she went out for a run, conscious that she'd been neglecting her training program and time was running out before the Turkey Trot. It was a misty November morning, and Libby's black coat was soon gray with dew drops as she ran along, just ahead of Lucy. Libby always had to be first, which Lucy had heard meant the Lab considered herself the leader of the pack. Lucy didn't agree. She preferred to think that Libby was clearing a path for *Lucy* and guarding *her*, the actual leader of this very small pack.

When she got home, Bill was standing at the sink, rinsing the egg off his breakfast dishes. "Good run?" he asked, opening the dishwasher and loading the dishes inside.

"Great," said Lucy, panting and gently shoving him aside so she could fill Libby's bowl with fresh water. That chore completed she returned to the sink to get a drink for herself.

Bill closed the dishwasher door and wrapped his arms around her, nuzzling the back of her neck, tickling her with his beard. She enjoyed the familiar embrace and leaned back against him while she drained the glass of water. Once refreshed, she turned around for a proper kiss.

"Napoleon famously wrote to Josephine, telling her not to

bathe before he returned from war as he enjoyed her natural scent," he said, stepping back, "but I gotta say a shower might not be a bad idea."

Lucy pouted. "You're not usually quite so fastidious and it seems to me that I put up with quite a bit of man sweat from time to time."

"Well, that's different. That's a sign that I've been working hard to bring home the bacon for you and the kids."

"Men are so weird. You just love all your various parts and bodily fluids. Must be the testosterone."

"Right," said Bill with a nod and a satisfied smile. "When you got it, flaunt it."

"Well, are you going to be flaunting it at the Cali Kitchen?" inquired Lucy, glancing at the antique Regulator clock that held pride of place on the wall between the windows. "It's getting late, isn't it?"

"That job's on hold," said Bill with a grimace. "The millwork truck was egged the other day when they were delivering windows and the tires on the electrician's van were slashed while he was working inside."

"Any idea who's doing this?"

"Probably some of those demonstrators. They're not holding protests anymore. They've turned to vandalism instead. I don't know where it's going to end."

"I'm surprised that Rey is giving up," said Lucy. "He seemed so determined to move forward on the restaurant."

"He's not giving up, at least that's what he told me," said Bill, sitting down at the round golden oak table and grabbing the sports section. "He's just waiting for things to settle down a bit. He and Matt are taking a little vacation. They're going back to the West Coast for Thanksgiving with their family."

"I thought he was suspect number one for Ed Franklin's murder."

Bill shrugged. "He hasn't been charged."

"Interesting," said Lucy, heading up the back stairway to the upstairs bathroom for a shower. Pausing at the bottom stair she turned, struck with a thought. "You know, since you'll be at loose ends for a bit, you could paint the family room. And there's that closet door in Sara's room that's off kilter, and—"

"Enough, enough," he said, holding up a hand in protest. "I'll check in with some of the guys, see if they need an extra hand."

"Yeah, you wouldn't want all that testosterone to go to waste," said Lucy before making a quick escape up the stairs.

Freshly showered and blown dry, Lucy dressed for the day, keeping in mind that she would be meeting her friends for breakfast. Sue usually had something critical to say about her appearance so she took a bit of extra care, applying lipstick and mascara and choosing her best jeans and a new sweater she'd bought on sale.

She felt quite pleased with herself as she started the car and headed into town. Her route took her past O'Brien's Turkey Farm and she planned to make a quick stop there to pick up a turkey for the food pantry. She wasn't going to be cooking a big dinner for the family this year, so she wanted to give the turkey she didn't need to a family that wouldn't otherwise have one.

She passed the farm every day on her way to work and had seen the little turkey chicks grow into big, table-ready birds. *Table-ready* was just about the nicest thing you could say about the beasts, she thought, remembering that even as chicks they hadn't been cute. There was something prehistoric about turkeys, with their naked necks and long scaly legs, and she was only too happy to see that the pens that once held the birds were empty and the barnyard was quiet. O'Brien's turkeys had gobbled their last gobbles and were sitting in the refrigerator case, plucked and trussed and ready for roasting.

The farm store was quiet with only a few early-morning customers. Lucy wasn't in a hurry so she browsed, checking out the various turkey-related items the store offered. There were oversized turkey platters, basters, roasting pans, and packs of the O'Brien's own brining mix. There were also the usual T-shirts picturing a handsome Tom turkey in full display as well as aprons, dish towels, and pot holders. There were little onesies for babies, proclaiming BABY'S FIRST THANKSGIVING in big orange letters, with either a cartoon version of a tom or a hen with chicks. There were even turkey suits for pet dogs.

Lucy couldn't resist taking a closer look at the onesies, wondering if Toby and Molly might be planning to have a second child now that Patrick was getting older and they were more financially secure. She was admiring the little piece of clothing and dreaming of having a little grandbaby girl when a woman's voice broke into her reverie.

"Those are so adorable!" shrieked the woman in a voice that was much too loud.

Lucy turned to acknowledge her and recognized Eudora Clare, smartly dressed in a short fur jacket and carrying a huge Louis Vuitton bag that contained a tiny Yorkshire terrier. All that was visible of the dog was a little face with bright eyes, and a plastic pumpkin barrette attached between its ears.

"They certainly are," said Lucy. "I only wish I had a little grandbaby so I could buy one."

"Don't you know anyone who's expecting?" asked Eudora, examining one of the little garments with an expensively gloved hand. "I do." She laid the onesie over one arm and stroked it as if it was a pet cat, "but I don't know if she's expecting a hen or a tom."

"In that case, I'd go with the hen and chicks. They're cuter," said Lucy, who had noticed that while Eudora's face was smooth as a baby's bottom, evidence of a face lift, her wrinkled neck boasted wattles that a turkey would be proud of.

"I really shouldn't get her anything," said Eudora, stroking the onesie so hard that Lucy feared she would rub the design right off. "The mother, I mean. Face it, these presents are really for the mother and this one is nothing but a husband-stealing slut."

Lucy realized Eudora must be talking about Mireille, and was surprised she'd consider buying a gift for the woman she believed had broken up her marriage. Some of the allegations from the lawsuit ran through Lucy's mind and she couldn't believe Eudora was ready to forgive and forget.

"Of course," continued Eudora, spitting out the words, "it's not the baby's fault that her mother is a conniving little gold digger, and now that Ed and Allie are gone, the baby will be my only link to Ed." She turned and stared at Lucy with tear-filled eyes. "Isn't that right?"

Lucy felt uncomfortable being put on the spot and wondered if

Eudora was somewhat unstable, perhaps even on some sort of medication. "I suppose you have photos and videos and memories . . ."

"It's not the same as a living person," said Eudora, dabbing at her eyes with a tissue in such a way that she wouldn't smear her heavy eye makeup. "That baby will have Ed's DNA. It might even be a boy and look like him."

"You have a son," said Lucy.

"Oh, Tag's not Ed's," Eudora said, crumpling the tissue in her hand. "I had him with my first husband. Ed adopted him, but he's nothing like my Ed."

"It's hard to let go of the past," said Lucy, "but you have to think of the family you do have, your son and husband."

"But don't you think I have a responsibility to this little mite? It's quite likely that a slut like you-know-who will be an unfit mother. What would happen then? Imagine, my Ed's child in foster care, abused and neglected." Eudora pressed her botoxed, glossy orange lips together. "It would be up to me. I would have to adopt the child. I would name him after Ed . . . Edward, Junior . . . or Edwina, if it's a girl."

"I think you're getting ahead of yourself," said Lucy, eager to get away from Eudora but somewhat concerned about her welfare. She was no psychologist, but this seemed extremely abnormal.

Fortunately, just as Lucy was looking around, hoping Eudora'd been accompanied by her husband or son, Jon Clare appeared, carrying a bulging shopping bag with the O'Brien's Turkey Farm logo.

"You mustn't chew this poor woman's ear off," he said, attempting to take Eudora's hand. "I've got the turkey—it's a beauty—and we can go home now."

"I'm not a child," hissed Eudora, yanking her hand away and stuffing the onesie into the Louis Vuitton bag, causing the dog to yip in protest. "Don't treat me like a child."

"Have a nice day," said Lucy, seizing the opportunity to make her escape. She crossed the store to the counter and placed her order, then watched as the squabbling couple made their way out of the store to a large Cadillac Escalade. As she watched Jon holding the bag with the shoplifted onesie while Eudora settled herself in the car, Lucy wondered if she should report the theft.

"This is a nice twenty-two pounder," said Carolyn O'Brien, grunting as she hoisted the heavy bird onto the counter and slid it into a reusable cloth shopping bag. "That'll be thirty-nine thirty-eight. The bag's complimentary."

Lucy couldn't believe that was right; she was used to buying Thanksgiving turkeys at the IGA for fifty-nine cents a pound. But when she checked the sign behind the counter, she saw that O'Brien's hormone-free, free-range turkeys were a dollar seventy-nine a pound. "Do you take checks?" she asked, deciding that O'Brien's Turkey Farm could certainly absorb the loss of the onesie.

Lucy was late for breakfast with the girls, having detoured to drop off the turkey at the food pantry. They were already seated at their usual table in Jake's when she arrived. Norine, the waitress, came and filled the mug that was waiting at Lucy's place while she seated herself and shrugged out of her jacket.

"Interesting choice of color, Lucy," said Sue, studying her new sweater. "I know orange was very big last year, but I think it's a tricky color for most people, and if you're going to go with orange I wouldn't combine it with blue. Brown or beige, maybe, even a creamy white, and, sweetheart, while I certainly appreciate the fact that you're wearing lipstick, nude would have been much better than that oh-so-sweet pink."

"It's my favorite lipstick and it's the only one I wear," said Lucy, who was used to Sue's critical comments and wasn't bothered in the least. Sue, she noticed, was immaculately turned out in a nubby white sweater and white wool slacks. "It's called Gentlemen Prefer Pink . . . and I got the sweater on sale."

"Cute name," said Rachel. "I think orange and pink together is very Lilly Pulitzer."

"That's what I thought," said Lucy, who didn't have a clue what or who Lilly Pulitzer was and wouldn't have recognized the company's colorful resort-wear designs.

"That sweater's the perfect color for this time of year," said Pam. "It's really more of a rust than orange, and they've done research that indicates warm colors like reds and oranges actually make you feel warmer and happier and thus more open to positive interactions with others."

"I had a very interesting interaction this morning," said Lucy, pausing to let Norine take their orders.

"Usual all round?" she asked, pen poised over her pad. Receiving nods she ambled off toward the kitchen, writing as she went.

"Who did you interact with in an interesting way?" asked Sue, who was running a perfectly manicured finger around the rim of her coffee mug.

"Eudora Clare," said Lucy, lifting her mug for that delicious first sip of coffee.

"Ed Franklin's first wife?" asked Rachel with a puzzled expression.

"The very same," said Lucy, setting her cup down. "It was at the turkey farm. She was acting kind of weird, talking about buying a Baby's First Thanksgiving onesie for Mireille's baby."

"Those onesies are really tacky," said Sue.

"I think they're cute," said Pam.

"In what way was she acting weird?" asked Rachel.

"She seemed kind of out of control, barely holding it together," said Lucy. "Her husband intervened and dragged her out of the store. She ended up shoplifting the onesie, but I don't think she meant to. She was pretty upset."

"Well, that's understandable. She must be grieving for her daughter and her ex-husband. I know they were divorced, but it's still traumatic when someone close to you is murdered," said Pam.

"Pam's right," said Rachel as Norine arrived with their breakfast orders. "She could be suffering from post-traumatic stress."

Norine plunked down a bowl of yogurt with granola for Pam, a sunshine muffin for Rachel, and hash and eggs for Lucy, then glared at Sue. "Anything I can get you?" she asked in a challenging tone.

"Just top off my coffee, thanks," said Sue, who, as far as anyone knew, existed on a diet of black coffee and white wine.

Norine went off to fetch the coffee pot, tut-tutting and shaking her head in disapproval.

"Just think about it," said Rachel. "Her husband left her for a younger woman then he divorced her, which research shows is every bit as stressful as a death. Then her daughter dies—that's a second stressor—her ex-husband is murdered, and to top it all off, the new, young wife is very visibly pregnant. That's a lot for anyone to deal with."

"I can't work up too much sympathy," said Sue, giving Norine a big thank-you smile as she added more coffee to her mug. "She's remarried, after all, and her son and the new husband seem very devoted to her, plus she's got plenty of dough. That's one thing she doesn't have to worry about."

"I guess she is worried, though," said Lucy, piercing the yolk of her sunny-side up egg with her fork. "She's contesting Ed's will, which leaves everything to the new baby."

"Going to court. That's another stressor," said Rachel, peeling the paper off her muffin.

"Well, I'll say this," said Lucy. "After seeing how she acted in the turkey store, I can understand why Alison went to live with her father and Mireille."

"That would be hard for a mother to take," said Pam. "It would be a real slap in the face."

"No rush. Any time you're ready," said Norine, tucking the bill between the salt and pepper shakers.

Sue picked it up and her eyebrows rose. "Talk about a slap in the face. Jake's raised the price of a cup of coffee."

CHAPTER 13

When Lucy stopped by at the office to pick up her check, Ted was doing a little jig.

"What's gotten into him?" she asked Phyllis, who was resplendent in a sweatshirt featuring a bejeweled Tom turkey in full display, his chest and neck covered with sequins and his tail dotted with faux diamonds, emeralds, and rubies.

"It's your story about the lawsuit," she said, peering over the granny glasses perched on her nose. "He says AP and Gateway are picking it up and paying for the privilege."

"That's right, Lucy," he said, giving her a huge smile. "You got us a gen-you-wine scoop!"

"How about a little bonus for me?" she suggested, giving him a sideways look as she opened the envelope that was lying on her desk and noticed the usual paltry sum.

"How about I pay the heat bill?" he replied. "I suppose you'd rather work in a warm office—"

"Actually, it's not all that warm," said Phyllis, interrupting and rubbing her upper arms. "Barely above freezing."

"Well, with adequate heat and electric lights and computers and all—" said Ted.

"Point taken," admitted Lucy, slipping into her chair and powering up her computer. While she waited she noticed the light on her phone indicating she had a voice mail and dialed the code. Much to her surprise, Mireille Franklin had called and left a message, requesting an interview. Lucy immediately returned the call and was invited to "come right over."

"Why do I feel like I slipped into an alternate universe?" she asked after telling Ted and Phyllis about the invitation.

"Well, it isn't often that Ted is actually in a good mood," said Phyllis. "That alone is rather disconcerting."

"It's her sweatshirt that's disconcerting," said Ted, chuckling at his little joke. "You need sunglasses to look at it."

"I got it at the Harvest Festival. It's handcrafted," said Phyllis, smoothing the sequins. "I think what's disconcerting Lucy is the fact that somebody actually called requesting an interview. I don't think that's ever happened before."

"Well, that guy who puts on magic shows in the summer always calls," said Lucy.

"The Amazing Mr. Magic," said Phyllis with a disapproving snort. "He just wants free publicity."

"Not quite in the same league as Mireille Franklin," said Ted.

"I bet she wants the same thing," said Lucy, "only in her case it's called *positive spin.*"

Whatever her motive, Mireille greeted Lucy at the door to the mansion, brushing aside the burly fellow dressed all in black—black shirt, black tie, black suit and shoes—who had opened the door. He had a rather obvious lump under his jacket that Lucy supposed was made by a gun.

"It's okay, Jack. I'm expecting company," said Mireille, grabbing Lucy by the arm and pulling her inside.

Jack looked Lucy up and down, frisking her visually, then asked for her bag so he could also check it. Finding no threat there, either, he handed it back to her. He turned to Mireille and said in a very serious tone, "I'll be right here in the hallway if you need me."

"Good to know," replied Mireille, who pressed one hand on her lower back and, with a bit of a waddle, led the way to a small library at the rear of the house. The shelves were largely empty, apart from a handful of best-selling thrillers and business books, but there was a huge, wall-mounted TV above the gas fireplace. A comfortable sofa and arm chairs that swiveled were arranged around a large coffee table covered with a messy pile of magazines and newspapers. Both the gas fireplace and TV were on.

Mireille had been watching an old black-and-white Cary Grant movie, which she quickly turned off.

"It's pure escapism. I watch these old romantic movies. I love *Bringing Up Baby, The Philadelphia Story,* stuff like that."

"Me, too," said Lucy, who was waiting for an invitation to sit down. She thought Mireille was one of those women who couldn't help looking beautiful, even if her eyes were rather red and swollen, evidence she'd been crying a lot.

She was small-boned and had a touching air of fragility despite being nine months pregnant. Her tummy was a huge beach ball covered by a tight, stretchy turquoise top, which Lucy knew was the current fashion. Her hair was long and wavy, and the blond color seemed to be natural, though Lucy wouldn't have bet money on it. She knew from Sue, who was always urging her to "do something" with her fading hair, that hair color products had come a long way in recent years.

Mireille was wearing black leggings and her feet, only slightly swollen, were tucked into black ballet flats.

"Oh, please sit down," she said, flopping onto the couch and putting her feet up. "Would you like something to drink? Coffee? Tea? Herb tea? Kefir? I drink a lot of that."

"No thanks. I'm fine," said Lucy, choosing one of the swivel chairs and noticing that Mireille was nervously twisting her fingers.

"It's no trouble. I can just ring and someone will bring it," said Mireille, sounding as if this was a phenomenon she had not yet grown accustomed to.

"If you want something, go ahead," said Lucy. "I'm training for the Turkey Trot—"

She stopped suddenly, embarrassed. She should never have mentioned the Turkey Trot, which Alison had also been training for.

"It's okay," said Mireille in a voice that was almost a whisper. "I know Alison was looking forward to running in the Turkey Trot. It was one of the positives in her life." She paused. "I'd run, too, if it wasn't for this," she said, patting her tummy.

"When are you due?" asked Lucy, pulling her notebook out of her bag. Spying her cell phone, and not wanting any interruptions during the interview, she turned it off.

"Any day," replied Mireille with a sigh.

"Well, thanks for the interview. I know our readers will be interested in what you have to say, and how you're coping with everything."

"Not very well, and that's the truth. The worst part is waking up and realizing this isn't a bad dream. It's my life." She snatched up a tabloid from the top of the pile and waved it around. "Anybody reading this rag would think I'm a coldhearted gold digger."

"Are you?" asked Lucy, taking advantage of the opening. She much preferred interviewing the defensive, angry Mireille than the weepy, grieving one.

"No! I don't care about money or houses or cars. I really don't. And I didn't break up Ed's marriage, either. He'd been wanting a divorce for a long time before we met and he pursued me, not the other way around. All that stuff that Eudora is alleging is absolutely false."

"How did you meet?" asked Lucy, jotting everything down in her notebook.

"I was working for a caterer, just to pay the bills. I was taking drama classes and going to auditions. I was making progress, starting to get callbacks. He was very persistent. At first I turned him down, but he was hard to resist. He kept calling and sending flowers and he really won me over. After our first date I knew. I knew that even though he was old enough to be my father, he was the man for me. I know he had a reputation for being brash and hard-nosed in business, and some of his ideas weren't exactly PC, but with me he was nothing but kind and considerate and loving. He never raised his voice to me . . . or to Alison, for that matter. He said he liked having a peaceful, pleasant atmosphere at home."

"What about Alison?" asked Lucy. "What was it like when she came to live with you?"

"It was great," said Mireille, looking Lucy right in the eye. "I know what people think, that she must have hated me and the baby, but it wasn't that way at all. We got on great together. We were like sisters. She was so much fun and so excited about having a baby in the house." Mireille paused and plucked a tissue from the box on the coffee table, blew her nose, and dabbed at her eyes. "I really miss her and I hate the way she died in that cold, icy water.

"You know what she loved more than anything? Sitting by that fireplace," Mireille said, pointing at the flickering flames. "I think of her every time I turn it on. She loved to curl up by a nice cozy fire, reading or watching movies with me."

"It's a bit unusual, isn't it, that she moved in with you and her father? Wouldn't she naturally want to be with her mother?"

"I guess not. She moved in with us right after the wedding. That was about a year ago. She was just out of rehab."

"What about that?" asked Lucy, recalling the accusation that Mireille had gotten Alison back on drugs. "There are rumors that she was back on drugs and died of an overdose."

"No way!" exclaimed Mireille. "She got hooked after an accident . . . when she broke her ankle and they gave her painkillers. She hated drugs and was determined to stay off them. She was happy. She had friends and was doing well at college."

Lucy looked around at the comfortable, cozy room and thought of the huge, empty house beyond the closed door. It struck her that Mireille had carved out a little space for herself, almost as if she was holed up in a bunker with a guard at the door. "What about you? Are you going to stay on in Tinker's Cove?"

"I don't think so," she replied, stroking her tummy. "I'm just waiting for the baby and then I'll decide what to do. I'm not really a small town girl. I grew up in New York and I really miss it. It wasn't so bad here when Ed and Allie were, well—" She stopped and grabbed another tissue, quickly wiping her eyes. "I really miss them. I'm still in shock. I don't understand why anybody would want to kill Ed. I mean, I know he made enemies. He was so outspoken, but he didn't deserve to get shot like that." She chewed her lip. "And I don't like living like this, with bodyguards and all. It's scary and not just for me. I have to think about the baby."

"What about the guards? Do you think whoever killed Ed might try to kill you, too?"

"I don't know what to think, but it's a definite possibility. At least that's what they tell me. And they haven't ruled out murder in Alison's death, either."

"Who's 'they'?" asked Lucy.

"Ed's people," Mireille said with a shrug. "You know, people who worked for him, like Howard Munn. And my mom. She's with me here. She says I can't be too careful."

"Will you be at the funeral?" asked Lucy.

"I really can't think about that now," Mireille answered, looking down at her tummy and giving it a pat. "I think a memorial service would be best after the baby's arrived and everyone's emotions have kind of settled down."

"Haven't you heard?" Lucy was so surprised that the words just tumbled out.

"What do you mean?"

"Howard Munn told me the funeral is this Saturday, eleven o'clock at Trinity Church."

"Which is Trinity?" asked Mireille. "The one with the big white steeple?"

"It's in Boston, at Copley Square," explained Lucy. "And there's a reception afterwards at the Copley Plaza Hotel."

"He must have called," Mireille said quickly, attempting a cover-up. "I haven't been checking my messages."

Lucy had a sudden realization Mireille was completely extraneous to the ongoing business empire that was Ed Franklin Enterprises, a situation that would certainly change once her infant child became the sole owner.

"I'm sorry," said Mireille, rising awkwardly from the sofa by pushing against the padded armrest. "I hope you don't mind, but I really need to rest now."

"Of course," said Lucy, jumping up and spilling the contents of her bag onto the floor. Embarrassed, she fell clumsily to her knees and started stuffing everything back inside, including her notebook. Struggling to her feet, she apologized. "Sorry about that . . ."

"No problem," said Mireille. Sunshine was streaming through

the window, backlighting her fair hair and making her look an-gelic.

"And thank you for your time," said Lucy.

"Thank you," said Mireille, suddenly dropping back down on the couch. "If you don't mind, I'm a bit . . . can you let your-self out?"

"Are you all right?" asked Lucy. "Can I get someone?"

"I'm ringing now," Mireille said, picking up a gadget like a TV remote.

A moment later, the door opened and a woman in nurse's scrubs hurried in and rushed to Mireille's side. Lucy was some-what relieved to know she was leaving Mireille in good hands and stepped out into the hallway where she encountered a middle-aged woman also hurrying toward the library.

Seeing Lucy, the woman quickly changed direction, veering to-ward the front door where the bodyguard was slouched on a chair.

"What do you think you're here for?" she demanded, con-fronting him. "How did this woman get in? Why aren't you doing your job?"

The bodyguard jumped to his feet and his right hand slipped beneath his jacket. "Mrs. Franklin told me to let her in. She said it was okay." His eyes were on Lucy, watching every move.

"It's true," said Lucy, making sure not to make any sudden movements and keeping her hands clearly in view. "I'm Lucy Stone from the *Pennysaver* and Mireille asked me to come and in-terview her."

"Oh, sorry, Lucy. I spoke to you on the phone. I'm Mimsy, Mireille's mom," said the woman, who Lucy realized was an older version of Mireille. She was heavier, and her frizzy hair was obvi-ously colored, but beneath her carefully moisturized wrinkles, she had the same enviable cheekbones and little pointed chin. Like her daughter, she was casually dressed in yoga pants and ballet flats, though she had topped her T-shirt with a matching hoodie.

"I'm sorry about this," she added, giving the bodyguard an apologetic smile. "I'm a bit paranoid these days and I can't wait to get out of here. Believe me, if Mireille wasn't due any minute and hadn't made arrangements to have the baby here, we'd be long gone."

"I think you might want to check on her. She just rang for the nurse," said Lucy.

"Thanks," said Mimsy, hurrying across the hall to the library.

The bodyguard was standing by the front door, which he opened for Lucy.

"Take good care of them," she said, catching his eye.

"I certainly will," he replied with a serious nod.

Pausing for a moment on the front porch to take in the million-dollar view of the bay dotted with pine-covered islets, she felt a sharp stab of envy. Imagine being able to live among all this beauty, she thought, in a big, beautiful house with plenty of helpers just waiting to satisfy every whim. She grabbed the handrail and descended the stone steps carefully, comparing them to the scuffed wooden steps that led to her back porch.

And then she remembered that her husband was healthy and alive and so were her children, and even though she lived in a modestly sized home, she didn't need a bodyguard. Ed Franklin's wealth hadn't protected him or his daughter from sudden death.

When she returned to the office, Ted was eager to hear all about the interview. "What's she like? What did she say?" he asked, looking up from his desk.

"I think she just wants everyone to know she's not a gold digger, she truly loved Ed, and she has nothing to do with his business affairs."

"If you believe that, I've got a bridge I'd like to sell you," said Phyllis.

"I do believe her," said Lucy, who was hanging up her jacket. "In fact, she didn't even know about the funeral Saturday. It came as quite a shock when I told her."

"That's weird," said Phyllis. "Planning a funeral without consulting the wife."

"That's what I think," said Lucy. "It's like Munn doesn't take her seriously, like she's kind of temporary."

"Well, she is very pregnant. Maybe he thought it would be too much for her," said Ted.

"I wonder whose side he's on," said Lucy, seating herself at her desk. "If the will stands, Mireille's baby will be the sole owner of Ed Franklin Enterprises. As the baby's guardian, she'll be running the show."

"I bet she's really a crafty little wench, out to make everybody think she's a little angel, while she makes off with the loot," said Phyllis.

"She's got the looks for the part," said Lucy, remembering how she'd been struck by Mireille's beauty. She went straight to her e-mails, catching up with the messages she'd missed while she was out. She couldn't miss the one from Zoe, which had arrived just minutes before, with the subject line in capitals: MATT ARRESTED.

Quickly opening the file, she found no details. There was only a terse message, also in caps. MOM, CALL ME.

CHAPTER 14

Lucy immediately reached for the phone on her desk and called Zoe's cell phone, which Zoe must have been holding in her hand because she answered immediately.

"Why don't you answer your phone?" she demanded. "I called and called, but all I got was voice mail."

"I turned it off. I had an important interview and didn't want to be interrupted," said Lucy, fumbling in her bag for the forgotten phone and switching it back on. "But I got your e-mail. Is this true?"

"Yeah. Mom, he called me from California. He said he got a call from the DA that he was being charged with Ed Franklin's murder and there was a warrant for his arrest. The DA said he should turn himself in, otherwise the California cops would arrest him and Maine would start extradition proceedings."

"Well, it was nice of Aucoin to give him that option," said Lucy, thinking of the police shootings that were getting so much attention these days. By turning himself in, Matt would avoid being seized on the street in some sort of risky armed confrontation.

"Are you crazy?" demanded Zoe. "Being charged with murder isn't nice . . . especially if you didn't happen to do it."

"Did he say why they think he did it?" asked Lucy.

"He says it's because he used to date Alison."

"What did you say?" demanded Lucy, who couldn't believe what she was hearing.

"Matt used to date Alison. I thought you knew."

"I didn't know, but it explains a lot," said Lucy, thinking of the antagonism she'd witnessed between Matt and Ed Franklin.

"He said it's that thing about husbands and boyfriends being automatic suspects. You know how her father gave him a lot of grief. Franklin kept saying how Matt was a Mexican, and wouldn't let him come to the house or anything. I guess they think there was some sort of confrontation and he got real mad and killed him."

"I think there must be more to it than that," said Lucy, suspecting that Matt hadn't given Zoe the whole story. "They wouldn't charge him without evidence."

"You know, Mom, you're every bit as bigoted as Ed Franklin! People of color, people with Hispanic names, they get arrested all the time for crimes they didn't commit."

"That may be true but I don't think that's the case here—" Lucy broke off in midsentence, aware that Ted was frantically waving his arms like a demented sailor signaling by semaphore to get her attention.

"He's the darkest person in Tinker's Cove, Mom. Face it!"

"Right. Look, I'll get right on it," said Lucy. "I gotta go."

"Let me know what you find out, okay?" Zoe's voice had changed; she sounded like the little girl who used to beg Lucy not to go to work and leave her home in the care of her older brother and sisters.

Ted was waving his hand in a circle, signaling to Lucy to wrap it up, and she glared back at him in response, holding her free hand up in a "hold-on-a-sec" signal. She couldn't leave Zoe out on a limb. "I will, sweetie. I'll call as soon as I find out anything. Hang in there. Try not to worry."

"Are you kidding?" Angry Zoe was back. "Innocent people get convicted all the time. Our so-called justice system's rigged—"

"Maybe it is sometimes and some places," said Lucy, "but our *system* is made up of people, people like Phil Aucoin and Lt. Horowitz and Barney and all those Kirwan kids. They'll do what's right."

"I suppose," said Zoe, sounding chagrined. "I guess I forgot."

Reassured that Zoe had calmed down, Lucy ended the call. As soon as she said good-bye, Ted was on her.

"Pam wants you to call her—" he began, only to be interrupted by Lucy.

"Hold on a sec. My daughter got a call from Matt Rodriguez in California. He says Aucoin is charging him with Ed Franklin's murder and he's supposed to turn himself in and await extradition."

Ted looked puzzled. "Matt Rodriguez? Really?"

"The good-looking Mexican kid with the Corvette?" asked Phyllis, equally puzzled.

"Yeah," said Lucy, who was also struggling to reconcile the young man she knew with this disturbing new information. "Apparently he dated Alison, which means he was personally involved with Ed Franklin. It wasn't just the business about the restaurant." As she spoke, it occurred to her that Mireille hadn't shared this bit of information with her, and began to wonder if Mireille had really been as open and forthright as she'd thought. What else was she hiding?

"Thwarted love," mused Phyllis. "That's a strong motive."

"Well, I think they need more than a motive," said Ted. "There are plenty of people in this town with a motive to kill Ed Franklin."

"Like pretty much anyone who had to deal with the board of health," said Lucy.

Ted was already on the phone, calling the DA's office. "Hey, Phil," he began, in a friendly tone that implied they were old buddies. "What's this I hear about Matt Rodriguez being charged with Ed Franklin's murder?"

Lucy and Phyllis were all ears, but all they got was a series of "I sees" and "Oh, reallys" and finally a "Thanks for your time."

Ted replaced the receiver thoughtfully and swiveled around in his desk chair, facing his two employees. Moving slowly and deliberately, he placed one hand on each thigh and pressed his lips together.

"So what did he say?" demanded Phyllis.

"What have they got on him?" asked Lucy.

"The murder weapon," said Ted, sounding surprised. "It was hidden inside the restaurant, dropped between two studs behind new Sheetrock."

"How'd they find it?" wondered Phyllis.

"She's right," said Lucy. "Unless they used a metal detector. And what were they doing searching the restaurant, anyway?"

"Aucoin said they got a tip and were legally obligated to get a warrant and follow up."

"This is fishy," said Lucy, beginning to wonder if Zoe might be on to something. "It sounds to me like somebody planted the gun to set him up."

"Like who?" asked Ted.

"Well, there's the anti-immigrant, anti-Mexican bunch."

"I don't think they're smart enough to think up something like this," said Phyllis.

"It doesn't take a lot of smarts to hide a gun, especially if you used it to kill somebody," said Lucy.

"I don't see those guys as killers," protested Ted.

"Well, there's Ed Franklin Enterprises," Lucy pointed out. "That's a major operation that we don't know much about."

"Right," said Ted, looking as if a lightbulb had turned on in the vacant space over his head. "We've got to find out who they are and what they do."

The phone rang and Phyllis answered, promptly transferring the call to Lucy. "It's your wife, Ted, and she wants to talk to Lucy."

Lucy picked up her extension and heard Pam's somewhat breathless voice. "Finally!" she exclaimed. "Didn't my husband tell you to call me?"

"He did," admitted Lucy, "but we're kind of caught up in a breaking story—"

"Well, this is breaking news, too. And good news, for a change. I want to get it in the paper. I'm here with the members of the Harvest Festival planning committee . . ."

Lucy could just picture the scene at Pam's kitchen table, where a group of earnest church ladies were listening as she made this big announcement.

"And we've just done the accounting and it turns out this year's festival was a record breaker, clearing just under ten thousand dollars!"

"That's terrific," said Lucy, eager to get back to the big story about Matt Rodriguez's arrest.

"It gets better," said Pam. "As you know, we usually distribute the money from the festival to local charities, but this year we decided to do something different."

Lucy had a somewhat disturbing thought, picturing the church ladies taking part in one of Pam's early-morning yoga classes on a Caribbean beach.

"We were discussing various options and one of our members mentioned that her nephew had become addicted to opioids and couldn't afford rehab and, well, everyone seemed to know someone affected by this opioid crisis and we came up with the idea of helping people who want to go to rehab."

"That's a great idea," said Lucy, "but ten thousand dollars will send only one person to rehab. Not that there's anything wrong with that. It means saving a life."

"Believe me, Lucy, between the five of us we knew quite a bit about addiction and rehab and that's something we discussed. It was Michelle, who is a social worker, who pointed out that simply giving an addict a free ride to rehab would be counterproductive. Addicts need to be accountable, she said, so we've come up with the idea of an interest-free loan program. Anyone who accepts the money will have to pay it back so we can help fund rehab for others. And we're not going to pay the whole cost, either. Some medical insurance plans provide partial coverage for rehab, and family members can usually help, too. And there are charitable groups like the fraternal organizations and the police and fire unions that would probably want to help."

Lucy had to admit the church ladies had come up with a workable plan. "I think you're really on to something."

"Well, we do, too, and we want to let everybody know all about it and get the ball rolling."

"How soon will this money be available?" asked Lucy, thinking of Hank.

"At the moment, it's just sitting in a bank account," said Pam.

"But that doesn't mean we're going to write a check to someone for ten thousand dollars. Every applicant will have to put together a financial package and formally request the amount they need and agree to pay it back on a regular payment schedule."

Lucy could just see those church ladies nodding along. "I see," she said, convinced that this was a rare opportunity for Hank, if she could convince him to take advantage of it.

"So you'll write the story?" asked Pam.

"Of course," said Lucy, struck by the absurdity of the question. "You're the boss's wife."

"Great. We'll write up an official press release and e-mail it to you today."

The wheels were already turning in Lucy's head, and she was convinced that simply writing up the details of the festival committee's plan was not enough. For the story to have a real impact it would have to show how the plan made a difference in someone's life, someone like Hank. But how was she going to pull something like this together?

First she'd have to convince him to agree to go to rehab, which he had said he wanted to do, but she wasn't entirely convinced he really meant it. And then he'd have to start putting a financial plan together, which seemed like a daunting challenge for someone struggling with drug dependency. He would definitely need help for that part, probably more help than she was in a position to provide. And finally, she realized, as her heart dropped with a thump, she didn't even know how to contact him. She knew he was no longer enrolled at the college, which meant he didn't have a dorm room of his own but most likely couch-surfed among his friends or even slept in his truck. She knew he still had his pickup because she'd seen him in it at Blueberry Pond . . .

"What does my wife want you to do?" asked Ted, crashing into her runaway train of thought.

"Hot lead. See you later," said Lucy, picking up her bag and grabbing her jacket as she hurried out the door.

Ted and Phyllis shared a puzzled glance.

"I thought I knew my wife," he said, shaking his head, "but now it seems she's brushing me off and giving news tips to Lucy."

Phyllis just shrugged and went back to editing the classified ads while Ted reached for his phone to call home.

Lucy knew it was a long shot, but it was the only shot she had. The drive home to the house took fifteen minutes or so, changing into her running clothes took another five, and then she was back on the trail to Blueberry Pond. Libby was thrilled at this unexpected treat and ran ahead with her tail held high, tongue and ears flapping.

Lucy suspected she was being ridiculous as she ran along the familiar path. There was only the slimmest chance that she would catch Hank buying drugs at the pond, and an even slimmer chance that she could get him to agree to go to rehab, much less figure out a plan to submit to the church ladies. *What will be, will be,* she told herself, repeating it like a mantra as her feet hit the path in an even pace. What will be, will be . . .

With a series of sharp barks, Libby announced their arrival in the Blueberry Pond parking lot and Lucy miraculously spotted Hank's parked pickup truck. She was panting as she approached the driver's side window where she could see Hank's head leaning against the glass. For a second she had a flashback to Ed Franklin's murder.

Then Hank moved his head and he saw her and the dog. "Hey," he said, rolling down the window

"Hey," said Lucy, eyeing him skeptically. He was unshaven and seemed lethargic, and he looked as if he could use a shower and clean clothes. "Are you high?"

He considered his state carefully. "Coming down, I'd say."

"You're good for a talk?" asked Lucy, chest heaving from exertion and also a certain amount of anxiety. She'd never done anything like this before.

"Sure. But I don't want a sermon."

"Funny you should say that," she began, launching into an outline of the church ladies' plan.

When she'd finished, Hank shook his head. "It's a great idea, but I wouldn't know how to begin."

"Your folks have got money," said Lucy.

"I'd have to tell them that I've been using," said Hank. "They don't even know I dropped out of college."

"Well, telling them would be an important step toward recovery. Believe me, I'm a mom and I'd rather know the truth about my kids. And besides, I think you're kidding yourself if you think they don't know. They certainly suspect something bad is going on with you."

He sat for a while and Lucy wondered if he was drifting off into a drug-induced haze. Then, all of a sudden, he shook his head and spoke. "And all that red tape with health insurance and finding a rehab place that'll take me . . ."

"I know a couple people who are brilliant at that stuff," said Lucy, suddenly inspired. "I'll bet they'll help you."

Again there was a long pause as Hank mulled things over. Lucy was feeling the chill and Libby had collapsed at her feet, resting her head on her paws. She was about to give up and head home when Hank made his decision.

"I'll do it," he said. "So who are these brilliant people who'll help me?"

Lucy was jogging in place. "Never mind that," she said, worried that the answer would cause him to immediately reject the idea, "just call this number."

"Hold on," he said, producing a cell phone. "Give it to me again," he requested, and Lucy obliged, with lots of stops and starts, until he got the right digits.

Back on the trail, she knew she'd done all she could and now it was up to Hank. She wondered if he would actually commit to getting clean or whether he would continue to use and simply slip away like so many others.

When she approached the house, she spotted Zoe's ancient little Civic in the driveway Her daughter met her at the door, ignoring the dog's enthusiastic tail-wagging greeting and demanding any news of Matt.

Lucy got herself a drink of water and filled Libby's bowl with clean water before sitting down at the golden oak table. She patted the chair Zoe usually used and waited for her to sit down, too, before breaking the news. "It's not good, I'm afraid," she said, somewhat out of breath. "The cops believe they found the gun that killed Ed Franklin. It was hidden in the restaurant."

As Lucy expected, Zoe promptly exploded, delivering an angry tirade. "That's absolutely unbelievable! It's so obvious that somebody set him up! How dumb are they? It's a construction site, right? Anybody could have gotten in and hidden the gun. Were there fingerprints? How do they know it was Matt's? That's crazy! It's . . . it's . . . it sucks," she finally said, running out of steam.

"It does," agreed Lucy, "but we don't know everything that the police know."

"Well, I know that Matt would never do something like that," said Zoe.

Lucy smiled. "Well, then, he's got nothing to worry about, right?"

"Oh, Mom," groaned Zoe, rolling her eyes. "You're so naïve."

Lucy stood up and rinsed out her water glass, then set it on the dish drainer. Zoe had remained at the table and was tapping away on her smartphone, which reminded Lucy that she needed to give Miss Tilley and Rachel a heads-up about Hank on the slim chance that he might follow up and call them for help.

Lucy knew that Miss Tilley had a way of getting her way and Hank wouldn't have a hope of evading rehab if he took that first step and called her. Rachel, who was Miss Tilley's companion and home aide, was a whiz with red tape and bureaucracy, and had the advantage of being able to get free legal advice from her lawyer husband, Bob.

"Ah, Lucy, I haven't seen much of you lately. Have you been avoiding me?" asked Miss Tilley when Lucy called.

"Not at all," said Lucy. "You're one of my favorite people."

"Well, I'd never know it, since you never visit," continued Miss Tilley.

"I know. It's been too long," said Lucy. "And now I'm going to ask a big favor of you and Rachel." She outlined the program the Harvest Festival planners had come up with and told Miss Tilley about Hank. "So I gave him your number, hoping you and Rachel could help him put together an application."

"That was rather presumptuous of you," said Miss Tilley, causing Lucy's hopes to wither.

"I know. I do hope you won't let that stand in the way . . ." she began, by means of apologizing.

"But of course we'll do it," said Miss Tilley. "Rachel has been so difficult lately, I've been at my wit's end trying to think of ways to keep her entertained."

"Right," said Lucy, suspecting that her old friend wasn't joking at all, but was quite serious.

She could only imagine how Rachel, who devoted herself to Miss Tilley's well-being, was reacting. Though, truth be told, she refused to let Miss Tilley's little jabs bother her, aware that the old woman's wit was her sole remaining defense against the inexorable deterioration of old age.

"I can't thank you enough for taking this on," said Lucy.

"We may not be taking on anything unless he calls," said Miss Tilley.

"I hope he does," said Lucy.

"So do I," replied her old friend. "So do I."

That task completed, Lucy glanced at the clock on the kitchen wall and realized it was time to think about starting supper. She opened the fridge and discovered it was quite empty; a look in the freezer revealed a whole chicken and nothing much else. She took out the chicken, which was frozen hard as a rock, and decided there was no way she could get it thawed and cooked before midnight. Nothing for it but to call for pizza.

CHAPTER 15

Lucy couldn't believe it when Rachel called on Friday evening, looking for a way to get Hank to New Beginnings rehab in Portsmouth, New Hampshire. "They say it's not a good idea for him to drive himself," she explained, "as he might get cold feet and decide not to come. I'd do it, but I've got a rehearsal tomorrow."

Rachel was a gifted amateur actress, who often starred in the town's Little Theater productions. This year she was playing Scrooge's housekeeper in the group's annual production of Dickens' *A Christmas Carol*.

"You've done all this in one day?" asked Lucy, incredulous. "Put together the application, raised the money, got Hank to commit . . ."

"Well, yeah," said Rachel as if it hadn't been much of an achievement. "He called shortly after you did and came over that evening and I have to say he was very sweet and grateful for our help. He called his father and got a thousand from him. It turns out he has a trust fund from his mother's family and Miss Tilley got her to release some funds from that. He's on his parents' health plan so they're covering fifty percent, so he only needed a couple thousand from Pam's fund—"

"You did all this in one day? Including finding a spot in a rehab place?"

"That was the toughest part," said Rachel. "We got a list off the Internet and started calling and there were no openings, including this New Beginnings outfit you mentioned, but then they called back later and said they could take him. I think somebody may have decided not to go at the last minute, which is why—"

"I can do it, but we'll have to leave early. I'm driving to Boston tomorrow for Ed Franklin's funeral."

"Well, that's great, Lucy. Hank's sleeping here at Miss Tilley's tonight. We'll have him up and packed bright and early."

When Lucy arrived at Miss Tilley's little Cape-style house on Saturday morning, Hank was waiting by the door, every bit as nervous as a kindergartener on the first day of school. Rachel gave him a big hug,

Miss Tilley took his strong young hand in her age-spotted and blue-veined arthritic claw and gave it a pat. "You'll do fine, young man, and don't forget to write."

Hank was puzzled. "Write? You mean like Twitter?"

"I mean letters. You take a pen and paper and write down everything that's happening. I'll be looking forward to hearing from you."

Hank was thinking hard. "Wouldn't I need stamps for that?"

"E-mail will be fine," said Rachel, giving him a pat on the back and a little shove toward the door.

"That Miss Tilley's a funny old bird, isn't she?" he asked as he walked down the brick path with Lucy, dragging a wheeled duffel behind him.

"A word of advice," said Lucy, opening the rear hatch on her SUV. "Don't underestimate her and don't disappoint her, or you'll be sorry."

Hank loaded the bag inside, then turned to her. "You've done so much for me. Not just you, but Miss Tilley and Rachel and my folks and the Harvest Festival ladies. I really don't want to let anybody down."

"Well, don't," said Lucy, yanking the driver's side door open and climbing inside. She waited until he was seated beside her with his seatbelt fastened, then started the car and began the three hour drive to Portsmouth.

Hank was very quiet and when Lucy glanced at him she noticed his eyes were closed as if he had dozed off. Just as well, she thought, relieved that she didn't have to keep up a conversation.

It wasn't until they were going over the Piscataqua Bridge linking Maine with New Hampshire that he woke up, yawning and rubbing his eyes. "We must be almost there."

"Pretty close, according to the GPS. Did you have a nice rest?"

"Sorry about that. I haven't been sleeping much lately."

Lucy remembered how her son, Toby, when he was Hank's age, used to sleep for twelve hours at a stretch. She and her friends used to be amazed at the amount of sleep their teenage boys needed, and how difficult it was to get them up in the morning in time for the seven o'clock school bus. "How come?" she asked, wondering if insomnia was a side effect of addiction.

"I keep thinking about Alison," he said. "I keep seeing her dead, you know, drowned and all wet and ghoulish."

"I saw her body," said Lucy. "She looked just like herself. Not ghoulish."

He was silent, looking out the window as they drove down a main avenue dotted with stores and houses. Some of the buildings looked ancient, perhaps dating from the eighteenth century. "She wasn't on drugs. They say she was, but I know for sure that she wasn't. I tried to get her to use with me, but she wouldn't. She used to get mad at me, tell me to get clean or get lost."

"Was she dating anyone?" asked Lucy, thinking of Matt Rodriguez.

"Maybe. I don't know," he answered. "We were good friends for a while. We both have kind of messed up families, but we kind of drifted apart when I stopped going to classes."

"Do you know why she didn't want to live with her mother?" asked Lucy. "It seems kind of odd that she chose to live with her father and his new, young wife."

"She hated her mom, and she really hated her stepdad. She called him a weasel. She didn't always agree with her dad, she told me, but at least he was honest, even if all he really cared about was having a lot of money."

"You have reached your destination," the GPS informed her in a crisp British accent.

Lucy spotted a small, discreet sign announcing NEW BEGIN-NINGS on a patch of grass in front of a large Federal-style brick building. "We're here," she said, noticing that Hank seemed to have lost all the color in his face. "Are you okay?"

"I will be," he said, opening the door and climbing out.

Lucy popped the rear hatch and he pulled out his duffel, then he came around the car to her door. She hit the power button and lowered the window, expecting him to say good-bye.

But there was something else on Hank's mind. "Alison was really excited about having a little half sister or brother. She loved kids." He swallowed hard. "It's too bad she never got to have any of her own."

Lucy reached out the window and squeezed his shoulder. "This is about you," she told him. "Time for you to concentrate on getting well."

He nodded, looking very serious. Then he walked around the car and started up the brick path, dragging the duffel behind him. As Lucy watched him mount the stairs, she saw someone opening the door for him, greeting him with a welcoming smile.

She remained parked for a few minutes, entering her next destination—Boston's Trinity Church—into her GPS, and then shifted into DRIVE. As she pulled out into the street, she left with mixed emotions. On one hand, she felt satisfied she'd done all she could for him. On the other, she hoped and prayed that Hank would do the work he needed to do.

Lucy was familiar enough with Boston to know that she wouldn't be able to pull up next to Trinity Church and park the car, so she was on the lookout for a parking garage when the GPS told her she was approaching her destination. She pulled into the first garage she saw and, after getting over the shock of the price listed on a sign by the entrance, took the ticket and began a long descent into the bowels of Boston. Finally finding a vacant spot, she parked, took the elevator to the surface, and began the short walk to Copley Square.

Her mother used to scoff that Boston was a "small town" compared to New York, but Lucy found Boston pretty exciting after living so long in Tinker's Cove. The streets were lined with tall buildings and the sidewalks were filled with people of all ages and ethnicities, all intent on going somewhere. The shop windows were filled with interesting, and no doubt expensive, temptations.

Arriving at Copley Square where a steel drum band was playing beneath the bare trees, she paused to take in the scene. The square itself was filled with people, some listening to the music, others feeding pigeons or simply taking a rest on one of the benches. The Boston Public Library faced the square on one side, the stately Fairmont Copley Plaza Hotel stood on another, and Trinity Church itself stood beneath the gleaming mirrored walls of the sleek Hancock Tower, which was designed to reflect an image of the church.

A steady stream of people were pouring into the church and Lucy joined them, making sure to have her ID and press pass ready for presentation. As she shuffled along in the line, she recognized some well-known people—the governor of Massachusetts, the mayor of Boston, the senior senator from Massachusetts, Bob Kraft, who owned the Patriots football team, and a couple newscasters she'd seen on TV. The line moved right along as people were identified and escorted to pews in the Romanesque church, but when Lucy handed over her credentials to the gatekeepers she was directed to a small doorway. There she encountered a steep staircase that led to the choir loft, which offered a terrific view of the church below, but was too small for the large number of media people assigned to cover the funeral.

She was fortunate enough to squeeze herself into a spot in the front row, where she stood in a corner and prayed that whoever designed the 150-year old church had thought to make sure the choir loft was strong enough to hold a large crowd. She wasn't the only one who had that thought.

The cameraman from Channel 5 was clearly uncomfortable. "I covered a balcony collapse—a triple-decker—last week," he told her. "Bunch of college kids. Two were killed."

"That's terrible," said Lucy. "I hope that doesn't happen to us."

"What are the chances?" he asked. "An old building, constructed before today's building codes . . ."

"Back when people weighed less," added newscaster Monique Washington, who was a beautiful, large black woman.

"We don't get no respect," said a young guy sporting a fashionable day-old beard whose lanyard identified him as working for the *Boston Globe*. "They want good press, but they don't want to provide decent accommodations for us. They just crowd us in behind fences like we're a bunch of cows or stick us up in the attic. Jeez, it's hot up here."

"You said it," agreed Monique, fanning herself with the order of service she'd picked up off a chair. "So do you think we'll have any drama? The wives encounter each other and start ripping off black veils?"

"That'd be something," said the guy from the *Globe* in a hopeful tone.

"Well, here comes the current wife, the show girl," said the cameraman, swinging his camera to focus on Mireille.

She was walking slowly down the aisle, leaning slightly backwards and holding onto her mother's arm. From her vantage point, Lucy could only see her back. Mireille was dressed in low heels and a simple black cloth coat that provided a dark contrast to her flowing blond hair. Mimsy was also dressed simply in a navy pantsuit. A navy and white checked beret was on her head. They were following an usher, who led them to the first pew on the left-hand side of the church.

"Very understated, very tasteful," admitted Monique with a raised eyebrow. "I'm kinda surprised. I thought she'd be brassier somehow."

Lucy wanted to defend Mireille but bit her tongue, unwilling to share her privileged one-on-one interview with the entire press corps.

"You gotta wonder with a young wife like that, if she's kinda glad the old boy is gone or whether she'll really miss him," said the cameraman.

"She won't have to go on Match.com, that's for sure, not with a billion or two in the bank," said the guy from the *Globe*.

"And she's got the looks, or will have, once she has the baby," said the cameraman. He was swinging the camera once again, this time picking up the arrival of Ed Franklin's divorced wife, Eudora. "Here comes the hag," he announced.

"Oh my gosh. She's gone over the top," said Monique, rolling her eyes.

Peering down, Lucy had to agree. Eudora had swathed herself in layers and layers of black gauze, which gave the impression that she was a Muslim woman required to cover every inch of herself with a suffocating chador. Apparently unable to support her grieving self, or perhaps unable to see through the dense layers of fabric, she was supported by her son, Tag, on one side and her husband, Jon, on the other. The trio were led by an usher and followed by an entourage that included two beady-eyed security agents and a couple assistants carrying briefcases and black leather portfolios.

Lucy would have loved to hear what her companions thought of Eudora and company, but anything they might have said was drowned out by the organ music, which began with a thunderous chord that practically blew the crowd of media representatives right off the balcony. The pipes of the church's organ were located behind the choir loft, giving the media the full benefit of that magnificent instrument's awesome power.

The service was long. Many famous people eulogized Ed Franklin. A famous opera singer sang his favorite song ("I Did It My Way"), and the congregation stumbled through a number of unfamiliar hymns, which didn't matter because the organ drowned everyone out. Lucy was feeling quite dizzy and nauseous when the casket containing Ed Franklin's remains was finally lifted off its support and carried down the aisle on the shoulders of six strong men. There was an anxious moment when Eudora and Mireille faced off on opposite sides of the aisle, but Mireille graciously yielded to Eudora, who was determined to be seen as the principal mourner.

"First wives go first," said Monique with a smirk.

Lucy regretted taking that prime spot in the front row of the choir loft as it meant she was one of the last to leave. She seemed to be having some sort of low blood sugar problem. Or maybe it was the noise of the organ or the heat in the church, or the fact she hadn't had anything to eat since breakfast. She was feeling quite unsteady when she finally reached the stairs and began descending. She held on to the railing for dear life and concentrated on getting through the crowd to the door, hoping that all she needed was some fresh air. At the bottom of the staircase she encountered Eudora's assistants, who were distributing packets of press releases. She grabbed the thick folder and slipped through the crowd to the porch, where she grabbed a handy pillar for support and breathed deep breaths.

She spotted a CVS store across the square and made a somewhat unsteady beeline to its candy counter, where she bought herself a lifesaving Snickers bar and a bag of peanut M&Ms. She ate them all while standing outside the store, watching the great and good—the celebrities and the politicians—stream from the church and make their way to the Copley Plaza. All except for Mireille and her mother, who Lucy saw leaving by a side door and getting into a waiting black town car unnoticed by the chattering crowd.

She felt much better after her chocolate and sugar binge and was sorely tempted to cruise down Boylston and back up Newbury for a bit of window-shopping . . . or maybe even some actual shopping if she found something irresistible that wasn't too expensive. Then she remembered the price of the parking garage where the meter was running and decided she'd better head back to Tinker's Cove. She had a long drive ahead of her, after all, and a long list of weekend chores that weren't going to do themselves. There were no little fairies (or even family members) who shopped for groceries like she did, taking advantage of coupons and sales, nor any who remembered to pick up the dry cleaning or knew which brand of dog food to buy.

She was somewhat nervous about the traffic in Boston, which was known for its notoriously bad drivers, but she made it to the expressway in one piece, and then joined the bumper-to-bumper traffic crawling through the Big Dig tunnels to the dramatic Zakim Bridge. Things gradually improved as she headed north and traffic steadily thinned out. She was approaching the Hampton tolls, where her EZPass allowed her to fly through the formerly clogged toll booths, when her cell phone rang.

She picked it up, she saw Zoe's picture, and quickly answered. "What's up?"

"It's Dad, Mom. He's in the hospital."

Lucy felt as though she'd been hit with a sledge hammer. What could it be? A heart attack? An accident? "What happened?"

"I'm not sure. I'm on my way there now. Barney called. He said the restaurant was firebombed."

Lucy had lots of questions, but the only thing that mattered was getting back to Tinker's Cove and Bill as fast as possible. That was all she thought about as she pushed her car beyond the speed limit, rushing to her husband's side.

CHAPTER 16

The drive from New Hampshire had never seemed so long to Lucy, even though she was risking getting a speeding ticket. She kept trying to call Zoe or Bill or even the Tinker's Cove police department on her cell phone, desperate to learn what had happened and, more important, Bill's condition. She struggled to divide her attention between the phone and the road, unwilling to lose time by pulling over into a rest area. Her fingers kept fumbling and she couldn't get a signal and when she nearly ran off the road, she gave up.

She ran out of freeway in Brunswick when she had to exit onto Route 1 and that was when the state trooper appeared in her rearview mirror, blue lights flashing, and she had to pull over.

"I know I was going too fast," she told the trooper, "but my husband's been injured. It was an explosion, and I'm desperate to get to the hospital in Tinker's Cove."

"License and registration," said the trooper, unmoved by her plea. "Turn off your engine."

She obeyed, turning the ignition key and producing the documents, and watched in her side mirror as he took them back to his cruiser, where she knew he'd run them on his computer. Minutes ticked by slowly and it seemed like hours before he returned and handed them back to her.

"It seems you're known to the department," he said, still expressionless. "I'm supposed to escort you to the hospital. Follow me."

"Great," said Lucy, amazed at this surprising turn of events. Moments later he passed her, blue lights flashing, and she followed as he sped along the local road clearing the way. Traffic was fairly heavy this time of day when people were heading home for supper, but vehicles scattered before him as drivers pulled over to the side. When an inattentive motorist failed to spot the cruiser and forced him to slow he hit the siren, producing a couple short barks, and the driver quickly moved out of the way.

Lucy found she had to pay close attention in order to keep up as they whizzed along the narrow two-lane road, sometimes pulling into the oncoming lane, and she had to put her worries about Bill out of her mind. She'd never driven like this, weaving through traffic at speeds approaching eighty miles per hour, and she found it terrifying. It was a huge relief when they finally made the turn onto Main Street in Tinker's Cove and she spotted the illuminated emergency room sign at the cottage hospital. The trooper turned off his flashing lights and drove off, giving her a cursory wave as she pulled into an empty parking space.

Getting out of the car, she was assailed by fear, dreading what she might find. What if Bill hadn't survived the blast? What would she do then? She couldn't imagine living a single day without her husband. It would be like losing part of herself. Or what if he was gravely injured and required constant care? How was her life going to change? Was he suffering?

It was that last thought that propelled her forward, toward the plate glass doors that opened automatically at her approach. She went straight to the reception desk where she was surprised to see Babs Culpepper, her friend Barney's sister.

"Lucy, you're here," she said in a bright voice. "Bill's in that first exam room. Go right on in."

"How is he?" Lucy asked.

"I'm not supposed to say," replied Babs. "But he's in pretty good shape, considering."

Lucy wasn't sure how to take that. "Pretty good shape, considering" could cover a lot of territory. But when she opened the door, she saw Bill was sitting up on the gurney, with his arm in a sling. Zoe was there, sitting on a chair, and State Police Lieutenant Horowitz was standing beside him, dressed as always in a gray suit. Lucy and Horowitz had a long history, and while they often conflicted, they shared a mutual respect for each other. She was rather dismayed to notice his hair was also entirely gray, and his pale blue eyes made him look more tired than ever.

"Did you enjoy the escort?" he asked, stepping aside so Lucy could reach her husband.

"Was that you?" she asked, occupied in studying Bill's condition and deciding if she could hug him.

His face and head were scraped and bruised, as was the hand that emerged from the black sling. He held out his other hand and she grabbed it with both hands.

"What's the damage?" she asked.

"Broken arm, a few bumps and bruises," he answered with a smile. "I was darned lucky. I was standing by the door, which happened to be open, and I was blown outside by the force of the explosion. I guess I must have instinctively used my arm to try and break my fall, which is why it's broken."

"You should see the place, Mom," said Zoe. "The entire front wall is gone and there was a lot of damage from the fire. It looks like a bomb hit it."

"That's what we're trying to determine," said Horowitz, looking very serious. "The fire marshal is investigating whether the explosion was caused by a device or a gas leak. I was just asking your husband if he smelled gas beforehand."

Lucy couldn't take her eyes off Bill. She was studying every scab and bruise, and kept hanging onto his hand as if afraid he'd disappear if she let go.

"I don't remember much," said Bill, mumbling a bit.

"Does it hurt to talk?" she asked, and he gave her a nod.

"Can you question him another time?" asked Lucy, turning to Horowitz. "He's clearly in pain."

"I really don't know what happened," said Bill, speaking slowly with effort. "I opened the door and pow! Next thing I knew I was flat on my back in the parking lot and the pub was in flames." He sighed. "I wish I could tell you more. I really do."

"Okay," said Horowitz with a decisive nod. "I'll be in touch."
He turned to go.

"Thanks for the police escort," said Lucy, walking the few steps to the door with him. "It was quite an experience."

"Glad to be of service," he said, opening the door. "Besides, from what I heard, you were a menace out there on the road."

"Well, thanks again," said Lucy as he stepped into the hallway.

Once she was sure he was gone, and the door closed, Lucy had a million questions for Bill and Zoe. She had to wait to ask them, however, as a nurse popped in with a clipboard full of papers for him to sign.

"Once we finish this business you can go," she announced, flipping the pages and pointing where to sign.

"Good thing it was my left arm," he said, scrawling his signature where she'd indicated. "I'm right-handed."

"I've got a prescription for painkillers for you," she said, handing him a blue square of paper. "Don't try to be a hero. They're not addictive and you'll be a lot more comfortable if you take them."

"Will do," said Bill. "I'm no hero."

"I can pick up the prescription on my way home," offered Zoe.

"That would be great," said Lucy, giving her the blue slip. "That way we won't have to stop and can go straight home with your dad."

The nurse gave him a hand and helped him off the gurney, and then they all walked through the ER and out through the waiting room to the door.

"Safe home," said Babs, and Lucy gave her a big smile and a little wave before stepping outside.

"Do you want to wait here and I'll bring the car over?" asked Lucy, but Bill shook his head and headed straight for her SUV, albeit walking rather more slowly than usual.

Zoe headed in the opposite direction, toward her little Civic.

Watching her go, Lucy had a sudden inspiration and called after her, "Zoe! Pick up a pizza for dinner!"

"Again?" asked Bill with a groan.

Zoe turned back and gave her a nod. "Will do!"

Bill grunted a bit as he settled himself in the passenger seat, and he winced as Lucy helped him with his seat belt, arranging it so it didn't press against his broken arm. Then she started the car and they were on the way home.

"So what really happened?" she asked, braking at the exit.

"It's like I told the lieutenant," said Bill. "I opened the door and the place blew up."

"Do you think it was a gas leak?" she asked, making the turn onto Main Street. "Or did somebody set a bomb, like maybe one or more of those anti-immigration demonstrators?"

"Could be either of those," said Bill. "Or it could have been Rey."

Lucy couldn't believe what he was saying. "Rey?"

"Yeah. Why not? He's running into a lot of problems here. His son is facing criminal charges, he's got to pay a lot of money for a lawyer to defend the kid, and he's already soaked a lot of money into a project that he probably figures is never going to be profitable."

"You think he did it himself for the insurance money?"

"Wouldn't be the first time somebody tried that," said Bill, leaning back and closing his eyes. "Or the last."

When they got home Lucy helped him into the house and got him settled on the sectional in the family room where he could rest and watch the evening news on TV while she threw together a salad. When the segment about the explosion came on, he called her and she hurried to watch.

Looking at the images of the damage, which was extensive, she thought it was a miracle that Bill had survived. As Zoe had told her, the entire front of the pub was gone, and the inside was a charred mess. Tables and chairs had been tossed this way and that, the remaining walls were streaked with soot, and the swinging door that led to the kitchen was hanging askew. A lace curtain that remained where a window had once been blew in the breeze.

"What happened here?" a reporter asked fire chief Buzz Bresnahan. "Was it arson?"

"We don't know yet. The fire marshal will conduct a complete investigation. I'm just glad it wasn't worse. One man was injured, but there were no fatalities."

Overcome by the thought of what might have been, Lucy plunked herself down on the coffee table and took Bill's good hand. When she started to talk he shushed her.

"All's well that ends well," he said with a wry grin. "And I think Zoe's here with the pizza—and the pills."

Lucy met Zoe in the kitchen and they put together trays so they all could eat in the family room. Lucy read the instructions on the bottle of painkillers and counted out two tablets, which she placed in a custard cup on Bill's tray. He swallowed them immediately when she gave him his dinner tray, washing them down with a big swallow of cola. He had switched off the news and found a college football game, and the roar of the huge crowd, punctuated by blasts from the college band, provided a welcome distraction as they ate their pizza and salad.

When there was a break in the action and the chains were brought out to determine if Iowa had made a first down, Zoe spoke up. "I don't think I should go to Montreal," she said, referring to her planned departure after class on the coming Tuesday, two days before Thanksgiving. "Dad's gonna need help while Mom's at work and I'm sure Renée will understand."

"But you've been looking forward to seeing Renée," said Lucy, referring to their young neighbor from the housing development on nearby Priscilla Path who was attending Concordia University.

"And I'll be fine," said Bill, who had polished off his first piece of pizza and was well into his second.

"I'm really nervous about leaving and I know I'd be terrible company. I'd just be worried about Dad and Matt and, well, it's just a lot coming on top of Alison's death."

"I think you should go, the sooner the better, for your own safety," said Lucy. "I've got a bad feeling that Tinker's Cove isn't safe right now."

Bill was about to take a bite of pizza but, hearing this, set it back down on his plate.

"Don't be silly, Lucy. That explosion was probably due to a loose gas connection, something like that."

"I don't think so, Bill. I think it was purposely set off by somebody, some evil person who didn't care if someone got hurt. Maybe it was for insurance, maybe it was to send a message. I don't know. But I do know that the whole town feels different. It's like people are afraid to meet each other's eyes. Admit it. You've felt it, too. There are people who don't like the fact that you've been working for Rey Rodriguez."

"Some idiot did throw some rotten garbage into my truck," he said with a shrug.

"When was this?" demanded Lucy. "Why didn't you tell me?"

"A couple days ago. I didn't think it was a big deal," he replied.

"It is a big deal!" exclaimed Lucy. "It's escalating and I'm afraid it's only going to get worse."

"Mom, you're being paranoid," said Zoe.

"Well, maybe so, but better safe than sorry. I think you should give Renée a call and say you can come earlier than you planned, okay?"

Zoe didn't answer but looked at her father, waiting for his thoughts.

"I'm not sure your mom is right, but I do think you could use a change of scene," said Bill. "It would be good for you to spend some time with Renée . . . and you can brush up on your French."

"I think you should give Renée a call. See if you can go tomorrow," suggested Lucy.

"But what about Matt? I want to support him . . ."

"I'm pretty sure he'll be relieved to know you're safe," said Lucy. "And he sure won't want you visiting him in jail."

"If he's got any decency at all," added Bill, who was never a fan of his daughter's boyfriends.

"Okay," agreed Zoe, deciding further resistance was futile, and turning her attention to her salad she speared a chunk of lettuce. "Will you keep me posted?"

"Absolutely," promised Lucy, taking a bite of pizza. She was chewing when a Notre Dame player made a ninety-yard run for a touchdown. Realizing Bill was strangely quiet, she turned to look at him and saw that he'd drifted off, still holding the tray with his half-eaten pizza in his lap. She gently removed it and covered him with an afghan, giving him a little kiss on his forehead as she tucked it around him.

Sunday morning was busy. Bill needed help getting showered and dressed, and took out his frustration with the situation on Lucy. She'd made him a big breakfast of ham and eggs, thinking it would please him, but he snapped at her when he couldn't manage to cut the ham by himself and had to ask for help. Zoe couldn't decide what clothes she needed to pack for Montreal and kept appearing in the kitchen, holding up various garments and asking her mother's opinion. Lucy was at her wits' end by the time Bill retreated to the family room, where he promptly fell asleep on the sectional sofa.

When the phone rang, she was surprised to hear Rey's voice.

"How is Bill?" he asked, concern in his voice.

"He's doing okay," said Lucy, taking the phone into the kitchen so she wouldn't disturb Bill. "He's in some pain, I think, but he doesn't want to admit it."

"What a terrible thing. I feel responsible. Let me know if there's anything I can do."

Lucy was tempted to say that he'd done enough, thank you, and to please leave them alone, but then she remembered that his son was facing murder charges, which was much more serious than a broken arm and a few bruises. "What's going on with Matt?"

"I believe they're transferring him today, bringing him back to Maine for arraignment on Monday. The lawyer says there's little chance he'll get bail, but we're going to try."

"I'm very sorry," said Lucy.

"I guess it was inevitable, given the situation, that they would try to pin Franklin's murder on him. He's innocent, of course, and I believe the truth will come out in the end."

"I certainly hope so," said Lucy.

"The reason I called is I'm coming to Maine for the arraignment, and to see Matt, and I'd like to meet with Bill about the restaurant project."

"I don't suppose you want to continue—" began Lucy.

"On the contrary," he said, interrupting her. "I'm determined to go ahead, I'm meeting with the insurance adjuster tomorrow and I'd like Bill to be there, if he's able."

"I'm not sure," said Lucy when Bill appeared in the doorway.

"Who's that?" he asked.

When she said it was Rey he took the phone himself and, before she could object, had agreed to meet him at the burned-out pub first thing in the morning.

Lucy was furious. "You're always telling me to mind my own business and to stay out of trouble," she reminded him, "and here you're walking right into a hornet's nest. Maybe you should take your own advice."

"I'm not committing myself to anything. I'm just going to a meeting," he said, turning his back on her and shuffling back to the family room.

A series of thumps emanating from the back staircase preceded Zoe, who appeared with her enormous duffel bag, ready to leave for Montreal. "You're sure you don't need me here, Mom?" she asked, setting the suitcase on the floor.

"No, we'll be fine. Give your dad a kiss."

Zoe disappeared into the family room, only to emerge a moment later. "He's gone back to sleep. You'll have to say good-bye for me."

"Okay," said Lucy, her voice thickening. "Drive carefully and be—well, you know, it's a big city. Take care of yourself."

"I will," said Zoe, laughing, as she put on her coat. "I won't go wandering off with any strangers, not even if they're incredibly cute and have charming French accents."

"If only I could believe that," said Lucy, tying a long scarf around her daughter's neck and giving her a big hug.

She stood at the kitchen window, watching as Zoe dragged the heavy bag down the path and loaded it into her car. She paused before getting in the car and gave her mother a wave, then she was gone.

Lucy was headed down to the cellar with a load of laundry when her cell rang and she saw the caller was Zoe. "What's up? Did you forget something?" she asked, resting the laundry basket on her hip.

"No, Mom, I didn't forget anything. It's this billboard. I thought you'd want to know about it. It must have just gone up, right out here on Route 1. It's a big blown-up version of the newspaper photo of those three drug dealers that got arrested a few weeks ago, with those police ID placards that have their names on them, all Latino of course, and then in big red, white, and blue letters it says AMERICA FOR AMERICANS!"

CHAPTER 17

Bill might have been able to drive one-handed, but the fact that he was also taking pain meds meant that Lucy had to chauffeur him to the early Monday morning meeting with Rey. His truck was damaged in the blast and was in the body shop, so they went in her SUV. The sun was just rising when they arrived at the harbor and shafts of morning light filled with dancing bits of dust streamed through the burned outer wall of the restaurant. The place reeked of smoke, charred wood, and melted plastic. Lucy and Bill stood outside the cordon of yellow tape and studied the scene, amazed that Bill survived the blast that created so much damage.

"I was sure lucky," he said, taking Lucy's hand.

"I can't think about what might have been," she said, turning away. Looking across the mostly empty parking lot dotted with a few pickup trucks and boats shrouded in white plastic, she spotted a white sedan coming down the hill. "I bet that's Rey."

Moments later the sedan slid into the parking spot next to Lucy's SUV and Rey got out, giving them a wave. The passenger side door opened and a young woman stepped out and came around the car to join him.

"This is my daughter, Luisa," said Rey, introducing her.

She was a petite version of her brother, with the addition of a gorgeous mane of black, wavy hair. She smiled, revealing dazzling white teeth and two dimples, one in each cheek.

"It's lovely to meet you," said Lucy. "We're both very sorry about Matt. Have you seen him?"

"Not yet," said Rey. "I imagine we'll be able to have a minute or two with him after the arraignment."

"He's very strong," said Luisa, sounding as if she was trying to reassure herself. "He'll be all right."

"I'm sure he will," said Bill. He indicated the burned out pub with a wave of his hand. "So what do you think?"

Rey stepped up to the yellow tape and walked along it, studying the damage and shaking his head. Bill, Lucy, and Luisa stood together, silently watching him.

"I'm interested to hear what the adjuster has to say," he said, joining them. "I think that may be him."

The *him* turned out to be a *her* dressed in mannish Carhartt overalls, sturdy work boots, and a hard hat. "I'm Donna Dewicki from National Assurance," she said, sticking out her hand.

"Rey Rodriguez." He shook hands with her and introduced the others.

"I've got permission from the fire department to take a look inside," she said, pulling a flashlight out of her pocket. "I'll be back in a jif."

The four stood together, watching as Donna stepped inside the burned shell of the pub and following the progress of her dancing flashlight.

After a few minutes she returned. "This is a total loss. It doesn't look to me like anything can be salvaged."

"So that means the company will pay the entire amount of the policy?" asked Luisa.

"That depends on the results of the fire marshal's investigation," said Donna, giving Rey a once-over. "If the explosion was caused by a gas leak or an electrical fault, then the company will pay, but if it's arson, there will need to be a further investigation."

"Are you implying I might have done this myself?" asked Rey.

"I'm not saying that. I'm saying that it's been done before and the company will want to be certain that it's not the case. We have a responsibility to our shareholders."

"I'd like to point out that I was in California when this happened," said Rey.

"Point taken," said Donna. "But there are people who would do the job for a price, and there are plenty of people who think a couple thousand dollars is a small price to pay for a million dollar payout."

"I can't believe this," fumed Rey, who was building up a head of steam.

Luisa rested a cautionary hand on his arm.

"It's okay, Papa. They have to investigate all the possibilities, but we know that we had nothing to do with this."

"I hope that's the case," said Donna, thrusting a clipboard in front of Rey. "Sign here, please. It's just an acknowledgement that I was here and examined the premises."

Rey scrawled an oversized signature on the small line marked with an X and handed the clipboard back with a little shove.

Donna responded with a raised eyebrow, but didn't say anything and quickly turned and strode across the parking lot to her van. No doubt she had learned through the years to avoid confrontations with policyholders. Lucy herself had been furious with her own insurance agent when he informed her that, even though their auto policy would cover some of the cost of repairs to the truck, they would have to pay a hefty deductible.

"Come on, Papa," said Luisa. "Let's look at the view before we leave."

Rey shook his head. "I want to talk to Bill. I want to know what he thinks."

"I'll walk with you," offered Lucy. "You can see Quissett Point from here."

"Okay," agreed Luisa with a smile.

The two women strolled to the end of the pier, watching in silence as a little red boat headed past the lighthouse, rounded the point, and went out to sea.

"It must be awfully cold out there," said Luisa with a little shiver.

"You bet." Lucy wondered if Luisa knew about the developing relationship between Matt and Zoe, but wasn't sure how to ask. After they stood in silence a few moments, gazing at the gleaming surface of the water and the little pine-covered islands and the boats bobbing on their moorings, she decided to just go for it. "You know, Matt seemed to be taking an interest in my daughter Zoe."

"He told me. He said she was the first girl since Alison that he really liked."

"Zoe's in Montreal, visiting a girlfriend there," said Lucy.

"Probably a smart move, considering all this," said Luisa with a nod in the direction of the burned-out pub.

Lucy was quick to add, "But she's very worried about Matt. She made me promise to keep her posted on developments."

"I'll let him know," said Luisa with a little smile.

"Thanks," said Lucy. "Was he very serious about Alison?"

"I think so. He dated her for quite a while. She was practically part of our family. They met in LA. She was a student at UCLA and he was working as a sous chef at the Four Seasons. I think they met when they were both running. You know, they had the same routine and saw each other every morning and finally started saying hi, that sort of thing. But then she had that accident and got into drugs and they broke up."

"Wow, it really is a small world. Girl from Maine meets boy in California."

"You know those Venn diagrams, those circles that overlap?" asked Luisa. "I'm into math and that's how I think about things. We all travel in circles, you know family groups, interest groups, economic groups, age groups, and when people share a certain number of factors it's pretty likely that their circles will overlap and they'll meet."

"So Matt and Alison shared a number of factors?" asked Lucy.

"Yeah. They were both young, they were both runners, they were in the same city, and they shared the same fantasy. She saw herself as a damsel in distress and he saw himself as a knight in shining armor."

"So what was Alison's dragon?" asked Lucy. "Drugs?"

"No. It was her family. She didn't get along with them at all. I used to think that it wasn't so much Matt who she liked as our whole extended family. You know, the parties and dinners with all the uncles and cousins and aunts."

"Well, Ed Franklin wasn't the easiest guy to get along with . . ." began Lucy.

"Oh, no, it wasn't her father. It was her monster mom and her slimy stepfather. Her words, not mine. And she hated the half brother, Trot or Trig. I forget his name. She said he was awful."

"In what way?" asked Lucy, fascinated.

"I'm not sure, exactly," admitted Luisa, "but Matt told me that she had him install a deadbolt on her bedroom door so she could lock herself in at night."

"Oh," said Lucy as they turned to walk back. She knew from her work as a reporter that sexual abuse in families was not uncommon and often had tragic consequences. "Do you think that she might have killed herself?"

"No. She would never have committed suicide," said Luisa, certainty in her voice. "I'm sure of that. And she didn't use drugs, either. She got addicted to pain killers after an accident, but she went to rehab and after that, she wouldn't even take an aspirin."

Bill and Rey were shaking hands and saying good-bye when the women returned and joined them.

Lucy also took Rey's hand and said, "I hope everything goes well at the arraignment. Be sure to give Matt our best wishes."

"I most certainly will," said Rey, taking Luisa's arm and walking with her to the rental car.

Lucy and Bill were quiet as they walked to the SUV, but as soon as they were inside Lucy asked if Rey had come to a decision about the future of the pub.

"He wants to go ahead," said Bill. "He says it's a blessing in disguise and he's hiring an architect to design his dream restaurant and he wants me to build it."

"I guess that depends on the insurance company."

"I guess it does."

Lucy took a detour on the way home, driving out to Route 1 to see the AMERICA FOR AMERICANS billboard. It was exactly as Zoe had described it, and it dominated the view. You couldn't avoid seeing it even if you wanted to. Lucy suspected a good number of people probably agreed with the anti-immigration sentiment.

"I wonder if Rey and Luisa saw it," said Bill as Lucy drove on past.

"I think they must have. Of course, they would have thought it utterly ridiculous since their family was here long before the American Revolution."

"But it's not really about immigration, is it? We're all descended from immigrants after all. It's about race and ethnicity. You know how they say a picture is worth a thousand words? Well there are only three words on the sign, but the picture of those mug shots of the three accused drug dealers says that Mexicans are criminals."

"I wonder who's behind it," said Lucy, switching into investigative reporter mode. "Those billboards are expensive."

"I have a feeling you're going to find out," said Bill as she turned off Route 1 onto Shore Road, heading back to Tinker's Cove and home.

Lucy was running late when she was finally able to leave for work, and she knew that Monday morning was always busy. There were usually new developments over the weekend, and a lot of people seemed to have nothing better to do on Sunday afternoon than to write e-mails to the local paper, which had to be answered.

Phyllis greeted her with a smile, and asked how Bill was doing. "Everybody's talking about that explosion," she said, peering over the zebra-striped cheaters perched on her nose. They matched her sweater and also her fingernails.

"Bill's got a broken arm," said Lucy, studying Phyllis's manicure. "How do you get stripes like that on your nails?"

"They're stickers. I heard the explosion, you know, and the sirens. It was scary. I thought the whole town was going to blow up."

"It was a heck of a blast," said Ted, turning away from his computer screen. "He was lucky he wasn't blown to bits."

"That's what he tells me," said Lucy, attempting a joke while hanging up her coat. She didn't like to think about the explosion and what might have been. Now she was realizing, for the first time, that the blast hadn't affected only her family and the Rodriguez family, but had literally sent tremors through the entire town.

"I'd like to interview Bill, if he's up to it," said Ted. "That blast is a big story and I'd love to get a first-person account."

Lucy plunked herself down at her desk, feeling overwhelmed. It was one thing to cover the news, quite another to *be* the news. "I was on my way home from Ed Franklin's funeral when Zoe called. I was only thinking of Bill. I wasn't thinking like a reporter."

"That's perfectly understandable," said Ted. "But it's the biggest thing that's happened in Tinker's Cove since the big rope-walk fire. I'm running it on page one."

"They had mutual aid," said Phyllis, referring to the system by which the local fire departments helped each other. "Trucks came from Gilead, Elna, and Dundee."

Lucy found herself growing misty, thinking of all those people who came to help Bill and put out the fire. "He says he doesn't remember much, but I'm sure he'd like to tell you as much as he can."

"Great," Ted said. "I'll give him a call and set a time. I want to interview him face-to-face. You're writing up the Franklin funeral. There's the selectmen's meeting and I think the finance committee is meeting—"

"What about the billboard? I want to do a piece on that, find out who's behind it," said Lucy.

"What billboard?" asked Ted.

"The one out on Route 1 that says *America for Americans*, with bigger than life mug shots of those three drug dealers that got arrested."

"I hate those things. They spoil the view," said Phyllis. "I was so happy when they finally took down that one of the governor."

"I'll swing out that way and take a look on my way to the interview," said Ted, reaching for his jacket. "Meanwhile you've got plenty to do, Lucy."

* * *

Lucy had finished up her story about the Franklin funeral and was trying to think of a way to write an interesting story about the selectmen's debate as to whether or not the town had an adequate supply of road salt for the coming winter when Ted called.

"I saw the sign and it's too big to ignore," he said. "Go ahead and find out who's behind it."

"Great," she said, only too happy to switch gears. She immediately called the owner of the sign, Maine Message, and spoke to a sales rep who was enthusiastic about the benefits of roadside advertisements.

"We have hundreds of billboards throughout the state. Surveys show that billboards are one of the most effective forms of advertising."

"I'm not interested in renting a billboard," said Lucy, explaining that she was a reporter with the *Pennysaver* newspaper. "I'm working on a story about a billboard that just went up on Route 1 and I need to know who is responsible for it. It's got an anti-immigrant message, *America for Americans*."

"I know the one. I sold that," said the rep. "We're not responsible for the message, you know. We just provide the space. We've had people propose marriage on our billboards. One guy rented one to announce the birth of his grandson. We do have limits. No profanity, no libel or slander, that sort of thing. If you want to call your neighbor a thief or a liar, you have to paint that on a piece of plywood yourself and nail it up on a tree on your own property."

"Good to know," said Lucy. "Can you tell me who put up the *America for Americans* sign?"

"Sure. I'm just checking my files . . . Ah, here it is. It's actually a group called America for Americans, and the contact person is Zeke Bumpus."

"Thanks," said Lucy, abruptly ending the call. She didn't need any further information. She knew exactly who Zeke Bumpus was and where to reach him.

He lived on Bumpus Road where his family had lived for hundreds of years without doing much to improve the place. The family home was a compound of ramshackle buildings surrounded by an assortment of things that might come in handy someday—

things like busted washing machines, old cars propped on cinder blocks, and various pieces of rusting machinery. Family members supported themselves by occasionally working on lobster boats or helping local building contractors, but generally avoided full-time jobs.

Zeke operated a firewood business, and Lucy found him in a patch of woods next to the family compound, running logs through a splitting machine. The machine was noisy and she caught his attention by waving her arms.

He reluctantly silenced the machine. "Whaddya want?" he asked, scowling. Zeke was only in his mid-twenties, but looked older due to his thinning hair and growing waistline. He was dressed for work in a faded plaid flannel shirt, filthy jeans, and a pair of unlaced work boots.

"Hi, Zeke. It's a nice day for outdoor work, right?"

He scowled at her. "I'd rather be hunting, but I gotta do this. We got a big order from the Queen Vic."

"Yeah, they advertise fireplaces in every room." Lucy was familiar with the town's upscale B&B.

Zeke cocked his head and looked at her with a puzzled expression. "Are you here for wood? I can give you a half-cord."

"No, I'm all set with firewood," she replied. "I'm actually here to ask about that billboard, the one that says *America for Americans.* How'd that come about?"

"Is this for the newspaper?" he asked, narrowing his pale blue eyes suspiciously.

"Of course. People are wondering who's behind the sign. It's causing quite a stir."

"Great. That's what we want. We want folks to realize that these immigrants, these Muslims and Mexicans and Somalis, are taking our country away from us. It's white people like you and me that built this country and now folks like us can't get jobs. All the jobs have gone overseas to places like Bangladesh and China. Do you know our country owes millions and billions of dollars to the Chinese? What's gonna happen if they decide it's time to pay up, huh? It's crazy the way we're letting these Mexicans flood the country with drugs, and they're sending us their criminals, too. Rapists and murderers, attacking white women and leaving them with little brown anchor babies."

"I'm sure a lot of folks agree with you," said Lucy when Zeke had run out of steam. She didn't want to risk angering him further, so she ventured cautiously into the territory she wanted to explore. "Do you have some sort of organization people can join?"

"Sure, America for Americans. We've got a website and everything."

"Those are expensive, aren't they? And that billboard must have cost a pretty penny, right?"

"Money's no problem. That's for sure."

"Really? How come?" Lucy seriously doubted Zeke's little firewood business earned the kind of money needed to rent a billboard.

"'Cause a rich donor gave us a big, fat check."

"Who was this donor?" asked Lucy, who had a good idea.

"Ed Franklin himself, before he died. I'm president, you see, but the sign was his idea. He worked out the design and the details. It came out real good."

"His death must be a huge loss to the organization," said Lucy.

"Yeah," agreed Zeke, nodding. "But we're going to have a big rally in his memory . . . on Thanksgiving Day, our national holiday."

Lucy couldn't resist. She had to say it. "But you know, Thanksgiving was started by the Pilgrims, who were actually immigrants."

"They were American immigrants," said Zeke, pointing a finger at her. "Remember that. American immigrants. America for Americans."

"It's been great talking to you, Zeke," she said, managing a halfhearted smile. It really wasn't worth pointing out that the Pilgrims arrived in 1620, a hundred and fifty-six years before the colonists rebelled against English rule. "Thanks."

"Anytime, Lucy," he said, picking up a log and starting up the log splitter. It roared into life and even though his lips were moving she couldn't hear what he was saying.

She gave him a wave and headed for her car, feeling somehow soiled by his hateful, ignorant words. If only you could wash off intolerance and prejudice like you rinse off salt after a swim in the sea. But all too often, it seemed, these ideas stuck and wormed their way into people's minds, where they grew like cancer.

Ed Franklin was dead, she thought, but he had left behind a hateful legacy that would live on, poisoning minds and quite possibly ripping the Tinker's Cove community apart.

CHAPTER 18

Lucy glanced at the dashboard clock when she started the car and was startled to realize it was almost noon. She wasn't far from home, so she decided to stop by to see how Bill was doing and have lunch with him before heading back to the office.

Reaching Red Top Road, which was usually deserted this time of day, she was surprised to see a number of cars coming the opposite way. The drivers usually stuck an arm out the window and gave her a wave or a friendly toot on the horn. When she got to the house perched on the top of hill, she saw an extra car in the driveway. Franny Small was bent over taking something out of her little Chevy, and when she stood up, Lucy saw she was holding a foil-covered dish.

"Hi, Lucy," she said, waiting while Lucy got of her SUV. "I hope Bill likes American chop suey. I made some for him. I thought he might like a hot lunch."

"Thanks, Franny. It's one of his favorite meals." Lucy neglected to mention that she hadn't made it for him in years, considering all that macaroni and ground beef much too fattening. "Why don't you come in and have lunch with us."

"Okay," said Franny, who was a single lady, now retired from a successful business career. "That would be nice. I do get a little tired of eating alone."

Once inside the kitchen, Lucy saw the golden oak table was full with a number of covered dishes. "What's all this?" she asked when Bill popped out of the family room.

"People have been stopping all morning, bringing food," he said. "There's cookies and banana bread and mac and cheese and I don't know what all."

"I guess I've brought coals to Newcastle," said Franny.

"Never you mind. I'm going to clear this away and we'll have your American chop suey," began Lucy, transferring a couple pies to the counter.

"American chop suey!" exclaimed Bill. "That's my favorite, and Lucy never makes it anymore."

Franny blushed, setting the foil-covered dish on the table. "I know it's the sort of hearty dish most men enjoy eating."

Lucy took Franny's coat and hung it up with her own, then quickly set the table with placemats, dishes, and silverware. She put the kettle on for tea and they all sat down to eat. Bill's broken arm hadn't spoiled his appetite, and he pleased Franny no end by eating seconds and thirds. When the kettle whistle sounded, Lucy made a pot of tea that they had along with Lydia Volpe's pizzelle cookies for dessert.

When they were finished eating, Franny insisted on helping Lucy with the dishes. Bill went off to the family room, rubbing his tummy and yawning as he went. The phone rang a couple times, but each time, he picked up the extension in the family room before Lucy could dry her hands to answer. When the dishes were done, Franny and Lucy exchanged thanks and good-byes— Franny thanked Lucy for inviting her to lunch and Lucy thanked Franny for bringing lunch and they both did this several times before Franny finally left. Lucy went into the family room expecting to find Bill sound asleep, but he was still talking on the phone.

"Waller's Garage has offered to cover the deductible when they fix the truck," he said when the call ended. "No charge."

"That's great," said Lucy, who had been fretting about that hefty deductible ever since her conversation with their insurance agent. She'd made the decision to raise the deductible some years ago in an effort to reduce the cost of their car insurance, which had increased sharply when the kids began driving.

"And the kids in the church youth group want to come and rake leaves for us."

"My goodness," said Lucy, feeling rather overwhelmed.

"Miss Tilley is going to bring me some books," he said, "and Hattie Gordon from the garden club is bringing a harvest-themed wreath, whatever that is."

Lucy was going to tell him, but the phone was already ringing again. She left him to answer it and headed back to work, taking along one of the four loaves of cranberry bread they had received. It would be good for an afternoon coffee break.

As she drove, she thought about all the good and kind people in Tinker's Cove who were always quick to reach out and help their neighbors in times of trouble, and she thought of Zeke Bumpus and the America for Americans faction. She wondered if the groups overlapped, like the circles in Luisa Rodriguez's Venn diagrams, or if they were clearly distinct circles. Reaching town and making the familiar turn onto Main Street, she concluded that they probably did. People weren't necessarily consistent and the woman who baked cranberry bread for her ailing neighbor might also fear that an influx of immigrants would change the character of her town.

Lucy was passing the town common when she noticed that the chamber of commerce's huge cornucopia had been erected in the bandstand and decided to snap a photo for the *Pennysaver*. Volunteers had built the horn of plenty, which was constructed of painted canvas stretched over a wood frame, and the chamber set it up every year to collect the canned foods that were the entry fee for the Turkey Trot race. A photo of the empty cornucopia would remind everyone to bring donations, whether or not they were competing in the 5K.

She parked alongside the green where the grass was now brown and grabbed her camera, noticing that the cornucopia had already drawn a couple passersby. Drawing closer, she recognized the two women who were studying the display as Mireille Franklin and her mother, Mimsy.

"Do you mind if I take a photo of you two admiring the cornucopia?" Lucy asked, raising her camera.

"Maybe not," said Mimsy, grabbing her daughter's hand in a protective gesture. "Mireille needs to keep a low profile."

"Don't be silly, Mom," said Mireille. "A couple figures will make the photo more interesting."

"I can take you from behind and I wouldn't have to identify you," offered Lucy.

"Okay," agreed Mimsy somewhat reluctantly.

"I was going to suggest that, in any case," said Mireille. "I'd rather not be photographed with this huge belly."

"I thought you'd be a mom by now," said Lucy, smiling.

"Me, too," said Mireille, stroking her baby bump. "This little one is in no hurry to come into the world, and I can't say I blame him."

"Or her," added Mimsy, holding up her hand with two fingers crossed.

"Are you still planning to leave Tinker's Cove after the baby's born?" asked Lucy.

Mimsy answered, her assertive tone leaving no doubt about the matter. "Absolutely. Mireille needs to get away. The sooner she gets that house on the market, the better."

"You haven't done that yet?" asked Lucy.

"I know I should," said Mireille with a sigh, "but I'm not ready to leave Ed and Alison. I know it's weird, but I like visiting their graves . . ."

"It's morbid. That's what it is," snapped Mimsy. "And you shouldn't go alone to that cemetery."

"No, it's not morbid. I like being with them, just me and them, remembering them as they were when they were alive." Mireille paused, smiling. "Sometimes when I go there I think I hear them talking to me. They don't seem sad. Ed's mad that he isn't around to manage everything. He's not convinced that I can get along without him. Alison is more at peace. She says she's watching over me and the baby."

Mimsy didn't like hearing this one bit. "Come on, Mireille. You must be tired. You need to go home and get some rest."

"I'm fine, Mom," said Mireille, protesting.

"That's what you think, but it's not true," countered Mimsy. "You're not yourself and you're not behaving sensibly." She took her daughter by the arm, then turned to face Lucy. "Do you know what she did? She fired the bodyguards. All of them. Says she doesn't need them. Now does that sound like a sensible thing to do?"

Put on the spot, Lucy didn't know how to respond. "I really don't know."

"I didn't like having strangers in the house," said Mireille with a wan smile.

"Well, they were there to protect you and your baby," said Mimsy. "And if you end up dead like Ed and Alison, I'm not going to be visiting your grave so you can just hold your peace. Don't try talking to me, because I won't be there to listen!"

"Point taken, Mom," replied Mireille, allowing Mimsy to lead her away across the dead brown lawn to their car.

Lucy decided to jog the short distance to the *Pennysaver* office, chiding herself for not taking her Turkey Trot training regimen more seriously. She had lots of excuses, she told herself, but she definitely needed to make her morning runs a priority. Time was running out with only a few days until the race.

When she got to the office, Phyllis was bursting with news. "Lucy!" she exclaimed, "You'll never guess what's happened."

"Martians landed?"

"No! Jason Sprinkle and Link Peterson have been arrested for torching the pub."

"That was quick," Lucy said, glancing at Ted.

"Those two are not the brightest bulbs in the pack," he said. "At first they claimed they were out of town, but the cops have witnesses who saw them at the harbor just before the explosion. There's even video from the harbormaster's shed of them leaving the parking lot moments before the explosion. The chief told me they're saying they didn't notice the blaze, and that's why they didn't call for help. Little bastards insist it was Hank DeVries who did it."

"There's no way he could've done it. I took him to rehab in New Hampshire on Saturday," said Lucy.

"Next thing they'll be saying Santa Claus did it," said Phyllis.

When Lucy called Bill to give him the news, he wasn't convinced that Link and Jason were the arsonists. "They're not bad kids. I can't believe they did it. They knew I was in the building. I spoke to them in the parking lot. They asked me what I was doing working for those Mexicans and I told them I'd probably be needing help and asked if they'd be interested in some work. I figured even they could do demo."

"Looks like they did it for free," said Lucy.

Bill chuckled. "I don't think so. They seemed pretty interested in the fifteen dollars an hour I offered to pay them."

"Who else was down there?" asked Lucy. "Did you see anyone?"

"Yeah. Lots of people. It was Saturday afternoon and there was lots of activity. Even some tourists."

She heard the doorbell ring and Bill ended the call, saying someone was at the door and so far they had received six loaves of banana bread, but only one with chocolate chips, which he was eating.

"I should take out an ad," she told Ted and Phyllis. "No more banana bread, please!"

When she fired up her computer, she wondered if Link and Jason had actually seen the arsonist, but mistook him for someone else. When you thought about it, you realized there were a number of fair, tall young men in town.

That impression was confirmed that evening when she was driving home from work. Lucy was approaching the stop sign at the intersection of Main and Summer streets when a speeding car shot right through, causing her to brake abruptly. She was thinking it was a good thing she hadn't been going too fast, and strained to see who was the reckless driver. At first she thought it was Hank, then remembered he was supposed to be in rehab in New Hampshire and also that he certainly wouldn't be driving a shiny new Audi. It was probably Tag Franklin, she decided, wondering if he could possibly be the arsonist who firebombed the pub. He seemed a more likely suspect than Link and Jason, if he subscribed to his adoptive father's anti-immigrant views. But it was also a terribly dangerous thing to do, and why would he risk blowing himself up, or getting caught and going to jail? All indications were that he had a cushy lifestyle as the pampered offspring of wealthy parents.

When she reached home she saw a MINI Cooper parked in the driveway and figured that Bill had yet another visitor. Poor guy, he certainly wasn't getting much rest, she thought, opening the back door and finding Rev. Marge standing in the kitchen.

"I was just leaving," she told Lucy. "But Bill and I worked it out that the youth group will come on Friday afternoon to clean up your yard."

"Great," said Lucy. "We really appreciate the help." Her eyes were traveling over the kitchen table and counters, which were loaded with every imaginable form of baked good.

As Bill had told her, there were indeed six loaves of banana bread, as well as three loaves of cranberry bread, numerous Bundt cakes, plastic containers of cookies, even a few pies. The freezer, too, was loaded to bursting with homemade soups and casseroles.

"I don't know what to do with all this," she said. "Can you use some for coffee hour at the church?"

"Coffee hour is all set," said Rev. Marge. "Why don't you take it to the jail?"

"The jail? Will they take donations of food?"

"Sure," said Rev. Marge. "As long as there's no saws or chisels inside."

"Not that I know of," said Lucy, chuckling.

"I visit there every week as part of my ministry and I often take day-old baked goods from the IGA. Joe Marzetti donates them and I drop them off around back at the kitchen. The gals really love the sweets, especially anything chocolate, but the men like them, too. They get good food, but it's very plain, institutional cooking. They appreciate the sweets. I think it's also the fact that somebody is thinking of them and believes they deserve a treat."

"I'll do it," said Lucy. "There's somebody there I ought to visit, anyway."

"Bless you," said Rev. Marge by way of farewell.

Next morning, Lucy ran in the woods despite a chilly drizzle. When she got home she asked Bill to pick a few baked goods to keep while she showered, then she loaded the rest into the SUV and drove off to Gilead and the county complex. She had never gone around back at the county jail as Rev. Marge had suggested, but found there was no problem at all gaining admission to the delivery entrance. A guard was stationed at the gate in the fence, which was topped with razor wire, but when she explained her mission and showed him the baked goods he opened the electronic gate and waved her in.

She pressed the buzzer at the door marked for deliveries and it was promptly opened by another guard, who summoned several prisoners assigned to work in the kitchen and supervised as they unloaded the goodies. Lucy had visited the prison many times before, but only to visit individual prisoners involved in stories she was covering who were awaiting trial; she had never had much contact with actual convicts. She knew that the prisoners in the county jail were usually serving sentences for lesser offenses, those convicted of serious felonies were sent to the state penitentiary. At first, she was somewhat wary of the men, but gradually realized that these criminals were folks just like the people on the outside, except for the fact that they had made a mistake that got them into trouble. The guys joked as they carried in the foil-wrapped desserts, and made a point of politely thanking her for the donation.

As she drove around to the front of the jail, she felt the happy glow of knowing that she'd done her good deed for the day. She parked in the visitors' lot and made her way to the forbidding entrance. There she presented identification and allowed the guard to search her bag, then walked through a metal detector before she was buzzed through a second door that led to the visitor's room. That area was busy on weekends as family members usually visited then, but on this weekday morning the large room was empty. She seated herself at one of the cafeteria-style tables and waited for Matt.

When he appeared and saw her she noticed that his face fell in disappointment, and she suspected he had expected to see Zoe, not her mother. He quickly recovered, however, and greeted her with a big smile as he seated himself opposite her on the round stool attached to the table.

"Thanks for coming," he said. "How's Zoe?"

"She's fine. She's in Montreal, visiting a friend."

"Just as well, considering everything that's happening. I heard about the pub. How is your husband?"

After telling him that Bill was recovering from his injuries, Lucy asked if he had any ideas as to who might have torched the pub.

"I heard they arrested two guys, but I haven't seen them. They've been keeping me kind of separate from the others. I think it's because I'm charged with such a serious crime."

"How are they treating you?" asked Lucy.

"I don't have any complaints. The guards seem pretty decent. Of course, I haven't been convicted. I'm still legally innocent. I've got a good lawyer and I'm hoping to get out on bail, though I know it's a long shot."

"You seem to be taking all this remarkably well," said Lucy, struck by his attitude.

"Well, I know I'm innocent. I didn't kill Ed Franklin, and I've got faith in the justice system. Plus, I've got a lot of advantages most people accused of crimes don't have. I've got money and can afford a good lawyer, I've got family and friends who support me and believe in my innocence, and I've got connections to influential people." He gave her an apologetic shrug. "The system might be rigged, but it's kind of rigged in my favor."

Lucy couldn't help smiling. "That's one way of looking at it."

"I'm a glass-half-full sorta guy. I doubt I'll be brought to trial. Dad's got a private investigator who is working with the lawyer, and I'm sure they'll turn up something. And Dad's already working on winning over public opinion. He's planning a big Thanksgiving dinner for the entire town."

"That's a really good idea," said Lucy. "But how's he going to pull it off?"

"Not problem. Trust me. If he says he's going to do something, he'll do it." Matt paused. "I only hope I get out of here, so I can go." He licked his lips. "I don't want to miss my dad's turkey tacos."

CHAPTER 19

Lucy had no sooner walked through the door at the *Pennysaver* before Ted sent her right back out on assignment. "Pam tells me the ladies at the Community Church have volunteered to help Rey with this Mexican Thanksgiving Feast and she wants me to run a story. Can you go over there and see what's cooking?"

Phyllis, dressed from head to toe in a blaze of autumnal orange, rolled her eyes and groaned at the pun. "I sense a headline: A Recipe for Reconciliation? Cooking Up Cooperation? Stirring Up a Better World?"

"Those are a good start," said Ted in all seriousness, "but they need work."

"I was joking," protested Phyllis, again rolling her eyes. "You know"—she turned to Lucy—"he has absolutely no sense of humor."

"Oh, I do, believe me," said Ted. "How else do you think I manage to put up with you two?"

"Well, I'm outta here," said Lucy. "I'll leave you guys to your verbal sparring." She was at the door when the perfect headline came to her. "How about A Feast for the Season?"

When she reached the church, she was encouraged to see the parking lot was almost full, and when she stepped inside the kit-

chen, she was met with a wave of delicious odors and a cheerful
bustling atmosphere. Rey was clearly in charge, passing out recipe
cards and answering questions from cooks who were unfamiliar
with the ingredients and techniques. Luisa was there, too, giving a
hand.

"You're sure this sausage goes in the pumpkin soup?" asked
Toni Williams, sounding very doubtful. "It's very spicy."

"That's chorizo. It's delicious," replied Rey.

"And how exactly do I cut this thing up?" asked Betsy Cool-
idge, holding up a mango as if it was a hand grenade about to go off.

"I'll show you," said Luisa, grabbing a paring knife. "It's going
to make the most delicious mango salsa."

Lucy snapped a few photos of the volunteers, then approached
Rey for a brief interview. "What's on the menu?"

"Oh, my goodness, everything but the kitchen sink," he said.
"We'll start with chorizo pumpkin soup, move on to turkey tacos
and enchiladas, roast stuffed pork, a variety of salsas, and for
dessert, we'll have flan, bread pudding, and traditional pies like
pumpkin and apple. How does that sound?"

"It sounds delicious," said Lucy. "Am I invited?"

"Everybody's invited," said Rey with a big smile. "It struck me,
when I realized Matt wouldn't be able to come home for our family feast, that there are a lot of people who are in similar situa-
tions—people who've lost loved ones, people who are separated
from their families by long distances, old folks who've outlived
their friends. I thought it would be nice to do something for them,
give them an opportunity to enjoy a delicious meal along with
good fellowship. We'll even have some music and dancing afterwards so people can burn off some calories."

"That sounds great," said Lucy, who recognized herself in Rey's
description. "You can count on me and Bill. The kids are all away
this year and it's just the two of us."

"Great. I'll see you on Thanksgiving," Rey said, turning his attention to Angie DiBello who had a couple prickly pear paddles
in her hands and a puzzled expression on her face.

Lucy didn't want to leave without saying hi to Pam, and spotted her and Rachel in a far corner of the large hall. The two were

unpacking groceries from a number of cardboard boxes and arranging them on a long table where the cooks could find them.

"Thanks for coming, Lucy," said Pam, as Lucy approached them. "Time is short, Thanksgiving is fast approaching, and we need to get the word out so people will come."

"Look at all this food," said Rachel, setting two huge cloth bags of corn meal on the table. "Rey must have spent a fortune on this stuff."

"Where did it all come from?" asked Lucy, who knew that Marzetti's IGA did not carry prickly pears, Mexican chocolate, and chorizo, or many of the other items she saw on the table.

"He had it trucked in from some ethnic grocery in Portland," said Pam, who was looking worried. "I'm just afraid this is all going for naught. Who wants to eat roast pork on Thanksgiving? Or turkey tacos?"

"I do," said Lucy. "I'm pretty excited about trying some new foods."

"I suspect you might be alone in that," said Pam. "It's not Thanksgiving without turkey and stuffing and cranberry sauce."

"There's going to be cranberry salsa," said Rachel.

"Not the same thing at all," said Pam, checking the recipe card. "It's got hot peppers!"

"I'd like to come, but I'm not sure Bob and I will be welcome," said Rachel. "Bob's defending Link and Jason, you know."

"I didn't know," said Lucy, "but I'm sure you'll be welcome. Rey will understand. He knows how the system works. Everybody's entitled to legal representation whether they're innocent or guilty."

"That's the thing," said Rachel, lowering her voice to a whisper. "Link and Jason still insist they're innocent, that if it couldn't have been Hank DeVries, it's someone who looks a lot like him, but Bob's not buying it. He thinks they probably did it, but they didn't act alone. He suspects they were egged on by someone else to firebomb the pub, but they won't say who."

"That's not like Link," said Lucy, thinking that he and Jason may have grown up but were still behaving like naughty children, relying on the bully's tried and true tactic of blaming others for their own misdeeds.

"A lot of people are saying it was Rey himself," said Pam.

"No way," said Lucy. "I know for a fact that Rey wants to re-build. He's hired an architect and he wants Bill to be the contractor. And look at this dinner. He wouldn't be doing all this if he wasn't sticking around. He wants to be part of the community."

"Bob thinks Zeke Bumpus was involved," said Rachel.

"There's a big difference between talking hate speech and committing hate crimes," said Pam.

"I heard someone say that it's not so much what people say as what people hear," said Lucy. "Maybe Jason and Link misconstrued something Zeke said."

"I don't think that gets him off the hook," said Rachel. "He still bears some responsibility."

"I wonder what Zeke's got to say about that," mused Lucy, planning to give him a call. But first she had to make her escape from the kitchen where her friends seemed to expect her to put down her notebook and camera and pick up a knife and a cutting board. "I wish I could stay and help"—she gave an apologetic shrug—"but I've got to take Bill to see the bone doctor today."

She made the call to Zeke while driving back home to pick up Bill.

As she expected, he vehemently denied any involvement in the firebombing.

"America for Americans is strictly nonviolent. We're sort of a National Association for the Advancement of White People, and we follow Dr. King's strategy of passive resistance."

Lucy found this claim hard to swallow. "But some of the statements you've made do seem to encourage violence. It seems pretty suspicious that the pub was firebombed after your anti-immigrant demonstration."

"America for Americans held a demonstration and put up a billboard, all activities that are protected by the Constitution. We didn't have anything to do with the explosion at the pub—no how, no way."

"But some folks might have taken your anti-immigrant rhetoric a step too far," said Lucy.

"Well, that's their problem, not mine. And what about folks like you, in the media?" he continued, challenging her. "Time after time I've seen my words twisted just so you guys can sell more newspapers."

Lucy knew this was an argument she couldn't win. Just as patriotism was said to be the last resort of scoundrels, blaming the media seemed to be their first, knee-jerk reaction. "So, for the record"—she spoke slowly and carefully—"you insist that America for Americans had nothing whatever to do with firebombing the old pub?"

"Absolutely not," said Zeke, "but I'll be amazed if you print that."

"Prepare to be amazed," said Lucy, ending the call as she reached the top of Red Top Road and turned into her driveway.

Bill was ready to go, waiting for her at the kitchen table where he'd been doing the word jumble in the morning paper. "Any idea what *c-l-e-t-t-e-u* could be?" he asked as he got to his feet.

"Lettuce," said Lucy, not missing a beat. "How's the arm?"

"Fine, thanks to the Vicodin, once it's in the sling, and I don't move it or bump it," said Bill.

Lucy knew he was putting on a brave front. She'd seen how badly bruised his arm and shoulder were, and how painful it was for him to get dressed and undressed. He couldn't wear anything that involved raising his arm, like a pull-on T-shirt or sweater, and instead chose shirts that buttoned. Even so, he couldn't shove his broken arm into a sleeve but had to carefully slide it on, inch by painful inch. Getting dressed was no longer a quick matter of automatically throwing on a few garments but was a slow process that left him white-faced and exhausted. He couldn't even tie his shoes and, too proud to ask for help, had switched to a pair of casual suede slip-ons.

"Well, we'll see what the doctor has to say," she said while he settled himself in the passenger seat and struggled to fasten the seatbelt with his good arm.

Coastal Orthopedics and Sports Medicine was housed in a modern office building that had only recently been built on the outskirts of town near the Winchester College campus. It took about fifteen minutes to drive there, and there was plenty of parking in the adjoining lot.

As she walked into the waiting room with Bill, Lucy was reminded of the many times she'd brought the kids to see Doc Ryder. The old family doctor was now retired, and Bill was her husband, not her child, but there was still a bit of that déjà vu feeling. She was on her way to the receptionist's desk to announce their arrival when Bill caught her by the wrist, signaling that he was fully capable of managing that business by himself. She took a seat, and he joined her in a few minutes, settling down on the next chair and watching CNN on the wall-mounted TV. When his name was called they both got up, but he gave her a little head shake, indicating that he would see the doctor by himself.

She waited for what seemed a very long time, flipping through tattered issues of *Real Simple*, and growing increasingly discouraged about the chaotic condition of her home, her finances, her health, and her wardrobe. After learning of the various options for simplifying her life by repackaging her liquid dish detergent in a variety of attractive containers she decided to abandon the quest for lifestyle improvement and looked up, glancing through the glass doors of the waiting room to the outer lobby. There, much to her surprise, she saw Jon and Eudora, along with Tag, coming through the outer doors. Curious as to what brought them to the professional building, she decided to head for the ladies room which was conveniently located in the lobby.

The three were standing together, waiting for the elevator, and didn't notice her walking behind them and down the hall toward the ladies room. The elevator arrived and they stepped in, so Lucy quickly ducked into the nearby staircase. Reaching the landing to the next floor she peeked through the small window in the fire door and spotted the group walking down the hallway. She waited a few seconds, then stepped out and followed them, careful to remain some distance behind.

Unlike the first floor where the orthopedics practice took up the entire floor, the second floor was occupied by a number of smaller offices arranged on a long hallway. Placards on the doors identified a CPA, a lawyer, a dentist, and other professionals, none of whom seemed to be terribly busy this morning. The hallway was empty apart from Eudora and the two men with her; they had stopped in front of an office and Eudora was shaking her head, refusing to step through the door. Wishing to advance closer,

Lucy pulled the notepaper on which she'd jotted down the time and place for Bill's appointment and studied it as if looking for the correct office. As she proceeded down the hallway, she made a show of checking the names on the doors against the paper in her hand. Approaching the trio, she heard Jon and Tag arguing, but when she passed them they lowered their voices and she couldn't catch the words.

She reached the end of the hallway where she turned and planned, if they noticed her, to say she must be on the wrong floor. That proved to be unnecessary, however, as Eudora suddenly exclaimed, "I'm not going in there!" and marched off down the hall toward the elevator, arm in arm with her son, Tag. Her husband, Jon, looking quite defeated, trailed behind them.

Lucy followed and saw them enter the elevator together just as she reached the office that Eudora had so vehemently refused to enter. She wasn't really surprised to see it was occupied by a psychiatrist.

Interesting, thought Lucy, hurrying down the stairs in hopes of returning to the waiting room before Bill's appointment was over. She was back in her seat, watching CNN announce that the president had officially pardoned a turkey, sparing it from certain death as the main course for someone's Thanksgiving dinner, when Bill appeared.

"How'd it go?" she asked.

"I got a prescription for more painkillers and an appointment to come back in four weeks."

"No surgery? Not even a cast?" she asked.

"Nope. They took X-rays and the break is too close to my shoulder for a cast. I'm supposed to stick with the sling and start physical therapy in a couple weeks." He paused. "The good news is that my shoulder's not dislocated."

"What about all that bruising?" asked Lucy as they left the waiting room and walked outside and across the parking lot.

"Normal."

"And how long before you can go back to work?" she asked.

"Six, maybe eight weeks."

"That's after Christmas." Dismayed, she opened the car door for him. "How are we going to manage?"

"We'll manage somehow," he said, climbing into the passenger seat. "We always do. I can probably pick up some work at the hardware store. They'll need extra help with Christmas coming and I don't need two hands to help people find Christmas lights and coffeemakers."

Lucy did some calculations involving the checking account, the savings account, and their usual monthly expenses while she walked around the car and got in the driver's seat. It wasn't an encouraging exercise, but they weren't in any immediate danger of bankruptcy or foreclosure so she shoved her concerns to the back of her mind and started the car. "You'll never believe who I saw while you were with the doctor."

"Who? Santa Claus?"

"No. Eudora Clare, Ed Franklin's ex-wife, along with her son and present husband. It looked to me like they were taking her to see a psychiatrist, but she balked at the door and wouldn't go in."

"She does seem to have a screw loose," said Bill as they turned out of the parking area and onto the road.

"What's really interesting is that it was Jon, the husband, who was pushing her to see the psychiatrist, but it seemed like Tag, the son, seemed to side with her against Jon," said Lucy, thinking aloud as she drove. "A witness identified Hank as the arsonist, but when you think about it, Hank and Tag look a lot alike. It might have been Tag who blew up the pub. Maybe Ed planned the whole thing before he was killed and Tag followed through as a sort of final tribute to him. Or maybe he had some sort of cockeyed idea that Mireille was on the same page with Ed about Mexicans and blowing up the restaurant would please her and she'd share her child's inheritance with him."

They were passing a little inlet where a couple handsome old houses sat on the shoreline overlooking a million-dollar view of rocky seacoast when Bill challenged her.

"Where exactly did you see this little drama? The sports med is the only office on the first floor."

Lucy knew she'd said too much. "Uh, well, I saw them come in and, um, followed them upstairs."

"Are you crazy? You can't follow people around. What if they saw you?"

"I was going to pretend I was looking for an office and was on the wrong floor."

"And you think that would convince them? You suspect this guy is an arsonist, someone who's willing to hurt and possibly kill other people, and you think it's smart to follow him around?"

They'd passed the inlet and were passing stands of leafless trees and fields of drooping cornstalks.

"It wasn't like I was creeping around in the dark or something. I was in a professional building in broad daylight, well, actually under bright fluorescent lights. There were no windows up there. It was a brightly lit hallway and I had every right to be there."

"Yeah, well, I had every right to go about my business in the pub and look at what happened to me," declared Bill.

"So you do think it might have been Tag?" asked Lucy, making the turn onto School Street.

"I don't know and I don't care," said Bill. "And I want you to promise to stop this crazy nonsense and mind your own business. You should hear yourself. You sound as crazy as this Eudora woman."

"Well, this is my business," argued Lucy, braking for the stop sign at the bottom of Red Top Road. "When you got blown up it became my business."

"Stop. Stop the car," ordered Bill.

"Why? Do you think you can drive one-armed?"

"I'm not driving, I'm getting out. I'll walk from here."

"That's crazy," said Lucy, beginning the climb up the hill.

"I mean it. Stop the car."

"Okay, okay," she grumbled, pulling off to the side of the road. She turned, giving him a questioning look, but he didn't notice.

He had already shoved the door open and was getting out. Then he shut the door hard without looking at her and marched off, striding up the hill without a backwards glance.

If only *Real Simple* had had an article advising how to have a productive argument with your husband, she thought, watching as he strode along, clearly driven by anger.

She made a three-point turn and headed for the office, aware that it wasn't only his arm that was injured in the blast, but also his pride. She knew she'd handled things badly. He'd given her clear signals that he didn't want to be mothered or babied, and that he would take responsibility for his injuries and for the family's welfare, too. By the time she reached the office she'd resolved to be more tactful in the future . . . and to keep her investigative reporting activities to herself until it was time to break the story in the *Pennysaver.*

When she got to the office, Phyllis greeted her with a stack of press releases to be entered in the listings, and Ted informed her that he'd sent her story about the selectmen's meeting back to her for a rewrite, so she knew she'd be working late. That was actually fine with her since she was in no hurry to go home and face Mister High and Mighty Grumpy Pants. If he was so darn independent, he could zap a frozen mini-pizza for himself. She was pretty sure he wouldn't need two arms for that little chore.

When she sat down at her desk she found a press release from the DA announcing that the state crime lab had found no trace of any opiates in Alison Franklin's body and therefore her death from drowning was considered accidental and the case was officially closed. There was also a voice mail from Mimsy, asking Lucy to give her a call as soon as possible, as it was a bit of an emergency. Lucy's curiosity was piqued, wondering if the call was a reaction to the news about Alison, and she returned the call immediately. The phone rang numerous times before it was answered.

"Sorry, I was stuck in a closet," said Mimsy, sounding rather breathless. "Mireille got a bee in her bonnet about getting the house ready for the Realtor and she's had me clearing out all sorts of junk."

"Maybe it's that nesting thing," said Lucy. "I bet she'll go into labor any minute."

"I can only hope," said Mimsy with a sigh. "She's working me ragged, and she's got me worried, too. You know she fired the bodyguards and I'm terrified for her safety, especially since I found"—she paused and dropped her voice to a whisper—"I found committal papers that Jon sent to Ed. He wanted to have Eudora committed and wanted information from Ed about their marriage. He specifically wanted to know about any incidents of violent behavior." Again she paused. "What if she goes after Mireille?"

"What do you mean? Do you really think Eudora is prone to violence?"

"It's not what *I* think. It's what her husband thinks. And Eudora's made it very clear that she hates Mireille."

Lucy thought about this and had to admit Mimsy had a point if Eudora truly was an unhinged psychopath. Lucy wasn't convinced that was the case. True, she'd witnessed Eudora refusing to see a psychiatrist, but that didn't mean she was a danger to herself or others. As her friend Rachel often said, mental health was a continuum, and people moved through various periods of stability and instability throughout their lives, but that didn't mean they were crazy. Eudora had clearly been through a lot, and she might very well be close to a breakdown, but her husband seemed to be dealing with the situation. He was clearly in contact with a psychiatrist and even if Eudora wasn't ready to cooperate was probably getting sound professional advice.

"I don't think you have anything to worry about," said Lucy, recalling her encounter with Eudora at the turkey farm. Then she'd seemed on the verge of hysteria, understandably shaken by the dual loss of her ex-husband and daughter. "Eudora is a small, slight middle-aged woman. If anything, she seems to be struggling with her emotions. Grief takes people differently. It's terrible to lose loved ones, even if you're estranged. Sometimes that makes it worse."

"I don't buy that," said Mimsy. "Eudora might look fragile, but she's been absolutely horrible to Mireille. She blames her for losing Ed. And remember, it doesn't take a lot of muscle to pull a trigger." Mimsy sighed. "I thought you'd be able to help me. That's why I called. I don't really know anybody but you in this stinky little town and I thought maybe you could talk some sense into Mireille."

Lucy sensed Ted looming over her and when she looked up, he handed her a freshly issued brochure from the state outlining new hunting regulations. A yellow sticky note had been attached to the front cover, on which the words *summarize this* were written in his neat block print.

"I've really got to get back to work," said Lucy, "and I don't see how I can help you. Mireille's all grown up. She seems quite capable of taking care of herself and her baby. If you're really worried about Eudora, I think you should share this information with the police."

"From what I've seen so far, they're a pretty useless bunch," said Mimsy.

Ted hadn't budged. He was still standing behind her chair.

"Well, that's all I can suggest," said Lucy. "Thanks for calling. I'll keep this information in mind." She hung up and turned to face him. "So what do you want now?" she demanded.

"I just wanted to tell you that Rey Rodriguez dropped off some apple cider and donuts. The cider's in the fridge and the donuts are by the coffee pot."

"Oh," said Lucy, somewhat deflated. "Thanks. I could use a donut."

Her emotions were in turmoil as she ate three donuts in quick succession and gulped down at least a pint of apple cider. She didn't really taste any of it as she tried to rationalize the way she brushed off poor Mimsy. She felt horribly guilty, but told herself that Mimsy and Mireille's problems weren't her problems. She had plenty of her own, the most pressing of which was the pile of work that was sitting on her desk. That wasn't all, however. Bill was languishing at home, coping not only with considerable pain but also with depression about his inability to work. It didn't help matters that they'd parted the way they did, with him stomping off in an angry huff.

It was bad enough that she was swamped at work, but knowing that Bill was mad at her made her feel completely overwhelmed. She didn't have time for self-pity, she told herself. All she could spare was a nod and a prayer. The nod was an acknowledgment of the whole messy situation—the deaths, the grieving families, the accusations against Matt Rodriguez, the simmering intolerance that had suddenly flared up in the little town, and Bill's injuries. The prayer was for help and guidance in seeing her own way through, for justice to be done, and for everyone involved to find peace and healing.

Even so, she couldn't forget the terrible morning when she'd discovered Alison's body and the whole mess began. No matter how hard she tried, she couldn't seem to erase the image of the lovely girl's drowned body and the streaming hair that floated around her bluish face in the freezing water. That popped into her mind with disturbing frequency. If only she could remember some clue, some bit of information she missed, that would shed light on Alison's death.

What could possibly have prompted Alison to venture out on thin ice? She wasn't a child. She was an intelligent young adult familiar with seasonal changes and she certainly would have known the danger. There must have been some reason, some very strong reason that caused her to disregard her own safety and go out onto the thin ice.

She wondered if Alison might have spotted a dog that was in trouble, or even a wild animal like a deer. It was heartrending to witness an animal struggling for survival and Lucy knew from her own experience that it was almost impossible to resist the impulse to help, even when you knew it could be life threatening. She had once seen a mother doe and her fawn stranded on a chunk of floating ice in the pond and had felt terrible about leaving them to their fate, even though she knew there was nothing she could do that wouldn't endanger her and possibly leave her own family motherless.

On impulse she hurried back to her desk and put in a call to her friend, Barney Culpepper, who had been one of the first police officers to respond to her call that awful morning.

"Barney, I was just wondering. Did you see anything the morning that Alison Franklin drowned that might explain why she went out on the ice? We just got a press release from the DA that says they didn't find any trace of drugs."

"Sorry, Lucy," he replied in a mournful tone. "I keep worrying about that myself. I can't seem to put that pretty young thing's face out of my mind."

"I think maybe she saw a dog or a deer that got in trouble."

"Could be, Lucy. It seems something like that happens every year. Some do-gooder tries to help and falls through. And half the time, the animal manages to save itself and is just fine. The stupid dog gets itself back on shore, gives a good shake, and wants to go home for a good meal."

"But did you see any sign of anything like that?"

"Nope. But that doesn't mean it didn't happen that way," said Barney. "That's most likely what happened. It's the only thing that makes any sense to me."

"Me, too," said Lucy, reaching for the booklet of revised hunting regulations. Flipping it open to the first page, she saw a bold red headline advising hunters to hunt safely. First on the list of dangers to watch for was thin ice.

CHAPTER 20

Thanksgiving Day dawned bright and clear, but with a cool breeze that made it perfect weather for running. Bill's temper had eventually cooled, helped by a Skype session with his grandson, Patrick, in Alaska and his favorite supper of meatloaf and mashed potatoes.

Both he and Lucy were in high spirits as they parked the car alongside the town common and joined the crowd of people gathered around the registration table for the 5K race. Everyone was talking about the cornucopia on the bandstand, which was already full to overflowing with donated food for the Food Pantry. Bill had volunteered to help collect the canned goods that were the entry fee for the race, along with a nominal $10 fee, but since he had to work with only one hand he was assigned instead to distributing the highly coveted Turkey Trot T-shirts. Many of the competitors were wearing shirts from previous years. Each featured the cartoon running turkey and the year in big, bold numbers. The older the shirt, the greater the prestige.

After signing in and receiving her T-shirt, Lucy pulled it on over her running togs and got busy stretching out her muscles. She didn't have any real hope of winning the race, especially since her training had been so spotty, but as she checked out the other runners who were also busy warming up, she realized that there were very few in her age category. Most women her age, she figured, were much too busy this morning getting their turkeys stuffed and in the oven to even think of running in the race. Maybe, she thought as her competitive spirit rose, she might actually have a chance of placing and getting a medal. It was certainly worth a try. Vowing to give the race every bit of energy she could, she joined the other runners assembling behind the starting line. She noticed lots of familiar faces, including Phyllis's husband Wilf, several of Dot Kirwan's kids, and even Roger Wilcox, chairman of the board of selectmen.

Rev. Marge offered a short prayer and announced that this year's donations for the Food Pantry had topped all previous records. Then she raised the starting gun, said the traditional "Ready, Set," and pulled the trigger.

They were off. Runners who had placed in previous years' races got the best positions just behind the starting line, and they led the pack. Others, like Lucy, had to wait a bit before they even reached the starting line. As she shuffled along, Lucy pictured the route in her mind, picturing the race course. The route was clearly signed and led from the town common along Parallel Street with its antique sea captain's homes, then gradually climbed up to Shore Road. There the route passed roomy shingle-style summer cottages and newer McMansions and offered beautiful views of the bay dotted with rocky, pine-covered islands and bound by Quissett Point in the distance. The course then turned at the gate to Pine Point, the Van Vorst estate, and continued along a pine needle strewn path through the woodsy Audubon sanctuary, emerging onto Church Street by the old cemetery and continuing down Main Street to Sea Street, where the runners descended to reach the finish line in the harbor.

Lucy was trapped in a crowd of runners when she reached the starting line where she gave a wave to the cheering crowd of onlookers and jogged along with the group. The pack of runners began to thin out as they proceeded alongside the town common and Lucy could finally begin running. The race attracted runners and walkers of various levels of fitness. Some were keen competitors who raced regularly, while others were simply out for a pleasant bit of exercise that also happened to benefit a good cause.

That meant that the pack stretched out for some distance along the course, with the dedicated competitors far out in front of the rest, followed by slower runners and finally, the walkers bringing up the rear.

Reaching Parallel Street, Lucy found her rhythm and began passing the slower walkers and joggers. The running became automatic. The steady *thump-thump* of her running shoes hitting the asphalt became a kind of background music, and her mind began to wander as she left Parallel Street and began the climb up Shore Road.

There, the air seemed to thin and a brisk ocean breeze refreshed and cooled her heated body. The sky and ocean were deep blue, a few oak trees still held on to rattling russet leaves, and dark green pointed firs stood sentinel on the rocky coast. The handsome homes that lined the road, most only occupied during the summer, had interesting architectural features that captured her imagination. Here a spacious porch where the railing was dotted with drying beach towels all summer long, there a tall tower where a telescope could be seen in the window, pointing out to the sea below.

Approaching the Franklin mansion, Lucy was struck once again by its enormous size. It almost seemed terribly foolish, perhaps even tempting fate, to build such a grand house. A house was meant to shelter its inhabitants, and this house had clearly failed. Ed was dead, so was his daughter, Alison, and now his pregnant wife couldn't wait to leave.

A water station had been set up in the mansion's driveway and Lucy grabbed a paper cup, slowing slightly to swig a few gulps before discarding the cup in one of the barrels set out for the purpose. Something about the house caught her fancy. She thought the large, hulking edifice looked a bit like Ed Franklin himself. There was something unsettling about it, just as there had been about the man. Something a bit off-kilter or out of proportion. Something not right. And then she saw a young woman with long blond hair stepping out of the house and she stopped in her tracks, certain it was Alison.

It wasn't, of course. She realized immediately it was one of the volunteers bringing a fresh pack of paper cups out to the water station. Lucy shook her head, trying to clear her mind as she resumed running, but she couldn't get that easy rhythm back. Once again, the image she couldn't seem to shake, the vision that kept reappearing—Alison's white face and long, swirling hair just beneath the surface of the water—came back to haunt her. What on earth possessed the girl to go out on that ice?

That was the question that bedeviled Lucy. It was such a foolish, dangerous thing to do. Why did Alison do it?

Lucy was running more steadily as she approached the gates at Pine Point. The *thump-thump* had become a *why-why, why-why*. And suddenly, clear as day, she remembered doing something remarkably similar. Something so foolish and risky, she could hardly believe she'd done it.

"My bag! I dropped my bag!"

Lucy heard the panic in the voice, and she quickly stooped down and grabbed the bag off the tracks moments before the train came thundering into the station.

She could still hear the frantic urgency, and the memory of that close call was so strong that it took her breath away and squeezed her heart, stopping it for a moment. The pain was excruciating, piercing, and then it began to ease.

She was running. She was running again and she was certain she knew who had sent Alison onto the ice.

But what about Ed Franklin? Did the same person kill Ed? It was possible, she thought, even likely. As Mimsy had pointed out, it didn't take a lot to pull a trigger, especially if you were gripped by a powerful emotion. Cops who feared for their lives shot unarmed people. It seemed to happen all the time. Gang members who'd been dissed took their revenge on city streets, often missing their intended targets and killing innocent bystanders. Lost souls were recruited by terrorist organizations and turned into lethal killers, and mentally unstable people heard voices that urged them to kill. Even love could sour and turn to murderous hate, as children rose up and killed parents or spouses took advantage of intimacy to pull a gun from beneath the pillow.

By the time she reached Church Street and the turn back toward town, Lucy found herself practically alone. She could see the backs of the elite runners ahead of her, but they were some distance away, and she knew that most of the others were behind her. She decided to try to catch up to the leading group of runners as she approached the ancient cemetery where former citizens of Tinker's Cove were presumably resting in peace beneath lichen-covered tombstones that leaned this way and that.

She turned to catch a glimpse of a favorite grave marker, a Victorian angel that bowed sadly over little Rose Williams, barely three years old when she died in 1854, but couldn't make it out as a flash of bright sunlight momentarily blinded her. Curious, she slowed. As her vision cleared and the angel came into view, she realized to her horror that the blinding flash had not come from the sun but came instead from a huge carving knife. That knife was held in Eudora Clare's hand and she was brandishing it wildly over Mireille's prone and struggling body.

Momentarily at a loss, Lucy didn't know what to do. She was alone, she was tired and out of breath, and she didn't have a weapon of any sort. She did hear the runners approaching from behind, however, and thinking quickly, grabbed one of the signs marking the course and turned it so it pointed to the road leading into the cemetery. Then she raced to intervene, praying that the other runners would be deceived and follow her into the grave-yard.

As she drew closer to the statue of the hovering angel, she realized that Mireille had been trussed up with duct tape and was lying on her back on a raised stone grave, twisting from side to side in a tremendous effort to avoid Eudora's knife thrusts. Lucy could hear Eudora's voice cooing like a demented mourning dove, admonishing Mireille to lie still.

"It won't hurt a bit and will be over in a minute." Eudora aimed the knife for Mireille's dome of baby belly. "Won't hurt a bit. Not a bit," she crooned over and over as she brandished the knife. "You took them all, my Ed and my little Alison, and now you have to give me your baby." The knife connected with Mireille's breast, slitting her shirt. "It's not your baby." Eudora shook her head sadly and thrust the knife yet again, slashing Mireille's upper arm which began to bleed. "It's my baby. My baby."

Lucy realized with horror that the unbelievable was actually happening. Eudora was attempting to cut Mireille's baby from her body.

"You can't do that! Stop! Stop!" Lucy yelled, leaping over gravestones and throwing herself at Eudora, attempting to knock the knife from her hand.

Eudora wouldn't let go, even though Lucy had grabbed her arm with both hands, desperately trying to pry the knife from her grip. She was surprisingly strong, and Lucy found she had a tiger by the tail. She had to hang on for dear life. She couldn't use her hand to punch or strike the crazed woman for fear Eudora would slash or stab her. She tried to use her feet, kicking at Eudora's shins in an attempt to knock the woman down, but Eudora was able to dodge her running shoes.

Lucy found herself weakening, tired from the race and the struggle. Her hands were slipping and she knew it was now or never. She had to gain control of Eudora. She took a deep breath and using both hands, forced Eudora's arm upward, then threw herself at the woman, knocking her down on the ground. Lucy was in an awkward position, and although she had pinned Eudora beneath her, she was stuck on top of the struggling woman. She was beginning to doubt she could continue to restrain her when the first of the pack of runners arrived, feet pounding, and yelling.

Eudora quickly dropped the knife and began screaming, claiming Lucy was trying to kill her.

"What's going on here?" inquired Roger Wilcox, giving Lucy a hand and helping her to her feet.

Wilf Lundgren did the same for Eudora, careful to place his substantial bulk between the two combatants.

"She attacked me," claimed Eudora, pointing at Lucy. "She tried to kill me with that knife!"

Her claim was quickly rebutted as Lily Kirwan, who was studying to be an EMT, pulled the duct tape off Mireille's mouth.

"Don't believe her!" Mireille cried. "Lucy saved me! Eudora was trying to take my baby!"

Hearing this there was a general gasp of horror, which gave Eudora a chance to attempt to dart away. She was stopped by the quick action of Wilf, who grabbed her arm and held her tight.

"Nobody's going anywhere till this is sorted out," he said as a siren was heard in the distance.

Lucy wanted to go to Mireille, but felt that since she'd been accused, she had to wait for the police. She had to be content to let Lily and a few of the runners attend to Mireille, comforting her, stripping off the duct tape, and bandaging her bleeding arm in fourteen-year-old Finn Thaw's T-shirt, which he had pulled off. Lucy was also concerned about keeping an eye on the knife, which was still lying on the ground, and keeping a wary eye on Eudora, who had given up struggling and stood silently in place with a sulky expression on her face.

The wailing siren grew closer, bringing Barney Culpepper to the scene in a squad car. He surveyed the scene, taking it all in. He saw Mireille sitting on the grave, accompanied by a handful of caregivers, her arm wrapped in a blood-stained cotton T-shirt with a pile of duct tape neatly arranged beside her. He saw the knife on the ground and collected it as evidence. He examined Eudora, noting the spatters of blood on her hands.

Finally, he turned to Lucy. "What's going on here? Some of the runners reported a scuffle at the cemetery."

"I was running in the race and I saw Eudora in the cemetery, flashing a knife. She had tied up Mireille and was trying to cut the baby from her body. She kept saying 'It's my baby,' over and over. I tried to stop her. I tried to get the knife."

"That's right," said Roger. "When I arrived, Lucy had tackled Eudora and was struggling with her on the ground."

"Lucy saved my life," said Mireille.

Barney nodded and produced handcuffs, which set Eudora into a fit of hysterics.

"They're lying. They're all lying," she screamed, twisting free of Wilf's grip and starting to dart away, but running instead right into Finn Thaw's wiry young body. A member of the high school JV wrestling team, he wrapped his arms around her, pinning her arms to her sides and restraining her until Barney applied the handcuffs.

They were all watching him escort a protesting Eudora to the squad car when Mireille suddenly moaned.

"I'm in labor," she said, panting and clutching her stomach. "I've got to get to the hospital!"

Nobody could talk about anything else at Rey's Mexican Thanksgiving Dinner, which had attracted a huge crowd that somehow managed to squeeze into the basement hall at the Community Church as evening fell.

"There's plenty of food, plenty of food for everyone," Rey said, busy ladling out bowls of spicy pumpkin soup and piling plates with turkey burritos, roast pork, and plenty of cranberry salsa.

Lucy had signed up to help serve at the dinner, but he had insisted that she should sit this one out, considering her heroic actions that morning. She and Bill were seated at one of the long tables, along with Miss Tilley, Rachel and Bob Goodman, and Miss Tilley's best friend, Rebecca Wardwell. Rebecca was almost as old as Miss Tilley, and was rumored to be a witch, but that was probably only because she kept a tiny owl as a pet.

"Well, as usual, Lucy, you seem to have been up to your shenanigans," said Miss Tilley, digging into her burrito with gusto.

"Honestly, I was just running when I saw Eudora raising that knife. If it hadn't been for the beam of sunlight that hit it, I never would have seen a thing."

"A higher force was at work," said Rebecca, taking a bite of a turkey taco.

"Talk about crazy," said Rachel, stirring her soup. "That woman was completely round the bend."

"What about your famous continuum?" asked Lucy. "You know, how our mental states fall along a continuum throughout our lives, sometimes more balanced and sometimes less."

"I can say with confidence that Eudora fell off the continuum," said Rachel with a nod. "Absolutely loony-tunes, completely crazy, psychopathic, out of her mind."

"Evil. She was possessed by the evil one," said Rebecca, sounding like someone who had firsthand knowledge of the demonic, and had the battle scars to prove it.

"Well, whatever you want to call it, we're all a lot better off now that she's in jail, along with her son."

"What I don't understand," said Miss Tilley, scooping up cranberry salsa, "is why her family didn't take care of her. At the very least, she should have been under the care of a psychiatrist, perhaps even confined."

"They tried," said Lucy. "Her husband tried to enlist Ed Franklin and Alison to commit her, but Eudora found out. That's what began her murder spree. First Alison, who she somehow managed to lure onto the ice—"

"Whoa there," said Bob. "Where'd you get that idea?"

"It came to me while I was running. I remembered how my mother had dropped her purse on a train track and I foolishly grabbed it for her just as the train arrived. I would never have done such a stupid thing except it was for my mother, and she was so upset about losing her bag." Lucy paused. "It's amazing, the things you'll do for your mother—especially if you feel guilty about something."

"Alison probably felt guilty about leaving her mother's house and moving in with Ed and Mireille," said Rachel.

"That is exactly why Eudora wanted to kill her," added Lucy. "If she couldn't have Alison, she certainly wasn't going to let Ed have her."

"But why wasn't killing Alison enough?" asked Bill.

"Mimsy said she found a letter from Jon to Ed asking him for help committing Eudora," said Lucy. "That's why Eudora killed Ed. She shot him while he was sitting in his car, supposedly waiting for Tag. Ironically, she used a gun which he had given her so she could protect herself. According to Barney, she confessed everything, even hiding the gun at the old pub to cast suspicion on Matt. She was quite proud of herself. And, believe it or not, she fingered her own son, Tag, for the firebombing. She said it was her idea . . . to divert attention from the murders of Alison and Ed."

"But what about Mireille? Did Eudora really think she could perform an al fresco caesarean?" asked Bill. "And how did she manage to truss up Mireille? She's a healthy young woman, even if she is pregnant."

"Eudora said she found Mireille sitting on that raised slab chatting with Ed's spirit, and she conked her on the head, then wrapped her up in duct tape."

"But what was Eudora thinking?" demanded Bob. "You can't carve a fetus out of a woman's body and expect it to live."

"It's hard to know what Eudora was thinking," said Lucy. "Maybe she did want the baby. Maybe she did believe that Mireille stole Alison and Ed from her, but there's also the fact that Ed's will left his entire estate to his children, which meant that Mireille's baby will get it all. Maybe Eudora wanted the baby in order to get the money or maybe she just wanted it out of the way."

"Quite extraordinary," said Miss Tilley, who had moved on to a large helping of refried beans.

"The one who puzzles me is Tag," said Bill. "He's smart and good looking. He's well-educated and has great connections. Why did he risk it all by firebombing the restaurant?"

"An Oedipus complex?" suggested Rachel. "To please his mother?"

"Probably, plus he might well be a bigot like Ed," suggested Bob. "And it could be he wanted to gain some cred with the America for Americans crowd."

"Maybe he's every bit as crazy as his mother," suggested Lucy.

"The evil one at work, again," said Rebecca with a sigh.

"Well, all's well that ends well," said Bill. "Mireille's in good hands in the hospital—"

He was interrupted by Rey, who was tapping a glass tumbler with a spoon and beaming.

"I have good news to report: Mireille has given birth to a healthy little boy."

Both Miss Tilley's and Rebecca's faces fell at this news, and they shared a look.

"A girl would have been so much nicer," whispered Rebecca.

"I have it here, eight pounds, fourteen ounces, and twenty-one inches long."

This news was met with great applause and a few cheers.

"And his name is Lucas," Rey added.

"Lucas," repeated Bill. "I think he's named after you, Lucy."

Hearing this, Lucy blushed. "I'm sure she just liked the name," she said.

"Let's all raise a glass to Lucas," said Rey. "May he have a long and happy life."

"To Lucas," they all said, standing and clinking glasses.

"And also, I'm happy to announce that my son Matt will soon be joining me and managing our new restaurant, Cali Kitchen, which my friend Bill Stone is building. Construction will begin immediately and Cali Kitchen will be open in time for the summer season."

This news was greeted with wild applause and a few whistles.

When the crowd quieted down, Rey approached Lucy and Bill's table.

"How do you like the food?" he asked.

"Delicious," said Lucy.

"Really good," said Bob.

"Terrific," said Rachel.

"And what about you, Miss Tilley?" asked Rey.

"Well . . ." she began. "Personally I prefer roast turkey, stuffing, and giblet gravy . . . but I think I could manage a bit more of that spicy cranberry salsa. And, oh dear, don't tell me the burritos are all gone?"

"For you," said Rey as they all laughed, "I will make some more."

Lucy's energy began to flag when dessert was served, but she wasn't about to miss tasting the pumpkin flan that everyone was raving about. She was clearly exhausted, however, and Bob drove her and Bill home in Lucy's SUV, followed by Rachel in their Volvo. The familiar route took them past the town green where Zeke Bumpus and the America for Americans group were scheduled to hold their much-publicized demonstration demanding tougher immigration policies.

"Where's the demonstration?" asked Lucy as they passed the green where Zeke stood entirely alone, draped in an American flag and holding an AMERICA FOR AMERICANS placard.

"I think they're all over at the church, eating Rey's Mexican Thanksgiving Dinner," said Bob, and they all laughed.

Please turn the page for an exciting sneak peek of
Leslie Meier's newest Lucy Stone mystery,
IRISH PARADE MURDER,
coming soon wherever print and e-books are sold!

CHAPTER 1

" I just want to say that this was absolutely the loveliest, most beautiful funeral I've ever attended," said the woman, grasping Lucy Stone's hand and leaning in a bit too close for Lucy's comfort. Some people were like that, and Lucy resisted the urge to draw away, and smiled instead at the woman, who was middle-aged and dressed appropriately for such a somber occasion in a simple navy blue dress and pearls. Her hair was a warm brown, probably colored, and she had applied her make-up with a light hand; a touch of foundation, mascara and soft pink lipstick. Lucy didn't know the woman, but she didn't know most of the people she was greeting in the reception line at her father-in-law's funeral and she assumed she was a friend or neighbor.

"You know, it made me feel as if I actually knew Mr. Stone," continued the woman, exploding that theory. "And what a wonderful family you have."

A bit weird, thought Lucy, wondering if the woman made a hobby of attending total strangers' funeral services. They were listed in the newspaper, after all, and anyone who had a passing interest could come. It was because of those listings that the funeral director had advised them to make sure someone stayed at the house, since burglars were known to take advantage of those listings, too.

"What a nice thing to say, and thank you for coming," said Lucy, passing the woman along to her husband, Bill, who was next in the reception line, and greeting Maria Dolan, who was Edna's best friend and one of the few people at the reception who she actually knew.

"Edna seems to be holding up," observed Maria, glancing at Lucy's newly widowed mother-in-law, "but I'll be keeping an eye on her and making sure she doesn't get lonely. I know you Maine folks can't be popping down to Florida every time she feels a bit blue."

"Thank you so much, I really appreciate that," said Lucy, who was finding her present situation somewhat surreal. It was only two weeks ago when Lucy was still clearing away the Christmas decorations that Edna had called, saying Bill Senior had suffered a heart attack, but was going to be just fine. She had insisted on downplaying the situation but Bill, an only child, had immediately booked a seat on the next flight to Tampa.

When he called Lucy from the hospital, he reported that Edna was either in denial or hadn't understood the seriousness of the situation, as his father was in the ICU in critical condition and wasn't expected to survive. He asked Lucy to inform the kids, and prepare them for their grandfather's death. He also urged her to book a flight as soon as possible, as they would have to plan a funeral and support his mother. But even as her husband lay dying, Edna refused to believe there was any cause for concern and insisted that her son was making too much of a fuss. And when her husband finally did slip away in the final days of January, she opted for a quick cremation to be followed by a simple memorial service. "No need for the kids to come all this way, my Bill wouldn't want a big fuss. He always said he hated funerals and didn't even want to attend his own," she said. "Elizabeth's in Paris, Toby's in Alaska, and Sara is just starting her new job in Boston and their granddad would want them to look to the future. Young people don't want to waste time at some dreary memorial service, and why should they?"

But much to Edna's surprise, the kids immediately made plans to come to Florida. Elizabeth insisted she had to say a final *adieu*

to her *bon pere*, Toby and his wife Molly brought Patrick to remember his Poppop, and Sara, who was waiting to start her new
job at the Museum of Science in Boston, offered to stay with her
grandma for a week or two to help out. Zoe, the youngest, who
was a still in college, wasn't sure she'd be able to make it but in
the end was able to postpone some exams and joined the grieving
family that had gathered in Edna's spacious ranch house.

Lucy wasn't sure what to expect, but it turned out that people
in Florida weren't much different from folks in Tinker's Cove,
Maine. There was a steady stream of visitors offering sympathy,
and many brought casseroles and desserts for the mourning family. And when they all finally gathered in the modern church, all
angles and abstract stained glass, which was so different from the
centuries-old church in Maine, with its clear glass windows and
tall white steeple, the memorial service wasn't dreary at all, but
was instead a true celebration of Bill Senior's life.

The service began with one of his favorite hymns, "For the
Beauty of the Earth," and was followed by a favorite Irish prayer,
that he often repeated: "May you be in heaven before the devil
knows you're dead." The kids all spoke of favorite memories they
cherished of their grandfather. Elizabeth remembered the rain-
bow colored Life Savers he always carried and shared with her,
Patrick remembered catching his first fish with Poppop's help,
Sara recalled the loud rock and roll he favored, that grew even
louder as his hearing began to fail, and Zoe remembered countless games of checkers that Poppop somehow never won. Toby
recalled that as a child he loved helping Poppop wash his car, but
admitted the time he tried to do it himself, as a surprise, didn't go
well because the car was a convertible and the top was down, but
Poppop just laughed and said it was about time the inside got
washed, too.

Lucy knew all these stories, of course, except for Toby's misad-
venture, which was a surprise to her. It was the minister's eulogy,
however, that revealed her father-in-law's deep spirituality and
faith, which she hadn't appreciated. "Bill Stone was a man who
practiced his faith through action," said Rev. Florence Robb, "and
he spent countless hours delivering Meals on Wheels, giving rides

to the homebound, and working at the local food pantry. He helped at worship services, sometimes as an usher, sometimes reading the lessons and prayers. If something was needed, he provided it, often before it was missed. He replaced light bulbs, tightened screws, polished the brass, and those were only the things he did inside the church. Outside, he mowed the grass, weeded the flower beds, pruned the bushes and repaired the church sign when it was torn down in a storm. In his quiet way he made a huge difference in many people's lives and he will be missed." She paused and, voice breaking, added, "Greatly missed."

All this was running through Lucy's mind as she smiled and accepted the condolences offered by the people who had attended the funeral—dear friends, neighbors, and people whose lives had been touched by Bill Stone Sr. And also, as the reception line finally petered out, at least one total stranger who admitted she hadn't known Bill Stone Sr. at all.

Finally released from her duties on the reception line, Lucy glanced around the room, making sure everyone was all right. Bill had taken charge of his mother, and had led her to the buffet table, where he was filling a plate for her. The kids were gathered in a corner, taking advantage of this rare opportunity to hang together and catch up with each other. There was plenty of food and drink, there was a steady buzz of conversation punctuated with laughter, as was usual after the solemnities had been dispensed with and people took the time to reminisce, renew acquaintances and enjoy each other's company. As she scanned the crowd, Lucy looked for the woman in the blue dress and pearls, but didn't see her. She did see Bill, however, trying to catch her eye and she quickly joined him and Edna.

"Quite a nice turnout," she said, taking Edna's arm and leading her to one of the chairs that were lined up against the wall. "It's good to know that Pop was appreciated by so many people."

"I suppose so," said Edna, pushing her potato salad around with a plastic fork. She sighed. "I don't know what I'm going to do with myself, now that he's gone."

"He was a force to be reckoned with, that's for sure," said Lucy, squeezing Edna's hand. "But you're not alone. We're here for a few more days, Sara plans to stay for a week or more, and I hope you'll come visit us in Maine very soon. There's always a place for you at our house, you know."

"I know," said Edna, but she didn't sound as if she really believed it.

A week later, the Florida sun was only a memory as Lucy was back at her job in late-winter Maine, working as a part-time reporter and feature writer for the *Pennysaver*, the weekly newspaper in the quaint coastal town of Tinker's Cove, but she was having a hard time concentrating on the intricacies of the rather complicated changes being proposed to the town's zoning laws. "What exactly is an overlay district?" she asked Phyllis, the paper's receptionist, who was seated at her desk across the room, tucked behind the counter where members of the public filled out orders for classified ads, renewed subscriptions, dropped off Letters to the Editor, and occasionally complained.

"Beats me," said Phyllis with a shrug of her shoulders. She was occupied with entering the week's new batch of classified ads and was peering through the heart-shaped reading glasses that were perched on her nose and that matched her colorful sweatshirt, which was bedecked with hearts and flowers in contrast to the dreary reality of lingering dirty snow outside. "I don't know where to put this thank-you to Sheriff Murphy," she groaned. "Is it an announcement?"

Lucy perked up, her curiosity piqued. "What thank-you?"

"All about his help for some fund drive."

"Who submitted it?"

"Uh, it's right here." Phyllis studied the slip. "Someone named Margaret Mary Houlihan, corresponding secretary of the Hibernian Knights Society. Do you know her?"

"No, can't say I do. The Hibernian Knights present the big St. Patrick's Day parade over in Gilead, but the thank-you is a new one on me."

"Where do you think I should put it?"

"That I don't know. Better ask Ted." Ted Stillings was the publisher, editor, and chief reporter for the paper, which he'd inherited from his grandfather who was a noted regional journalist. Times had changed since his day, however, and Lucy knew that

Ted was hard-pressed to keep the little weekly paper afloat. Like newspapers throughout the country, the *Pennysaver* was faced with a diminishing list of advertisers and subscribers, and constantly increasing production costs.

"Well, I would if he was here but he hardly ever is these days," complained Phyllis. After a pause she added, "Is it me, or do things seem a bit weird around here?"

"Weirder than usual?" asked Lucy, who hadn't really been paying much attention since she'd returned from Florida. She'd been focused on staying in touch with Edna and keeping Bill's spirits up.

"Yeah. While you were gone Ted's had a lot of meetings with, well, folks who aren't from around here. Fancy types, in city slicker clothes."

"Really?" Lucy's interest was piqued. "Like who?"

"Well, there was a middle-aged man, with quite a big belly, dressed in a suit and tie. He was nice enough, made a lot of jokes and laughed a lot, but didn't give his name or business. Then Ted arrived and whisked him off, took him out to lunch I think."

"And when Ted got back from lunch did he offer any explanation?"

"Nope. I asked if he was buying life insurance, it kind of just popped out. I guess the guy seemed kind of like a salesman, but Ted just chuckled and gave me a big pile of listings for the Events column." Phyllis paused to polish her glasses. "I definitely got the feeling he didn't want to continue the discussion."

"He is always complaining about the rising cost of newsprint . . ." said Lucy.

"And the declining number of subscribers," added Phyllis. "And that's another thing. He had me research all sorts of facts and figures, like ad revenue, classified ad revenue, production costs . . ." She let out a big sigh. "Not exactly my cup of tea, if you know what I mean."

"How did the figures look?" asked Lucy, beginning to feel rather uneasy. Was it possible that Ted wasn't just worrying out loud but that the *Pennysaver* was really in dire financial straits? Was he thinking of selling the paper, or even shutting it down permanently?

"Not good," admitted Phyllis, "but I'm no accountant. I can't even balance my checkbook."

"Neither can I," admitted Lucy. "I just cross my fingers and if the bank says I have more money than I think I have, then it's a good month."

"Wilf manages our money," confessed Phyllis, sounding a bit smug as she referred to her husband. They had married late in life and she was clearly enjoying married life. "And then there was that woman, done up to the nines, with high-heel boots and that bleached blond hair that looks natural so you know it must cost a fortune."

Lucy noticed that Phyllis's tone had changed; she sounded worried when she spoke about the woman. "I'm confused," admitted Lucy. "Does Wilf know this woman?"

"No way," Phyllis dismissed that idea with a flap of her hand. "She came here to the office and, again, no introduction, Ted just dragged her off. He was gone for a couple of hours and when he got back, not a word. He just sat down and started pounding out his weekly editorial."

"You have no idea who she was?" Lucy considered possible identities for a woman with a city hairdo and high heels. "Maybe she was some sort of sales rep? A high-flying real estate agent?"

"Your guess is as good as mine," said Phyllis, "but she looked like trouble to me."

Lucy was inclined to agree. She tended to be suspicious of women in high heels, who clearly did not have to negotiate the icy sidewalks and muddy driveways that were an annual feature in Maine as winter began to loosen its grip and temperatures began to rise above freezing in the day, only to refreeze at night. Everyone she knew, male and female, wore duck boots beginning with the first February thaw and right on through June.

"Any other suspicious characters?" asked Lucy, thinking this was beginning to sound like a Sherlock Holmes story. Of course, Sherlock would immediately identify the jovial man as having come from Portland where he'd recently stopped for gas and a stale tuna sandwich. The woman, he would assert, undoubtedly came from Chestnut Hill where she raised Dobermans and ran a sado-masochistic dungeon patronized by wealthy men with guilty consciences.

"A tall, skinny man in a plaid shirt and jeans with a big Adam's apple," offered Phyllis, interrupting Lucy's thoughts. "He had a deep voice. He greeted me politely, 'Good morning, ma'am,' he said. That's how I know about his voice."

Ah, thought Lucy, a radio announcer for the country-western channel. "No introduction?"

"Nothing. He asked for Ted, called him 'Mr. Stillings.' Ted happened to be in the morgue, but popped out like a jack-in-a-box when he heard the man's voice. Then they were gone, and again, no explanation when he returned."

"I dunno," said Lucy, shaking her head in puzzlement. "Either he's working on a feature story of some sort about little-known celebrities, or it's got something to do with the business. Maybe he's once again on the brink of bankruptcy and is trying to refinance, or . . . ," here she stopped, unwilling to continue and voice the notion that Ted might be selling the *Pennysaver*.

The bell on the door jangled, and they both turned to see who their next visitor might be. This time the stranger was tall, dark and undeniably handsome. He was also young and dressed in brand-new country duds: ironed jeans with a crease down the leg, a plaid shirt topped with a barn jacket, and fresh-from-the-box duck shoes that hadn't yet ventured into muddy territory.

"What can I do for you?" asked Phyllis in her polite receptionist voice.

"I have an appointment with Ted Stillings. Will you let him know I'm here?"

Phyllis and Lucy both perked up, presented with an opportunity to ascertain the fellow's name. "Gladly," said Phyllis with a big smile. "Who shall I say is here?"

"Rrr," he began, then caught himself. "Just say his eleven o'clock is here."

Phyllis's ample bosom seemed to deflate a trifle. "Actually, you'd better take a seat. Ted's not here, but I expect him shortly, Mr. Rrrr . . ."

"Thanks," he said, smiling and revealing a dazzling white perfect bite. He sat down on one of the chairs next to the door, opposite the reception counter, and even bent at the knee his long legs pretty much filled the intervening space. He picked up the latest copy of the *Pennysaver* from the table between the chairs and began reading it.

Lucy took this opportunity to study him, taking in his thick, Kennedyesque hair, his sweeping black brows, hawkish nose, square jaw, broad shoulders, and large hands. Dudley Doright? she wondered, recalling the cartoon character. Clearly, she was no Sherlock Holmes.

"Did you travel far?" she asked.

"Not too far," he said with a shrug.

"So you're familiar with Maine?" she continued.

"Sure," he said. "Lobsters, blueberries, and moose."

"Would you like some coffee while you wait?" asked Phyllis.

"No, thanks." He nodded. "I'm good."

"We also have tea," offered Lucy. "If you're a tea drinker."

"Thanks, but I'm all set," he answered, turning the page of the paper and burying his nose in it. Lucy doubted he was really all that interested in the Tinker's Cove high school's basketball team's recent defeat at the hands of the Dover Devils, and figured he was trying to avoid conversation. But why? Why were all these recent visitors so secretive, and what was Ted trying to hide?

She glanced at the antique Regulator clock that hung on the wall above the stranger's head, just as the big hand clicked into place at twelve, indicating it was exactly eleven o'clock. Like clockwork, the bell jangled as the door opened and Ted arrived, bristling with energy and rubbing his hands together. "Ah, you're already here," he said, extending his hand.

The stranger stood up and took Ted's hand, giving it a manly shake. "Good to meet you," he said.

"Same here," said Ted. "Did you have a good drive?"

"Not bad," said the stranger. "Bit of traffic in Portland but otherwise clear sailing."

Lucy and Phyllis picked up on that last, and their eyes met. Was this a clue to his identity? Was he a fisherman? A yachtsman?

"That's great," said Ted. "Well, I don't know about you, but

I'm usually ready for a coffee around now. We don't have Starbucks, but we've got our own Jake's. How about it?"

"Sounds great," said the stranger.

Ted opened the door, holding it for the visitor, who stepped outside. Ted followed and the two walked past the plate glass window with the old-fashioned wooden blinds, their progress followed by the two women inside the office. Then they were out of view, leaving nothing behind except questions.

"Who is he?" asked Phyllis.

"Why is here?" asked Lucy.

"What's Ted up to?" asked Phyllis.

"I wish we had some answers," said Lucy.

Made in the USA
Middletown, DE
05 October 2023

40296014R00239